JOHN BUCHAN

SUPERNATURAL
Tales

Edited & Introduced by
REV. JAMES C. G. GREIG

B&W PUBLISHING

This edition first published 1997
by B&W Publishing Ltd
Edinburgh

Copyright © The Lord Tweedsmuir
and Jean, Lady Tweedsmuir
Introduction & notes © Rev. James C. G. Greig 1997

ISBN 1 873631 78 2

British Library Cataloguing in Publication Data:
A catalogue record for this book is available
from the British Library

Cover illustration:
Dr Lee by D. O. Hill & Robert Adamson
reproduced by kind permission
of the National Galleries of Scotland

Cover Design: Winfortune *&* Associates

Printed by Werner Söderström

CONTENTS

INTRODUCTION

REV. JAMES C. G. GREIG

Pan playing on his aiten reed
And shepherds him attending,

THE BALLAD OF LEADER HAUGH

One may take "supernatural" to mean simply whatever fascinates because it is inexplicable, mysterious and sometimes perturbing— analogous to the theologians' *mysterium tremendum fascinans* but not limited to specifically Christian theology.

The ancient Greeks, with their many gods and creatures such as nymphs and monsters, were very familiar with the idea that there are "more things in Heaven and earth than are dreamt of in your philosophy"; but in their philosophies too they naturally kept open a place for the "ground of being". Plato, pre-eminently, liked to look behind the visible universe to the world of "forms" or "ideas".

John Buchan (1875-1940), the son of a minister of the Free Church of Scotland (later of the United Free Church of Scotland), tried hard to marry the philosophy inspired in him by his reading of Walter Pater's *Plato and Platonism* with his family's inherited Calvinism, and at the same time to pay homage to his own literary Muse, writing from an early age short stories and novels, and poems.

His short stories present us with a *mélange* of philosophical, mythic[1] and mystical perceptions which seem to demonstrate a continuing attempt to grapple with the inexplicable, and especially with certain types of unusual human situations, not only as a philosopher but as an existentially involved seer, what the Greeks would have called a *mantis*.

In an early book of essays, *Scholar Gipsies* (1896), his use of our epigraph already signals a mystical strain in dealing with nature, even when the content is simply a re-telling of his early encounters with shepherds and nature in Peeblesshire. That sensitivity to the incalculable, sometimes uncanny *deus absconditus*, the God—to the ancient Greeks the gods—behind Nature in all her moods—*Benigna* and *Maligna*—pervades the short stories.

Here we look only at some of those stories. I have chosen those that represent a fairly broad canvas of Buchan's interests.

Many of the tales have a supernatural flavour which at first sight might seem at odds with Professor Daniell's emphasis on Buchan's undoubted Platonism. Nevertheless we need hardly go farther than the famous story of the Cave in the *Republic* to recognize the affinity between the Platonic philosophy of transcendental "ideas" and the ancient mythopoeic presentation of nature and the human situation. What we do not see may nevertheless exist. But what is the nature of its existence?

Contemporary interest in Buchan's stories springs from at least three main sources; Janet Adam Smith's *John Buchan* (1965, paper-back 1985), David S. Daniell's *The Best Short Stories of John Buchan* (two volumes, 1980 and 1982) and Andrew Lownie's *John Buchan: The Complete Short Stories* (volume 1, 1996; volumes 2 and 3, 1997).

This new introduction,[2] inevitably drawing on the raw facts already made available, seeks to add a modest further dimension of depth to these studies. The Blackwood 1936 edition of *The Watcher by the Threshold*[3] (1902) and *The Moon Endureth* (1912) and the Hodder and Stoughton edition of *The Runagates Club* (1928) have been used, also David Daniell's text (1980) of "The Herd of Standlan" (1899).

As a Scot Buchan read widely on Scottish historical themes and his father's interest in old Scottish ballads and fairy tales left its mark on his imagination.

As a classicist who studied the classics first at the University of Glasgow, then at Brasenose College, Oxford, Buchan could and did draw on the story-telling tradition of Scott and Stevenson, and also on the worlds of Greek myth and drama, at first sight frequently at odds with Platonism.

As an undergraduate at Oxford he reviewed books for John Lane, and in the climate of the day acquired an acquaintance with writing such as that of the occultist Arthur Machen. But his classical studies also drew him to sources containing a rich mine of material he was able to exploit in his stories.

He completed his studies in law at the Temple and so added a further judicial element to his make-up which must have increased his ability to stand back from his subject-matter. (Scott, Stevenson and Goethe, who all had an interest in the supernatural, also had a legal training.)

The stories with a supernatural colouring fall into several categories. These are not mutually exclusive, but each has a distinctiveness that signals its importance for our understanding of Buchan's mindset.

We may conveniently consider the following themes: (1) dual personality, (2) the sacred grove (the *temenos* of the ancient Greeks), (3) the mystical, (4) philosophy in mystical guise, (5) the challenge to ambition and (6) the use of artificial devices.

(1) *Dual Personality*

At Oxford Buchan's work had included study of Byzantium, and therefore of the age of Justinian (A.D. 482–565). This was an essential foundation for legal studies: Justinian is famed for his codification of Roman Law in four books, and some traces of this legal interest of Buchan's crop up in some of the stories. But another side to Justinian was presented by the historian Procopius' *Secret History* (*Anecdota* or *Historia Arcana*) and Buchan was to make use of this in "The Watcher by the Threshold" (published in 1902), the most substantive of his short stories of the supernatural.

His technique there, and in his other tales in this genre, is more sophisticated than Stevenson's in *Dr Jekyll and Mr Hyde* (1886). (Only in one of them—"A Lucid Interval", to which we shall return—does he make use of the artificial medium of a drug as a generator of abnormal conduct.) In "The Watcher . . .", for instance, we have almost a case study of something like temporary schizophrenia (a term on record lexicographically only since 1911). There the Calvinist narrator encounters in Mr Ladlaw—whose wife bears the significant name of Sybil[5]—a commonplace, rationalistic justice of the peace and amateur antiquary, plunged by obsessive studies and contact with a bust of the Byzantine Emperor Justinian into a state of near madness. Ladlaw's recovery is effected by contact with a country minister of the Kirk whose modernist theology is challenged by the uncanny nature of Ladlaw's devil-possessed condition. This prompts the minister to think of producing a philosophy that would outdo Nietzsche in its unorthodoxy. "The Watcher . . ." is set in the ancient Pictish Manann (roughly east of central Scotland, a boggy moorland with "ugly red burns" and a depressive air). Procopius has been said to present Justinian's court as a veritable "*diabolorum lerna*" (*Dictionary of Christian Biography*, 1887, quoting Cave—and possibly consulted by Buchan). Lerna was the forest and marshland four miles from Argos, where Hercules slew the many-headed Hydra. This description of Procopius' book as a real "devil-filled bog" links well with Buchan's adaptation of Procopius for his story. Moreover, the Lernaean Hydra is mentioned in Virgil's *Aeneid* VI. Buchan was not only familiar with the *Aeneid*, Book 6, which describes Aeneas' journey into the underworld, but draws on this (and on Euripides' *Bacchae*) again in *Witch Wood* (1927)[6]. It is also worth noting that Virgil gives the Sybil of Cumae an important presiding role in *Aeneid* VI, and the underworld guardian—that is, watcher—and the threshold are significantly present there too. (Cf. Virgil, *The Aeneid*, Penguin Classics, translated by W. F. Jackson Knight, 1956, pp147ff, 160, 164, 165.) At all events there is good reason to suppose that the title, "The Watcher by the Threshold", was the product in its author's mind of a conjunction of Virgil's and Procopius' work with Scottish topography. A dependence on Bulwer-Lytton's *Zanoni* (1842) is, as Lownie (vol. II, p7) indicates, possible; but hardly necessary, even allowing for the "Dweller of the Threshold" to be found in that book.

The observant reader will note that a naturalistic explanation for Ladlaw's illness may also be found: his wife thought his illness involved "something about the heart" but this is to be interpreted primarily as a metaphor. The narrator's later supposition that Ladlaw's difficulties with his left hand are the product of heart trouble is contradicted when the occult nature of his difficulty is made clear. If not to his heart, however, Ladlaw's voracious reading in ancient lore has, in the common phrase, "gone to his head". That Buchan presents him as possessed can likewise be discerned from the atmosphere of terror that he builds up; and not only Ladlaw but even the local minister is depicted, rather like one of the Gadarene swine, as suddenly seized by the mysterious force that had been in Ladlaw.

This tale is only one of several in which the rational and the non-rational are closely interwoven in Buchan's writing. He is not a victim of his own magic, but his choice of subject-matter may nevertheless throw light on areas of conflict within his mind. He needs his modernist minister who is shocked into a less modernist faith by his encounter with Ladlaw; for Buchan's own father was no modernist, and Buchan's Calvinism was challenged both by his own mythopoeic imagination and by his encounter with Greek tragedies and the whole range of his classical studies, even down to references to the occult force of the left side of the body ("sinister" means "left" in Latin), which explains the reference to "heart" trouble: the spiritual sense of the word "heart" is intended. (Given the importance of topography in the story, we may also keep in mind Buchan's likely familiarity with Sir James Frazer's *Golden Bough*, as Professor Christopher Harvie has pointed out in another connection. This is particularly relevant to the *temenos* theme discussed below.[7])

Dual personality appears in a less gruesome form in "The Kings of Orion" (written in 1905, published in *Blackwood's Magazine* in 1906, and in *The Moon Endureth* in 1912). It is still linked with the Byzantine Emperor as "Emperor of the World"— *kosmokrator* would seem to be the underlying Greek, a word referring initially to ruling gods or spirits good or evil (cf. Ephesians 6:12, "the world-rulers—*tous kosmokratoras*—of this darkness") and later to a Roman Emperor.[8] Buchan's purpose would ultimately be theological and a product of his Presbyterian up-bringing, as if he were subconsciously grappling with the problem of the spiritual sources of human evil. The text in Ephesians is a highly relevant counterpart to the material he uses from the classics. We find him tackling the theme obliquely, and not always negatively. Thus, in "The Kings of Orion", there is a sample of the two souls in Goethe's Faust's human breast.

Fundamentally, the prosaic conscious personality of Buchan's hero seems humdrum, but he has an underlying secret world in which he apparently suffers from delusions of grandeur. This, however, may erupt beneficially into his life if he is presented with a crisis; which is precisely what happens.

In the much later "Tendebant Manus", one of the tales in *The Runagates Club* (1928), the hero becomes a greater self through self-identification with a brother held in high regard but killed in the First World War. (Buchan lost his youngest brother at Arras in 1917.)

In "The Kings of Orion" the key reference is to an ancient legend of supernatural kings driven out of the constellation of Orion and "sent to this planet and given each his habitation in some mortal soul". He quotes Ausonius, who does mention Orion, but I have not so far found a precise correspondence.

Buchan seems never to have lost the sense of awe, not only for the thin partition that divides civilization from barbarism in any age, but specifically for the equally thin line that separated his present life from the Greek and Roman—or any other—past. One of his major later historical works, *Augustus* (1937), presents us with the rational, historically perceptive side of his thinking and research. But the mythopoeic undercurrent that emerged in Buchan's fiction remained till the end, not least with the glimpse of a kind of sacred grove ("Clairefontaine") in his posthumous novel, *Sick Heart River* (1941).

(2) *The Sacred Grove (temenos)*

Perhaps the most significant early story that takes up this theme is "No-Man's-Land" (1899). The raw material is drawn from many sources. The narrator is a young Oxford don of Scots origin, at home in the field of northern antiquities. In a fictitious Allermuir, based (but perhaps not exclusively) on the ancient Pictish Manann (which would have included Allermuir Hill near Edinburgh) he finds himself confronted with a remnant of hill-dwelling ancient Picts. They are presented as far less civilized than we know the historical Picts to have been, and more like Brownies; and the landscape is not dissimilar to that in "The Watcher . . .". Elements of Celtic folklore add to the sense of mystery. But the crux lies in the narrator's discovery of the "remnants of a ritual and mythology". And for his Picts there is a "holy season . . . when sacrifices were offered to the gods". Indeed he and the destined victim both narrowly escape falling prey to the custom by which "every twentieth summer a woman was sacrificed to some devilish god, and by the hand of one of the stranger race". The setting is a cave where the intended victim is tied to a stake; but the cave is simply the transmutation onto Scottish soil of a pagan Greek *temenos* or sacred grove—and of the Greek ritual Buchan makes use of in the much later novel *The Dancing Floor* (1926), where a *kouros* (young man) and *koré* (young woman) are in a similar predicament.

The remaining tales we have selected for this theme treat it with varying light and shade.

In "Fountainblue" (1901) the title already suggests one of the features of a *temenos*—the clear, sparkling water of a spring; but the real *temenos* is quite different, except in so far as the title is also the rather odd name of the Highland estate which is the setting for the hero's childhood love of nature in all its moods. Maitland becomes a hard politician and financier who has worked his way up from nothing, but revisits the scenes of his childhood and is aware of the contrast between past simplicities and present arid sophistication; he is also capable of falling into "abstractions", in one of which the ancient motto of his family dances in his brain and clearly demonstrates his need of a woman's love.[9] To be a whole person he has to integrate his boyhood with what he has become, and marriage might be the answer; but it ultimately eludes him when ironically he saves from drowning the girl's other suitor, a gentler personality, after a gruelling shipwreck. Two elements of the real *temenos* theme have led up to this. First, a reference to an island that contains the cell of an ancient saint—Eilean na Cille ("the isle of the cell" in Gaelic), which was the planned destination for an expedition that ends in disaster; secondly a calm before the storm, probably really the eye of the storm, described in terms of Celtic myth—the "Ocean Quiet"—as a phenomenon that helps the "hard man" to realise the emptiness of his worldly success. This realisation coincides—but is not identical—with the moment when he becomes aware that he has lost a love that would have integrated the better self of his boyhood with what he had ultimately become; and the change in him is described by a brief allusion to a verse in 1 John 2:16, and at length by his abandonment of a glittering career at home for an African governorship.

Buchan too went to South Africa in 1901 to work under Lord Milner! A number of parallels may be drawn between his stories and his own early life and that of his acquaintances at Oxford but this may sometimes be a rather hazardous enterprise.

If this suggestion of "fragments of a great confession" (Goethe's phrase) does not apply, one might nevertheless be prepared to compare the psychology of the story with Jung's theory of archetypes, not least because of the brief appearances of a formidable though generous old lady—surely an anticipation of Jung's *anima*, and perhaps reflecting the possessive character of Buchan's mother.

(Paul Webb, *A Buchan Companion*, p34, is surely wrong in claiming that "Fountainblue" is "the only short story in the *Watcher* collection that is not supernatural". It is quite as supernatural as the others, with its mystical use of the *temenos* theme.)

"The Far Islands" (1899) had already broached the use of an island sanctuary—a theme recurring in *A Prince of the Captivity* (1933)—as a formative influence on character. This too is related to the *temenos* theme. The hero, Colin Raden, is descended from sea-rovers and Scottish aristocrats, some of whom intermarried with great English houses and were ultimately "of the common over-civilised type, graceful, well-mannered, . . . but only once in a generation reverting to the rugged northern strength". (This only eight years or so before Buchan—in 1907—married one from a "great English house"!)

Colin has known the West Highland coast and its islands as

a boy and has experienced a kind of mystical vision in which repeatedly he travels mentally, with little or no success, to "far islands"—beyond a neighbouring island called Cuna, where more than one of his ancestors had drowned. Later in life as a schoolboy at Eton, as an undergraduate (at Oxford, of course!) and, improbably, in the Guards, the vision returns, linked by one of the other characters with a form of hallucination that runs in a family for generations. (This is not far from Highland second sight.) Colin reaches the stage of confusing external phenomena with his vision. Finally, as he dies in battle, he has clearly penetrated beyond Cuna to his far islands.

At one point in the story there is a fairly clear identification of these far islands with the Isle of Avilion, the Greek Hesperides; equally interesting is the ambivalence of Cuna—once the scene of an ancient forswearing of the church's way, sometimes for Colin "blotting out his own magic way", sometimes simply the neighbouring island. But there may well be more than coincidence in the fact that *cunae* is "cradle" in Latin, while *cuan* is "ocean" in Gaelic. The story is thus something of a proleptic version of "Fountainblue"; but it is also perhaps intended as a psychological parable of the Death Wish: the cradle is the gateway from eternity to temporality; conversely death is a kind of retrogression to eternity, passing through a different gateway, but one that is parallel—a return to the prenascent state. This is *Tìr nan Òg*, the Highland "land of the (ever) young", unreachable till life ends.

Buchan develops the theme in *A Prince of the Captivity* (1933) where the island known as Eilean Bàn—"the fair island" in Gaelic—is Adam Melfort's necessary paradise to which in spirit he can frequently return.

Another contrasting version of the *temenos* theme is to be found in "The Outgoing of the Tide" (1903). At first sight we are simply in the world of witchcraft; but the drama is created by a river in spate and by the "witching" hour of twelve till one in the morning at the ebbing of the tide—and at the time of the pagan Beltane festival, still celebrated conventionally in some Scottish places such as the Peebles Buchan knew. This enables us to place the tale loosely in the *temenos* category. The narrator is a minister, who is used again by Buchan in the Epilogue to *Witch Wood* (1927), and the tone of the narrative is typical of Scots seventeenth-century Presbyterianism, though with an unexpected demonstration of grace to the villain at the very end.

One man's religion is another man's witchcraft: so at least Margaret Murray would have claimed, in *The Witch-Cult in Western Europe*, 1922 (Oxford pb 1962). This might almost be a text for analysis of "The Grove of Ashtaroth" (1910; in *The Moon Endureth*, 1912), one of the most powerful instances of the *temenos* theme at work.

The scene is in a wild area north of South Africa, the narrator is a Christian, the chief character is a friend who is part-Jewish, appropriately named Lawson, thus bringing out the contrast between Calvinist "justification by grace through faith" and the legalism often attributed without due qualification to Judaism. The narrator finds himself almost having to say "there but for the grace of God go I"; but the tale suggests not the triumph of grace over Judaism, but over the narrator's apprehensiveness. Hence he can rescue—save the soul (sic!) of—Lawson who, fascinated by the worship of the pagan Astarte, is in danger of forsaking his ancestral Jewish faith. The *temenos* is situated where Lawson ultimately has his house, in a glen near a wooded stream— "not a copse, but a 'grove'—one such as Artemis may have flitted through in the moonlight . . . the *temenos* of some strange and lovely divinity" where a flock of green doves forgathered.— Doves are associated with Astarte, an oriental equivalent of Aphrodite but also of Artemis/Diana of the Ephesians (cf. Acts 19:28), Ashtoreth in the KJV. (Ashtaroth is strictly the plural of Ashtoreth/Ashtereth.)—Central to the scene is a little ancient conical tower. (Buchan associates this with the usually now discredited theory of a Phoenician origin for the tower, and thus strengthens the notion of a Canaanite paganism at work on the scene.)[10]

As the story develops, Buchan uses his knowledge of the Old Testament (1 Kings 11) to good effect, and finally portrays Lawson as exhausted from frequent visits to the *temenos* to dance in a frenzy round the central tower.

Here we have another example of Buchan's linking the distant past and the present supernaturally, as in the story of Ladlaw (another laid low by the Law—and by the past?). The pagan past exercises a sweet fascination; and it is difficult not to believe that here again Buchan is unconsciously exorcising that pagan inclination in himself: his Calvinist superego, mellowed by philosophy, particularly Plato's, was still in control. Or in Nietzschean terms the Apollonian has to triumph over the Dionysiac. Buchan, as we have seen, knew something of Nietzsche, just as he knew something of Euripides' *Bacchae*, where Dionysos is central. (There is a quotation in *Witch Wood* from Clement of Alexandria which provides a clue to the influence of the *Bacchae* on the structure of that novel.) Interestingly Buchan claims in *Memory Hold-the-Door* (1940) that he had "never greatly cared for" Euripides but "for some obscure reason I took to reading him on the veld" (i.e. between 1901 and 1903).[11] This seems just a little disingenuous!

At this point we may do well to switch to the year 1928, when in the *Runagates Club* a story entitled "The Wind in the Portico" again reveals the fascination antiquity held for Buchan.

This tale is perhaps the most brilliant example of the *temenos* theme.

The narrator of the substance of the tale is a classical scholar from Cambridge, engaged in work on Theocritus. He has to consult a rare manuscript in private possession, but finds the owner, Dubellay, a scholarly but amateurish recluse in Shropshire, whose hobby has virtually turned his head. Dubellay, living in a wooded environment, has found and excavated an ancient British (Welsh) temple, then built in classical style a new temple— carefully hidden from the public gaze—dedicated to Vaunus, the ancient local god.

Vaunus is a variant of Faunus, a Roman equivalent of Pan. To this we return later.

A strange hot wind seems explicable initially from Dubellay's mention of a hypocaust (the Roman method for producing heating for rooms or baths)—but is in the end linked more closely with a sacrificial altar in the temple. The narrator finds him "a naked body, already charred and black. There was nothing else, except that the Gorgon's head in the wall seemed to glow like a sun in hell."

Thus Dubellay is not as lucky as Ladlaw: the narrator has been too late to save him from his madness and in the tailpiece to the story natural explanations for the subsequent burning of his house are suggested but left unresolved. "You may believe if you like that the god Vaunus inhabited the temple . . . and when his votary grew scared . . . became angry and slew him with his flaming wind."

As happens frequently, Buchan alludes to genuine ancient sources, this time Ausonius (ca. 310–ca. 395) and Sidonius, bishop of Clermont-Ferrand (ca. 430–ca. 486), and some classical allusions; but these are necessary for the story, not obtrusive. Likely sources are Ausonius X, *The Moselle*, 318–348 and Sidonius, *Letters* II: ii, 10. In the latter we read of a portico overlooking a lake.

Mention of Ludlow in Shropshire at the beginning of the tale, and of the untamed landscape near the temple, remind one of Ladlaw in Pictish Manann in "The Watcher . . ." but the later story is stylistically more economical, though the note of tragedy replaces the redemptive success of the narrator in the early one. This may be taken as a signal of Buchan's "naturalisation" as an Englishman; but his Scottish Presbyterian roots are never far from the scene. One hint of this is the epigraph to the story: a quotation from Jeremiah 4:11f. which summons Jerusalem to repentance. Was Buchan perturbed at preferring secular literature to the life of a minister? We know that in earlier years he reacted strongly against the narrowness of some in the Free Church of Scotland. Nevertheless his work is often didactic, not to say theologically conditioned and spiritually edifying.[12]

"The Lemnian" (written in 1911, included in *The Moon Endureth*) contrasts with the previous stories in having a genuinely ancient setting: the Battle of Thermopylae (480 B.C.), a Greek disaster, and its aftermath. Buchan draws not only on his initial classical studies but also, as David Daniell pointed out in *The Best Short Stories of John Buchan*, II (1982), on Gilbert Murray's *The Rise of the Greek Epic* (Harvard lectures of 1907). There is also much detail on the relevant Greek geography, and Buchan's visit to the Aegean in 1910 will have been the immediate prompting for the story which Sir Arthur Quiller-Couch thought "any man in my generation might be proud to sign". It is certainly a fine piece of craftsmanship where Buchan himself has, as it were, taken on the mantle of Atta, marrying scholarship and imagination in a profound unity.

As the whole tale is steeped in the atmosphere of ancient Greece it is not surprising to find in it references to the pre-Greek Pelasgian islanders, the Spartans, and Apollo's shrine at Delphi.

The *temenos* theme is only a shadow of itself in these latter references, but it comes into its own in the closing pages of the story, where the Lemnian Atta, dying after the failure of the Spartan resistance to the Persians, sings yearningly:

> I will sing of thee,
> Great Sea-Mother,
> Whose white arms gather
> Thy sons in the ending:
> And draw them homeward . . .
>
> Soothe them and guide them
> By shining pathways
> Homeward to thee.
>
> Far in the sunrise,
> Nestled in thy bosom,
> Lies my own green isle.
> Thither wilt thou bear me . . .

All the poems in *The Moon Endureth* link up well with the stories they accompany, but none better than this one, with its echoes of Euripides and the Greek Anthology, as the narrator (Buchan hardly in disguise) reminds us.

"The Wise Years", a poem attached to "The Green Glen" (a story written in 1911 and included in *The Moon Endureth*, 1912) is a good example. It is attributed to Lapidarius, one of three monks who in the story were regarded by the chapter of Melrose as of ill repute. After him came one "Andrew de Faun . . . who had the unpleasing gift *diabolos convocandi*"—conjuring up devils.

The poem generates the quotation from Psalm 72—"while the moon endures"—which is alluded to in the epigraph to the entire collection of 1912. Lapidarius is an unorthodox mystic, the "devil's minion" to the countryfolk, but befriended by the children and persuaded that "he findeth God who finds the earth He made".

Fawn is the name of the stream in the Green Glen, dignified by a Latin couplet attributed—dubiously, claims the narrator—to Thomas the Rhymer, the medieval Borderer reputedly carried off for a season by the Queen of Elfland.

The couplet—*Ubi Faunus fluit/Spes mortalis ruit* is interpreted as

> Where Fawn flows
> Man's hope goes.

It is first introduced in the course of a seemingly inordinately long introduction to the story. But this is a prerequisite to the *dénouement*.

The narrator, wandering as an eleven-year-old into this Border glen is frightened by its inordinate greenness, but in later life returns to it and investigates its history. This enables Buchan to conjoin the idea of a pagan *temenos* with medieval Scots history and balladry and with the atmosphere of faerie typified by Thomas the Rhymer.

There follows the tale of a diffident lover and a somewhat ethereal beloved, the latter in the end dying in her lover's arms in the Green Glen—arguably of heart failure through too strenuous a walk, but rather because she is a reincarnation of a medieval ancestor who had saved her beloved there.

Once again we have the opportunity for a naturalistic solution, but the story compels us rather to believe in the supernatural power at work in the Green Glen. Once again, too, distant past and present are linked. *The Path of the King* (1921) provides another variant of this with its picture of kingly characteristics re-emerging from time to time through the history of a family.

(3) *The Mystical*

Turning from the *temenos* we may choose an example of a more broadly mystical theme. As early as *Grey Weather* (1899) we find this, in "The Herd of Standlan", which is thoroughly Scottish and rural in its background. The herd saves a rising politician from drowning but is himself injured in his effort in the waters, losing normal consciousness and convinced he speaks to his dead grandmother. His granny tells of her experiences in a state between Heaven and hell. Recovered, the herd goes to England as the employee of the rescued politician, but eventually returns to Scotland disillusioned. Drama and humour are happily combined in this tale and the telling of it already places Buchan almost on the same plane as Stevenson or Scott. But it signals his own early awareness of the gap between the rural Scotland he knew and the culture-shock of his early Oxford years as an undergraduate. This is part and parcel of the syndrome that found literary expression in later short stories.

(4) *Philosophy in Mystical Guise*

A more philosophically mystical story is to be found in "Space" (*Blackwood's Magazine*, 1911 and in *The Moon Endureth*, 1912). Buchan had been gaining an acquaintance of the work of Jules Henri Poincaré (the mathematician, astronomer and philosopher) and Henri Bergson (of *élan vital* fame). It is possible that he also knew something of Georg Cantor (1845-1918) the German mathematician who developed the idea of transfinite numbers but who from 1884 suffered from mental illness. One should also remember that Einstein's first theory of relativity dates from 1905.

Nevertheless the story also depends in part on a verse from the seventeenth-century poet Traherne, as we shall see.

"Space", with Leithen as the involved narrator, tells of Hollond, a mathematician and professor, but also an alpinist (like Buchan). Hollond has an epistemological theory. Might Space not be "really full of things we cannot see and as yet do not know?" Space may be "made up of corridors and alleys" . . . "fourth-dimensional inwardness or involution was part of it". Moreover, "Number has no place in nature. It is an invention of the human mind to atone for a bad memory. But figures are a different matter. All the mysteries of the world are in them, and the old magicians knew that at least". Hollond, however, is more intuitionist than experimenter, and his theory becomes an obsession. His behaviour resembles Ladlaw's: "he would . . . come into a room with a quick look round him, and sometimes for no earthly reason he would swerve". His loneliness knows no bounds and is accompanied by a kind of intellectual fear; he has become conscious of "Presences" in his intellectual world of Space. Leithen offers explanations for Hollond's experiences and is fascinated. "You may discover the meaning of Spirit".

Hollond is certain that Traherne, the poet, was talking (in "Shadows in the Water") about his "Presences" and not about angels:

> Within the region of the air,
> Compassed about with heavens fair,
> Great tracts of lands there may be found,
>   Where many numerous hosts,
>   in those far distant coasts
> For other great and glorious ends
> Inhabit, my yet unknown friends.[13]

But soon he thinks his private intellectual world is close to the biblical Abomination of Desolation: "I am on the edge of a terror . . . that no mortal can think of and live".—A far cry from Addison's "spangled heavens, a shining frame"!

Visiting Chamonix, Leithen discovers Hollond has fallen to his death. "He had seen . . . the little bit too much".

Here the *temenos* has become internalised in Hollond's mind. It has become the idea, the form, behind Plato's forms: "Let no-one who is ignorant of geometry enter here". Ironically, the *akademeia* where Plato taught was a grove of olive trees sacred to Akademos! It was closed in A.D. 529 by *Justinian*!

The present writer is happily very ignorant of geometry.

(5) *The Challenge to Ambition*

Some light relief is afforded in "The Rime of True Thomas", originally written in 1897 and included in *Grey Weather* (1899) as "The Moor-Song", but finding its eventual home in *The Moon Endureth* (1912). As the last paragraph in it suggests, there is a quest for a compromise between the Romantic and the Classical, and it is Buchan's own quest. In a sense it is also an anticipatory

(1897) colophon to the story of Hollond (1911). And it is a reiteration of the fruitlessness of uninhibited ambition.

The narrator claims to have been told the tale by the "King of the Numidians"—a reference to the Border gipsies, but this gipsy is a scholar gipsy as we later learn. The setting is Scottish and is highly humorous but with a touch of faerie throughout. A whaup (curlew) addresses a godly shepherd in Scots, and contrasts ancient faiths and cultures with the world of the "black-gowned" Presbyterian minister known to the shepherd. The bird prompts the man to look beyond his shepherding to the wider world and indeed to the wild deeds of his ancestors.

The shepherd is gradually fascinated by what the whaup has to say and the whaup persuades him to participate in a magic spell, on ground known to Thomas the Rhymer. He falls into a trance and levitates, hearing a melody which (like the Pied Piper) prompts him to take to the Open Road (a popular literary fad of the day). The tune changes to "the Ballad of Grey Weather, which makes him who hears it sick all the days of his life for something he cannot name". (This tallies with the *Sehnsucht* of the German Romantics.) A conversation next day with his minister and with a Wise Woman does not prevent his taking the road south. He is prepared to abandon the routine "ministrations" of his faith and ignores the woman's claim that while a woman too may hear the "Rime" of the melody she will "lay it up in her soul and bide at hame". Nevertheless, ". . . let none" says the King, "pray to have the full music; for it will make him who hears it a footsore traveller in the ways o' the world and a masterless man till death".

By the time he wrote the story, Buchan was already well on the way to "hearing the full music".

(6) *The Use of Artificial Devices*

By way of tailpiece, we may turn to "A Lucid Interval", written in 1910, published in *The Moon Endureth* (1912). This shows Buchan again in humorous mood, but it is also satirical, aimed at what he regarded as the unctuousness of contemporary Liberal politicians. An Indian wants the government to right a wrong relating to land tenure in the Nepal border. (Buchan's brother Willie was an Indian civil servant under the Raj till his death in 1912.) He fails and resorts to the use of a drug which he ensures will be used by a dependent of his own family in a meal the latter will cook for a dinner to be held in the former Viceroy of India's house in London. Those attending include members of the (then Liberal) government. The effect of the drug is to provide some of them with a "lucid" interval in which they depart from their unctuous, platitudinous political stances. This has further effects in parliament. But when the drug has worn off through the cook's administration (on behalf of his Indian superior) of an antidote—to prevent the implementing of a policy of enforced Indian emigration to Africa—everything returns to normal.

Here we see a different Buchan—the Buchan at the centre of things, the politician who in 1911 stood as parliamentary candidate for Peebles and Selkirk.

John Buchan's story-telling is the product of a complex personality. His early literary enterprise may be regarded a projection of his own need to detach from influences that could have destroyed him, as they nearly destroyed Ladlaw and the several other characters we have looked at. These stories represent only a fraction of his vast output.[14] But, taking them together, we can see that his inherited Calvinism, his classics and his happy childhood with its store of Scots folklore provided him with a balance which enabled him to end his career as a latter-day Justinian of sorts: from 1935 till his death in 1940 he was Governor General of Canada.

J. C. G. G.
September 1997

Notes

1. David Daniell, *The Interpreter's House* (1975) has already drawn attention to Buchan's ability to create myths. Their source must surely be in his imaginative perceptiveness in handling the classics, itself the product of his father's communication of his interest in Scottish ballads and fairy tales to his family.

2. The basis for the new approach is in an unpublished essay of mine produced in the 1980s.

3. The Blackwood edition is fuller than Lownie's and has been used here.

4. This term is used for the fictitious story-teller set up by Buchan to distance himself from his creation.

5. The name is that given to Greek prophetesses, such as the Erythraean Sybil, named after the red earth of her alleged birthplace, and the Sybil of Cumae. In "The Watcher" one of the topographical features is red rock, which the narrator speaks of as "sickening red stone". Several paragraphs are devoted to building up the atmosphere of dread on the basis of the Scottish moorland topography. (The young Buchan liked to compare other parts of the Scottish landscape more favourably with that of Greece.)

6. I refer to this in my Introduction and Notes to *Witch Wood*, O.U.P. World's Classics (1993).

7. Article in *The John Buchan Journal*, 9 (1989) pp14-26. Nevertheless, the *Aeneid* VI would have been enough, together with his knowledge of Old Testament references to pagan groves, to launch Buchan into the *temenos* theme.

8. *Kosmokrator* ultimately is contrastable with *Pantokrator*—ruler of all things—used as a Jewish and Christian description of God. In *A Lodge in the Wilderness* (1906— the same date as that in which the present story was initially published in *Blackwood's Magazine*) there is a circumstantial development of the idea that a nineteenth-century political personality might have a secret world, at odds with his everyday public character, in which he sees himself as a usurping Byzantine ruler.

9. In *The Northern Muse* (1924), Buchan—the editor of that anthology of Scots poetry—rightly refers to the poet Dunbar as being of "that fantastic house of March which had for its motto *Parmi ceu haut bois conduyrai m'amie*". The link with Maitland's name is, as far as I know, fictitious, though the Maitlands were a powerful Borders family.

10. It can be no coincidence that in 1909 Buchan was asked to examine Lady Lovelace's archives to reach some conclusion on the quarrel between Byron and his wife—Lord Lovelace having written *Astarte* to vindicate his grandmother, the lady in question (Janet Adam Smith, *John Buchan*, p175). As to the conical tower, Aphrodite/Astarte in Paphos was symbolized by a cone!

11. *Memory Hold-the-Door*, reprinted 1964, p121.

12. cf. also his use of *The Pilgrim's Progress* in *Mr Standfast* (1919).

13. Traherne (1637/8-1674) was a member of Brasenose College, Oxford—Buchan's college. According to Helen Gardner, *The Metaphysical Poets* (Penguin Books 1972, p321f.) his poems were discovered by Bertram Dobell in 1896 or 1897. In these years Buchan was an undergraduate at Brasenose! Buchan was interested in the seventeenth-century metaphysical poets, and in particular in the Cambridge Platonists.

14. Our selection illustrates the major themes in Buchan's treatment of the supernatural.

THE WATCHER
BY THE THRESHOLD

CHAPTER I

THE HOUSE OF MORE

I

I HAVE told this story to many audiences with diverse results, and once again I take my reputation in my hands and brave the perils. To the common circle of my friends it was a romance for a winter's fire, and I, the most prosaic of men, was credited with a fancy. Once I repeated it to an acquaintance, who, scenting mystery, transcribed it in a notebook, and, with feigned names, it figured in the publications of a Learned Society. One man only heard me with true appreciation; but he was a wandering spirit with an ear open to marvels, and I hesitate to advance his security. He received it simply, saying that God was great, and I cannot improve upon his comment.

A chill evening in the early October of the year 189– found me driving in a dogcart through the belts of antique woodland which form the lowland limits of the hilly parish of More. The Highland express, which brought me from the North, took me no farther than Perth. Thence it had been a slow journey in a disjointed local train, till I emerged on the platform at Morefoot, with a bleak prospect of pit-stalks, coal-heaps, certain sour corn-lands, and far to the west a line of moor where the sun was setting. A neat groom and a respectable trap took the edge off my discomfort, and soon I had forgotten my sacrifice and found eyes for the darkening landscape. We were driving through a land of thick woods, cut at rare intervals by old long-frequented highways. The More, which at Morefoot is an open sewer, became a sullen woodland stream, where the brown leaves of the season drifted. At times we would pass an ancient lodge, and through a gap in the trees would come a glimpse of a chipped crow-step gable. The names of such houses, as told me by my companion, were all famous. This one had been the home of a drunken Jacobite laird, and a kind of north-country Medmenham. Unholy revels had waked the old halls, and the Devil had been toasted at many a hell-fire dinner. The next was the property of a great Scots law family, and there the old Lord of Session who built the place, in his frowsy wig and carpet slippers, had laid down the canons of Taste for his day and society. The whole country had the air of faded and bygone gentility. The mossy roadside walls had stood for two hundred years, the few wayside houses were toll-bars or defunct hostelries. The names, too, were great—Scots baronial with a smack of France—Chatelray and Reiverslaw, Black Holm and Champertoun. The place had a cunning charm, mystery dwelt in every cranny, and yet it did not please me. The earth smelt heavy and raw, the roads were red underfoot, all was old, sorrowful, and uncanny. Compared with the fresh Highland glen I had left, where wind and sun and flying showers were never absent, all was chilly and dull and dead. Even when the sun sent a shiver of crimson over the crests of certain firs, I felt no delight in the prospect. I admitted shamefacedly to myself that I was in a very bad temper.

I had been staying at Glenaicill with the Clanroydens, and for a week had found the proper pleasure in life. You know the house with its old rooms and gardens, and the miles of heather which defend it from the world. The shooting had been extraordinary for a wild place far on in the season, for there are few partridges and the woodcock are notoriously late. I had done respectably in my stalking, more than respectably on the river, and creditably on the moors. Moreover, there were pleasant people in the house—and there were the Clanroydens. I had had a hard year's work, sustained to the last moment of term, and a fortnight in Norway had been disastrous. It was therefore with real comfort that I had settled myself down for another ten days in Glenaicill, when all my plans were shattered by Sybil's letter.

Sybil is my cousin and my very good friend, and in old days when I was briefless I had fallen in love with her many times. But she very sensibly chose otherwise, and married a man Ladlaw—Robert John Ladlaw—who had been at school with me. He was a cheery, good-humoured fellow, a great sportsman, a justice of the peace and deputy-lieutenant for his county, and something of an antiquary in a mild way. He had a box in Leicestershire to which he went in the hunting season; but from February till October he lived in his moorland home. The place was called the House of More, and I had shot there once or twice in recent years. I remembered its loneliness and its comfort, the charming diffident Sybil and Ladlaw's genial welcome. And my recollections set me puzzling again over the letter which that morning had broken into my comfort. "You promised us a visit this autumn," Sybil had written, "and I wish you would come as soon as you can." So far common politeness. But she had gone on to reveal the fact that Ladlaw was ill, she did not know how exactly, but something she thought, about his heart. Then she had signed herself my affectionate cousin, and then had come a short violent postscript, in which, as it were, the fences of convention had been laid low. "For Heaven's sake come and see us!" she scrawled below. "Bob is terribly ill, and I am crazy. Come at once." And then she finished with an afterthought, "Don't bother about bringing doctors. It is not their business."

She had assumed that I would come, and dutifully I set out. I could not regret my decision, but I took leave to upbraid my luck. The thought of Glenaicill with the woodcock beginning to arrive, and the Clanroydens imploring me to stay, saddened my journey in the morning, and the murky, coally midland country of the afternoon completed my depression. The drive through the woodlands of More failed to raise my spirits. I was anxious about Sybil and Ladlaw, and the accursed country had always given me a certain eeriness on my first approaching it. You may call it silly; but I have no nerves, and am little susceptible to vague sentiment. It was sheer physical dislike of the rich deep soil, the woody and antique smells, the melancholy roads and trees, and the flavour of old mystery. I am aggressively healthy and wholly Philistine. I love clear outlines and strong colours,

3

and More, with its half-tints and hazy distances, depressed me
miserably. Even when the road crept uphill and the trees ended,
I found nothing to hearten me in the moorland which succeeded.
It was genuine moorland, close on 800 feet above the sea, and
through it ran this old grass-grown coach-road. Low hills rose to
the left, and to the right after some miles of peat flared the
chimneys of pits and oil-works. Straight in front the moor ran
out into the horizon, and there in the centre was the last dying
spark of the sun. The place was as still as the grave save for the
crunch of our wheels on the grassy road; but the flaring lights
to the north seemed to endow it with life. I have rarely felt so
keenly the feeling of movement in the inanimate world. It was
an unquiet place, and I shivered nervously. Little gleams of loch
came from the hollows, the burns were brown with peat, and
every now and then there rose in the moor jags of sickening red
stone. I remembered that Ladlaw had talked about the place as
the old Manann, the holy land of the ancient races. I had paid
little attention at the time, but now it struck me that the old
peoples had been wise in their choice. There was something
uncanny in this soil and air. Framed in dank mysterious woods,
and a country of coal and ironstone, no great distance, too, from
the capital city, it was a sullen relic of a lost barbarism. Over the
low hills lay a green pastoral country with bright streams and
valleys, but here in this peaty desert there were few sheep and
little cultivation. The House of More was the only dwelling, and,
save for the ragged village, the wilderness was given over to the
wild things of the hills. The shooting was good; but the best
shooting on earth would not persuade me to make my abode in
such a place. Ladlaw was ill; well, I did not wonder. You can
have uplands without air, moors that are not health-giving, and
a country life which is more arduous than a townsman's. I
shivered again, for I seemed to have passed in a few hours from
the open noon to a kind of dank twilight.

We passed the village and entered the lodge-gates. Here there
were trees again, little innocent new-planted firs, which flourished
badly. Some large plane-trees grew near the house, and there
were thickets upon thickets of the ugly elder. Even in the half-
darkness I could see that the lawns were trim and the flower-beds

respectable for the season; doubtless Sybil looked after the gardeners. The oblong whitewashed house, more like a barrack than ever, opened suddenly on my sight, and I experienced my first sense of comfort since I left Glenaicill. Here I should find warmth and company, and, sure enough, the hall door was wide open, and in the great flood of light which poured from it Sybil stood to welcome me.

She ran down the steps as I dismounted, and, with a word to the groom, caught my arm and drew me into the shadow. "Oh, Henry, it was so good of you to come. You mustn't let Bob think that you know he is ill. We don't talk about it. I'll tell you afterwards. I want you to cheer him up. Now we must go in, for he is in the hall expecting you."

While I stood blinking in the light, Ladlaw came forward with outstretched hand and his usual cheery greeting. I looked at him and saw nothing unnatural in his appearance: a little drawn at the lips, perhaps, and heavy below the eyes, but still fresh-coloured and healthy. It was Sybil who showed change. She was very pale, her pretty eyes were deplorably mournful, and in place of her delightful shyness there was the self-confidence and composure of pain. I was honestly shocked and, as I dressed, my heart was full of hard thoughts about Ladlaw. What could his illness mean? He seemed well and cheerful, while Sybil was pale, and yet it was Sybil who had written the postscript. As I warmed myself by the fire, I resolved that this particular family difficulty was my proper business.

II

The Ladlaws were waiting for me in the drawing-room. I noticed something new and strange in Sybil's demeanour. She looked to her husband with a motherly protective air, while Ladlaw, who had been the extreme of masculine independence, seemed to cling to his wife with a curious appealing fidelity. In conversation he did little more than echo her words. Till dinner was announced he spoke of the weather, the shooting, and Mabel Clanroyden. Then he did a queer thing, for, when I was about to offer my arm to Sybil, he forestalled me, and, clutching her right arm with his left hand, led the way to the dining-room, leaving me to follow in some bewilderment.

I have rarely taken part in a more dismal meal. The House of More has a pretty Georgian panelling through most of the rooms; but in the dining-room the walls are level, and painted a dull stone colour. Abraham offered up Isaac in a ghastly picture in front of me. Some photographs of the Quorn hung over the mantelpiece, and five or six drab ancestors filled up the remaining space. But one thing was new and startling. A great marble bust, a genuine antique, frowned on me from a pedestal. The head was in the late Roman style, clearly of some emperor, and in its commonplace environment the great brows, the massive neck, and the mysterious solemn lips had a surprising effect. I nodded towards the thing, and asked what it represented.

Ladlaw grunted something which I took for "Justinian," but he never raised his eyes from his plate. By accident I caught Sybil's glance. She looked towards the bust, and laid a finger on her lips.

The meal grew more doleful as it advanced. Sybil scarcely touched a dish, but her husband ate ravenously of everything. He was a strong, thick-set man, with a square, kindly face, burned brown by the sun. Now he seemed to have suddenly coarsened. He gobbled with undignified haste, and his eye was extraordinarily vacant. A question made him start, and he would turn on me a face so strange and inert that I repented the interruption.

I asked him about the autumn's sport, and he collected his wits with difficulty. He thought it had been good on the whole, but he had shot badly. He had not been quite so fit as usual. No, he had had nobody staying with him—Sybil had wanted to be alone. He was afraid the moor might have been under-shot, but he would make a big day with keepers and farmers before the winter.

"Bob has done pretty well," Sybil said. "He hasn't been out often, for the weather has been very bad here. You can have no idea, Henry, how horrible this moorland place of ours can be when it tries. It is one great sponge sometimes, with ugly red burns, and mud to the ankles."

"I don't think it's healthy," said I.

Ladlaw lifted his face. "Nor do I: I think it's intolerable; but I am so busy, I can't get away."

Once again I caught Sybil's warning eye as I was about to question him on his business.

Clearly the man's brain had received a shock, and he was beginning to suffer from hallucinations. This could be the only explanation, for he had always led a temperate life. The *distrait* wandering manner was the only sign of his malady, for otherwise he seemed normal and mediocre as ever. My heart grieved for Sybil, alone with him in this wilderness.

Then he broke the silence. He lifted his head and looked nervously around till his eye fell on the Roman bust.

"Do you know that this countryside is the old Manann?" he said.

It was an odd turn to the conversation, but I was glad of a sign of intelligence. I answered that I had heard so.

"It's a queer name," he said oracularly; "but the thing it stood for was queerer. Manann, Manaw," he repeated, rolling the words on his tongue. As he spoke, he glanced sharply, and, as it seemed to me, fearfully, at his left side.

The movement of his body made his napkin slip from his left knee and fall on the floor. It leaned against his leg, and he started from its touch as if he had been stung by a snake. I have never seen a more sheer and transparent terror on a man's face. He got to his feet, his strong frame shaking like a rush. Sybil ran round to his side, picked up the napkin, and flung it on a sideboard. Then she stroked his hair as one would stroke a frightened horse. She called him by his old boy's name of Robin, and at her touch and voice he became quiet. But the particular course then in progress was removed untasted.

In a few minutes he seemed to have forgotten his behaviour, for he took up the former conversation. For a time he spoke well and briskly.

"You lawyers," he said, "understand only the dry framework of the past. You cannot conceive the rapture, which only the antiquary can feel, of constructing in every detail an old culture. Take this Manann. If I could explore the secret of these moors, I would write the world's greatest book. I would write of that

7

prehistoric life when man was knit close to nature. I would describe the people who were brothers of the red earth and the red rock and the red streams of the hills. Oh, it would be horrible, but superb, tremendous! It would be more than a piece of history; it would be a new gospel, a new theory of life. It would kill materialism once and for all. Why, man, all the poets who have deified and personified nature would not do an eighth part of my work. I would show you the unknown, the hideous, shrieking mystery at the back of this simple nature. Men would see the profundity of the old crude faiths which they affect to despise. I would make a picture of our shaggy, sombre-eyed forefather, who heard strange things in the hill-silences. I would show him brutal and terror-stricken, but wise, wise, God alone knows how wise! The Romans knew it, and they learned what they could from him, but he did not tell them much. But we have some of his blood in us, and we may go deeper. Manann! A queer land nowadays! I sometimes love it and sometimes hate it, but I always fear it. It is like that statue, inscrutable."

I would have told him that he was talking mystical nonsense; but I had looked towards the bust, and my rudeness was checked on my lips. The moor might be a common piece of ugly wasteland, but the statue was inscrutable—of that there was no doubt. I hate your cruel, heavy-mouthed Roman busts; to me they have none of the beauty of life, and little of the interest of art. But my eyes were fastened on this as they had never before looked on marble. The oppression of the heavy woodlands, the mystery of the silent moor, seemed to be caught and held in this face. It was the intangible mystery of culture on the verge of savagery, a cruel, lustful wisdom, and yet a kind of bitter austerity which laughed at the game of life and stood aloof. There was no weakness in the heavy-veined brow and slumbrous eyelids. It was the face of one who had conquered the world and found it dust and ashes, one who had eaten of the tree of the knowledge of good and evil and scorned human wisdom. And at the same time it was the face of one who knew uncanny things, a man who was the intimate of the half-world and the dim background of life. Why on earth I should connect the

Roman grandee[1] with the moorland parish of More, I cannot say; but the fact remains, that there was that in the face which I knew had haunted me through the woodlands and bogs of the place, a sleepless, dismal, incoherent melancholy.

"I bought that at Colenzo's," Ladlaw said, "because it took my fancy. It matches well with this place."

I thought it matched very ill with his drab walls and Quorn photographs, but I held my peace.

"Do you know who it is?" he asked. "It is the head of the greatest man the world has ever seen. You are a lawyer and know your Justinian."

The Pandects are scarcely part of the daily work of a common-law barrister. I had not looked into them since I left college.

"I know that he married an actress," I said, "and was a sort of all-round genius. He made law and fought battles and had rows with the Church. A curious man! I And wasn't there some story about his selling his soul to the Devil and getting law in exchange? Rather a poor bargain!"

I chattered away sillily enough, to dispel the gloom of that dinner-table. The result of my words was unhappy. Ladlaw gasped, and caught at his left side as if in pain. Sybil, with tragic eyes, had been making signs to me to hold my peace. Now she ran round to her husband's side and comforted him like a child. As she passed me she managed to whisper in my ear to talk to her only and let her husband alone.

For the rest of dinner I obeyed my orders to the letter. Ladlaw ate his food in gloomy silence, while I spoke to Sybil of our relatives and friends, of London, Glenaicill, and any random subject. The poor girl was dismally forgetful, and her eye would wander to her husband with wifely anxiety. I remember being suddenly overcome by the comic aspect of it all. Here were we three fools alone in this dank upland, one of us sick and nervous,

[1] I have identified the bust, which, when seen under other circumstances, had little power to affect me. It was a copy of the head of Justinian in the Tesci Museum at Venice, and several duplicates exist, dating apparently from the seventh century, and showing traces of Byzantine decadence in the scrollwork on the hair. It is engraved in M. Delacroix's *Byzantium*, and, I think, in Windscheid's *Pandektenlehrbuch*.

talking out-of-the-way nonsense about Manann and Justinian, gobbling his food and getting scared at his napkin, another gravely anxious, and myself at my wits' end for a solution. It was a Mad Tea-party with a vengeance, Sybil the melancholy little Dormouse, and Ladlaw the incomprehensible Hatter. I laughed aloud, but checked myself when I caught my cousin's eye. It was really no case for finding humour. Ladlaw was very ill, and Sybil's face was getting deplorably thin.

I welcomed the end of that meal with unmannerly joy, for I wanted to speak seriously with my host. Sybil told the butler to have the lamps lit in the library. Then she leaned over to me and spoke low and rapidly: "I want you to talk with Bob. I'm sure you can do him good. You'll have to be very patient with him and very gentle. Oh please try and find out what is wrong with him. He won't tell me, and I can only guess."

The butler returned with word that the library was ready to receive us, and Sybil rose to go. Ladlaw half rose, protesting, making the most curious, feeble clutches at his side. His wife quieted him. "Henry will look after you, dear," she said. "You are going into the library to smoke." Then she slipped from the room, and we were left alone.

He caught my arm fiercely with his left hand, and his grip nearly made me cry out. As we walked down the hall I could feel his arm twitching from the elbow to the shoulder. Clearly he was in pain, and I set it down to some form of cardiac affection, which might possibly issue in paralysis.

I settled him in the biggest armchair, and took one of his cigars. The library is the pleasantest room in the house, and at night, when a peat-fire burned on the old hearth and the great red curtains were drawn, it used to be the place for comfort and good talk. Now I noticed changes. Ladlaw's bookshelves had been filled with the proceedings of antiquarian societies and many light-hearted works in *belles-lettres*. But now the Badminton Library had been cleared out of a shelf where it stood most convenient to the hand, and its place taken by an old Leyden reprint of Justinian. There were books on Byzantine subjects of which I never dreamed he had heard the names. There were volumes of history and speculation, all of a slightly bizarre kind;

and to crown everything, there were several bulky medical works with gaudily coloured plates. The old atmosphere of sport and travel had gone from the room, with the medley of rods, whips, and gun-cases which used to cumber the tables. Now the place was moderately tidy and slightly learned—and I did not like it.

Ladlaw refused to smoke, and sat for a little while in silence. Then of his own accord he broke the tension—

"It was devilish good of you to come, Harry. This is a lonely place for a man who is a bit seedy."

"I thought you might be alone," I said, "so I looked you up on my way down from Glenaicill. I'm sorry to find you looking ill."

"Do you notice it?" he asked sharply.

"It's tolerably patent," I said. "Have you seen a doctor?"

He said something uncomplimentary about doctors, and kept looking at me with his curious dull eyes.

I remarked the strange posture in which he sat—his head screwed round to his right shoulder, and his whole body a protest against something at his left hand.

"It looks like your heart," I said. "You seem to have pains in your left side."

Again a spasm of fear. I went over to him and stood at the back of his chair.

"Now, for goodness' sake, my dear fellow, tell me what is wrong? You're scaring Sybil to death. It's lonely work for the poor girl, and I wish you would let me help you."

He was lying back in his chair now, with his eyes half shut, and shivering like a frightened colt. The extraordinary change in one who had been the strongest of the strong kept me from realising its gravity. I put a hand on his shoulder, but he flung it off.

"For God's sake sit down!" he said hoarsely. "I'm going to tell you; but I'll never make you understand."

I sat down promptly opposite him.

"It's the Devil," he said very solemnly.

I am afraid that I was rude enough to laugh. He took no notice, but sat with the same tense, miserable air, staring over my head.

"Right," said I. "Then it is the Devil. It's a new complaint, so it's as well I did not bring a doctor. How does it affect you?"

He made the old impotent clutch at the air with his left hand. I had the sense to become grave at once. Clearly this was some mental affection, some hallucination born of physical pain.

Then he began to talk in a low voice, very rapidly, with his head bent forward like a hunted animal's. I am not going to set down what he told me in his own words, for they were incoherent often, and there was much repetition. But I am going to write the gist of the odd story which took my sleep away on that autumn night, with such explanations and additions as I think needful. The fire died down, the wind arose, the hour grew late, and still he went on in his mumbling recitative. I forgot to smoke, forgot my comfort—everything but the odd figure of my friend and his inconceivable romance. And the night before I had been in cheerful Glenaicill!

He had returned to the House of More, he said, in the latter part of May, and shortly after he fell ill. It was a trifling sickness—influenza or something—but he had never quite recovered. The rainy weather of June depressed him, and the extreme heat of July made him listless and weary. A kind of insistent sleepiness hung over him, and he suffered much from nightmare. Towards the end of July his former health returned; but he was haunted with a curious oppression. He seemed to himself to have lost the art of being alone. There was a perpetual sound in his left ear, a kind of moving and rustling at his left side, which never left him by night or day. In addition he had become the prey of nerves and an insensate dread of the unknown.

Ladlaw, as I have explained, was a commonplace man, with fair talents, a mediocre culture, honest instincts, and the beliefs and incredulities of his class. On abstract grounds I should have declared him an unlikely man to be the victim of a hallucination. He had a kind of dull, bourgeois rationalism, which used to find reasons for all things in Heaven and earth. At first he controlled his dread with proverbs. He told himself it was the sequel of his illness, or the light-headedness of summer heat on the moors. But it soon outgrew his comfort. It became a living second presence, an *alter ego* which dogged his footsteps. He became acutely afraid of it. He dared not be alone for a moment, and clung to Sybil's company despairingly. She went off for a week's visit in the beginning of August, and he endured for seven days the tortures of the lost. His malady advanced upon him with swift steps. The presence became more real daily. In the early dawning, in the twilight, and in the first hours of the morning it seemed at times to take a visible bodily form. A kind of amorphous featureless shadow would run from his side into the darkness, and he would sit palsied with terror. Sometimes in lonely places his footsteps sounded double, and something would brush elbows with him. Human society alone exorcised it. With Sybil at his side he was happy; but as soon as she left him the thing came slinking back from the unknown to watch by him. Company might have saved him, but joined to his affliction was a crazy dread of his fellows. He would not leave his moorland home, but must bear his burden alone among the wild streams and mosses of that dismal place.

The Twelfth came, and he shot wretchedly, for his nerve had gone to pieces. He stood exhaustion badly, and became a dweller about the doors. But with this bodily inertness came an extraordinary intellectual revival. He read widely in a blundering way, and he speculated unceasingly. It was characteristic of the man that, as soon as he left the paths of the prosaic, he should seek his supernatural in a very concrete form. He assumed that he was haunted by the Devil—the visible, personal Devil in whom our fathers believed. He waited hourly for the shape at his side to speak, but no words came. The Accuser of the Brethren in all but tangible form was his ever-present companion. He felt, he declared, the spirit of old evil entering subtly into his blood. He sold his soul many times over, and yet there was no possibility of resistance. It was a Visitation more undeserved than Job's, and a thousandfold more awful.

For a week or more he was tortured with a kind of religious mania. When a man of a healthy, secular mind finds himself adrift on the terrible ocean of religious troubles, he is peculiarly helpless, for he has not the most rudimentary knowledge of the winds and tides. It was useless to call up his old carelessness; he had suddenly dropped into a new world where old proverbs did not apply. And all the while, mind you, there was the shrieking terror of it—an intellect all alive to the torture and the most unceasing physical fear. For a little he was on the near edge of idiocy.

Then by accident it took a new form. While sitting with Sybil one day in the library, he began listlessly to turn over the leaves of an old book. He read a few pages, and found the hint of a story like his own. It was some French life of Justinian, one of the unscholarly productions of last century, made up of stories from Procopius and tags of Roman law. Here was his own case written down in black and white; and the man had been a king of kings! This was a new comfort, and for a little—strange though it may seem—he took a sort of pride in his affliction. He worshipped the great emperor and read every scrap he could find on him, not excepting the Pandects and the Digest. He sent for the bust in the dining-room, paying a fabulous price. Then he settled himself to study his imperial prototype, and the study became an idolatry. As I have said, Ladlaw was a man of ordinary talents and certainly of meagre imaginative power. And yet from the lies of the *Secret History* and the crudities of German legalists he had constructed a marvellous portrait of a man. Sitting there in the half-lit room, he drew the picture—the quiet, cold king with his inheritance of Dacian mysticism, holding the great world in fee, giving it law and religion, fighting its wars, building its churches, and yet all the while intent upon his own private work of making his peace with his soul. The churchman and warrior whom all the world worshipped, and yet one going through life with his lip quivering, the Watcher by the Threshold ever at his left side. Sometimes at night in the great Brazen Palace, warders heard the emperor walking in the dark corridors, alone and yet not alone; for once, when a servant entered with a lamp, he saw his master with a face as of another world, and something beside him which had no face or shape, but which he knew to be that hoary Evil which is older than the stars. Crazy nonsense! I had to rub my eyes to assure myself that I was not sleeping. No! There was my friend with his suffering face, and it was the library of More.

And then he spoke of Theodora—actress, harlot, *devotée*, empress. For him the lady was but another part of the uttermost horror, a form of the shapeless thing at his side. I felt myself falling under the fascination. I have no nerves and little imagination, but in a flash I seemed to realise something of that awful featureless face, crouching ever at a man's hand, till darkness and loneliness comes and it rises to its mastery. I shivered as I looked at the man in the chair before me. Those dull eyes of his were looking upon things I could not see, and I saw their terror. I realised that it was grim earnest for him. Nonsense or no, some devilish fancy had usurped the place of sanity, and he was being slowly broken upon the wheel. And then, when his left hand twitched, I almost cried out. I had thought it comic before; now it seemed the last proof of tragedy.

He stopped, and I got up with loose knees and went to the window. Better the black night than the intangible horror within. I flung up the sash and looked out across the moor. There was no light, nothing but an inky darkness and the uncanny rustle of elderbushes. The sound chilled me, and I closed the window.

"The land is the old Manann," Ladlaw was saying. "We are beyond the pale here. Do you hear the wind?"

I forced myself back into sanity and looked at my watch. It was nearly one o'clock.

"What ghastly idiots we are!" I said. "I am off to bed."

Ladlaw looked at me helplessly. "For God's sake don't leave me alone!" he moaned. "Get Sybil."

We went together back to the hall, while he kept the same feverish grip on my arm. Someone was sleeping in a chair by the hall fire, and to my distress I recognised my hostess. The poor child must have been sadly wearied. She came forward with her anxious face.

"I'm afraid Bob has kept you very late, Henry," she said. "I hope you will sleep well. Breakfast at nine, you know." And then I left them.

Over my bed there was a little picture, a reproduction of some Italian work of Christ and the Demoniac. Some impulse made me hold my candle up to it. The madman's face was torn with passion and suffering, and his eye had the pained furtive look which I had come to know. And by his left side there was a dim shape crouching.

I got into bed hastily, but not to sleep. I felt that my reason must be going. I had been pitchforked from our clear and cheerful modern life into the mists of old superstition. Old tragic stories of my Calvinist upbringing returned to haunt me. The man dwelt in by a devil was no new fancy; but I believed that Science had docketed and analysed and explained the Devil out of the world. I remembered my dabblings in the occult before I settled down to law—the story of Donisarius the monk of Padua, the unholy legend of the Face of Proserpina, the tales of *succubi* and *incubi*, the Leannain Sith and the Hidden Presence. But here was something stranger still. I had stumbled upon that very possession which fifteen hundred years ago had made the monks of New Rome tremble and cross themselves. Some devilish occult force, lingering through the ages, had come to life after a long sleep. God knows what earthly connection there was between the splendid Emperor of the World and my prosaic friend, or between the glittering shores of the Bosphorus and this moorland parish! But the land was the old Manann! The spirit may have lingered in the earth and air, a deadly legacy from Pict and Roman. I had felt the uncanniness of the place; I had augured ill of it from the first. And then in sheer disgust I rose and splashed my face with cold water.

I lay down again, laughing miserably at my credulity. That I, the sober and rational, should believe in this crazy fable, was too palpably absurd. I would steel my mind resolutely against such harebrained theories. It was a mere bodily ailment—liver out of order, weak heart, bad circulation, or something of that sort. At the worst it might be some affection of the brain to be treated by a specialist. I vowed to myself that next morning the best doctor in Edinburgh should be brought to More.

The worst of it was that my duty compelled me to stand my ground. I foresaw the few remaining weeks of my holiday blighted. I should be tied to this moorland prison, a sort of keeper and nurse in one, tormented by silly fancies. It was a charming prospect, and the thought of Glenaicill and the woodcock made me bitter against Ladlaw. But there was no way out of it. I might do Ladlaw good, and I could not have Sybil worn to death by his vagaries.

My ill-nature comforted me, and I forgot the horror of the thing in its vexation. After that, I think I fell asleep and dozed uneasily till morning. When I awoke I was in a better frame of mind. The early sun had worked wonders with the moorland. The low hills stood out fresh-coloured and clear against the pale October sky, the elders sparkled with frost, the raw film of morn was rising from the little loch in tiny clouds. It was a cold rousing day, and I dressed in good spirits and went down to breakfast.

I found Ladlaw looking ruddy and well, very different from the broken man I remembered of the night before. We were alone, for Sybil was breakfasting in bed. I remarked on his ravenous appetite, and he smiled cheerily. He made two jokes during the meal, he laughed often, and I began to forget the events of the previous day. It seemed to me that I might still flee from More with a clear conscience. He had forgotten about his illness. When I touched distantly upon the matter he showed a blank face.

It might be that the affection had passed: on the other hand, it might return to him at the darkening—I had no means to decide. His manner was still a trifle *distrait* and peculiar, and I did not like the dulness in his eye. At any rate, I should spend the day in his company, and the evening would decide the question.

I proposed shooting, which he promptly vetoed. He was no good at walking, he said, and the birds were wild. This seriously limited the possible occupations. Fishing there was none, and hill-climbing was out of the question. He proposed a game at billiards, and I pointed to the glory of the morning. It would have been sacrilege to waste such sunshine in knocking balls about. Finally we agreed to drive somewhere and have lunch, and he ordered the dogcart.

In spite of all forebodings I enjoyed the day. We drove in the opposite direction from the woodland parts, right away across the moor to the coal-country beyond. We lunched at the little mining town of Borrowmuir, in a small and noisy public-house.

The roads made bad going, the country was far from pretty, and yet the drive did not bore me. Ladlaw talked incessantly, talked as I had never heard man talk before. There was something indescribable in all he said—a different point of view, a lost groove of thought, a kind of innocence and archaic shrewdness in one. I can only give you a hint of it by saying that it was like the mind of an early ancestor placed suddenly among modern surroundings. It was wise with a remote wisdom, and silly (now and then) with a quite antique and distant silliness.

I will give you instances of both. He provided me with a theory of certain early fortifications, which must be true, which commends itself to the mind with overwhelming conviction, and yet which is so out of the way of common speculation that no man could have guessed it. I do not propose to set down the details, for I am working at it on my own account. Again, he told me the story of an old marriage custom, which till recently survived in this district—told it with full circumstantial detail and constant allusions to other customs which he could not possibly have known of. Now for the other side. He explained why well-water is in winter warmer than a running stream, and this was his explanation. At the Antipodes our winter is summer; consequently the water of a well which comes through from the other side of the earth must be warm in winter and cold in summer, since in our summer it is winter there. You perceive what this is. It is no mere silliness, but a genuine effort of an early mind which had just grasped the fact of the Antipodes, to use it in explanation.

Gradually I was forced to the belief that it was not Ladlaw who was talking to me, but something speaking through him, something at once wiser and simpler. My old fear of the Devil began to depart. This spirit, this exhalation, whatever it was, was ingenuous in its way, at least in its daylight aspect. For a moment I had an idea that it was a real reflex of Byzantine thought, and that by cross-examining I might make marvellous discoveries. The ardour of the scholar began to rise in me, and I asked a question about that much-debated point, the legal status of the *apocrissiarii*. To my vexation he gave no response. Clearly the intelligence of this familiar had its limits.

It was about three in the afternoon, and we had gone half of our homeward journey, when signs of the old terror began to appear. I was driving, and Ladlaw sat on my left. I noticed him growing nervous and silent, shivering at the flick of the whip, and turning half-way round towards me. Then he asked me to change places, and I had the unpleasant work of driving from the wrong side. After that I do not think he spoke once till we arrived at More, but sat huddled together with the driving-rug almost up to his chin—an eccentric figure of a man.

I foresaw another such night as the last, and I confess my heart sank. I had no stomach for more mysteries, and somehow with the approach of twilight the confidence of the day departed. The thing appeared in darker colours, and I could have found it in my mind to turn coward. Sybil alone deterred me. I could not bear to think of her alone with this demented being. I remembered her shy timidity, her innocence. It was monstrous that the poor thing should be called on thus to fight alone with phantoms. So I braced myself for another evening.

When we came to the House it was almost sunset. Ladlaw got out very carefully on the right side, and for a second stood by the horse. The sun was making our shadows long, and as I stood beyond him, it seemed for a moment that his shadow was double. It may have been mere fancy, for I had not time to look twice. He was standing, as I have said, with his left side next the horse. Suddenly the harmless elderly cob fell into a very panic of fright, reared upright, and all but succeeded in killing its master. I was in time to pluck Ladlaw from under its feet, but the beast had become perfectly unmanageable, and we left a groom struggling to quiet it.

In the hall the butler gave me a telegram. It was from my clerk, summoning me back at once to an important consultation.

CHAPTER II

THE MINISTER INTERVENES

HERE was a prompt removal of my scruples! There could be no question of my remaining, for the case was one of the first importance, which I had feared might break up my holiday. The consultation fell in vacation-time to meet the convenience of certain people who were going abroad, and there was the most instant demand for my presence. I must go, and at once; and, as I hunted in the timetable, I found that in five hours' time a night-train for the South would pass Borrowmuir, which might be stopped by special wire. This would give me time for dinner and a comfortable departure.

But I had no pleasure in my freedom, for I was in despair about Sybil. I must return to More—that was clear; and I must find someone to look after Ladlaw. I found my cousin in the drawing-room alone and told her my plans.

She was very pale and fragile, and she seemed to shiver as the prospect of solitude returned to her. I spoke with all the carelessness I could muster. "I am coming back," I said. "Don't think you have got rid of me so easily. It is most unpleasant to have to travel eight hundred miles in thirty-six hours, but there is no help for it. I ought to be back again by Friday morning. And you know Bob is much better. He was quite like his old self driving today."

My words comforted the poor child, and I went away with the novel feeling of a good conscience. Frankly, I hate the sordid and unpleasant. I am honestly a sun-worshipper; I have small taste for arduous duty, and the quixotic is my abhorrence. My professional success is an accident, for Lord knows I had no impulse to contend and little ambition. But somewhere or other I have the rudiments of an austere conscience. It gives me no peace, and as I love a quiet life, I do its bidding with a grumble. Now I grumbled fiercely in spirit, but outwardly I was a model of virtuous cheerfulness.

But to find somebody to keep Ladlaw company—there was the rub. I racked my brains to think of a substitute. It must be a man of some education and not a mere servant, and it must be somebody in the parish of More; the conjunction seemed for the moment impossible. Then a brilliant idea struck me. There was the minister of Morebrig, the ugly village by the roadside. I remembered him on previous visits. He was a burly young man, with a high complexion and a drooping blonde moustache, who smoked cheap cigarettes incessantly, and spat. He had been what they call a "brilliant student", and he was reported to be something of an orator, eagerly sought after by city congregations, but at present hiding his light under the bushel of Morebrig to allow him time to prepare some great theological work. Ladlaw had liked him in a half-amused and tolerant way, and he used to come sometimes to dine. His name was Bruce Oliphant, and he inhabited a dark manse at the outskirts of the village.

I had an hour before dinner, and I set out for Mr. Oliphant's dwelling. I remember the curious dull village street, without colour or life, drab women looking out of dingy doorways, and a solitary child playing in the red mud. The manse stood at the back of the usual elder thicket, a little place with small windows and a weather-stained front door. A gaunt old servant ushered me into Mr. Oliphant's study, where I found that young man smoking and reading a weekly paper. It was a room well stocked with books in the popular religious vein, and the Poets in gilt editions adorned his shelves. Mr. Oliphant greeted me with the nervous ease of one who would fain cultivate a good manner. The first sight of him sent my hopes down. He had a large calf-like face, mildly arrogant eyes, and a chin which fell sharply away beneath the eaves of his moustache. This was not one to do Ladlaw much good; indeed I questioned if I could ever make him understand, for the man before me had an impenetrable air of omniscience.

"I have come to ask you a great favour on behalf of the Ladlaws," said I. "You are the only other gentleman in the parish of More, and it is your duty to help your neighbours."

He bowed, with pleased eyes. "Anything," he said, "I'll be very glad."

"I am staying there just now, you know, and as it happens I

must go back to town by the night-train. I'll only be gone a day, but you know that Ladlaw is a melancholy beggar and gets low-spirited. Now I want you to go up and stay at the House for a couple of nights while I am away."

It was an odd request, and he stared at me. "Why, what's wrong with Mr. Ladlaw?" he asked. "I should never have called him melancholy. Now, his lady is different. She always looks a little pale. Did she send you to ask me?" Mr. Oliphant was a stickler for the usages of polite society.

I sat down in a chair and took one of his cigarettes. "Now, look here, Oliphant," I said. "You are a man of education and common sense, and I am going to do you the honour to tell you a story which I would not tell to a stupid man. A stupid man would laugh at me. I hope you will see the gravity of the thing."

I told him briefly the points in Ladlaw's case. His eyes grew very round as I went on, and when I finished he laughed nervously. He was clearly impressed; but he was too ignorant and unimaginative to understand fully, and he had his credit as a representative of modern thought to support. "Oh, come now! You don't mean all that; I never heard the like of it. You can't expect me as a Christian man to believe in a Pagan spirit. I might as well believe in ghosts at once. What has the familiar of a heathen emperor to do with this parish?"

"Justinian was a Christian," I said.

He looked puzzled. "It's all preposterous. Meaning no disrespect to you, I must decline to believe it. My profession compels me to discourage such nonsense."

"So does mine," I said wearily. "Good Lord! man, do you think I came here to tell you a fairy tale? It's the most terrible earnest. Now I want you to give me an answer, for I have very little time."

He was still incredulous and inclined to argue. "Do you know if Mr. Ladlaw has been—eh—a strictly temperate man?" he asked.

With this my patience departed. I got up to go, with rude thoughts on the stupidity of the clergy. But Mr. Oliphant was far from a refusal. He had no objection to exchange the barren comfort of the manse for the comparative luxury of the House, and he had no distrust of his power to enliven. As he accompanied me to the door he explained his position. "You see, if they really want me I will come. Tell Mrs. Ladlaw that I shall be delighted. Mrs. Ladlaw is a lady for whom I have a great respect."

"So have I," I said crossly. "Very well. A trap shall be sent for you after dinner. Good evening, Mr. Oliphant. It is a pleasure to have met you."

When I reached the House, I told Sybil of my arrangement. For the first time since my arrival she smiled. "It's very kind of him, but I am afraid he won't do much good. Bob will frighten him away."

"I fancy he won't. The man is strong in his self-confidence and remarkably dense. He'll probably exasperate Bob into sanity. In any case I'll be back by Friday morning."

As I drove away the trap arrived at the door, bringing Mr. Oliphant and his portmanteau.

The events of the next twenty-four hours, during which I was travelling in the Scotch express or transacting dreary business in my chambers, are known only from the narrative of the minister. He wrote it out some weeks after at my request, for I wished to have all the links in the tale. I propose to give the gist of it, as he wrote it, stripped of certain reflections on human life and an inscrutable Providence, with which he had garnished it.

Narrative of the Reverend Mr. Oliphant.

I arrived at the House of More at a quarter past eight on the Wednesday evening. The family had dined early, as Mr. Grey was leaving for London, and when I arrived I was taken to the library, where I found Mr. Ladlaw. I had not seen him for some time, and thought him looking pale and a little haggard. He seemed glad to see me, and made me sit down in a chair on his left and draw it up close to him. I wondered at his manner, for though we had always been on good terms he had never admitted me to any close intimacy. But now he was more than amiable. He made me ring for toddy, and though he refused to taste it himself, he pressed the beverage on me. Then he gave me a large cigar, at which I trembled, and finally he said that we should play at picquet. I declined resolutely, for it is part of my conscience to refuse to join in any card games; but he made no trouble, and indeed in a moment seemed to have forgotten his proposition.

The next thing he did startled my composure. For he asked abruptly, "Do you believe in a living personal Devil, Oliphant?"

I was taken aback, but answered that to the best of my light I did not.

"And why not?" he asked sharply.

I explained that it was an old, false, anthropomorphic fiction, and that the modern belief was infinitely more impressive. I quoted the words of Dr. Rintoul, one of our Church leaders. I am sorry to say that Mr. Ladlaw's words were, "Dr. Rintoul be d—d!"

"Who the deuce are you to change the belief of centuries?" he cried. "Our forefathers believed in him. They saw him at evening slinking about the folds and peatstacks, or wrapped up in a black gown standing in the pulpits of the Kirk. Are we wiser men than they?"

I answered that culture had undoubtedly advanced in our day.

Mr. Ladlaw replied with blasphemous words on modern culture. I had imagined him to be a gentleman of considerable refinement, and I knew he had taken a good degree at college. Consequently, I was disagreeably surprised at his new manner.

"You are nothing better than an ignorant parson,"—these were his words—"and you haven't even the merits of your stupid profession. The old Scots ministers were Calvinists to the backbone, and they were strong men—strong men, do you hear?—and they left their mark upon the nation. But your new tea-meeting kind of parson, who has nothing but a smattering of bad German to commend him, is a nuisance to God and man. And they don't believe in the Devil! Well, he'll get them safe enough some day."

I implored him to remember my cloth, and curb his bad language.

"I say the Devil will get you all safe enough some day," he repeated.

I rose to retire in as dignified a manner as possible, but he was before me and closed the door. I began to be genuinely frightened.

"For God's sake, don't go!" he cried. "Don't leave me alone. Do sit down, Oliphant, like a good chap, and I promise to hold my tongue. You don't know how horrible it is to be left alone."

I sat down again, though my composure was shaken. I remembered Mr. Grey's words about the strange sickness.

Then Mr. Ladlaw fell into an extraordinary moodiness. He sat huddled up in his chair, his face turned away from me, and for some time neither of us spoke a word. I thought that I had seriously offended him, and prepared to apologise, so I touched his left shoulder to attract his attention. Instantly he jumped to his feet, screaming, and turned on me a face of utter terror. I could do nothing but stare at him, and in a second he quieted down and returned to his seat.

Then he became partially sane, and murmured a sort of excuse. I thought that I would discover what truth lay in Mr. Grey's singular hypothesis. I did not ask him bluntly, as an ordinary man would have done, what was his malady, but tactfully, as I thought then, I led the conversation to demoniacal possession in the olden time, and quoted Pellinger's theory on the Scriptural cases. He answered with extraordinary vehemence, showing a childish credulity I little expected from an educated man.

"I see that you hold to the old interpretation," I said pleasantly. "Nowadays, we tend to find the solution in natural causes."

"Heavens, man!" he cried. "What do you mean by natural? You haven't the most rudimentary knowledge of nature. Listen to me, and I will tell you something."

And with this he began a long rambling account of something which I could not understand. He talked much about a name which sounded like Canaan, and then he wandered to another subject and talked about Proserpina, whom I remembered from Mr. Matthew Arnold's poem. I would have thought him trying to ridicule me, if I had not seen his face, which was white and drawn with pain; and, again, I would have thought him drunk, but for his well-known temperate habits. By-and-by even my nerves, which are very strong, began to suffer. I understood fragments of his talk, and the understanding did not reassure me. It was poisonous nonsense, but it had a terrible air of realism. He had a queer habit of catching at his heart like a man with the heart disease, and his eyes were like a mad dog's I once saw, the pupil drawn to a pin-point with fear. I could not bear it, so I tried to break the spell. I offered, against my conscience, to play a card game, but his face showed that he did not understand me. I began to feel a sort of languor of terror. I could hardly rise from my chair, and when at last I got up the whole room seemed haunted. I rushed to the bell and rang it violently, and then tried to open the door. But he was before me again, and gripped my arm so fiercely that I cried out between the pain and my dread of him.

"Come back!" he cried hoarsely. "Don't leave me alone. For God's sake, Oliphant!"

Just then the manservant opened the door, and found the two of us standing like lunatics. I had the sense to save the situation, and I asked him to bring more coals for the fire. Then as soon as he turned to go, I stepped out of the open door before Mr. Ladlaw could prevent me.

The hall seemed empty, but to my surprise I found Mrs. Ladlaw sleeping in a chair by the fire. I did not like to waken her, but I was at my wits' end with fright. If I had known the way to the kitchen, I should have sought the servants' company. I ran down a passage, but it seemed to end in a blind wall, and in a great fear I turned and ran upstairs. But the upper lobbies seemed to be unlit, and I was turning back when I heard Ladlaw's voice behind me. It was muffled and queer, and the sound drove me into the darkness. When I turned a corner, to my relief I saw a lamp burning on a table and recognised my bedroom door. Here was sanctuary at last, and I ran in and shut it behind me.

My nerves were so shaken by the evening's performances that I found it impossible to get to sleep. I sat up the better part of the night by the fire, and smoked several cigarettes, which in

26

ordinary circumstances I should never have dared to do in a strange bedroom. About four o'clock, I think, I dozed off in my chair, and awoke about nine, very stiff and cold, to find Ladlaw laughing at me in the doorway.

I was at first so confused that I did not remember what had scared me the night before. Then, as it came back to me, I was amazed at my host's appearance. He looked fresh and well, and in excellent spirits. He laughed immoderately when he found I had not gone to bed.

"You do look cheap," he said. "Breakfast's in half an hour. You will feel better when you have had a tub."

I bathed reluctantly, feeling ill and bitterly cold; but I was comforted by a good breakfast. Then I had an opportunity of talking to Mrs. Ladlaw. As I remembered her, she had been full of gaiety, and even, I thought, a little frivolous; but now she was so pale and silent that I pitied her sincerely. I began to feel an intense dislike of her husband, partly for the fright he had given me the night before, and partly for the effect his silliness seemed to be having on his wife. The day was a fine one, but after breakfast he showed no intention of going out. I expected to be asked to shoot, a sport which I sometimes try; but he never spoke of it, and insisted on my coming to the billiard-room. As we were leaving the table Mrs. Ladlaw touched my arm, and asked me in a low tone if I would promise to stay all day with her husband. "I want to go down to Morefoot," she said, "and you know he cannot be left alone." I promised willingly, for in the daylight Mr. Ladlaw had no terrors for me. I thought that Mrs. Ladlaw looked relieved. Poor thing! she badly needed a respite.

We hung aimlessly about the place till lunch, playing a few games of billiards, and in the intervals looking at stables and harness-rooms and the now barren gardens. At lunch Mrs. Ladlaw appeared, but immediately after I heard wheels on the gravel and knew that she had gone to Morefoot. Then I began to feel nervous again. I was the only responsible person left in the place, and Mr. Ladlaw might at any moment relapse into craziness. I watched his moods anxiously, and talked all the nonsense I knew to keep him in good humour. I told him stories, I talked wildly of sport, I made ridiculous jokes at which I felt myself blushing. At first he seemed amused, but soon I felt that my words were falling on deaf ears. He himself began to talk, violently, incessantly, and, I may say, brilliantly. If my memory had been better and my balance less upset, I might have made my reputation, though it would have been a reputation, perhaps, that a minister of the Gospel might well look askance at. I could have written a terrible romance from that man's babbling. Nay, I could have done more: I could have composed a new philosophy which would have cast Nietzsche in the shade for ever. I do not wish to exaggerate, but I have never been so impressed with a sense of a crazy intellectual acumen. This Mr. Ladlaw, whom I had known as a good landlord and a respectable country gentleman, now appeared as a kind of horrible genius, a brilliant and malignant satyr. I was shocked and confounded, and at the same time filled with admiration. I remember that we passed through the dining-room, where there was a great marble bust of a Roman emperor, an old discoloured thing, but wonderful in its way. Mr. Ladlaw stopped before it and pointed out its merits. The thing seemed simple enough, and yet after the description I fled from it as if it had been a devil. He followed me, still talking, and we found ourselves in the library.

I remember that I suggested tea, but he scarcely heeded me. The darkness was falling, Mrs. Ladlaw had not returned, and I felt horribly uncomfortable. I tried to draw him away from the room which I feared, but he made no sign of understanding. I perceived that the malady of the last night was returning. I hated that library, with its low fire, its ghastly white books, and its dreary outlook. I picked up one volume, and it was lettered on the back "Sancti Adelberti Certamina". I dropped it, only to feel Mr. Ladlaw clutching my right arm and dragging me to one of those horrible armchairs.

"The night is coming on, the old *Nox Atra* that the monks dreaded. Promise me that you won't go away."

I promised feebly, and prayed for Mrs. Ladlaw's return. I suggested that the lamps should be lit. He rose and tried to light the hanging central one, and I noticed how his hands trembled.

His awkwardness upset the thing, and it fell with a crash on the floor. He jumped back with a curious scream like an animal.

I was so miserably scared that I had not the heart to do the work for him, so we sat on in the darkness. Any sound from the out-of-doors would have comforted me, but the whole world was as silent as death. I felt that a little more would drive me mad, and the thought roused me to make a final effort after safety. In spite of all my promises I must get away. A man's first duty was to himself, and the hour had come for me. I thought with longing of my little bare manse and my solemn house-keeper. And yet how was I to escape, for this man was the stronger, and he would never let me go.

I begged him to come into the hall, but he refused. Then I became very cunning. I suggested that we should go to the door and receive Mrs. Ladlaw. He did not know that she had gone, and the news made him so nervous that he accepted my proposal. He caught my arm as before, and, leaning heavily upon me, went into the hall. There was no one about, and the fire had died down; but at the far end there was a pale glimmer from the glass door. We opened it and stood on the top step, looking over the dark lawns. Now was the time for an effort for freedom. If I could only get rid of his hand I might escape across the fields. I believed him to be too weak on his legs to follow me, and in any case I was a respectable runner. Out-of-doors he seemed less formidable: it was only in that haunted room that I shuddered.

I took the only way of escape which presented itself. There was a flowering-shrub in a pot on the top of the parapet. I caught this with my elbow and knocked it over, so that it broke with a clatter on the stone. As I expected, he screamed and jumped aside, letting go my arm for one instant. The next I was down the steps and running hard across the lawns to the park beyond.

For a little I heard him stumbling after me, breathing heavily and with little short cries. I ran with the speed of fear, for till I was within my own doors I could feel no security. Once I turned, and there he was, a field behind me, running with his head down like a blind dog. I skirted the village, broke through the little fir plantation, and came out on the highway. I saw the light from Jean's little window, and it was like a beacon of hope.

In a few minutes I was at the door, and my servant stared as I rushed in, without hat or overcoat, and wet with perspiration. I insisted on barring the doors, and bolting and shuttering every window. Then I had the unusual luxury of a fire in my bedroom, and there I supped, and sat till I fell asleep.

End of Mr. Oliphant's Statement.

CHAPTER III

EVENTS ON THE UPLANDS

I RETURNED from town by the night express, which landed me at Borrowmuir about seven on the Friday morning. To my surprise there was no dogcart to meet me, as had been arranged, and I was compelled to hire from the inn. The omission filled me with forebodings. Things must have gone badly at More in my absence, or the careful Sybil would never have forgotten. I grudged the time occupied in that weary drive. The horse seemed intolerably slow, the roads unaccountably steep. It was a sharp morning, with haze on the fields and promise of bright sunshine at midday; but, tired as I was with my two days' journey, I was in the humour to see little good in my case. I was thankful when we drew up at the house door, and, cold and stiff, I hobbled up the steps.

The door was open, and I entered. The hall was empty, there was no sign of any servant, and all the doors were wide to the wall. I tried one room after another without success. Then I made my voice heard in that place. I shouted for Ladlaw, and then I shouted for Sybil. There came no answer, and in despair I rushed to the kitchen wing. There I found a cluster of frightened maids, and by dint of much questioning learned the truth.

Ladlaw, it seemed, had disappeared from the house about a quarter past six on the previous night. The minister had decamped and found sanctuary in the manse; but there was no trace of the other. Sybil had gone to Morefoot in the afternoon, and, returning about half-past six, found her husband gone. She had been distracted with anxiety, had gone to the manse, where she found Mr. Oliphant in a state of nervous collapse and quite unable to make any coherent statement, and had then roused some of the neighbouring shepherds and organised a search-party. They had searched all night, but so far no word had come of the result. Meanwhile, Sybil, utterly wearied and a little hysterical, was in bed, sleeping, for her anxiety of the past week had culminated in a sort of deep languor, which in the circumstances was the best thing that could have happened. There was no question of wakening her; but, as I snatched a hurried breakfast, it seemed to me that I must at once follow the search. They were to meet in the morning at a farm called Mossrigging, beneath a hill of the same name, and if I went there I might get word of them. In the meantime I must interview Mr. Oliphant.

I found him in bed, unshaven, and very hollow about the eyes. He told me a lame story, and indeed his fright was so palpable that I had not the heart to blame him. But I insisted that he should get up and come with me, for every man would be needed to search those mossy uplands. I was dog-tired, sleepy, and irritable, and yet I must go: why should not this man, who had had his night's rest?

He made some feeble objection; but he had a conscience of his own and rose obediently. We set out to the nearest part of the moor, he in his clergyman's garb, and I in a dark suit and a bowler; and I remember thinking how oddly unsuited was our dress for this stalking game. I was wretchedly anxious, for I liked Ladlaw, and God alone knew where he might have got to in the night. There were deep bogs and ugly old pit-shafts on the moor, and there were ravines with sheer red sides. At any moment we might find tragedy, and I dreaded the report of the searchers at Mossrigging. When we left the road, we followed an old cart-track up a shallow glen, where stood some curious old stone chimneys, which had been built by a speculator who hoped to make a fortune from peat. The sun was beginning to break through the haze, and miles of low moorland were disclosed to left and right. But the hills in front were still cloudy, and we were close on the cottage before we knew its whereabouts. It stood high in a crinkle of hill, with a wide prospect north and east to the sea, and as I turned I saw Morebrig smoking clear in the autumn light, and the chimneys of the House above the fir-trees. Out on the waters three ships were sailing like toy boats, a reminder of the bustling modern life beyond this antique place of horrors.

The house was full of men, devouring their morning porridge. They were shepherds of the neighbourhood, and two boys from the village, as well as John Ker, the head-keeper from More. One man, Robert Tod by name, answered my unspoken question. "We havena gotten him, but we've gotten his whereabouts. We got a glisk o' him about six this mornin' on the backside o' the Lowe Moss. I kent him fine by the way he ran. Lord, but he was souple! Nane o' us could come within a hunner yairds o' him. We'll hae to wyse him gently, sir, and some o' us'll hae to tak a lang cast round the hill."

I had no ambition to "tak a lang cast round the hill"; but these men had been abroad all night, and I and the minister must undertake the duty. Tod agreed to come with us, and the shaggy silent men of the party expounded the plan of campaign. The Lowe Moss was impassable on one side, on another bounded by a steep hill-shoulder, and on the others by two narrow glens. They would watch the glens; we three should make a circuit and come back over the hill, driving the fugitive before us. Once enclosed between the moss and our three parties, he should be an easy capture. I implored them to go to work gently, for I feared that he might be driven into the bog. They shook their heads and laughed: it was all a kind of crazy sport to them, and their one idea was to carry out their orders.

I confess I was desperately tired before we had forded the upper waters of the More, crossed the Redscaurhead, and looked over the green pasture-lands to the south. It was a most curious sight; for whereas one side of the range was rough and mossy and hideous with red scaurs, the other was a gentle slope with sweet hill-grass and bright shallow waters. It was a new country where the old curse could not reign, and an idea took possession of me that if once Ladlaw came into the place he would be healed of his malady. The air seemed clearer, the sky softer, the whole world simple and clean. We fetched a circuit down one of the little streams till we came to the back of the hill which on its face is called Mossrigging. I was abominably tired, but in better spirits. As for the minister, he groaned occasionally, but never spoke a word.

At the foot we separated to the distance of half a mile, and began the ascent. So far there was no sign of our man. Tod was on the far east, I was in the centre, and Mr. Oliphant took the west. I cannot profess to remember exactly all the incidents of that climb. I was too stupid with sleep and exertion, and the little distant figures of my companions danced in a kind of haze. The ascent was simple—short grass, varied by short heather, with at wide intervals a patch of shingle. The shepherd walked with an easy swing, the minister stumbled and groaned, while I, in sheer bravado and irritation at my weakness, kept up a kind of despairing trot. The Devil and Ladlaw combined might confront me, but I was too tired to care. Indeed, in a little I had forgotten all about the purpose of our quest.

Then, quite suddenly, almost at the summit, in a little hollow of the ridge, I saw our man. He was sitting on the ground, directly in the minister's line, and his head was sunk on his breast. I remember being taken with a horrid thought that he was dead, and quickened my trot to a run. Meanwhile the minister was approaching very near, but apparently quite unconscious of his presence. His eyes were in the ends of the earth, and he ambled along with no purpose in the world.

What happened rests mainly on my authority; but Robert Tod, shepherd in Nether Mossrigging, is ready to swear to the essentials. Mr. Oliphant stumbled on into the hollow till he was within ten yards of the sitting figure. Ladlaw never moved; but the subtle influence which tells of human presence came suddenly upon the minister's senses, for he lifted his eyes and started. The man was still scared to death, and he naturally turned to run away, when something happened which I cannot well explain. Ladlaw was still sitting with his head on his breast, and yet it was clear to my mind that Ladlaw had somehow risen and was struggling with the minister. I could see the man's wrists strained and twisted as if in a death-grapple, and his white face reddening with exertion. He seemed to be held round the middle, for his feet tottered several times, and once he lurched to the left side, so that I thought he was thrown. And yet he was only battling with the air, for there was Ladlaw sitting quietly some yards from him.

And then suddenly the contest seemed to cease. Mr. Oliphant ran straight past the sitting man and over the brow of the hill. Surprise had held Tod and myself motionless. Now the spell was broken, and from our several places we ran towards Ladlaw. I heard the shepherd's loud voice crying, "Look at Oliphant! Oliphant's no wise!" and thought I heard a note of sardonic mirth. In any case, it was the minister he was after, for a moment later he disappeared down the farther slope.

Mr. Oliphant might go where he pleased, but my business was with my friend. I caught Ladlaw by the shoulder and shook him fiercely. Then I pulled him to his feet, let him go, and he rolled over. The sight was so comic that I went into a fit of nervous laughter; but the shock seemed to have restored his wits, for he opened sleepy eyes and regarded me solemnly. I do not propose to analyse my reasons, but I was conscious that it was the old Ladlaw who was looking at me. I knew he was healed of his malady, but how I knew it I do not know. He stuck both fists into his eyes like a sleepy child. Then he yawned, and looked down ruefully at soaked, soiled, and ragged clothing. Then he looked reproachfully at me.

"What's up?" he asked. "Stop that hideous row and tell me what has happened. Have I had an accident?"

Then I spoke cunningly. "Nothing much. A little bit of a fall, but you'll be all right soon. Why, you look better already." And again I went into a fit of laughter.

He grew wholesomely cross. "Oh, don't be a confounded jackass!" he cried. "I feel as if I hadn't slept for a week, and I'm hungry and thirsty."

He swallowed the contents of my flask, and wolfed my sandwiches in a disgusting way. Then he proposed that we should go home. "I'm tired, and I'm sick of shooting for the day. By-the-by, where's my gun?"

"Broken," I said, "broken in the fall. The keeper is going to

34

look after it." And with the aid of my arm he began with feeble steps his homeward journey.

The minister—this is the tale of Robert Tod and his colleagues—ran down the precipitous part of Mossrigging like a thing inspired. Tod, labouring heavily in his wake, declared that he went down the hillside like a loose stone, slipping, stumbling, yet never altogether losing his feet, and clearing dangers solely by the grace of God. As he went, said the men, he made clutches at the air, and his face was the face of one distraught. They ran together from their different places to intercept him on the edge of the bog, for at first they thought he was Ladlaw. When they saw their mistake they did not stop, for Tod was making frantic signals for pursuit. John Ker, the More keeper, was nearest, and he declared afterwards that he never approached a business so unwillingly. "I wad hae grippit a wild stot or a daft staig suner nor yon man," he said. But the business was too public for sheer cowardice. John assaulted him on the left flank while the other attacked in front, and John was bowled over like a ninepin. It was not the minister, he said, but something else, something with an arm two yards long, which flew out like a steam-hammer. But the others were more fortunate. One caught Mr. Oliphant's right arm, another hung on to the flaps of his coat, while a third tripped him up gallantly, till the whole body of them rolled on the ground. Then ensued an indescribable fray, Tod got a black eye from some unknown source, and one of the boys lost several front teeth. Howls of rage filled the moorland air, and all the while, they declared, the minister was praying with an unction which was never heard in the kirk. "Lord, give me peace!" he cried. "Lord, take the thing away!" and then again, "Get thee behind me, Satan!"

The end came very suddenly, for the company rolled into the bog. The minister, being lowest, saved the others, but he floundered in the green slime up to his middle. The accident seemed to inspire sobriety. He ceased his prayers, his face lost its horror, and took on a common human fear. Then Tod and his friends laboured heroically to rescue him, and all the while, they declared, something was pommelling them and bruising them, and they showed for long black marks on their bodies. Slowly they raised Mr. Oliphant from the slough, and on a bridge of coats he crept back to solid land. And then something happened which was the crowning marvel of the business. It was a still sharp day; but suddenly there came a wind, hot and harsh, and like nothing they had ever known, It stung them like nettles, played for a moment in their midst, and then in a kind of visible cloud passed away from them over the bog in the direction of the Red Loch. And with the wind went the Thing which had so long played havoc in the place; and the men were left with an unkempt figure, coated with slime and shivering with fright, but once more the sane and prosaic Mr. Oliphant, the minister of the parish of More.

We got Ladlaw and the minister back to the house with much trouble, for both were weak on their legs, and one was still in a pitiable fright. The two kept eyeing each other, one with a sort of disgusted amusement, the other with a wondering fear. The shepherds were mystified; but they were matter-of-fact beings, who, having fulfilled their orders, gave no more thought to the business. The wounded nursed their bruises and swore cheerfully, and the boy with the broken teeth whistled his complaints. A good dinner restored them to humour, and the last I saw was Ker and Tod going over the Odyssey of their adventures to a circle of critical spectators.

When Ladlaw and the minister had washed and fed, and sat smoking in the library, I went to talk to Sybil. I have often wondered how much she understood. At any rate she took my word that the trouble had passed, and in a fit of tears thanked me for my labours. Then she said she would go to her husband, and I led her to the library, where the two heroes were smoking the pipe of peace.

Ladlaw greeted her cheerily as if nothing had happened. "I feel a bit shaken," he said, "but I'll be all right after a night's rest. You needn't be nervous, Sib. By-the-bye, Harry, where's that gun?"

Then he wandered round the room, casting an unfriendly eye on his new acquisitions. "Look here! Somebody has been playing the fool in this place. I can't see a single Badminton, and where did this stuff come from?" And he tapped a row of books in old vellum. "I never remember the things before. St. Adelbert! Who on earth was he? Why, anyone who came in suddenly and did not know me might think I was a minor poet. I wish you'd tell Harrison to clear all this truck away."

The minister sat by the fire and said nothing. The marvellous had intruded upon his easy life and spoiled the balance. I was sorry for the man as I thanked him in a low tone and asked how he felt.

The words came from between chattering teeth.

"I am getting b-better," he said, "but I have had a terrible sh-shock—I am a Christian man and I have been tempted. I thought we lived in a progressive age, but now I know that we d-d-don't. And I am going to write to Dr. Rintoul."

THE KINGS OF ORION

"An ape and a lion lie side by side in the heart of a man."

PERSIAN PROVERB

SPRING-FISHING in the North is a cold game for a man whose blood has become thin in gentler climates. All afternoon I had failed to stir a fish, and the wan streams of the Laver, swirling between bare grey banks, were as icy to the eye as the sharp gusts of hail from the north-east were to the fingers. I cast mechanically till I grew weary, and then with an empty creel and a villainous temper set myself to trudge the two miles of bent to the inn. Some distant ridges of hill stood out snow-clad against the dun sky, and half in anger, half in a dismal satisfaction, I told myself that fishing tomorrow would be as barren as today.

At the inn door a tall man was stamping his feet and watching a servant lifting rod-cases from a dogcart. Hooded and wrapped though he was, my friend Thirlstone was an unmistakable figure in any landscape. The long, haggard, brown face, with the skin drawn tightly over the cheek-bones, the keen blue eyes finely wrinkled round the corners with staring at many suns, the scar which gave his mouth a humorous droop to the right, made up a whole which was not easily forgotten. I had last seen him on the quay at Funchal bargaining with some rascally boatman to take him after mythical wild goats in Las Desertas. Before that we had met at an embassy ball in Vienna, and still earlier at a hill-station in Persia to which I had been sent post-haste by an anxious and embarrassed Government. Also I had been at school with him, in those far-away days when we rode nine stone and dreamed of cricket averages. He was a soldier of note, who had taken part in two little wars and one big one; had himself conducted a political mission through a hard country with some success, and was habitually chosen by his superiors to keep his eyes open as a foreign attaché in our neighbours' wars. But his fame as a hunter had gone abroad into places where even the name of the British army is unknown. He was the hungriest shikari I have ever seen, and I have seen many. If you are wise you will go forthwith to some library and procure a little book entitled *Three Hunting Expeditions* by A. W. T. It is a modest work, and the style is that of a leading article, but all the lore and passion of the Red Gods are in its pages.

The sitting-room at the inn is a place of comfort, and while Thirlstone warmed his long back at the fire I sank contentedly into one of the well-rubbed leather armchairs. The company of a friend made the weather and the scarcity of salmon less the intolerable grievance they had seemed an hour ago than a joke to be laughed at. The landlord came in with whisky, and banked up the peats till they glowed beneath a pall of blue smoke.

"I hope to goodness we are alone," said Thirlstone, and he turned to the retreating landlord and asked the question.

"There's naebody bidin' the nicht forbye yoursels," he said, "but the morn there's a gentleman comin'. I got a letter frae him the day. Maister Wiston, they ca' him. Maybe ye ken him?"

I started at the name, which I knew very well. Thirlstone, who knew it better, stopped warming himself and walked to the window, where he stood pulling his moustache and staring at the snow. When the man had left the room, he turned to me with the face of one whose mind is made up on a course but uncertain of the best method.

"Do you know this sort of weather looks infernally unpromising? I've half a mind to chuck it and go back to town."

I gave him no encouragement, finding amusement in his difficulties.

"Oh, it's not so bad," I said, "and it won't last. Tomorrow we may have the day of our lives."

He was silent for a little, staring at the fire. "Anyhow," he said at last, "we were fools to be so far up the valley. Why shouldn't we go down to the Forest Lodge? They'll take us in, and we should be deucedly comfortable, and the water's better."

"There's not a pool on the river to touch the stretch here," I said. "I know, for I've fished every inch of it."

He had no reply to this, so he lit a pipe and held his peace for a time. Then, with some embarrassment but the air of having made a discovery, he announced that his conscience was troubling him about his work, and he thought he ought to get back to it at once. "There are several things I have forgotten to see to, and they're rather important. I feel a beast behaving like this, but you won't mind, will you?"

"My dear Thirlstone," I said, "what is the good of hedging? Why can't you say you won't meet Wiston?"

His face cleared. "Well, that's the fact—I won't. It would be too infernally unpleasant. You see, I was once by way of being his friend, and he was in my regiment. I couldn't do it."

The landlord came in at the moment with a basket of peats. "How long is Capt—Mr. Wiston staying here?" I asked.

"He's no bidin' ony time. He's just comin' here in the middle o' the day for his denner, and then drivin' up the water to Altbreac. He has the fishin' there."

Thirlstone's face showed profound relief. "Thank God!" I heard him mutter under his breath, and when the landlord had gone he fell to talking of salmon with enthusiasm. "We must make a big day of it tomorrow, dark to dark, you know. Thank Heaven, our beat's downstream, too." And thereafter he made frequent excursions to the door, and bulletins on the weather were issued regularly.

Dinner over, we drew our chairs to the hearth and fell to talk and the slow consumption of tobacco. When two men from the ends of the earth meet by a winter fire, their thoughts are certain to drift overseas. We spoke of the racing tides off Vancouver, and the lonely pine-clad ridges running up to the snow-peaks of the Selkirks, to which we had both travelled once upon a time in search of sport. Thirlstone on his own account had gone wandering to Alaska, and brought back some bearskins and a frostbitten toe as trophies, and from his tales had consorted with the finest band of rogues which survives unhanged on this planet. Then some casual word took our thoughts to the south, and our memories dallied with Africa. Thirlstone had hunted in Somaliland and done mighty slaughter; while I had spent some never-to-be-forgotten weeks long ago in the hinterland of

Zanzibar, in the days before railways and game-preserves. I have gone through life with a keen eye for the discovery of earthly paradises, to which I intend to retire when my work is over, and the fairest I thought I had found above the Rift valley, where you have a hundred miles of blue horizon and the weather of Scotland. Thirlstone, not having been there, naturally differed, and urged the claim of a certain glen in Kashmir, where you may hunt two varieties of bear and three of buck in thickets of rhododendron, and see the mightiest mountain-wall on earth from your tent door. The mention of the Indian frontier brought us back to our professions, and for a little we talked "shop" with the unblushing confidence of those who know each other's work and approve it. As a very young soldier Thirlstone had gone shooting in the Pamirs, and had blundered into a Russian party of exploration which contained Kuropatkin. He had in consequence grossly outstayed his leave, having been detained for a fortnight by an arbitrary hospitality; but he had learned many things, and the experience had given him strong views on frontier questions. Half an hour was devoted to a masterly survey of the East, until a word pulled us up.

"I went there in '99," Thirlstone was saying, "the time Wiston and I were sent—" and then he stopped, and his eager face clouded. Wiston's name cast a shadow over our reminiscences.

"What did he actually do?" I asked after a short silence.

"Pretty bad! He seemed a commonplace, good sort of fellow, popular, fairly competent, a little bad-tempered perhaps. And then suddenly he did something so extremely blackguardly that everything was at an end. It's no good repeating details, and I hate to think about it. We know little about our neighbours, and I'm not sure that we know much about ourselves. There may be appalling depths of iniquity in every one of us, only most people are fortunate enough to go through the world without meeting anything to wake the devil in them. I don't believe Wiston was bad in the ordinary sense. Only there was something else in him—*somebody else*, if you like—and in a moment it came uppermost, and he was a branded man. Ugh! it's a gruesome thought."

Thirlstone had let his pipe go out, and was staring moodily into the fire.

"How do you explain things like that?" he asked. "I have an idea of my own about them. We talk glibly of ourselves and our personality and our conscience, as if every man's nature were a smooth, round, white thing, like a chuckie-stone. But I believe there are two men—perhaps more—in every one of us. There's our ordinary self, generally rather humdrum; and then there's a bit of something else, good, bad, but never indifferent—and it is that something else which may make a man a saint or a great villain."

" 'The Kings of Orion have come to earth'," I quoted.

Something in the words struck Thirlstone, and he asked me what was the yarn I spoke of.

"It's an old legend," I explained. "When the kings were driven out of Orion, they were sent to this planet and given each his habitation in some mortal soul. There were differences of character in that royal family, and so the *alter ego* which dwells alongside of us may be virtuous or very much the reverse. But the point is that he is always greater than ourselves, for he has been a king. It's a foolish story, but very widely believed. There is something of the sort in Celtic folklore, and there's a reference to it in Ausonius. Also the bandits in the Bakhtiari have a version of it in a very excellent ballad."

"Kings of Orion," said Thirlstone musingly. "I like that idea. Good or bad, but always great! After all, we show a kind of belief in it in our daily practice. Every man is always making fancies about himself; but it is never his workaday self, but something else. The bank clerk who pictures himself as a financial Napoleon knows that his own thin little soul is incapable of it; but he knows, too, that it is possible enough for that other bigger thing which is not his soul, but yet in some odd way is bound up with it. I fancy myself a field-marshal in a European war; but I know perfectly well that if the job were offered me, I should realise my incompetence and decline. I expect you rather picture yourself now and then as a sort of Julius Caesar and empire-maker, and yet, with all respect, my dear chap, I think it would be rather too much for you."

"There was once a man," I said, "an early Victorian Whig, whose chief ambitions were to reform the criminal law and abolish slavery. Well, this dull, estimable man in his leisure moments was Emperor of Byzantium. He fought great wars and built palaces, and then, when the time for fancy was past, went into the House of Commons and railed against militarism and Tory extravagance. That particular king from Orion had a rather odd sort of earthly tenement."

Thirlstone was all interest. "A philosophic Whig and the throne of Byzantium. A pretty rum mixture! And yet—yet," and his eyes became abstracted. "Did you ever know Tommy Lascelles?"

"The man who once governed Deira? Retired now, and lives somewhere in Kent? Yes, I've met him once or twice. But why?"

"Because," said Thirlstone solemnly, "unless I'm greatly mistaken, Tommy was another such case, though no man ever guessed it except myself. I don't mind telling you the story, now that he is retired and vegetating in his ancestral pastures. Besides, the facts are all in his favour, and the explanation is our own business. . . .

"His wife was my cousin, and when she died Tommy was left a very withered, disconsolate man, with no particular object in life. We all thought he would give up the service, for he was hideously well off; and then one fine day, to our amazement, he was offered Deira, and accepted it. I was short of a job at the time, for my battalion was at home, and there was nothing going on anywhere, so I thought I should like to see what the East Coast of Africa was like, and wrote to Tommy about it. He jumped at me, cabled offering me what he called his Military Secretaryship, and I got seconded, and set off. I had never known him very well, but what I had seen I had liked; and I suppose he was glad to have one of Maggie's family with him, for he was still very low about her loss. I was in pretty good spirits, for it meant new experiences, and I had hopes of big game.

"You've never been to Deira? Well, there's no good trying to describe it, for it's the only place in the world like itself. God made it and left it to its own devices. The town is pretty enough, with its palms and green headland, and little scrubby islands in the river's mouth. It has the usual half-Arab, half-Portugee look—white green-shuttered houses, flat roofs, sallow little men in duck, and every type of nigger from the Somali to the Shangaan. There are some good buildings, and Government House was the mansion of some old Portugee seigneur, and was built when people in Africa were not in such a hurry as today. Inland there's a rolling, forest country, beginning with decent trees and ending in mimosa-thorn, when the land begins to rise to the stony hills of the interior; and that poisonous yellow river rolls through it all, with a denser native population along its banks than you will find anywhere else north of the Zambesi. For about two months in the year the climate is Paradise, and for the rest you live in a Turkish bath, with every known kind of fever hanging about. We cleaned out the town and improved the sanitation, so there were few epidemics, but there was enough ordinary malaria to sicken a crocodile.

"The place was no special use to us. It had been annexed in spite of a tremendous Radical outcry, and, upon my soul, it was one of the few cases where the Radicals had something to say for themselves. All we got by it was half a dozen of the nastiest problems an unfortunate governor can have to face. Ten years before it had been a decaying strip of coast, with a few trading firms in the town, and a small export of ivory and timber. But some years before Tommy took it up there had been a huge discovery of copper in the hills inland, a railway had been built, and there were several biggish mining settlements at the end of it. Deira itself was filled with offices of European firms, it had got a Stock Exchange of its own, and it was becoming the usual cosmopolitan playground. It had a knack, too, of getting the very worst breed of adventurer. I know something of your South African and Australian mining towns, and with all their faults they are run by white men. If they haven't much morals, they have a kind of decency which keeps them fairly straight. But for our sins we got a brand of Levantine Jew, who was fit for nothing but making money and making trouble. They were always defying the law, and then, when they got into a hole, they squealed to Government for help, and started a racket in the home papers about the weakness of the Imperial power. The crux of the whole difficulty was the natives, who lived along the river and in the foot-hills. They were a hardy race of Kaffirs, sort of far-away cousins to the Zulu, and till the mines were opened they had behaved well enough. They had arms, which we had never dared to take away, but they kept quiet and paid their hut-taxes like men. I got to know many of the chiefs, and liked them, for they were upstanding fellows to look at and Heaven-born shikaris. However, when the Jews came along they wanted labour, and, since we did not see our way to allow them to add to the imported coolie population, they had to fall back upon the Labonga. At first things went smoothly. The chiefs were willing to let their men work for good wages, and for a time there was enough labour for everybody. But as the mines extended, and the natives, after making a few pounds, wanted to get back to their kraals, there came a shortage; and since the work could not be allowed to slacken, the owners tried other methods. They made promises which they never intended to keep, and they stood on the letter of a law which the natives did not understand, and they employed touts who were little better than slave-dealers. They got the labour, of course, but soon they had put the Labonga into a state of unrest which a very little would turn into a rising.

"Into this kettle of fish Tommy was pitchforked, and when I arrived he was just beginning to understand how unpleasant it was. As I said before, I did not know him very well, and I was amazed to find how bad he was at his job. A more curiously incompetent person I never met. He was a long, thin man, with a grizzled moustache, and a mild sleepy eye—not an impressive figure, except on a horse; and he had an odd lisp which made even a shrewd remark sound foolish. He was the most indus-trious creature in the world, and a model of official decorum. His papers were always in order, his despatches always neat and correct, and I don't believe anyone ever caught him tripping in office work. But he had no more conception than a child of the kind of trouble that was brewing. He never knew an honest man from a rogue, and the result was that he received all unofficial communications with a polite disbelief. I used to force him to see people—miners, prospectors, traders, anyone who had something to say worth listening to, but it all glided smoothly off his mind. He was simply the most incompetent being ever created, living in the world as not being of it, or rather creating a little official world of his own, where all events happened on lines laid down by the Colonial Office, and men were like papers, to be rolled into packets and properly docketed. He had an Executive Council of people like himself, competent officials and blind bats at anything else. Then there was a precious Legislative Council, intended to represent the different classes of the population. There were several good men on it—one old trader called Mackay, for instance, who had been thirty years in the country— but most were nominees of the mining firms, and very seedy rascals at that. They were always talking about the rights of the white man, and demanding popular control of the Government, and similar twaddle. The leader was a man who hailed from Hamburg, and called himself Le Foy—descended from a Crusader of the name of Levi—who was a jackal of one of the chief copper firms. He overflowed with Imperialist sentiment, and when he wasn't waving the flag he used to gush about the beauties of English country life and the grandeur of the English tradition. He hated me from the start, for when he talked of going 'home' I thought he meant Hamburg, and said so; and then a thing happened which made him hate me worse. He was infernally rude to Tommy, who, like the dear sheep he was, never saw it, and, if he had, wouldn't have minded. But one day I chanced to overhear some of his impertinences, so I hunted out my biggest sjambok and lay in wait for Mr. Le Foy. I told him that he was a representative of the sovereign people, that I was a member of an effete bureaucracy, and that it would be most painful if unpleasantness arose between us. But, I added, I was prepared, if necessary, to sacrifice my official career to my private feelings, and if he dared to use such language again to His Majesty's representative I would give him a hiding he would remember till he found himself in Abraham's bosom. Not liking my sjambok, he became soap and butter at once, and held his tongue for a month or two.

"But though Tommy was no good at his job, he was a tremendous swell at other things. He was an uncommonly good linguist, and had always about a dozen hobbies which he slaved at; and when he found himself at Deira with a good deal of leisure, he became a bigger crank than ever. He had a lot of books which used to follow him about the world in zinc-lined boxes—your big paperbacked German books which mean research—and he was a Fellow of the Royal Society, and corresponded with half a dozen foreign shows. India was his great subject, but he had been in the Sudan and knew a good deal about African races. When I went out to him, his pet hobby was the Bantu, and he had acquired an amazing amount of miscellaneous learning. He knew all about their immigration from the North, and the Arab and Phoenician trade-routes, and the Portuguese occupation, and the rest of the history of that unpromising seaboard. The way he behaved in his researches showed the man. He worked hard at the Labonga language— which, I believe, is a linguistic curiosity of the first water—from missionary books and the conversation of tame Kaffirs. But he never thought of paying them a visit in their native haunts. I was constantly begging him to do it, but it was not Tommy's way. He did not care a straw about political expedience, and he liked to look at things through the medium of paper and ink. Then there were the Phoenician remains in the foot-hills where the copper was mined—old workings, and things which might have been forts or temples. He knew all that was to be known about them, but he had never seen them, and never wanted to. Once only he went to the hills, to open some new reservoirs and make the ordinary Governor's speech; but he went in a special train and stayed two hours, most of which was spent in lunching and being played to by brass bands.

"But, oddly enough, there was one thing which stirred him with an interest that was not academic. I discovered it by accident one day when I went into his study and found him struggling with a map of Central Asia. Instead of the mild, benevolent smile with which he usually greeted my interruptions, he looked positively furtive, and, I could have sworn, tried to shuffle the map under some papers. Now it happens that Central Asia is the part of the globe that I know better than most men, and I could not help picking up the map and looking at it. It was a wretched thing, and had got the Oxus two hundred miles out of its course. I pointed this out to Tommy, and to my amazement he became quite excited. 'Nonsense,' he said. 'You don't mean to say it goes south of that desert. Why, I meant to—' and then he stammered and stopped. I wondered what on earth he had meant to do, but I merely observed that I had been there, and knew. That brought Tommy out of his chair in real excitement. 'What!' he cried, 'you! You never told me,' and he started to fire off a round of questions which showed that if he knew very little about the place, he had it a good deal in his mind. I drew some sketch-plans for him, and left him brooding over them.

"That was the first hint I got. The second was a few nights later, when we were smoking in the billiard-room. I had been reading Marco Polo, and the talk got on to Persia and drifted all over the north side of the Himalaya. Tommy, with an abstracted eye, talked of Alexander and Timour and Genghis Khan, and particularly of Prester John, who was a character that took his fancy. I had told him that the natives in the Pamirs were true Persian stock, and this interested him greatly. 'Why was there never a great state built up in those valleys?' he asked. 'You get nothing but a few wild conquerors rushing east and west, and then some squalid khanates. And yet all the materials were there—the stuff for a strong race, a rich land, the traditions of an old civilisation, and natural barriers against all invasion.'

" 'I suppose they never found the man,' I said.

"He agreed. 'Their princes were sots, or they were barbarians of genius who could devastate to the gates of Peking or Constantinople, but could never build. They did not recognise their limits, and so they went out in a whirlwind. But if there had been a man of solid genius he might have built up the strongest nation on the globe. In time he could have annexed Persia and nibbled at China. He would have been rich, for he could tap all the inland trade-routes of Asia. He would have had to be a conqueror, for his people would be a race of warriors, but first and foremost he must have been a statesman. Think of such a civilisation, the Asian civilisation, growing up mysteriously behind the deserts and the ranges! That's my idea of Prester John. Russia would have been confined to the line of the Urals. China would have been absorbed. There would have been no

Japan. The whole history of the world for the last few hundred years would have been different. It is the greatest of all the lost chances in history.' Tommy waxed pathetic over the loss.

"I was a little surprised at his eloquence, especially when he seemed to remember himself and stopped all of a sudden. But for the next week I got no peace with his questions. I told him all I knew of Bokhara, and Samarkand, and Tashkend, and Yarkand. I showed him the passes in the Pamirs and the Hindu Kush. I traced out the rivers, and I calculated distances; we talked over imaginary campaigns, and set up fanciful constitutions. It was a childish game, but I found it interesting enough. He spoke of it all with a curious personal tone which puzzled me, till one day when we were amusing ourselves with a fight on the Zarafshan, and I put in a modest claim to be allowed to win once in a while. For a second he looked at me in blank surprise. 'You can't,' he said; 'I've got to enter Samarkand before I can—' and he stopped again, with a glimmering sense in his face that he was giving himself away. And then I knew that I had surprised Tommy's secret. While he was muddling his own job, he was salving his pride with fancies of some wild career in Asia, where Tommy, disguised as the lord knows what Mussulman grandee, was hammering the little states into an empire.

"I did not think then as I think now, and I was amused to find so odd a trait in a dull man. I had known something of the kind before. I had met fellows who after their tenth peg would begin to swagger about some ridiculous fancy of their own— their little private corner of soul showing for a moment when the drink had blown aside their common sense. Now, I had never known the thing appear in cold blood and everyday life, but I assumed the case to be the same. I thought of it only as a harmless fancy, never imagining that it had anything to do with character. I put it down to that kindly imagination which is the old opiate for failures. So I played up to Tommy with all my might, and though he became very discreet after the first betrayal, having hit upon the clue, I knew what to look for, and I found it. When I told him that the Labonga were in a devil of a mess, he would look at me with an empty face and change the subject; but once among the Turcomans his eye would kindle, and he

49

would slave at his confounded folly with sufficient energy to reform the whole East Coast. It was the spark that kept the man alive. Otherwise he would have been as limp as a rag, but this craziness put life into him, and made him carry his head in the air and walk like a free man. I remember he was very keen about any kind of martial poetry. He used to go about crooning Scott and Macaulay to himself, and when we went for a walk or a ride he wouldn't speak for miles, but keep smiling to himself and humming bits of songs. I daresay he was very happy—far happier than your stolid, competent man, who sees only the one thing to do and does it. Tommy was muddling his particular duty, but building glorious palaces in the air.

"One day Mackay, the old trader, came to me after a sitting of the precious Legislative Council. We were very friendly, and I had done all I could to get the Government to listen to his views. He was a dour, ill-tempered Scotsman, very anxious for the safety of his property, but perfectly careless about any danger to himself.

" 'Captain Thirlstone,' he said, 'that Governor of yours is a damned fool.'

"Of course I shut him up very brusquely, but he paid no attention. 'He just sits and grins, and lets yon Pentecostal crowd we've gotten here as a judgment for our sins do what they like wi' him. God kens what'll happen. I would go home tomorrow, if I could realise without an immoderate loss. For the day of reckoning is at hand. Maark my words, Captain—at hand.'

"I said I agreed with him about the approach of trouble, but that the Governor would rise to the occasion. I told him that people like Tommy were only seen at their best in a crisis, and that he might be perfectly confident that when it arrived he would get a new idea of the man. I said this, but of course I did not believe a word of it. I thought Tommy was only a dreamer, who had rotted any grit he ever possessed by his mental opiates. At that time I did not understand about the kings from Orion.

"And then came the thing we had all been waiting for—a Labonga rising. A week before I had got leave and had gone up country, partly to shoot, but mainly to see for myself what trouble was brewing. I kept away from the river, and therefore missed the main native centres, but such kraals as I passed had a look I did not like. The chiefs were almost always invisible, and the young bloods were swaggering about and bukking to each other, while the women were grinding maize as if for some big festival. However, after a bit the country seemed to grow more normal, and I went into the foot-hills to shoot, fairly easy in my mind. I had got up to a place called Shimonwe, on the Pathi River, where I had ordered letters to be sent, and one night coming in from a hard day after kudu I found a post-runner half-dead of fatigue with a chit from Utterson, who commanded a police district twenty miles nearer the coast. It said simply that all the young men round about him had cleared out and appeared to be moving towards Deira, that he was in the devil of a quandary, and that, since the police were under the Governor, he would take his orders from me.

"It looked as if the heather were fairly on fire at last, so I set off early next morning to trek back. About midday I met Utterson, a very badly scared little man, who had come to look for me. It seemed that his policemen had bolted in the night and gone to join the rising, leaving him with two white sergeants, barely fifty rounds of ammunition, and no neighbour for a hundred miles. He said that the Labonga chiefs were not marching to the coast, as he had thought, but north along the eastern foot-hills in the direction of the mines. This was better news, for it meant that in all probability the railway would remain open. It was my business to get somehow to my chief, and I was in the deuce of a stew how to manage it. It was no good following the line of the natives' march, for they would have been between me and my goal, and the only way was to try and outflank them by going due east, in the Deira direction, and then turning north, so as to strike the railway about half-way to the mines. I told Utterson we had better scatter, otherwise we should have no chance of getting through a densely populated native country. So, about five in the afternoon I set off with my chief shikari, who, by good luck, was not a Labonga, and dived into the jungly bush which skirts the hills.

"For three days I had a baddish time. We steered by the stars, travelling chiefly by night, and we showed extraordinary skill in missing the water-holes. I had a touch of fever and got light-headed, and it was all I could do to struggle through the thick grass and wait-a-bit thorns. My clothes were torn to rags, and I grew so footsore that it was agony to move. All the same we travelled fast, and there was no chance of our missing the road, for any route due north was bound to cut the railway. I had the most sickening uncertainty about what was to come next. Hely, who was in command at Deira, was a good enough man, but he had only three companies of white troops, and the black troops were as likely as not to be on their way to the rebels. It looked as if we should have a Cawnpore business on a small scale, though I thanked Heaven there were no women in the case. As for Tommy, he would probably be repeating platitudes in Deira and composing an intelligent despatch on the whole subject.

"About four in the afternoon of the third day I struck the line near a little station called Palala. I saw by the look of the rails that trains were still running, and my hopes revived. At Palala there was a coolie stationmaster, who gave me a drink and a little food, after which I slept heavily in his office till wakened by the arrival of an up train. It contained one of the white companies and a man Davidson, of the 101st, who was Hely's second in command. From him I had news that took away my breath. The Governor had gone up the line two days before with an A.D.C. and old Mackay. 'The sportsman has got a move on him at last,' said Davidson, 'but what he means to do Heaven only knows. The Labonga are at the mines, and a kind of mine-guard has been formed for defence. The joke of it is that most of the magnates are treed up there, for the railway is cut and they can't get away. I don't envy your chief the job of schooling that nervous crowd.'

"I went on with Davidson, and very early next morning we came to a broken culvert and had to stop. There we stuck for three hours till the down train arrived, and with it Hely. He was for ordinary a stolid soul, but I never saw a man in such a fever of excitement. He gripped me by the arm and fairly shook me. 'That old man of yours is a hero,' he cried. 'The Lord forgive me! and I have always crabbed him.'

"I implored him in Heaven's name to tell me what was up, but he would say nothing till he had had his pow-wow with Davidson. It seemed that he was bringing all his white troops up the line for some great demonstration that Tommy had conceived. Davidson went back to Deira, while we mended the culvert and got the men transferred to the other train. Then I screwed the truth out of Hely. Tommy had got up to the mines before the rebels arrived, and had found as fine a chaos as can be imagined. He did not seem to have had any doubts what to do. There were a certain number of white workmen, hard fellows from Cornwall mostly, with a few Australians, and these he got together with Mackay's help and organised into a pretty useful corps. He set them to guard the offices, and gave them strict orders to shoot at sight anyone attempting to leave. Then he collected the bosses and talked to them like a father. What he said Hely did not know, except that he had damned their eyes pretty heartily, and told them what a set of swine they were, making trouble which they had not the pluck to face. Whether from Mackay, or from his own intelligence, or from a memory of my neglected warnings, he seemed to have got a tight grip on the facts at last. Meanwhile the Labonga were at the doors, chanting their battle-songs half a mile away, and shots were heard from the far pickets. If they had tried to rush the place then, all would have been over, but, luckily, that was never their way of fighting. They sat down in camp to make their sacrifices and consult their witch-doctors, and presently Hely arrived with the first troops, having come in on the northern flank when he found the line cut. He had been in time to hear the tail-end of Tommy's final address to the mine-owners. He told them, in words which Hely said he could never have imagined coming from his lips, that they would be well served if the Labonga cleaned the whole place out. Only, he said, that would be against the will of Britain, and it was his business, as a loyal servant, to prevent it. Then, after giving Hely his instructions, he had put on his uniform, gold lace and all, and every scrap of bunting he possessed—all the orders and 'Golden Stars' of half a dozen Oriental States where he had served. He made Ashurst, the A.D.C., put on his best Hussar's kit, and Mackay rigged himself out in a frock-coat and a topper; and the three set out on horseback for the Labonga. 'I believe he'll bring it off,' said Hely, with wild eyes, 'and, by Heaven, if he does, it'll be the best thing since John Nicholson!'

"For the rest of the way I sat hugging myself with excitement. The miracle of miracles seemed to have come. The old, slack, incompetent soul in Tommy seemed to have been driven out by that other spirit, which had hitherto been content to dream of crazy victories on the Oxus. I cursed my folly in having missed it all, for I would have given my right hand to be with him among the Labonga. I envied that young fool Ashurst his luck in being present at that queer transformation scene. I had not a doubt that Tommy would bring it off all right. The kings from Orion don't go into action without coming out on top. As we got near the mines I kept my ears open for the sound of shots; but all was still—not even the kind of hubbub a native force makes when it is on the move. Something had happened, but what it was no man could guess. When we got to where the line was up, we made very good time over the five miles to the mines. No one interfered with us, and the nearer we got the greater grew my certainty. Soon we were at the pickets, who had nothing to tell us; and then we were racing up the long sandy street to the offices, and there, sitting smoking on the doorstep of the hotel, surrounded by everybody who was not on duty, were Mackay and Ashurst.

"They were an odd pair. Ashurst still wore his uniform; but he seemed to have been rolling about in it on the ground; his sleek hair was wildly ruffled, and he was poking holes in the dust with his sword. Mackay had lost his topper, and wore a disreputable cap, his ancient frock-coat was without buttons, and his tie had worked itself up behind his ears. They talked excitedly to each other, now and then vouchsafing a scrap of information to an equally excited audience. When they saw me they rose and rushed for me, and dragged me between them up the street, while the crowd tailed at our heels.

" 'Ye're a true prophet, Captain Thirlstone,' Mackay began, 'and I ask your pardon for doubting you. Ye said the Governor only needed a crisis to behave like a man. Well, the crisis has come; and if there's a man alive in this sinful world, it's that chief o' yours.' And then his emotion overcame him, and, hard-bitten devil as he was, he sat down on the ground and gasped with hysterical laughter, while Ashurst, with a very red face, kept putting the wrong end of a cigarette in his mouth and swearing profanely.

"I never remember a madder sight. There was the brassy blue sky and reddish granite rock and acres of thick red dust. The scrub had that metallic greenness which you find in all copper places. Pretty unwholesome it looked, and the crowd, which had got round us again, was more unwholesome still. Fat Jew boys, with diamond rings on dirty fingers and greasy linen cuffs, kept staring at us with twitching lips; and one or two smarter fellows in riding-breeches, mine-managers and suchlike, tried to show their pluck by nervous jokes. And in the middle was Mackay, with his damaged frocker, drawling out his story in broad Scots.

" 'He made this laddie put on his braws, and he commandeered this iniquitous garment for me. I've raxed its seams, and it'll never look again on the man that owns it. Syne he arrayed himself in purple and fine linen till he was like the king's daughter, all glorious without; and says he to me, "Mackay," he says, "we'll go and talk to these uncovenanted deevils in their own tongue. We'll visit them at home, Mackay," he says. "They're none such bad fellows, but they want a little humouring from men like you and me." So we got on our horses and started the procession—the Governor with his head in the air, and the laddie endeavouring to look calm and collected, and me praying to the God of Israel and trying to keep my breeks from working up above my knees. I've been in Kaffir wars afore, but I never thought I would ride without weapon of any kind into such a black Armageddon. I am a peaceable man for ordinar', and a canny one, but I wasna myself in that hour. Man, Thirlstone, I was that overcome by the spirit of your chief, that if he had bidden me gang alone on the same errand, I wouldna say but what I would have gone.

" 'We hadna ridden half a mile before we saw the indunas and their men, ten thousand if there was one, and terrible as an army with banners. I speak feeguratively, for they hadna the scrap of a flag among them. They were beating the war-drums, and the young men were dancing with their big skin shields and wagging their ostrich feathers, so I saw they were out for business. I'll no' say but what my blood ran cold, but the Governor's eye got brighter and his back stiffer. "Kings may be blest," I says to myself, "but thou art glorious."

" 'We rode straight for the centre of the crowd, where the young men were thickest and the big war-drums lay. As soon as they saw us a dozen lifted their spears and ran out to meet us. But they stopped after six steps. The sun glinted on the Governor's gold lace and my lum hat, and no doubt they thought we were heathen deities descended from the heavens. Down they went on their faces, and then back like rabbits to the rest, while the drums stopped, and the whole body awaited our coming in a silence like the tomb.

" 'Never a word we spoke, but just jogged on with our chins cocked up till we were forenent the big drum, where yon old scoundrel Umgazi was standing with his young men looking as black as sin. For a moment their spears were shaking in their hands, and I heard the click of a breech-bolt. If we had winked an eye we would have become pincushions that instant. But some unearthly power upheld us. Even the laddie kept a stiff face, and for me I forgot my breeks in watching the Governor. He looked as solemn as an archangel, and comes to a halt opposite Umgazi, when he glowers at the old man for maybe three minutes, while we formed up behind him. Their eyes fell before his, and by-and-by their spears dropped to their sides. "The father has come to his children," says he in their own tongue. "What do the children seek from their father?"

" 'Ye see the cleverness of the thing. The man's past folly came to help him. The natives had never seen the Governor before till they beheld him in gold lace and a cocked hat on a muckle horse, speaking their own tongue and looking like a destroying angel. I tell you the Labonga's knees were loosed under them. They durstna speak a word until the Governor repeated the question in the same quiet, steely voice. "You seek something," he said, "else you had not come out to meet me in your numbers. The father waits to hear the children's desires."

" 'Then Umgazi found his tongue and began an uneasy speech. The mines, he said, truly enough, were the abode of devils, who compelled the people to work under the ground. The crops were unreaped and the buck went unspeared, because there were no young men left to him. Their father had been away or asleep, they thought, for no help had come from him; therefore it had seemed good to them, being freemen and warriors, to seek help for themselves.

" 'The Governor listened to it all with a set face. Then he smiled at them with supernatural assurance. They were fools, he said, and people of little wit, and he flung the better part of the Book of Job at their heads. The Lord kens where the man got his uncanny knowledge of the Labonga. He had all their heathen customs by heart, and he played with them like a cat with a mouse. He told them they were damned rascals to make such a stramash, and damned fools to think they could frighten the white man by their demonstrations. There was no brag about his words, just a calm statement of faact. At the same time, he said, he had no mind to let anyone wrong his children, and if any wrong had been done it should be righted. It was not meet, he said, that the young men should be taken from the villages unless by their own consent, though it was his desire that such young men as could be spared should have a chance of earning an honest penny. And then he fired at them some stuff about the British Empire and the King, and you could see the Labonga imbibing it like water. The man in a cocked hat might have told them that the sky was yellow, and they would have swallowed it.

" ' "I have spoken," he says at last, and there was a great shout from the young men, and old Umgazi looked pretty foolish. They were coming round our horses to touch our stirrups with their noses, but the Governor stopped them.

" ' "My children will pile their weapons in front of me," says he, "to show me how they have armed themselves and likewise to prove that their folly is at an end. All except a dozen," says he, "whom I select as a bodyguard." And there and then he picked twelve lusty savages for his guard while the rest without a cheep stacked their spears and guns forenent the big drum.

" 'Then he turned to us and spoke in English. "Get back to the mines hell-for-leather, and tell them what's happening, and see that you get up some kind of a show for tomorrow at noon. I will bring the chiefs, and we'll feast them. Get all the bands you can, and let them play me in. Tell the mines fellows to look active, for it's the chance of their lives." Then he says to the Labonga, "My men will return," he says, "but as for me I will spend the night with my children. Make ready food, but let no beer be made, for it is a solemn occasion."

" 'And so we left him. I will not describe how I spent last night mysel', but I have something to say about this remarkable phenomenon. I could enlarge on the triumph of mind over matter. . . .'

"Mackay did not enlarge. He stopped, cocked his ears, and looked down the road, from which came the strains of 'Annie Laurie' played with much spirit but grievously out of tune. Followed 'The British Grenadiers,' and then an attempt at 'The March of the Priests.' Mackay rose in excitement and began to crane his disreputable neck, while the band—a fine scratch collection of instruments—took up their stand at the end of the street, flanked by a piper in khaki who performed when their breath failed. Mackay chuckled with satisfaction. 'The deevils have entered into the spirit of my instructions,' he said. 'In a wee bit the place will be like Falkirk Tryst for din.'

"Punctually at twelve there came a great hullabaloo up the road, the beating of drums and the yelling of natives, and presently the procession hove in sight. There was Tommy on his horse, and on each side of him six savages with feather head-dress, and shields and war-paint complete. After him trooped about thirty of the great chiefs, walking two by two, for all the world like an Aldershot parade. They carried no arms, but the bodyguard shook their spears, and let yells out of them that would have scared Julius Caesar. Then the band started in, and the piper blew up, and the mines people commenced to cheer, and I thought the heavens would fall. Long before Tommy came abreast of me I knew what I should see. His uniform looked as if it had been slept in, and his orders were all awry. But he had his head flung back, and his eyes very bright, and his jaw set square. He never looked to right or left, never recognised me or anybody, for he was seeing something quite different from the red road and the white shanties and the hot sky."

The fire had almost died out. Thirlstone stooped for a moment and stirred the peats.

"Yes," he said, "I knew that in his fool's ear the trumpets of all Asia were ringing, and the King of Bokhara was entering Samarkand."

BABYLON[1]

(THE SONG OF NEHEMIAH'S WORKMEN)

How many miles to Babylon?
Three score and ten.
Can I get there by candle-light?
Yes, and back again.

We are come back from Babylon,
  Out of the plains and the glare,
To the little hills of our own country
  And the sting of our kindred air;
To the rickle of stones on the red rock's edge
  Which Kedron cleaves like a sword.
We will build the walls of Zion again,
  To the glory of Zion's Lord.

Now is no more of dalliance
  By the reedy waters in spring,
When we sang of home, and sighed, and dreamed,
  And wept on remembering.
Now we are back in our ancient hills
  Out of the plains and the sun;
But before we make it a dwelling-place
  There's a wonderful lot to be done.

The walls are to build from west to east,
  From Gihon to Olivet,
Waters to lead and wells to clear,
  And the garden furrows to set.
From the Sheep Gate to the Fish Gate
  Is a welter of mire and mess;
And southward over the common lands
  'Tis a dragon's wilderness.

---

[1] [Each of the stories in *The Moon Endureth* (1912), of which we have included only a few, are, with one exception, accompanied by a poem. The poems used in the present shorter collection were all written between 1909 and 1911, except

The Courts of the Lord are a heap of dust
    Where the hill winds whistle and race,
And the noble pillars of God His House
    Stand in a ruined place.
In the Holy of Holies foxes lair,
    And owls and night-birds build.
There's a deal to do ere we patch it anew
    As our father Solomon willed.

Now is the day of the ordered life
    And the law which all obey.
We toil by rote and speak by note
    And never a soul dare stray.
Ever among us a lean old man
    Keepeth his watch and ward,
Crying, "The Lord hath set you free:
    Prepare ye the way of the Lord."

A goodly task we are called unto,
    A task to dream on o' nights,—
Work for Judah and Judah's God,
    Setting our land to rights;
Everything fair and all things square
    And straight as a plummet string.—
Is it mortal guile, if once in a while
    Our thoughts go wandering? . . .

We were not slaves in Babylon,
    For the gate of our souls lay free,
There in that vast and sunlit land
    On the edges of mystery.
Daily we wrought and daily we thought,
    And we chafed not at rod and power,
For Sinim, Sabæa, and dusky Hind
    Talked to us hour by hour.

for "Babylon" (1906). All the poems link up with the subject matter of the tales—cf. in "Babylon" the eight line stanzas 7, 8, 9 especially. Thus, in stanza 8 we read: "The man who lives in Babylon/May poorly sup and fare,/. . . Next year he too may have sailed strange seas/And conquered a diadem;/For kings are as common in Babylon/As crows in Bethlehem." See also the introduction. The dated poems can also be found as individual items in *John Buchan's Collected Poems*, ed. Lownie & Milne (1996).]

The man who lives in Babylon
    May poorly sup and fare,
But loves and lures from the ends of the earth
    Beckon him everywhere.
Next year he too may have sailed strange seas
    And conquered a diadem;
For kings are as common in Babylon
    As crows in Bethlehem.

Here we are bound to the common round
    In a land which knows not change.
Nothing befalleth to stir the blood
    Or quicken the heart to range;
Never a hope that we cannot plumb
    Or a stranger visage in sight,—
At the most a sleek Samaritan
    Or a ragged Amorite.

Here we are sober and staid of soul,
    Working beneath the law,
Settled amid our fathers' dust,
    Seeing the hills they saw.
All things fixed and determinate,
    Chiselled and squared by rule;—
Is it mortal guile once in a while
    To try and escape from school?

We will go back to Babylon,
    Silently one by one,
Out from the hills and the laggard brooks
    To the streams that brim in the sun.
Only a moment, Lord, we crave,
    To breathe and listen and see.—
Then we start anew with muscle and thew
    To hammer trestles for Thee.

TENDEBANT MANUS

Send not on your soul before
To dive from that beguiling shore,
And let not yet the swimmer leave
His clothes upon the sands of eve.

                                        A. E. HOUSMAN

ONE night we were discussing Souldern, who had died a
week before and whose memorial service had been held
that morning in St. Margaret's. He had come on amazingly in
Parliament, one of those sudden rises which were common in the
immediate post-war years, when the older reputations were being
questioned and the younger men were too busy making a
livelihood to have time for hobbies. His speeches, his member-
ship of a commission where he had shown both originality and
courage, and his reputed refusal, on very honourable grounds, of
a place in the Cabinet, had given him in the popular mind a
flavour of mystery and distinction. The papers had devoted a
good deal of space to him, and there was a general feeling that
his death—the result of a motor smash—was a bigger loss to the
country than his actual achievement warranted.

"I never met him," Palliser-Yeates said. "But I was at school
with his minor. You remember Reggie Souldern, Charles? An
uncommon good fellow—makings of a fine soldier, too—disappeared with most of his battalion in March '18, and was never
heard of again. Body committed to the pleasant land of France
but exact spot unknown—rather like a burial at sea."

"I knew George Souldern well enough," said Lamancha,
whom he addressed. "I sat in the House with him for two years
before the War. That is to say, I knew as much of him as
anybody did, but there was very little you could lay hold of. He

used to be a fussy, ineffective chap, very fertile in ideas which he never thought out, and always starting hares that he wouldn't hunt. But just lately he seems to have had a call, and he looked as if he might have a career. Rotten luck that a sharp corner and a lout of a motorcyclist should have put an end to it."

He turned to his neighbour. "Wasn't he a relation of yours, Sir Arthur?"

The man addressed was the oldest member of the Club and by far the most distinguished. Sir Arthur Warcliff had been a figure of note when most of us were in our cradles. He began life in the Sappers, and before he was thirty had been in command of a troublesome little Somaliland expedition; then he had governed a variety of places with such success that he was seriously spoken of for India. In the War he would have liked to have returned back to soldiering, but they used him as the Cabinet handyman, and he had all the worst diplomatic and administrative jobs to tackle. You see, he was a master of detail and had to translate the generalities of policy into action. He had never, as the jargon goes, got his personality over the footlights, so he was only a name to the public—but a tremendous name, of which every party spoke respectfully. He had retired now, and lived alone with his motherless boy. Usually, for all his sixty-five years, he seemed a contemporary, for he was curiously young at heart, but every now and then we looked at his wise, worn face, realised what he had been and was, and sat at his feet.

"Yes," he said in reply to Lamancha. "George Souldern was my wife's cousin, and I knew him well for the last twenty years. Since the War I knew him better, and in the past eighteen months I was, I think, his only intimate friend."

"Was he a really big man?" Sandy Arbuthnot asked. "I don't take much stock in his profession—but I thought—just for a moment—in that Irish row—that I got a glimpse of something rather out of the ordinary."

"He had first-class brains."

Sandy laughed. "That doesn't get you very far," he said. The phrase "first-class brains" had acquired at the time a flavour of comedy.

"No. It doesn't. If you had asked me the question six years

64

ago I should have said that George was a brilliant failure. Immensely clever in his way, really well educated—which very few of us are—laborious as a beaver, but futile. The hare that is always being passed by every kind of tortoise. He had everything in his favour, but nothing ever came out as he wanted it. I only knew him after he came down from Oxford, but I believe that at the University he was a nonpareil."

"I was up with him," said Peckwether, the historian. "Oh, yes, he was a big enough figure there. He was head of Winchester, and senior scholar of Balliol, and took two Firsts and several University prizes in his stride. He must have sat up all night, for he never appeared to work—you see, it was his pose to do things easily—a variety of the Grand Manner. He was a most disquieting undergraduate. In his political speeches he had the air of having just left a Cabinet meeting."

"Was he popular?" someone asked.

"Not a bit," said Peckwether. "And for all his successes we didn't believe in him. He was too worldly-wise—what we used to call 'banausic'—too bent on getting on. We felt that he had all his goods in the shop window, and that there was no margin to him."

Sir Arthur smiled. "A young man's contemporaries are pretty shrewd judges. When I met him first I felt the same thing. He wasn't a prig, and he had a sense of humour, and he had plenty of ordinary decent feeling. But he was the kind of man who could never forget himself and throw his cap over the moon. One couldn't warm to him. . . . But, unlike you, I thought he would succeed. The one thing lacking was money, and within two years he had remedied that. He married a rich wife; the lady died, but the fortune remained. I believe it was an honest love match, and for a long time he was heartbroken, and when he recovered he buried himself in work. You would have said that something was bound to happen. Young, rich, healthy, incredibly industrious, able, presentable—you would have said that any constituency would have welcomed him, that his party would have jumped at him, that he would have been a prodigious success.

"But he wasn't. He made a bad candidate, and had to stand

65

three times before he got into the House. And there he made no kind of impression, though he spoke conscientiously and always on matters he knew about. He wrote a book on the meaning of colonial nationalism—fluent, well expressed, sensible, even in parts eloquent, but somehow it wasn't read. He was always making speeches at public dinners and at the annual meetings of different kinds of associations, but it didn't seem to signify what he said, and he was scarcely reported. There was no conspiracy of silence to keep him down, for people rather liked him. He simply seemed to have no clear boundary lines and to be imperfectly detached from the surrounding atmosphere. I could never understand why."

"Lack of personality," said Lamancha. "I remember feeling that."

"Yes, but what is personality? He had the things that make it—brains and purpose. One liked him—was impressed by his attainments, but, if you understand me, one wasn't impressed by the man. . . . It wasn't ordinary lack of confidence, for on occasion he could be aggressive. It was the lack of a continuity of confidence in himself and in other things. He didn't *believe* enough. That was why, as you said, he was always starting hares that he wouldn't hunt. Some excellent and unanswerable reason would occur to him why he should slack off. He was what I believe you call a good party man and always voted orthodoxly, but, after four years in the House, instead of being a leader he was rapidly becoming a mere cog in the machine. He didn't seem to be able to make himself count.

"That was his position eight years ago, and it was not far from a tragedy. He was as able as any man in the Cabinet, but he lacked the demonic force which even stupid people sometimes possess. I can only describe him in paradoxes. He was at once conceited and shy, inordinately ambitious and miserably conscious that he never got the value of his abilities out of life. . . . Then came the War."

"He served, didn't he?" Leithen asked. "I remember running across him at G.H.Q."

"You may call it serving, if you mean that he was never out of uniform for four years. But he didn't fight. I wanted him to.

I thought a line battalion might make a man of him, but he shrank from the notion. It wasn't lack of courage—I satisfied myself of that. But he hadn't the nerve to sink himself into the ranks of ordinary men. You understand why? It would have meant the realisation of what was the inmost fear of his heart. He had to keep up the delusion that he was some sort of a swell—had to have authority to buttress his tottering vanity.

"So he had a selection of footling staff jobs—*liaison* with this and that, deputy-assistant to Tom, Dick and Harry, quite futile, but able to command special passes and staff cars. He ranked, I think, as a full colonel, but an Army Service Corps private was more useful than ten of him. And he was as miserable as a man could be. He liked people to think that his trouble was the strain of the War, but the real strain was that there was no strain. He knew that he simply didn't matter. At least he was candid with himself, and he was sometimes candid with me. He rather hoped, I think, that I would inspan him into something worth doing, but in common honesty I couldn't, for you see I too had come to disbelieve in him utterly.

"Well, that went on till March 1918, when his brother Reggie was killed in the German push. Ninth Division, wasn't it?"

Palliser-Yeates nodded. "Ninth. South African Brigade. He went down at Marrières Wood, but he and his lot stuck up the enemy for the best part of a Sunday, and, I solemnly believe, saved our whole front. They were at the critical point, you see, the junction of Gough and Byng. His body was never found."

"I know," said Sir Arthur, "and that is just the point of my story."

He stopped. "I suppose I'm right to tell you this. He left instructions that if anything happened to him I was to have his diary. He can't have meant me to keep it secret. . . . No, I think he would have liked one or two people to know."

He looked towards Palliser-Yeates. "You knew Reggie Souldern? How would you describe him?"

"The very best stamp of British regimental officer," was the emphatic reply.

"Clever?"

"Not a bit. Only average brains, but every ounce of them

useful. Always cheery and competent, and a born leader of men. He was due for a brigade when he fell, and if the War had lasted another couple of years he might have had a corps. I never met the other Souldern, but from what you say he must have been the plumb opposite of Reggie."

"Just so. George had a great opinion of his brother—in addition to the ordinary brotherly love, for there were only the two of them. I thought the news of his death would break him altogether. But it didn't. He took it with extraordinary calm, and presently it looked as if he were actually more cheerful. . . . You see, they never found the body. He never saw him lying dead, or even the grave where he was buried, and he never met anybody who had. Reggie had been translated mysteriously out of the world, but the melancholy indisputable signs of death were lacking."

"You mean he thought he was only missing and might turn up some day?"

"No. He *knew* he was dead—the proof was too strong, the presumption was too heavy. . . . But while there was enough to convince his reason, there was too little for his imagination—no white face and stiff body, no wooden cross in the cemetery. He could *picture* him as still alive, and George had a queer sensitive imagination about which most people knew nothing."

Sir Arthur looked round the table and saw that we were puzzled.

"It is a little difficult to explain. . . . Do you remember a story of the French at Verdun making an attack over ground they had been fighting on for months? They shouted 'En avant, les morts,' and they believed that the spirits of the dead responded and redressed the balance. I think it was the last action at Vaux. . . . I don't suppose the *poilu* thought the dead came back to help him, but he pretended they were still combatants, and got a moral support from the fancy. . . . That was something like George Souldern's case. If you had asked him, you would have found that he had no doubt that what was left of Reggie was somewhere in the churned-up wilderness north of Péronne. And there was never any nonsense about visitations or messages from the dead. But the lack of *visible* proofs enabled his

68

imagination to picture Reggie as still alive, and going from strength to strength. He nursed the fancy till it became as real to him as anything in his ordinary life. Reggie was becoming a great man and would soon be the most famous man in the world, and something of Reggie went into him and he shared in Reggie's glory. In March '18 a partnership began for George Souldern with his dead brother, and the dead, who in his imagination was alive and triumphant, lifted him out of the sticky furrow which he had been ploughing since he left Oxford."

We were all silent except Pugh, who said that he had come across the same thing in the East—some Rajput prince, I think.

"How did you know this?" Lamancha asked.

"From the diary. George set down very fully every stage of his new career. But I very nearly guessed the truth for myself. You see, knowing him as I did, I had to admit a sudden and staggering change."

"How soon?"

"The week after the news came. I had been in Paris, and on my return ran across George in the Travellers' and said the ordinary banal words of sympathy. He looked at me queerly, as he thanked me, and if I had not known how deeply attached the brothers were, I would have said that he was exhilarated by his loss. It was almost as if he had been given a drug to strengthen his arteries. He seemed to me suddenly a more substantial fellow, calmer, more at peace with himself. He said an odd thing too. 'Old Reggie has got his chance,' he said, and then, as if pulling himself up, 'I mean, he had the chance he wanted.'

"In June it was clear that something had happened to George Souldern. Do you remember how about that time a wave of dejection passed over all the Allied countries? It was partly the mess in Russia, partly in this country a slight loss of confidence in the Government, which seemed to have got to loggerheads with the soldiers, but mainly the 'drag' that comes in all wars. It was the same in the American Civil War before Gettysburg. Foch was marking time but he was doing it by retreating pretty fast on the Aisne. Well, our people needed a little cheering up, and our politicians tried their hand at it. There was a debate in Parliament, and far the best speech was George's. The rest were mere platitude and rhetoric, but he came down on the point like a steam-hammer."

"I know," said Lamancha. "I read it in *The Times* in a field hospital in Palestine."

"In his old days nobody would have paid much attention. He would have been clever and epigrammatic—sound enough, but 'precious'. His speech would have read well, if it had been reported, but it wouldn't have mattered a penn'orth to anybody. . . . Instead he said just the wise, simple, stalwart thing that every honest man had at the back of his head, and he said it with an air which made everybody sit up. For the first time in his life he spoke as one having authority. The press reported him nearly verbatim, for the journalists in the Gallery have a very acute sense of popular values.

"The speech put George, as the phrase goes, on the political map. The Prime Minister spoke to me about him, and there was some talk of employing him on a mission which never materialised. I met him one day in the street and congratulated him, and I remember that I was struck by the new vigour in his personality. He made me come home with him to tea, and to talk to him was like breathing ozone. He asked me one or two questions about numbers, and then he gave me his views on the War. At the time it was fashionable to think that no decision would be reached till the next summer, but George maintained that, if we played our cards right, victory was a mathematical certainty before Christmas. He showed a knowledge of the military situation which would have done credit to any soldier, and he could express himself, which few soldiers can do. His arguments stuck in my head, and I believe I used them in the War Cabinet. I left with a very real respect for one whom I had written off as a failure.

"Well, then came the last battle of the Marne, and Haig's great advance, and all the drama and confusion of the autumn months. I lost sight of George, for I was busy with the peace overtures, and I don't think I even heard of him again till the new year. . . . But the diary tells all about those months. I am giving you the bones of the story, but I am going to burn the diary, for it is too intimate for other eyes. . . . According to it

Reggie finished the War as a blazing hero. It was all worked out in detail with maps and diagrams. He had become a corps commander by August, and in October he was the chief fighting figure on the British front, the conduit pipe of Foch's ideas, for he could work out in practice what the great man saw as a vision. It sounds crazy, but it was so convincingly done that I had to rub my eyes and make myself remember that Reggie was lying in a nameless grave on the Somme and not a household word in two hemispheres. . . . George, too, shared in his glory, but just how was not very clear. Anyway, the brothers were in the front of the stage, Reggie the bigger man and George his civilian adviser and opposite number. I can see now how he got his confidence. He was no longer a struggler, but a made man; he had arrived, he was proved, the world required him. Whatever he said or did must be attended to, and, because he believed this, it was."

Lamancha whistled long and low. "But how could his mind work, if he lived among fairy tales?" he asked.

"He didn't," said Sir Arthur. "He lived very much in the real world. But he had all the time his private imaginative preserve, into which his normal mind did not penetrate. He drew his confidence from this preserve, and, having once got it, could carry it also into the real world."

"Wasn't he intolerably conceited?" someone asked.

"No, for the great man was Reggie and he was only a satellite. He was Reggie's prophet, and assured enough on that side, but there was no personal arrogance. His dead brother had become, so to speak, his familiar spirit, his *dæmon*. The fact is that George was less of an egotist than he had ever been before. His vanity was burned up in a passion of service.

"I saw him frequently during the first half of '19, and had many talks with him. He had been returned to Parliament by a big majority, but he wasn't much in the public eye. He didn't like the way things were going, but at the same time as a good citizen he declined to make things more difficult for the Government. The diary gives his thoughts at that time. He considered that the soldiers should have had the chief share in the settlement of the world—Foch and Haig and Hindenburg—and Reggie. He held that they would have made a cleaner and fairer job of it than the kind of circus that appeared at Versailles. Perhaps he was right—I can't be dogmatic, for I was a performer in the circus.

"That, of course, I didn't know till the other day. But the change in George Souldern was soon manifest to the whole world. There was the Irish business, when he went down to the worst parts of the South and West, and seemed to be simply asking for a bullet in his head. He was half Irish, you know. He wrote and said quite frankly that he didn't care a straw whether Ireland was inside or outside the British Empire, that the only thing which mattered was that she should find a soul, and that she had a long road to travel before she got one. He told her that at present she was one vast perambulating humbug, and that till she got a little discipline and sense of realities she would remain on the level of Haiti. Why some gunman didn't have a shot at him I can't imagine, except that such naked candour and courage was a new thing and had to be respected. . . . Then there was the Unemployment Commission. You remember the majority report—pious generalities and futile compromises. George's dissenting report made him for a month the best abused man in Britain, for he was impartially contemptuous of all sides. Today—well, I fancy most of us would agree with George, and I observe that he is frequently quoted by the Labour people.

"What struck me about his line of country was that it was like that of a good soldier's. He had the same power of seeing simple facts and of making simple syllogisms, which the clever intellectual—such as George used to be—invariably misses. And there was the soldier's fidelity and sense of service. George plainly had no axe to grind. He had intellectual courage and would back his views as a general backs his strategy, but he kept always a curious personal modesty. I tell you it seemed nothing short of a miracle to one who had known him in the old days.

"I accepted it as the act of God and didn't look for any further explanation. I think that what first set me questioning was his behaviour about Reggie's memorial. The family wanted a stone put up in the churchyard of the family place in Gloucestershire. George absolutely declined. He stuck his toes into the ground and gave nothing but a flat refusal. One might have thought that the brothers had been estranged, but it was common knowledge that they had been like twins and had written to each other every day.

"Then there was the business about a memoir of Reggie. The regiment wanted one, and his Staff College contemporaries. Tollett—you remember him, the man on the Third Army Staff—volunteered to write it, of course with George's assistance. George refused bluntly and said that he felt the strongest distaste for the proposal. Tollett came to me about it, and I had George to luncheon and thrashed it out with him. I found his reasons very difficult to follow, for he objected even to a regimental history being compiled. He admitted that Tollett was as good a man as could be found for the job, but he said he hated the idea. Nobody understood Reggie but himself. Someday, he suggested, he might try to do justice to him in print—but not yet. I put forward all the arguments I could think of, but George was adamant.

"Walking home, I puzzled a good deal about the affair. It couldn't be merely the jealousy of a writer who wanted to reserve a good subject for himself—that wasn't George's character, and he had no literary vanity. Besides, that wouldn't explain his aversion to a prosaic regimental chronicle, and still less his objection to the cenotaph in the Gloucestershire churchyard. I wondered if there was not some quirk in George, some odd obsession about his brother. For a moment I thought that he might have been dabbling in spiritualism and have got some message from Reggie, till I remembered that I had heard him a week before declare his unbridled contempt for such mumbo-jumbo.

"I thought a good deal about it, and the guess I made was that George was living a double life—that in his subconsciousness Reggie was still alive for him. It was only a guess, but it was fairly near the truth, and last year I had it from his own lips.

"We were duck-shooting together on Croftsmoor, the big marsh near his home. That had been Reggie's pet game; he used to be out at all hours in the winter dawns and dusks stalking wildfowl. George never cared for it, or indeed for any field sport. He would take his place at a covert shoot or a grouse drive and was useful enough with a gun, but he would have been the first to disclaim the title of sportsman. But now he was as keen and tireless as Reggie. He kept me out for eight hours in a filthy day of rain wading in trench boots in Gloucestershire mud.

"We did fairly well, and just before sunset the weather improved. The wind had gone into the north, and promised frost, and as we sat on an old broken-backed stone bridge over one of the dykes, waiting for the birds to be collected from the different stands, the western sky was one broad band of palest gold. We were both tired and the sudden change from blustering rain to a cold stillness, and from grey mist to colour and light, had a strange effect upon my spirits. I felt peaceful and solemnised. I lit a pipe, but let it go out, for my attention was held by the shoreless ocean in the west, against which the scarp of the Welsh hills showed in a dim silhouette. The sharp air, the wild marsh scents, the faint odour of tobacco awoke in me a thousand half-sad and half-sweet recollections.

"I couldn't help it. I said something about Reggie.

"George was sitting on the bridge with his eyes fixed on the sky. I thought he hadn't heard me, till suddenly he repeated 'Reggie. Yes, old Reggie.'

" 'This was what he loved,' I said.

" ' 'He still loves it,' was the answer, spoken very low. And then he repeated—to himself as it were:

> " 'Fight on, fight on,' said Sir Andrew Barton.
> 'Though I be wounded I am not slain.
> I'll lay me down and bleed awhile
> And then I'll rise and fight again.'

"He turned his fine-drawn face to me.

" 'You think Reggie is dead?'

"I didn't know what to say. 'Yes,' I stammered, 'I suppose—'

" 'What do you mean by death?' His voice was almost shrill. 'We know nothing about it. What does it matter if the body is buried in a shell-hole—?'

74

"He stopped suddenly, as a lamp goes out when you press the switch. I had the impression that those queer shrill words came not from George but from some other who had joined us.

" 'I believe that the spirit is immortal,' I began.

" 'The spirit—' again the shrill impersonal voice—'I tell you the whole man lives. . . . He is nearer to me than he ever was . . . we are never parted. . . .'

"Again the light went out. He seemed to gulp, and when he spoke it was in his natural tones.

" 'I apologise,' he said, 'I must seem to you to be talking nonsense. . . . You don't understand. *You* would understand, if anyone could, but I can't explain—yet—someday . . .'

"The head-keeper, the beaters and the dogs came out of the reed beds, and at the same time the uncanny glow in the west was shrouded with the film of the coming night. It was almost dark when we turned to walk home, and I was glad of it, for neither of us wished to look at the other's face.

"I felt at once embarrassed and enlightened. I had been given a glimpse into the cloudy places of a man's soul, and had surprised his secret. My guess had been right. In George's subconscious mind Reggie was still alive—nay more, was progressing in achievement as if he had never disappeared in the March battle. It was no question of a disembodied spirit establishing communication with the living—that was a business I knew nothing about, nor George either. It was a question of life, complete life, in a peculiar world, companionship in some spiritual fourth dimension, and from that companionship he was drawing sustenance. He had learned Reggie's forthrightness and his happy simplicity. . . . I wondered and I trembled. There is a story of an early Victorian statesman who in his leisure moments played at being Emperor of Byzantium. The old Whig kept the two things strictly separate—he was a pious humanitarian in his English life, though he was a ruthless conqueror in the other. But in George's case the two were mingling. He was going about his daily duties with the power acquired from his secret world; that secret world, in which, with Reggie, he had become a master, was giving him a mastery over our common life. . . . I did not believe it would last. It was against nature that a man could continue to live as a parasite on the dead.

"I am almost at the end of my story. Two months later, George became a figure of national importance. It was he who chiefly broke up the Coalition at the Grafton House meeting, and thereby, I suppose, saved his party. His speech, you remember, clove through subtleties and irrelevances with the simple declaration that he could not work with what he could not trust, and, unless things changed, must go out of public life. That was Reggie's manner, you know—pure Reggie. Then came the general election and the new Government, and George, very much to people's surprise, refused Cabinet office. The reason he gave was that on grounds of principle he had taken a chief part in wrecking the late Ministry, and he felt he could not allow himself to benefit personally by his action. We all thought him high-minded, if finical and quixotic, but the ordinary man liked it—it was a welcome change from the old gang of *arrivistes*. But it was not the real reason. I found that in the diary."

Sir Arthur stopped, and there was a silence while he seemed to be fumbling for words.

"Here we are walking on the edge of great mysteries," he continued. "The reason why he refused the Prime Minister's offer was Reggie. . . . Somehow the vital force in that subconscious world of his was ebbing. . . . I cannot explain how, but Reggie was moving away from what we call realities and was beckoning him to follow. . . . The Grafton House speech was George's last public utterance. Few people saw him after that, for he rarely attended the House. I saw him several times in Gloucestershire. . . . Was he happy? Yes, I should say utterly happy, but too detached, too peaceful, as if he had done with the cares of this world. . . . I think I guessed what was happening, when he told me that he had consented to the cenotaph in the churchyard. He took a good deal of pains about it, too, and chose an inscription, which his maiden aunts thought irreligious. It was Virgil's *'Tendebant manus ripæ ulterioris amore.'* . . . He withdrew his objection to the memoir, too, and Tollett got to work, but he gave him no help—it was as if he had lost interest. . . . It is an odd thing to say, but I have been waiting for the news which was in last week's paper."

"You don't mean that he engineered the motor smash?" Lamancha asked.

"Oh no," said Sir Arthur gently. "As I said, we are treading on the brink of great mysteries. Say that it was predestined, fore-ordained, decreed by the Master of Assembly. . . . I know that it had to be. If you join hands with the dead they will pull you over the stream."

NO-MAN'S-LAND

CHAPTER I

THE SHIELING OF FARAWA

IT was with a light heart and a pleasing consciousness of holiday that I set out from the inn at Allermuir to tramp my fifteen miles into the unknown. I walked slowly, for I carried my equipment on my back—my basket, fly-books and rods, my plaid of Grant tartan (for I boast myself a distant kinsman of that house), and my great staff, which had tried ere then the front of the steeper Alps. A small valise with books and some changes of linen clothing had been sent on ahead in the shepherd's own hands. It was yet early April, and before me lay four weeks of freedom—twenty-eight blessed days in which to take fish and smoke the pipe of idleness. The Lent term had pulled me down, a week of modest enjoyment thereafter in town had finished the work; and I drank in the sharp moorish air like a thirsty man who has been forwandered among deserts.

I am a man of varied tastes and a score of interests. As an undergraduate I had been filled with the old mania for the complete life. I distinguished myself in the Schools, rowed in my college eight, and reached the distinction of practising for three weeks in the Trials. I had dabbled in a score of learned activities, and when the time came that I won the inevitable St. Chad's fellowship on my chaotic acquirements, and I found myself compelled to select if I would pursue a scholar's life, I had some toil in finding my vocation. In the end I resolved that the ancient life of the North, of the Celts and the Northmen and the unknown Pictish tribes, held for me the chief fascination. I had acquired a smattering of Gaelic, having been brought up as a boy in Lochaber, and now I set myself to increase my store of languages. I mastered Erse and Icelandic, and my first book—a monograph on the probable Celtic elements in the Eddic songs—brought me the praise of scholars and the deputy-professor's chair of Northern Antiquities. So much for Oxford. My vacations had been spent mainly in the North—in Ireland, Scotland, and the Isles, in Scandinavia and Iceland, once even in the far limits of Finland. I was a keen sportsman of a sort, an old-experienced fisher, a fair shot with gun and rifle, and in my hillcraft I might well stand comparison with most men. April has ever seemed to me the finest season of the year even in our cold northern altitudes, and the memory of many bright Aprils had brought me up from the South on the night before to Allerfoot, whence a dogcart had taken me up Glen Aller to the inn at Allermuir; and now the same desire had set me on the heather with my face to the cold brown hills.

You are to picture a sort of plateau, benty and rock-strewn, running ridge-wise above a chain of little peaty lochs and a vast tract of inexorable bog. In a mile the ridge ceased in a shoulder of hill, and over this lay the head of another glen, with the same doleful accompaniment of sunless lochs, mosses, and a shining and resolute water. East and west and north, in every direction save the south, rose walls of gashed and serrated hills. It was a grey day with blinks of sun, and when a ray chanced to fall on one of the great dark faces, lines of light and colour sprang into being which told of mica and granite. I was in high spirits, as on the eve of holiday; I had breakfasted excellently on eggs and salmon-steaks; I had no cares to speak of, and my prospects were not uninviting. But in spite of myself the landscape began to take me in thrall and crush me. The silent vanished peoples of the hills seemed to be stirring; dark primeval faces seemed to stare at me from behind boulders and jags of rock. The place was so still, so free from the cheerful clamour of nesting birds, that it seemed a *temenos* sacred to some old-world god. At my feet the lochs lapped ceaselessly; but the waters were so dark that one could not see bottom a foot from the edge. On my right the links of green told of snake-like mires waiting to crush the unwary wanderer. It seemed to me for the moment a land of death, where the tongues of the dead cried aloud for recognition.

My whole morning's walk was full of such fancies. I lit a pipe to cheer me, but the things would not be got rid of. I thought of the Gaels who had held those fastnesses; I thought of the Britons before them, who yielded to their advent. They were all strong peoples in their day, and now they had gone the way of the earth. They had left their mark on the levels of the glens and on the more habitable uplands, both in names and in actual forts, and graves where men might still dig curios. But the hills—that black stony amphitheatre before me—it seemed strange that the hills bore no traces of them. And then with some uneasiness I reflected on that older and stranger race who were said to have held the hilltops. The Picts, the Picti—what in the name of goodness were they? They had troubled me in all my studies, a sort of blank wall to put an end to speculation. We knew nothing of them save certain strange names which men called Pictish, the names of those hills in front of me—the Muneraw, the Yirnie, the Calmarton. They were the *corpus vile* for learned experiment; but Heaven alone knew what dark abyss of savagery once yawned in the midst of this desert.

And then I remembered the crazy theories of a pupil of mine at St. Chad's, the son of a small landowner on the Aller, a young gentleman who had spent his substance too freely at Oxford, and was now dreeing his weird in the Backwoods. He had been no scholar; but a certain imagination marked all his doings, and of a Sunday night he would come and talk to me of the North. The Picts were his special subject, and his ideas were mad. "Listen to me," he would say, when I had mixed him toddy and given him one of my cigars; "I believe there are traces—ay, and more than traces—of an old culture lurking in those hills and waiting to be discovered. We never hear of the Picts being driven from the hills. The Britons drove them from the lowlands, the Gaels from Ireland did the same for the Britons; but the hills were left unmolested. We hear of no one going near them except outlaws and tinklers. And in that very place you have the strangest mythology. Take the story of the Brownie. What is that but the story of a little swart man of uncommon strength and cleverness, who does good and ill indiscriminately, and then disappears? There are many scholars, as you yourself confess, who think that the origin of the Brownie was in some mad belief in the old race of the Picts, which still survived somewhere in the hills. And do we not hear of the Brownie in authentic records right down to the year 1756? After that, when people grew more incredulous, it is natural that the belief should have begun to die out; but I do not see why stray traces should not have survived till late."

"Do you not see what that means?" I had said in mock gravity. "Those same hills are, if anything, less known now than they were a hundred years ago. Why should not your Picts or Brownies be living to this day?"

"Why not, indeed?" he had rejoined, in all seriousness.

I laughed, and he went to his rooms and returned with a large leather-bound book. It was lettered, in the rococo style of a young man's taste, *Glimpses of the Unknown*, and some of the said glimpses he proceeded to impart to me. It was not pleasant reading; indeed, I had rarely heard anything so well fitted to shatter sensitive nerves. The early part consisted of folk-tales and folk-sayings, some of them wholly obscure, some of them with a glint of meaning, but all of them with some hint of a mystery in the hills. I heard the Brownie story in countless versions. Now the thing was a friendly little man, who wore grey breeches and lived on brose; now he was a twisted being, the sight of which made the ewes miscarry in the lambing-time. But the second part was the stranger, for it was made up of actual tales, most of them with date and place appended. It was a most Bedlamite catalogue of horrors, which, if true, made the wholesome moors a place instinct with tragedy. Some told of children carried away from villages, even from towns, on the verge of the uplands. In almost every case they were girls, and the strange fact was their utter disappearance. Two little girls would be coming home from school, would be seen last by a neighbour just where the road crossed a patch of heath or entered a wood and then—no human eye ever saw them again. Children's cries had startled outlying shepherds in the night, and when they had rushed to the door they could hear nothing but the night wind. The instances of such disappearances were not very common—

perhaps once in twenty years—but they were confined to this one tract of country, and came in a sort of fixed progression from the middle of last century, when the record began. But this was only one side of the history. The latter part was all devoted to a chronicle of crimes which had gone unpunished, seeing that no hand had ever been traced. The list was fuller in last century;[1] in the earlier years of the present it had dwindled; then came a revival about the 'Fifties; and now again in our own time it had sunk low. At the little cottage of Auchterbrean, on the roadside in Glen Aller, a labourer's wife had been found pierced to the heart. It was thought to be a case of a woman's jealousy, and her neighbour was accused, convicted, and hanged. The woman, to be sure, denied the charge with her last breath; but circumstantial evidence seemed sufficiently strong against her. Yet some people in the glen believed her guiltless. In particular, the carrier who had found the dead woman declared that the way in which her neighbour received the news was a sufficient proof of innocence; and the doctor who was first summoned professed himself unable to tell with what instrument the wound had been given. But this was all before the days of expert evidence, so the woman had been hanged without scruple. Then there had been another story of peculiar horror, telling of the death of an old man at some little lonely shieling called Carrickfey. But at this point I had risen in protest, and made to drive the young idiot from my room.

"It was my grandfather who collected most of them," he said. "He had theories,[2] but people called him mad, so he was wise enough to hold his tongue. My father declares the whole thing mania; but I rescued the book, had it bound, and added to the collection. It is a queer hobby; but, as I say, I have theories, and there are more things in Heaven and earth—"

[1] The narrative of Mr. Graves was written in the year 1898.

[2] In the light of subsequent events I have jotted down the materials to which I refer. The last authentic record of the Brownie is in the narrative of the shepherd of Clachlands, taken down towards the close of last century by the Reverend Mr. Gillespie, minister of Allerkirk, and included by him in his *Songs and Legends of Glen Aller*. The authorities on the strange carrying-away of children are to be found in a series of articles in a local paper, the *Allerfoot Advertiser*,

But at this he heard a friend's voice in the Quad, and dived out, leaving the banal quotation unfinished.

Strange though it may seem, this madness kept coming back to me as I crossed the last few miles of moor. I was now on a rough tableland, the watershed between two lochs, and beyond and above me rose the stony backs of the hills. The burns fell down in a chaos of granite boulders, and huge slabs of grey stone lay flat and tumbled in the heather. The full waters looked prosperously for my fishing, and I began to forget all fancies in anticipation of sport.

Then suddenly in a hollow of land I came on a ruined cottage. It had been a very small place, but the walls were still half-erect, and the little moorland garden was outlined on the turf. A lonely apple-tree, twisted and gnarled with winds, stood in the midst.

From higher up on the hill I heard a loud roar, and I knew my excellent friend the shepherd of Farawa, who had come thus far to meet me. He greeted me with the boisterous embarrassment which was his way of prefacing hospitality. A grave reserved man at other times, on such occasions he thought it proper to relapse into hilarity. I fell into step with him, and we set off for his dwelling. But first I had the curiosity to look back to the tumbledown cottage and ask him its name.

A queer look came into his eyes. "They ca' the place Carrickfey," he said. "Naebody has daured to bide there this twenty year sin'—but I see ye ken the story." And, as if glad to leave the subject, he hastened to discourse on fishing.

September and October 1878, and a curious book published anonymously at Edinburgh in 1848, entitled *The Weathergaw*. The records of the unexplained murders in the same neighbourhood are all contained in Mr. Fordoun's *Theory of Expert Evidence*, and an attack on the book in the *Law Review* for June 1881. The Carrickfey case has a pamphlet to itself—now extremely rare—a copy of which was recently obtained in a bookseller's shop in Dumfries by a well-known antiquary, and presented to the library of the Supreme Court in Edinburgh.

CHAPTER II

TELLS OF AN EVENING'S TALK

THE shepherd was a masterful man; tall, save for the stoop which belongs to all moorland folk, and active as a wild goat. He was not a new importation, nor did he belong to the place; for his people had lived in the remote Borders, and he had come as a boy to this shieling of Farawa. He was unmarried, but an elderly sister lived with him and cooked his meals. He was reputed to be extraordinarily skilful in his trade; I know for a fact that he was in his way a keen sportsman; and his few neighbours gave him credit for a sincere piety. Doubtless this last report was due in part to his silence, for after his first greeting he was wont to relapse into a singular taciturnity. As we strode across the heather he gave me a short outline of his year's lambing. "Five pair o' twins yestreen, twae this morn; that makes thirty-five yowes that hae lambed since the Sabbath. I'll dae weel if God's willin'." Then, as I looked towards the hilltops whence the thin mist of morn was trailing, he followed my gaze. "See," he said with uplifted crook—"see that sicht. Is that no what is written of in the Bible when it says, 'The mountains do smoke.'" And with this piece of exegesis he finished his talk, and in a little we were at the cottage.

It was a small enough dwelling in truth, and yet large for a moorland house, for it had a garret below the thatch, which was given up to my sole enjoyment. Below was the wide kitchen with box-beds, and next to it the inevitable second room, also with its cupboard sleeping-places. The interior was very clean, and yet I remember to have been struck with the faint musty smell which is inseparable from moorland dwellings. The kitchen pleased me best, for there the great rafters were black with peat-reek, and the uncovered stone floor, on which the fire gleamed dully, gave an air of primeval simplicity. But the walls spoiled all, for tawdry things of today had penetrated even there. Some grocers' alma-nacs—years old—hung in places of honour, and an extraordinary lithograph of the Royal Family in its youth. And this, mind you, between crooks and fishing-rods and old guns, and horns of sheep and deer.

The life for the first day or two was regular and placid. I was up early, breakfasted on porridge (a dish which I detest), and then off to the lochs and streams. At first my sport prospered mightily. With a drake-wing I killed a salmon of seventeen pounds, and the next day had a fine basket of trout from a hill-burn. Then for no earthly reason the weather changed. A bitter wind came out of the north-east, bringing showers of snow and stinging hail, and lashing the waters into storm. It was now farewell to fly-fishing. For a day or two I tried trolling with the minnow on the lochs, but it was poor sport, for I had no boat, and the edges were soft and mossy. Then in disgust I gave up the attempt, went back to the cottage, lit my biggest pipe, and sat down with a book to await the turn of the weather.

The shepherd was out from morning till night at his work, and when he came in at last, dog-tired, his face would be set and hard, and his eyes heavy with sleep. The strangeness of the man grew upon me. He had a shrewd brain beneath his thatch of hair, for I had tried him once or twice, and found him abundantly intelligent. He had some smattering of an education, like all Scottish peasants, and, as I have said, he was deeply religious. I set him down as a fine type of his class, sober, serious, keenly critical, free from the bondage of superstition. But I rarely saw him, and our talk was chiefly in monosyllables—short interjected accounts of the number of lambs dead or alive on the hill. Then he would produce a pencil and notebook, and be immersed in some calculation; and finally he would be revealed sleeping heavily in his chair, till his sister wakened him, and he stumbled off to bed.

So much for the ordinary course of life; but one day—the second I think of the bad weather—the extraordinary happened. The storm had passed in the afternoon into a resolute and blinding snow, and the shepherd, finding it hopeless on the hill, came home about three o'clock. I could make out from his way of entering that he was in a great temper. He kicked his feet savagely against the doorpost. Then he swore at his dogs, a thing I had never heard him do before. "Hell!" he cried, "can ye no keep out o' my road, ye britts?" Then he came sullenly into the kitchen, thawed his numbed hands at the fire, and sat down to his meal. I made some aimless remark about the weather.

"Death to man and beast," he grunted. "I hae got the sheep doun frae the hill, but the lambs will never thole this. We maun pray that it will no last."

His sister came in with some dish. "Margit," he cried, "three lambs away this morning, and three deid wi' the hole in the throat."

The woman's face visibly paled. "Guid help us, Adam; that hasna happened this three year."

"It has happened noo," he said surlily. "But, by God! if it happens again I'll gang mysel' to the Scarts o' the Muneraw."

"O Adam!" the woman cried shrilly, "haud your tongue. Ye kenna wha hears ye." And with a frightened glance at me she left the room.

I asked no questions, but waited till the shepherd's anger should cool. But the cloud did not pass so lightly. When he had finished his dinner he pulled his chair to the fire and sat staring moodily. He made some sort of apology to me for his conduct. "I'm sore troubled, sir; but I'm vexed ye should see me like this. Maybe things will be better the morn." And then, lighting his short black pipe, he resigned himself to his meditations.

But he could not keep quiet. Some nervous unrest seemed to have possessed the man. He got up with a start and went to the window, where the snow was drifting unsteadily past. As he stared out into the storm I heard him mutter to himself, "Three away, God help me, and three wi' the hole in the throat."

Then he turned round to me abruptly. I was jotting down notes for an article I contemplated in the *Revue Celtique*, so my thoughts were far away from the present. The man recalled me by demanding fiercely, "Do ye believe in God?"

I gave him some sort of answer in the affirmative.

"Then do ye believe in the Devil?" he asked.

The reply must have been less satisfactory, for he came forward and flung himself violently into the chair before me.

"What do ye ken about it?" he cried. "You that bides in a southern toun, what can ye ken o' the God that works in thae hills and the Devil—ay, the manifold devils—that He suffers to bide here? I tell ye, man, that if ye had seen what I have seen ye wad be on your knees at this moment praying to God to pardon your unbelief. There are devils at the back o' every stane and hidin' in every cleuch, and it's by the grace o' God alone that a man is alive upon the earth." His voice had risen high and shrill, and then suddenly he cast a frightened glance towards the window and was silent.

I began to think that the man's wits were unhinged, and the thought did not give me satisfaction. I had no relish for the prospect of being left alone in this moorland dwelling with the cheerful company of a maniac. But his next movements reassured me. He was clearly only dead-tired, for he fell sound asleep in his chair, and by the time his sister brought tea and wakened him, he seemed to have got the better of his excitement.

When the window was shuttered and the lamp lit, I set myself again to the completion of my notes. The shepherd had got out his Bible, and was solemnly reading with one great finger travelling down the lines. He was smoking, and whenever some text came home to him with power he would make pretence to underline it with the end of the stem. Soon I had finished the work I desired, and, my mind being full of my pet hobby, I fell into an inquisitive mood, and began to question the solemn man opposite on the antiquities of the place.

He stared stupidly at me when I asked him concerning monuments or ancient weapons.

"I kenna," said he. "There's a heap o' queer things in the hills."

"This place should be a centre for such relics. You know that the name of the hill behind the house, as far as I can make it out, means the 'Place of the Little Men'. It is a good Gaelic word, though there is some doubt about its exact interpretation. But clearly the Gaelic peoples did not speak of themselves when they gave the name; they must have referred to some older and stranger population."

The shepherd looked at me dully, as not understanding.

"It is partly this fact—besides the fishing, of course—which interests me in this countryside," said I gaily.

Again he cast the same queer frightened glance towards the

window. "If ye'll tak the advice of an aulder man," he said slowly, "ye'll let well alane and no meddle wi' uncanny things."

I laughed pleasantly, for at last I had found out my hard-headed host in a piece of childishness. "Why, I thought that you of all men would be free from superstition."

"What do ye call supersteetion?" he asked.

"A belief in old wives' tales," said I, "a trust in the crude supernatural and the patently impossible."

He looked at me beneath his shaggy brows. "How do ye ken what is impossible? Mind ye, sir, ye're no in the toun just now, but in the thick of the wild hills."

"But, hang it all, man," I cried, "you don't mean to say that you believe in that sort of thing? I am prepared for many things up here, but not for the Brownie—though, to be sure, if one could meet him in the flesh, it would be rather pleasant than otherwise, for he was a companionable sort of fellow."

"When a thing pits the fear o' death on a man he aye speaks well of it."

It was true—the Eumenides and the Good Folk over again; and I awoke with interest to the fact that the conversation was getting into strange channels.

The shepherd moved uneasily in his chair. "I am a man that fears God, and has nae time for daft stories; but I havena traivelled the hills for twenty years wi' my een shut. If I say that I could tell ye stories o' faces seen in the mist, and queer things that have knocked against me in the snaw, wad ye believe me? I wager ye wadna. Ye wad say I had been drunk, and yet I am a God-fearing temperate man."

He rose and went to a cupboard, unlocked it, and brought out something in his hand, which he held out to me. I took it with some curiosity, and found that it was a flint arrow-head.

Clearly a flint arrow-head, and yet like none that I had ever seen in any collection. For one thing it was larger, and the barb less clumsily thick. More, the chipping was new, or comparatively so; this thing had not stood the wear of fifteen hundred years among the stones of the hillside. Now there are, I regret to say, institutions which manufacture primitive relics; but it is not hard for a practised eye to see the difference. The chipping has either a regularity and a balance which is unknown in the real thing, or the rudeness has been overdone, and the result is an implement incapable of harming a mortal creature. But this was the real thing if it ever existed; and yet—I was prepared to swear on my reputation that it was not half a century old.

"Where did you get this?" I asked with some nervousness.

"I hae a story about that," said the shepherd. "Outside the door there ye can see a muckle flat stane aside the buchts. One simmer nicht I was sitting there smoking till the dark, and I wager there was naething on the stane then. But that same nicht I awoke wi' a queer thocht, as if there were folk moving around the hoose—folk that didna mak' muckle noise. I mind o' lookin' out o' the windy, and I could hae sworn I saw something black movin' amang the heather and intil the buchts. Now I had maybe three-score o' lambs there that nicht, for I had to tak' them many miles off in the early morning. Weel, when I gets up about four o'clock and gangs out, as I am passing the muckle stane I finds this bit errow. 'That's come here in the nicht,' says I, and I wunnered a wee and put it in my pouch. But when I came to my faulds what did I see? Five o' my best hoggs were away, and three mair were lying deid wi' a hole in their throat."

"Who in the world—?" I began.

"Dinna ask," said he. "If I aince sterted to speir about thae maitters, I wadna keep my reason."

"Then that was what happened on the hill this morning?"

"Even sae, and it has happened mair than aince sin' that time. It's the most uncanny slaughter, for sheep stealing I can understand, but no this pricking o' the puir beasts' wizands. I kenna how they dae't either, for it's no wi' a knife or ony common tool."

"Have you never tried to follow the thieves?"

"Have I no?" he asked grimly. "If it had been common sheep-stealers I wad hae had them by the heels, though I had followed them a hundred miles. But this is no common. I've tracked them, and it's ill they are to track; but I never got beyond ae place, and that was the Scarts o' the Muneraw that ye've heard me speak o'."

"But who in Heaven's name are the people? Tinklers or poachers or what?"

"Ay," said he drily. "Even so. Tinklers and poachers whae work wi' stane errows and kill sheep by a hole in their throat. Lord, I kenna what they are, unless the Muckle Deil himsel'."

The conversation had passed beyond my comprehension. In this prosaic hard-headed man I had come on the deadrock of superstition and blind fear.

"That is only the story of the Brownie over again, and he is an exploded myth," I said, laughing.

"Are ye the man that exploded it?" said the shepherd rudely. "I trow no, neither you nor ony ither. My bonny man, if ye lived a twalmonth in thae hills, ye wad sing safter about exploded myths, as ye call them."

"I tell you what I would do," said I. "If I lost sheep as you lose them, I would go up the Scarts of the Muneraw and never rest till I had settled the question once and for all." I spoke hotly, for I was vexed by the man's childish fear.

"I daresay ye wad," he said slowly. "But then I am no you, and maybe I ken mair o' what is in the Scarts o' the Muneraw. Maybe I ken that whilk, if ye kenned it, wad send ye back to the South Country wi' your hert in your mouth. But, as I say, I am no sae brave as you, for I saw something in the first year o' my herding here which put the terror o' God on me, and makes me a fearfu' man to this day. Ye ken the story o' the gudeman o' Carrickfey?"

I nodded.

"Weel, I was the man that fand him. I had seen the deid afore and I've seen them since. But never have I seen aucht like the look in that man's een. What he saw at his death I may see the morn, so I walk before the Lord in fear."

Then he rose and stretched himself. "It's bedding-time, for I maun be up at three," and with a short good-night he left the room.

CHAPTER III

THE SCARTS OF THE MUNERAW

THE next morning was fine, for the snow had been intermittent, and had soon melted except in the high corries. True, it was deceptive weather, for the wind had gone to the rainy south-west, and the masses of cloud on that horizon boded ill for the afternoon. But some days' inaction had made me keen for a chance of sport, so I rose with the shepherd and set out for the day.

He asked me where I proposed to begin.

I told him the tarn called the Loch o' the Threshes, which lies over the back of the Muneraw on another watershed. It is on the ground of the Rhynns Forest, and I had fished it of old from the Forest House. I knew the merits of the trout, and I knew its virtues in a south-west wind, so I had resolved to go thus far afield.

The shepherd heard the name in silence. "Your best road will be ower that rig, and syne on to the water o' Caulds. Keep abune the moss till ye come to the place they ca' the Nick o' the Threshes. That will take ye to the very lochside, but it's a lang road and a sair."

The morning was breaking over the bleak hills. Little clouds drifted athwart the corries, and wisps of haze fluttered from the peaks. A great rosy flush lay over one side of the glen, which caught the edge of the sluggish bog-pools and turned them to fire. Never before had I seen the mountain-land so clear, for far back into the east and west I saw mountain-tops set as close as flowers in a border, black crags seamed with silver lines which I knew for mighty waterfalls, and below at my feet the lower slopes fresh with the dewy green of spring. A name stuck in my memory from the last night's talk.

"Where are the Scarts of the Muneraw?" I asked.

The shepherd pointed to the great hill which bears the name, and which lies, a huge mass, above the watershed.

"D'ye see yon corrie at the east that runs straucht up the side? It looks a bit scart, but it's sae deep that it's aye derk at the bottom o't. Weel, at the tap o' the rig it meets anither corrie that runs doun the ither side, and that one they ca' the Scarts. There is a sort o' burn in it that flows intil the Dule and sae intil the Aller, and, indeed, if ye were gaun there it wad be from Aller Glen that your best road wad lie. But it's an ill bit, and ye'll be sair guidit if ye try't."

There he left me and went across the glen, while I struck upwards over the ridge. At the top I halted and looked down on the wide glen of the Caulds, which there is little better than a bog, but lower down grows into a green pastoral valley. The great Muneraw still dominated the landscape, and the black scaur on its side seemed blacker than before. The place fascinated me, for in that fresh morning air the shepherd's fears seemed monstrous. "Some day," said I to myself, "I will go and explore the whole of that mighty hill." Then I descended and struggled over the moss, found the Nick, and in two hours' time was on the loch's edge.

I have little in the way of good to report of the fishing. For perhaps one hour the trout took well; after that they sulked steadily for the day. The promise, too, of fine weather had been deceptive. By midday the rain was falling in that soft soaking fashion which gives no hope of clearing. The mist was down to the edge of the water, and I cast my flies into a blind sea of white. It was hopeless work, and yet from a sort of ill-temper I stuck to it long after my better judgment had warned me of its folly. At last, about three in the afternoon, I struck my camp, and prepared myself for a long and toilsome retreat.

And long and toilsome it was beyond anything I had ever encountered. Had I had a vestige of sense I would have followed the burn from the loch down to the Forest House. The place was shut up, but the keeper would gladly have given me shelter for the night. But foolish pride was too strong in me. I had found my road in mist before, and could do it again.

Before I got to the top of the hill I had repented my decision; when I got there I repented it more. For below me was a dizzy chaos of grey; there was no landmark visible; and before me I knew was the bog through which the Caulds Water twined. I had crossed it with some trouble in the morning, but then I had light to pick my steps. Now I could only stumble on, and in five minutes I might be in a bog-hole, and in five more in a better world.

But there was no help to be got from hesitation, so with a rueful courage I set off. The place was if possible worse than I had feared. Wading up to the knees with nothing before you but a blank wall of mist and the cheerful consciousness that your next step may be your last—such was my state for one weary mile. The stream itself was high, and rose to my armpits, and once again I only saved myself by a violent leap backwards from a pitiless green slough. But at last it was past, and I was once more on the solid ground of the hillside.

Now, in the thick weather I had crossed the glen much lower down than in the morning, and the result was that the hill on which I stood was one of the giants which, with the Muneraw for centre, guard the watershed. Had I taken the proper way, the Nick o' the Threshes would have led me to the Caulds, and then once over the bog a little ridge was all that stood between me and the glen of Farawa. But instead I had come a wild cross-country road, and was now, though I did not know it, nearly as far from my destination as at the start.

Well for me that I did not know, for I was wet and dispirited, and had I not fancied myself all but home, I should scarcely have had the energy to make this last ascent. But soon I found it was not the little ridge I had expected. I looked at my watch and saw that it was five o'clock. When, after the weariest climb, I lay on a piece of level ground which seemed the top, I was not surprised to find that it was now seven. The darkening must be at hand, and sure enough the mist seemed to be deepening into a greyish black. I began to grow desperate. Here was I on the summit of some infernal mountain, without any certainty where my road lay. I was lost with a vengeance, and at the thought I began to be acutely afraid.

I took what seemed to me the way I had come, and began to descend steeply. Then something made me halt, and the next instant I was lying on my face trying painfully to retrace my steps. For I had found myself slipping, and before I could stop, my feet were dangling over a precipice with Heaven alone knows how many yards of sheer mist between me and the bottom. Then I tried keeping the ridge, and took that to the right, which I thought would bring me nearer home. It was no good trying to think out a direction, for in the fog my brain was running round, and I seemed to stand on a pin-point of space where the laws of the compass had ceased to hold.

It was the roughest sort of walking, now stepping warily over acres of loose stones, now crawling down the face of some battered rock, and now wading in the long dripping heather. The soft rain had begun to fall again, which completed my discomfort. I was now seriously tired, and, like all men who in their day have bent too much over books, I began to feel it in my back. My spine ached, and my breath came in short broken pants. It was a pitiable state of affairs for an honest man who had never encountered much grave discomfort. To ease myself I was compelled to leave my basket behind me, trusting to return and find it, if I should ever reach safety and discover on what pathless hill I had been strayed. My rod I used as a staff, but it was of little use, for my fingers were getting too numb to hold it.

Suddenly from the blankness I heard a sound as of human speech. At first I thought it mere craziness—the cry of a weasel or a hill-bird distorted by my ears. But again it came, thick and faint, as through acres of mist, and yet clearly the sound of "articulate-speaking men". In a moment I lost my despair and cried out in answer. This was some forwandered traveller like myself, and between us we could surely find some road to safety. So I yelled back at the pitch of my voice and waited intently.

But the sound ceased, and there was utter silence again. Still I waited, and then from some place much nearer came the same soft mumbling speech. I could make nothing of it. Heard in that drear place it made the nerves tense and the heart timorous. It was the strangest jumble of vowels and consonants I had ever met.

A dozen solutions flashed through my brain. It was some maniac talking Jabberwock to himself. It was some belated traveller whose wits had given out in fear. Perhaps it was only some shepherd who was amusing himself thus, and whiling the way with nonsense. Once again I cried out and waited.

Then suddenly in the hollow trough of mist before me, where things could still be half discerned, there appeared a figure. It was little and squat and dark; naked, apparently, but so rough with hair that it wore the appearance of a skin-covered being. It crossed my line of vision, not staying for a moment, but in its face and eyes there seemed to lurk an elder world of mystery and barbarism, a troll-like life which was too horrible for words.

The shepherd's fear came back on me like a thunderclap. For one awful instant my legs failed me, and I had almost fallen. The next I had turned and ran shrieking up the hill.

If he who may read this narrative has never felt the force of an overmastering terror, then let him thank his Maker and pray that he never may. I am no weak child, but a strong grown man, accredited in general with sound sense and little suspected of hysterics. And yet I went up that brae-face with my heart fluttering like a bird and my throat aching with fear. I screamed in short dry gasps; involuntarily, for my mind was beyond any purpose. I felt that beast-like clutch at my throat; those red eyes seemed to be staring at me from the mist; I heard ever behind and before and on all sides the patter of those inhuman feet.

Before I knew I was down, slipping over a rock and falling some dozen feet into a soft marshy hollow. I was conscious of lying still for a second and whimpering like a child. But as I lay there I awoke to the silence of the place. There was no sound of pursuit; perhaps they had lost my track and given up. My courage began to return, and from this it was an easy step to hope. Perhaps after all it had been merely an illusion, for folk do not see clearly in the mist, and I was already done with weariness.

But even as I lay in the green moss and began to hope, the faces of my pursuers grew up through the mist. I stumbled madly to my feet; but I was hemmed in, the rock behind and my enemies before. With a cry I rushed forward and struck wildly with my rod at the first dark body. It was as if I had struck an animal, and the next second the thing was wrenched from my grasp. But still they came no nearer. I stood trembling there in the centre of those malignant devils, my brain a mere weather-cock, and my heart crushed shapeless with horror. At last the end came, for with the vigour of madness I flung myself on the nearest, and we rolled on the ground. Then the monstrous things seemed to close over me, and with a choking cry I passed into unconsciousness.

CHAPTER IV

THE DARKNESS THAT IS UNDER THE EARTH

THERE is an unconsciousness that is not wholly dead, where a man feels numbly and the body lives without the brain. I was beyond speech or thought, and yet I felt the upward or downward motion as the way lay in hill or glen, and I most assuredly knew when the open air was changed for the close underground. I could feel dimly that lights were flared in my face, and that I was laid in some bed on the earth. Then with the stopping of movement the real sleep of weakness seized me, and for long I knew nothing of this mad world.

Morning came over the moors with bird-song and the glory of fine weather. The streams were still rolling in spate, but the hill-pastures were alight with dawn, and the little seams of snow were glistening like white fire. A ray from the sunrise cleft its path somehow into the abyss, and danced on the wall above my couch. It caught my eye as I wakened, and for long I lay crazily wondering what it meant. My head was splitting with pain, and in my heart was the same fluttering nameless fear, I did not wake to full consciousness; not till the twinkle of sun from the clean bright out-of-doors caught my senses did I realise that I lay in a great dark place with a glow of dull firelight in the middle.

In time things rose and moved around me, a few ragged shapes of men, without clothing, shambling with their huge feet and looking towards me with curved beast-like glances. I tried to marshal my thoughts, and slowly, bit by bit, I built up the present. There was no question to my mind of dreaming; the past hours had scored reality upon my brain. Yet I cannot say that fear was my chief feeling. The first crazy terror had subsided, and now I felt mainly a sickened disgust with just a tinge of curiosity. I found that my knife, watch, flask, and money had gone, but they had left me a map of the countryside. It seemed strange to look at the calico, with the name of a London printer stamped on the back, and lines of railway and highroad running through every shire. Decent and comfortable civilisation! And here was I a prisoner in this den of nameless folk, and in the midst of a life which history knew not.

Courage is a virtue which grows with reflection and the absence of the immediate peril. I thought myself into some sort of resolution, and lo! when the Folk approached me and bound my feet I was back at once in the most miserable terror. They tied me, all but my hands, with some strong cord, and carried me to the centre, where the fire was glowing. Their soft touch was the acutest torture to my nerves, but I stifled my cries lest someone should lay his hand on my mouth. Had that happened, I am convinced my reason would have failed me.

So there I lay in the shine of the fire, with the circle of unknown things around me. There seemed but three or four, but I took no note of number. They talked huskily among themselves in a tongue which sounded all gutturals. Slowly my fear became less an emotion than a habit, and I had room for the smallest shade of curiosity, I strained my ear to catch a word, but it was a mere chaos of sound. The thing ran and thundered in my brain as I stared dumbly into the vacant air. Then I thought that unless I spoke I should certainly go crazy, for my head was beginning to swim at the strange cooing noise.

I spoke a word or two in my best Gaelic, and they closed round me inquiringly. Then I was sorry I had spoken, for my words had brought them nearer, and I shrank at the thought. But as the faint echoes of my speech hummed in the rock-chamber, I was struck by a curious kinship of sound. Mine was sharper, more distinct, and staccato; theirs was blurred, formless, but still with a certain root-resemblance.

Then from the back there came an older being, who seemed to have heard my words. He was like some foul grey badger, his red eyes sightless, and his hands trembling on a stump of bog-oak. The others made way for him with such deference as they were capable of, and the thing squatted down by me and spoke.

To my amazement his words were familiar. It was some manner of speech akin to the Gaelic, but broadened, lengthened, coarsened. I remembered an old book-tongue, commonly supposed to be an impure dialect once used in Brittany, which I had met in the course of my researches. The words recalled it, and as far as I could remember the thing, I asked him who he was and where the place might be.

He answered me in the same speech—still more broadened, lengthened, coarsened. I lay back with sheer amazement. I had found the key to this unearthly life.

For a little an insatiable curiosity, the ardour of the scholar, prevailed. I forgot the horror of the place, and thought only of the fact that here before me was the greatest find that scholarship had ever made. I was precipitated into the heart of the past. Here must be the fountainhead of all legends, the chrysalis of all beliefs. I actually grew light-hearted. This strange folk around me were now no more shapeless things of terror, but objects of research and experiment. I almost came to think them not unfriendly.

For an hour I enjoyed the highest of earthly pleasures. In that strange conversation I heard—in fragments and suggestions—the history of the craziest survival the world has ever seen. I heard of the struggles with invaders, preserved as it were in a sort of shapeless poetry. There were bitter words against the Gaelic oppressor, bitterer words against the Saxon stranger, and for a moment ancient hatreds flared into life. Then there came the tale of the hill-refuge, the morbid hideous existence preserved for centuries amid a changing world. I heard fragments of old religions, primeval names of god and goddess, half-understood by the Folk, but to me the key to a hundred puzzles. Tales which survive to us in broken disjointed riddles were intact here in living form. I lay on my elbow and questioned feverishly. At any moment they might become morose and refuse to speak. Clearly it was my duty to make the most of a brief good fortune.

And then the tale they told me grew more hideous. I heard of the circumstances of the life itself and their daily shifts for existence. It was a murderous chronicle—a history of lust and rapine and unmentionable deeds in the darkness. One thing they had early recognised—that the race could not be maintained within itself; so that ghoulish carrying away of little girls from the lowlands began, which I had heard of but never credited. Shut up in those dismal holes, the girls soon died, and when the new race had grown up the plunder had been repeated. Then there were bestial murders in lonely cottages, done for God knows what purpose. Sometimes the occupant had seen more than was safe, sometimes the deed was the mere exuberance of a lust of slaying. As they gabbled their tales my heart's blood froze, and I lay back in the agonies of fear. If they had used the others thus, what way of escape was open for myself? I had been brought to this place, and not murdered on the spot. Clearly there was torture before death in store for me, and I confess I quailed at the thought.

But none molested me. The elders continued to jabber out their stories, while I lay tense and deaf. Then to my amazement food was brought and placed beside me—almost with respect. Clearly my murder was not a thing of the immediate future. The meal was some form of mutton—perhaps the shepherd's lost ewes—and a little smoking was all the cooking it had got. I strove to eat, but the tasteless morsels choked me. Then they set drink before me in a curious cup, which I seized on eagerly, for my mouth was dry with thirst. The vessel was of gold, rudely formed, but of the pure metal, and a coarse design in circles ran round the middle. This surprised me enough, but a greater wonder awaited me. The liquor was not water, as I had guessed, but a sort of sweet ale, a miracle of flavour. The taste was curious, but somehow familiar; it was like no wine I had ever drunk, and yet I had known that favour all my life. I sniffed at the brim, and there rose a faint fragrance of thyme and heather honey and the sweet things of the moorland. I almost dropped it in my surprise; for here in this rude place I had stumbled upon that lost delicacy of the North, the heather ale.

For a second I was entranced with my discovery, and then the wonder of the cup claimed my attention. Was it a mere relic of pillage, or had this Folk some hidden mine of the precious metal?

Gold had once been common in these hills. There were the traces of mines on Cairnsmore; shepherds had found it in the gravel of the Gled Water; and the name of a house at the head of the Clachlands meant the "Home of Gold".

Once more I began my questions, and they answered them willingly. There and then I heard that secret for which many had died in old time, the secret of the heather ale. They told of the gold in the hills, of corries where the sand gleamed and abysses where the rocks were veined. All this they told me, freely, without a scruple. And then, like a clap, came the awful thought that this, too, spelled death. These were secrets which this race aforetime had guarded with their lives; they told them generously to me because there was no fear of betrayal. I should go no more out from this place.

The thought put me into a new sweat of terror—not at death, mind you, but at the unknown horrors which might precede the final suffering. I lay silent, and after binding my hands they began to leave me and go off to other parts of the cave. I dozed in the horrible half-swoon of fear, conscious only of my shaking limbs, and the great dull glow of the fire in the centre. Then I became calmer. After all, they had treated me with tolerable kindness: I had spoken their language, which few of their victims could have done for many a century; it might be that I had found favour in their eyes. For a little I comforted myself with this delusion, till I caught sight of a wooden box in a corner. It was of modern make, one such as grocers use to pack provisions in. It had some address nailed on it, and an aimless curiosity compelled me to creep thither and read it. A torn and weather-stained scrap of paper, with the nails at the corner rusty with age; but something of the address might still be made out. Amid the stains my feverish eyes read, "To Mr. M——, Carrickfey, by Allerfoot Station." The ruined cottage in the hollow of the waste with the single gnarled apple-tree was before me in a twinkling. I remembered the shepherd's shrinking from the place and the name, and his wild eyes when he told me of the thing that had happened there. I seemed to see the old man in his moorland cottage, thinking no evil; the sudden entry of the nameless things; and then the eyes glazed in unspeakable terror. I felt my lips dry and burning. Above me was the vault of rock; in the distance I saw the fire-glow and the shadows of shapes moving around it. My fright was too great for inaction, so I crept from the couch, and silently, stealthily, with tottering steps and bursting heart, I began to reconnoitre.

But I was still bound, my arms tightly, my legs more loosely, but yet firm enough to hinder flight. I could not get my hands at my leg-straps, still less could I undo the manacles. I rolled on the floor, seeking some sharp edge of rock, but all had been worn smooth by the use of centuries. Then suddenly an idea came upon me like an inspiration. The sounds from the fire seemed to have ceased, and I could hear them repeated from another and more distant part of the cave. The Folk had left their orgy round the blaze, and at the end of the long tunnel I saw its glow fall unimpeded upon the floor. Once there, I might burn off my fetters and be free to turn my thoughts to escape.

I crawled a little way with much labour. Then suddenly I came abreast an opening in the wall, through which a path went. It was a long straight rock-cutting, and at the end I saw a gleam of pale light. It must be the open air; the way of escape was prepared for me; and with a prayer I made what speed I could towards the fire.

I rolled on the verge, but the fuel was peat, and the warm ashes would not burn the cords. In desperation I went farther, and my clothes began to singe, while my face ached beyond endurance. But yet I got no nearer my object. The strips of hide warped and cracked, but did not burn. Then in a last effort I thrust my wrists bodily into the glow and held them there. In an instant I drew them out with a groan of pain, scarred and sore, but to my joy with the band snapped in one place. Weak as I was, it was now easy to free myself, and then came the untying of my legs. My hands trembled, my eyes were dazed with hurry, and I was longer over the job than need have been. But at length I had loosed my cramped knees and stood on my feet, a free man once more.

I kicked off my boots, and fled noiselessly down the passage to the tunnel mouth. Apparently it was close on evening, for the white light had faded to a pale yellow. But it was daylight, and that was all I sought, and I ran for it as eagerly as ever runner ran to a goal. I came out on a rock-shelf, beneath which a moraine of boulders fell away in a chasm to a dark loch. It was all but night, but I could see the gnarled and fortressed rocks rise in ramparts above, and below the unknown screes and cliffs which make the side of the Muneraw a place only for foxes and the fowls of the air.

The first taste of liberty is an intoxication, and assuredly I was mad when I leaped down among the boulders. Happily at the top of the gully the stones were large and stable, else the noise would certainly have discovered me. Down I went, slipping, praying, my charred wrists aching, and my stockinged feet wet with blood. Soon I was in the jaws of the cleft, and a pale star rose before me. I have always been timid in the face of great rocks, and now, had not an awful terror been dogging my footsteps, no power on earth could have driven me to that descent. Soon I left the boulders behind, and came to long spouts of little stones, which moved with me till the hillside seemed sinking under my feet. Sometimes I was face downwards, once and again I must have fallen for yards. Had there been a cliff at the foot, I should have gone over it without resistance; but by the providence of God the spout ended in a long curve into the heather of the bog.

When I found my feet once more on soft boggy earth, my strength was renewed within me. A great hope of escape sprang up in my heart. For a second I looked back. There was a great line of shingle with the cliffs beyond, and above all the unknown blackness of the cleft. There lay my terror, and I set off running across the bog for dear life. My mind was clear enough to know my road, If I held round the loch in front I should come to a burn which fed the Farawa stream, on whose banks stood the shepherd's cottage. The loch could not be far; once at the Farawa I would have the light of the shieling clear before me.

Suddenly I heard behind me, as if coming from the hillside, the patter of feet. It was the sound which white hares make in the winter-time on a noiseless frosty day as they patter over the snow. I have heard the same soft noise from a herd of deer when they changed their pastures. Strange that so kindly a sound should put the very fear of death in my heart. I ran madly, blindly, yet thinking shrewdly. The loch was before me. Somewhere I had read or heard, I do not know where, that the brutish aboriginal races of the North could not swim. I myself swam powerfully; could I but cross the loch I should save two miles of a desperate country.

There was no time to lose, for the patter was coming nearer, and I was almost at the loch's edge. I tore off my coat and rushed in. The bottom was mossy, and I had to struggle far before I found any depth. Something plashed in the water before me, and then something else a little behind. The thought that I was a mark for unknown missiles made me crazy with fright, and I struck fiercely out for the other shore. A gleam of moonlight was on the water at the burn's exit, and thither I guided myself. I found the thing difficult enough in itself, for my hands ached, and I was numb from my bonds. But my fancy raised a thousand phantoms to vex me. Swimming in that black bog water, pursued by those nameless things, I seemed to be in a world of horror far removed from the kindly world of men. My strength seemed inexhaustible from my terror. Monsters at the bottom of the water seemed to bite at my feet, and the pain of my wrists made me believe that the loch was boiling hot, and that I was in some hellish place of torment.

I came out on a spit of gravel above the burn mouth, and set off down the ravine of the burn. It was a strait place, strewn with rocks; but now and then the hill turf came in stretches, and eased my wounded feet. Soon the fall became more abrupt, and I was slipping down a hillside, with the water on my left making great cascades in the granite. And then I was out in the wider vale where the Farawa water flowed among links of moss.

Far in front, a speck in the blue darkness, shone the light of the cottage. I panted forward, my breath coming in gasps and my back shot with fiery pains. Happily the land was easier for the feet as long as I kept on the skirts of the bog. My ears were sharp as a wild beast's with fear, as I listened for the noise of pursuit. Nothing came but the rustle of the gentlest hill-wind and the chatter of the falling streams.

Then suddenly the light began to waver and move athwart the

window. I knew what it meant. In a minute or two the household at the cottage would retire to rest, and the lamp would be put out. True, I might find the place in the dark, for there was a moon of sorts and the road was not desperate. But somehow in that hour the lamplight gave a promise of safety which I clung to despairingly.

And then the last straw was added to my misery. Behind me came the pad of feet, the pat-patter, soft, eerie, incredibly swift. I choked with fear, and flung myself forward in a last effort. I give my word it was sheer mechanical shrinking that drove me on. God knows I would have lain down to die in the heather, had the things behind me been a common terror of life. I ran as man never ran before, leaping hags, scrambling through green well-heads, straining towards the fast-dying light. A quarter of a mile and the patter sounded nearer. Soon I was not two hundred yards off, and the noise seemed almost at my elbow. The light went out, and the black mass of the cottage loomed in the dark.

Then, before I knew, I was at the door, battering it wearily and yelling for help. I heard steps within and a hand on the bolt. Then something shot past me with lightning force and buried itself in the wood. The dreadful hands were almost at my throat, when the door was opened and I stumbled in, hearing with a gulp of joy the key turn and the bar fall behind me.

CHAPTER V

THE TROUBLES OF A CONSCIENCE

MY body and senses slept, for I was utterly tired, but my brain all the night was on fire with horrid fancies. Again I was in that accursed cave; I was torturing my hands in the fire; I was slipping barefoot among jagged boulders; and then with bursting heart I was toiling the last mile with the cottage light—now grown to a great fire in the heavens—blazing before me.

It was broad daylight when I awoke, and I thanked God for the comfortable rays of the sun. I had been laid in a box-bed off the inner room, and my first sight was the shepherd sitting with folded arms in a chair regarding me solemnly. I rose and began to dress, feeling my legs and arms still tremble with weariness. The shepherd's sister bound up my scarred wrists and put an ointment on my burns; and, limping like an old man, I went into the kitchen.

I could eat little breakfast, for my throat seemed dry and narrow; but they gave me some brandy-and-milk, which put strength into my body. All the time the brother and sister sat in silence, regarding me with covert glances.

"Ye have been delivered from the jaws o' the Pit," said the man at length. "See that," and he held out to me a thin shaft of flint. "I fand that in the door this morning."

I took it, let it drop, and stared vacantly at the window. My nerves had been too much tried to be roused by any new terror. Out-of-doors it was fair weather, flying gleams of April sunlight and the soft colours of spring. I felt dazed, isolated, cut off from my easy past and pleasing future, a companion of horrors and the sport of nameless things. Then suddenly my eye fell on my books heaped on a table, and the old distant civilisation seemed for the moment inexpressibly dear.

"I must go—at once. And you must come too. You cannot stay here. I tell you it is death. If you knew what I know you would be crying out with fear. How far is it to Allermuir? Eight, fifteen miles; and then ten down Glen Aller to Allerfoot, and then the railway. We must go together while it is daylight, and perhaps we may be untouched. But quick, there is not a moment to lose." And I was on my shaky feet, and bustling among my possessions.

"I'll gang wi' ye to the station," said the shepherd, "for ye're clearly no fit to look after yourself. My sister will bide and keep the house. If naething has touched us this ten year, naething will touch us the day."

"But you cannot stay. You are mad," I began; but he cut me short with the words, "I trust in God."

"In any case let your sister come with us. I dare not think of a woman alone in this place."

"I'll bide," said she. "I'm no feared as lang as I'm indoors and there's steeks on the windies."

So I packed my few belongings as best I could, tumbled my books into a haversack, and, gripping the shepherd's arm nervously, crossed the threshold. The glen was full of sunlight. There lay the long shining links of the Farawa burn, the rough hills tumbled beyond, and far over all the scarred and distant forehead of the Muneraw. I had always looked on moorland country as the freshest on earth—clean, wholesome, and homely. But now the fresh uplands seemed like a horrible pit. When I looked to the hills my breath choked in my throat, and the feel of soft heather below my feet set my heart trembling.

It was a slow journey to the inn at Allermuir. For one thing, no power on earth would draw me within sight of the shieling of Carrickfey, so we had to cross a shoulder of hill and make our way down a difficult glen, and then over a treacherous moss. The lochs were now gleaming like fretted silver; but to me, in my dreadful knowledge, they seemed more eerie than on that grey day when I came. At last my eyes were cheered by the sight of a meadow and a fence; then we were on a little byroad; and soon the fir-woods and corn-lands of Allercleuch were plain before us.

The shepherd came no farther, but with brief goodbye turned his solemn face hillwards. I hired a trap and a man to drive, and down the ten miles of Glen Aller I struggled to keep my thoughts from the past. I thought of the kindly South Country, of Oxford, of anything comfortable and civilised. My driver pointed out the objects of interest as in duty bound, but his words fell on unheeding ears. At last he said something which roused me indeed to interest—the interest of the man who hears the word he fears most in the world. On the left side of the river there suddenly sprang into view a long gloomy cleft in the hills, with a vista of dark mountains behind, down which a stream of considerable size poured its waters.

"That is the Water o' Dule," said the man in a reverent voice. "A graund water to fish, but dangerous to life, for it's a' linns. Awa' at the heid they say there's a terrible wild place called the Scarts o' Muneraw—that's a shouther o' the muckle hill itsel' that ye see—but I've never been there, and I never kent ony man that had either."

At the station, which is a mile from the village of Allerfoot, I found I had some hours to wait on my train for the south. I dared not trust myself for one moment alone, so I hung about the goods-shed, talked vacantly to the porters, and when one went to the village for tea I accompanied him, and to his wonder entertained him at the inn. When I returned I found on the platform a stray bagman who was that evening going to London. If there is one class of men in the world which I heartily detest it is this; but such was my state that I hailed him as a brother, and besought his company. I paid the difference for a first-class fare, and had him in the carriage with me. He must have thought me an amiable maniac, for I talked in fits and starts, and when he fell asleep I would wake him up and beseech him to speak to me. At wayside stations I would pull down the blinds in case of recognition, for to my unquiet mind the world seemed full of spies sent by that terrible Folk of the Hills. When the train crossed a stretch of moor I would lie down on the seat in case of shafts fired from the heather. And then at last with utter weariness I fell asleep, and woke screaming about midnight to find myself well down in the cheerful English midlands, and red blast-furnaces blinking by the railwayside.

In the morning I breakfasted in my rooms at St. Chad's with a dawning sense of safety. I was in a different and calmer world. The lawn-like quadrangles, the great trees, the cawing of rooks, and the homely twitter of sparrows—all seemed decent and settled and pleasing. Indoors the oak-panelled walls, the shelves of books, the pictures, the faint fragrance of tobacco, were very different from the gimcrack adornments and the accursed smell of peat and heather in that deplorable cottage. It was still vacation-time, so most of my friends were down; but I spent the day hunting out the few cheerful pedants to whom term and vacation were the same. It delighted me to hear again their precise talk, to hear them make a boast of their work, and narrate the childish little accidents of their life. I yearned for the childish once more; I craved for women's drawing-rooms, and women's chatter, and everything which makes life an elegant game. God knows I had had enough of the other thing for a lifetime!

That night I shut myself in my rooms, barred my windows,

drew my curtains, and made a great destruction. All books or pictures which recalled to me the moorlands were ruthlessly doomed. Novels, poems, treatises I flung into an old box, for sale to the second-hand bookseller. Some prints and watercolour sketches I tore to pieces with my own hands. I ransacked my fishing-book, and condemned all tackle for moorland waters to the flames. I wrote a letter to my solicitors, bidding them go no further in the purchase of a place in Lorn I had long been thinking of. Then, and not till then, did I feel the bondage of the past a little loosed from my shoulders. I made myself a nightcap of rum-punch instead of my usual whisky-toddy, that all associations with that dismal land might be forgotten, and to complete the renunciation I returned to cigars and flung my pipe into a drawer.

But when I woke in the morning I found that it is hard to get rid of memories. My feet were still sore and wounded, and when I felt my arms cramped and reflected on the causes, there was that black memory always near to vex me.

In a little term began, and my duties—as deputy-Professor of Northern Antiquities—were once more clamorous. I can well believe that my hearers found my lectures strange, for instead of dealing with my favourite subjects and matters, which I might modestly say I had made my own, I confined myself to recondite and distant themes, treating even these cursorily and dully. For the truth is, my heart was no more in my subject. I hated—or I thought that I hated—all things Northern with the virulence of utter fear. My reading was confined to science of the most recent kind, to abstruse philosophy, and to foreign classics. Anything which savoured of romance or mystery was abhorrent; I pined for sharp outlines and the tangibility of a high civilisation.

All the term I threw myself into the most frivolous life of the place. My Harrow schooldays seemed to have come back to me. I had once been a fair cricketer, so I played again for my college, and made decent scores. I coached an indifferent crew on the river. I fell into the slang of the place, which I had hitherto detested. My former friends looked on me askance, as if some freakish changeling had possessed me. Formerly I had been ready for pedantic discussion, I had been absorbed in my work, men had spoken of me as a rising scholar. Now I fled the very mention of things I had once delighted in. The Professor of Northern Antiquities, a scholar of European reputation, meeting me once in the Parks, embarked on an account of certain novel rings recently found in Scotland, and to his horror found that, when he had got well under weigh, I had slipped off unnoticed. I heard afterwards that the good old man was found by a friend walking disconsolately with bowed head in the middle of the High Street. Being rescued from among the horses' feet, he could only murmur, "I am thinking of Graves, poor man! And a year ago he was as sane as I am!"

But a man may not long deceive himself. I kept up the illusion valiantly for the term; but I felt instinctively that the fresh schoolboy life, which seemed to me the extreme opposite to the ghoulish North, and as such the most desirable of things, was eternally cut off from me. No cunning affectation could ever dispel my real nature or efface the memory of a week. I realised miserably that sooner or later I must fight it out with my conscience. I began to call myself a coward. The chief thoughts of my mind began to centre themselves more and more round that unknown life waiting to be explored among the wilds. One day I met a friend—an official in the British Museum—who was full of some new theory about primitive habitations. To me it seemed inconceivably absurd; but he was strong in his confidence, and without flaw in his evidence. The man irritated me, and I burned to prove him wrong, but I could think of no argument which was final against his. Then it flashed upon me that my own experience held the disproof; and without more words I left him, hot, angry with myself, and tantalised by the unattainable.

I might relate my *bona-fide* experience, but would men believe me? I must bring proofs, I must complete my researches, so as to make them incapable of disbelief. And there in those deserts was waiting the key. There lay the greatest discovery of the century—nay, of the millennium. There, too, lay the road to wealth such as I had never dreamed of. Could I succeed, I should be famous for ever. I would revolutionise history and anthropology; I would systematise folklore; I would show the world of men the pit whence they were digged and the rock whence they were hewn.

And then began a game of battledore between myself and my conscience.

"You are a coward," said my conscience.

"I am sufficiently brave," I would answer. "I have seen things and yet lived. The terror is more than mortal, and I cannot face it."

"You are a coward," said my conscience.

"I am not bound to go there again. It would be purely for my own aggrandisement if I went, and not for any matter of duty."

"Nevertheless you are a coward," said my conscience.

"In any case the matter can wait."

"You are a coward."

Then came one awful midsummer night, when I lay sleepless and fought the thing out with myself. I knew that the strife was hopeless, that I should have no peace in this world again unless I made the attempt. The dawn was breaking when I came to the final resolution; and when I rose and looked at my face in a mirror, lo! it was white and lined and drawn like a man of sixty.

CHAPTER VI

SUMMER ON THE MOORS

THE next morning I packed a bag with some changes of clothing and a collection of notebooks, and went up to town. The first thing I did was to pay a visit to my solicitors. "I am about to travel," said I, "and I wish to have all things settled in case any accident should happen to me." So I arranged for the disposal of my property in case of death, and added a codicil which puzzled the lawyers. If I did not return within six months, communications were to be entered into with the shepherd at the shieling of Farawa—post-town Allerfoot. If he could produce any papers, they were to be put into the hands of certain friends, published, and the cost charged to my estate. From my solicitors I went to a gunmaker's in Regent Street and bought an ordinary six-chambered revolver, feeling much as a man must feel who proposed to cross the Atlantic in a skiff and purchased a small lifebelt as a precaution.

I took the night express to the North, and, for a marvel, I slept. When I awoke about four we were on the verge of Westmorland, and stony hills blocked the horizon. At first I hailed the mountain-land gladly; sleep for the moment had caused forgetfulness of my terrors. But soon a turn of the line brought me in full view of a heathery moor, running far to a confusion of distant peaks. I remembered my mission and my fate, and if ever condemned criminal felt a more bitter regret I pity his case. Why should I alone among the millions of this happy isle be singled out as the repository of a ghastly secret, and be cursed by a conscience which would not let it rest?

I came to Allerfoot early in the forenoon, and got a trap to drive me up the valley. It was a lowering grey day, hot and yet sunless. A sort of heat-haze cloaked the hills, and every now and then a smurr of rain would meet us on the road, and in a minute be over. I felt wretchedly dispirited; and when at last the whitewashed kirk of Allermuir came into sight and the broken-backed bridge of Aller, man's eyes seemed to have looked on no drearier scene since time began.

I ate what meal I could get, for, fears or no, I was voraciously hungry. Then I asked the landlord to find me some man who would show me the road to Farawa. I demanded company, not for protection—for what could two men do against such brutish strength?—but to keep my mind from its own thoughts.

The man looked at me anxiously.

"Are ye acquaint wi' the folks, then?" he asked.

I said I was, that I had often stayed in the cottage.

"Ye ken that they've a name for being queer. The man never comes here forbye once or twice a year, and he has few dealings wi' other herds. He's got an ill name, too, for losing sheep. I dinna like the country ava. Up by yon Muneraw—no that I've ever been there, but I've seen it afar off—is enough to put a man daft for the rest o' his days. What's taking ye thereaways? It's no the time for the fishing?"

I told him that I was a botanist going to explore certain hill-crevices for rare ferns. He shook his head, and then after some delay found me an ostler who would accompany me to the cottage.

The man was a shock-headed, long-limbed fellow, with fierce red hair and a humorous eye. He talked sociably about his life, answered my hasty questions with deftness, and beguiled me for the moment out of myself. I passed the melancholy lochs, and came in sight of the great stony hills without the trepidation I had expected. Here at my side was one who found some humour even in those uplands. But one thing I noted which brought back the old uneasiness. He took the road which led us farthest from Carrickfey, and when to try him I proposed the other, he vetoed it with emphasis.

After this his good spirits departed, and he grew distrustful. "What mak's ye a freend o' the herd at Farawa?" he demanded a dozen times.

Finally, I asked him if he knew the man, and had seen him lately.

"I dinna ken him, and I hadna seen him for years till a fortnicht syne, when a' Allermuir saw him. He cam doun one afternoon to the public-hoose, and begood to drink. He had aye been kenned for a terrible godly kind o' a man, so ye may believe folk wondered at this. But when he had stuck to the drink for twae days, and filled himsel' blind-fou half-a-dozen o' times, he took a fit o' repentance, and raved and blethered about siccan a life as he led in the muirs. There was some said he was speakin' serious, but maist thocht it was juist daftness."

"And what did he speak about?" I asked sharply.

"I canna verra weel tell ye. It was about some kind o' bogle that lived in the Muneraw—that's the shouthers o't ye see yonder—and it seems that the bogle killed his sheep and frichted himsel'. He was aye bletherin', too, about something or somebody ca'd Grave; but oh! the man wasna wise." And my companion shook a contemptuous head.

And then below us in the valley we saw the shieling, with a

thin shaft of smoke rising into the rainy grey weather. The man left me, sturdily refusing any fee. "I wantit my legs stretched as weel as you. A walk in the hills is neither here nor there to a stoot man. When will ye be back, sir?"

The question was well-timed. "Tomorrow fortnight," I said, "and I want somebody from Allermuir to come out here in the morning and carry some baggage. Will you see to that?"

He said "Ay," and went off, while I scrambled down the hill to the cottage. Nervousness possessed me, and though it was broad daylight and the whole place lay plain before me, I ran pell-mell, and did not stop till I reached the door.

The place was utterly empty. Unmade beds, unwashed dishes, a hearth strewn with the ashes of peat, and dust thick on everything, proclaimed the absence of inmates. I began to be horribly frightened. Had the shepherd and his sister, also, disappeared? Was I left alone in this bleak place, with a dozen lonely miles between me and human dwellings? I could not return alone; better this horrible place than the unknown perils of the out-of-doors. Hastily I barricaded the door, and to the best of my power shuttered the windows; and then with dreary forebodings I sat down to wait on fortune.

In a little I heard a long swinging step outside and the sound of dogs. Joyfully I opened the latch, and there was the shepherd's grim face waiting stolidly on what might appear.

At the sight of me he stepped back. "What in the Lord's name are ye daein' here?" he asked. "Didna ye get enough afore?"

"Come in," I said, sharply. "I want to talk."

In he came with those blessed dogs—what a comfort it was to look on their great honest faces! He sat down on the untidy bed and waited.

"I came because I could not stay away. I saw too much to give me any peace elsewhere. I must go back, even though I risk my life for it. The cause of scholarship demands it as well as the cause of humanity."

"Is that a' the news ye hae?" he said. "Weel, I've mair to tell ye. Three weeks syne my sister Margit was lost, and I've never seen her mair."

My jaw fell, and I could only stare at him.

"I cam hame from the hill at nightfa' and she was gone. I lookit for her up hill and doun, but I couldna find her. Syne I think I went daft. I went to the Scarts and huntit them up and doun, but no sign could I see. The Folk can bide quiet enough when they want. Syne I went to Allermuir and drank mysel' blind—me, that's a God-fearing man and a saved soul; but the Lord help me, I didna ken what I was at. That's my news, and day and night I wander thae hills, seekin' for what I canna find."

"But, man, are you mad?" I cried. "Surely there are neighbours to help you. There is a law in the land, and you had only to find the nearest police-office and compel them to assist you."

"What guid can man dae?" he asked. "An army o' sodgers couldna find that hidey-hole. Forby, when I went into Allermuir wi' my story the folk thocht me daft. It was that set me drinking, for—the Lord forgive me!—I wasna my ain maister. I threepit till I was hairse, but the bodies just lauch'd." And he lay back on the bed like a man mortally tired.

Grim though the tidings were, I can only say that my chief feeling was of comfort. Pity for the new tragedy had swallowed up my fear. I had now a purpose, and a purpose, too, not of curiosity but of mercy.

"I go tomorrow morning to the Muneraw. But first I want to give you something to do." And I drew roughly a chart of the place on the back of a letter. "Go into Allermuir tomorrow, and give this paper to the landlord at the inn. The letter will tell him what to do. He is to raise at once all the men he can get, and come to the place on the chart marked with a cross. Tell him life depends on his hurry."

The shepherd nodded. "D'ye ken the Folk are watching for you? They let me pass without trouble, for they've nae use for me, but I see fine they're seeking you. Ye's no gang half a mile the morn afore they grip ye."

"So much the better," I said. "That will take me quicker to the place I want to be at."

"And I'm to gang to Allermuir the morn," he repeated, with the air of a child conning a lesson. "But what if they'll no believe me?"

"They'll believe the letter."

"Maybe," he said and relapsed into a doze.

I set myself to put that house in order, to rouse the fire, and prepare some food. It was dismal work; and meantime outside the night darkened, and a great wind rose, which howled round the walls and lashed the rain on the windows.

CHAPTER VII

IN TUAS MANUS, DOMINE!

I HAD not gone twenty yards from the cottage door ere I knew I was watched. I had left the shepherd still dozing, in the half-conscious state of a dazed and broken man. All night the wind had wakened me at intervals, and now in the half-light of morn the weather seemed more vicious than ever. The wind cut my ears, the whole firmament was full of the rendings and thunders of the storm. Rain fell in blinding sheets, the heath was a marsh, and it was the most I could do to struggle against the hurricane which stopped my breath. And all the while I knew I was not alone in the desert.

All men know—in imagination or in experience—the sensation of being spied on. The nerves tingle, the skin grows hot and prickly, and there is a queer sinking of the heart. Intensify this common feeling a hundredfold, and you get a tenth part of what I suffered. I am telling a plain tale, and record bare physical facts. My lips stood out from my teeth as I heard, or felt, a rustle in the heather, a scraping among stones. Some subtle magnetic link seemed established between my body and the mysterious world around. I became sick—acutely sick—with the ceaseless apprehension.

My fright became so complete that when I turned a corner of rock, or stepped in deep heather, I seemed to feel a body rub against mine. This continued all the way up the Farawa water, and then up its feeder to the little lonely loch. It kept me from looking forward; but it likewise kept me in such a sweat of fright that I was ready to faint. Then the notion came upon me to test this fancy of mine. If I was tracked thus closely, clearly the trackers would bar my way if I turned back. So I wheeled round and walked a dozen paces down the glen.

Nothing stopped me. I was about to turn again, when something made me take six more paces. At the fourth something rustled in the heather, and my neck was gripped as in a vice. I had already made up my mind on what I would do. I would be perfectly still, I would conquer my fear, and let them do as they pleased with me so long as they took me to their dwelling. But at the touch of the hands my resolutions fled. I struggled and screamed. Then something was clapped on my mouth, speech and strength went from me, and once more I was back in the maudlin childhood of terror.

In the cave it was always a dusky twilight. I seemed to be lying in the same place, with the same dull glare of firelight far off, and the same close stupefying smell. One of the creatures was standing silently at my side, and I asked him some trivial question. He turned and shambled down the passage, leaving me alone.

Then he returned with another, and they talked their guttural talk to me. I scarcely listened till I remembered that in a sense I was here of my own accord, and on a definite mission. The purport of their speech seemed to be that, now I had returned, I must beware of a second flight. Once I had been spared; a second time I should be killed without mercy.

I assented gladly. The Folk, then, had some use for me. I felt my errand prospering.

Then the old creature which I had seen before crept out of some corner and squatted beside me. He put a claw on my shoulder, a horrible, corrugated, skeleton thing, hairy to the fingertips and nailless. He grinned, too, with toothless gums, and his hideous old voice was like a file on sandstone.

I asked questions, but he would only grin and jabber, looking now and then furtively over his shoulder towards the fire.

I coaxed and humoured him, till he launched into a narrative of which I could make nothing. It seemed a mere string of names, with certain words repeated at fixed intervals. Then it flashed on me that this might be a religious incantation. I had discovered remnants of a ritual and a mythology among them. It was possible that these were sacred days, and that I had stumbled upon some rude celebration.

I caught a word or two and repeated them. He looked at me curiously. Then I asked him some leading question, and he replied with clearness. My guess was right. The midsummer week was the holy season of the year, when sacrifices were offered to the gods.

The notion of sacrifices disquieted me, and I would fain have asked further. But the creature would speak no more. He hobbled off, and left me alone in the rock-chamber to listen to a strange sound which hung ceaselessly about me. It must be the storm without, like a park of artillery rattling among the crags. A storm of storms surely, for the place echoed and hummed, and to my unquiet eye the very rock of the roof seemed to shake!

Apparently my existence was forgotten, for I lay long before anyone returned. Then it was merely one who brought food, the same strange meal as before, and left hastily. When I had eaten I rose and stretched myself. My hands and knees still quivered nervously; but I was strong and perfectly well in body. The empty, desolate, tomb-like place was eerie enough to scare anyone; but its emptiness was comfort when I thought of its inmates. Then I wandered down the passage towards the fire which was burning in loneliness. Where had the Folk gone? I puzzled over their disappearance.

Suddenly sounds began to break on my ear, coming from some inner chamber at the end of that in which the fire burned. I could scarcely see for the smoke; but I began to make my way towards the noise, feeling along the sides of rock. Then a second gleam of light seemed to rise before me, and I came to an aperture in the wall which gave entrance to another room.

This in turn was full of smoke and glow—a murky orange glow, as if from some strange flame of roots. There were the squat moving figures, running in wild antics round the fire. I crouched in the entrance, terrified and yet curious, till I saw something beyond the blaze which held me dumb. Apart from the others and tied to some stake in the wall was a woman's figure, and the face was the face of the shepherd's sister.

My first impulse was flight. I must get away and think—plan, achieve some desperate way of escape. I sped back to the silent chamber as if the gang were at my heels. It was still empty, and I stood helplessly in the centre, looking at the impassable walls of rock as a wearied beast may look at the walls of its cage. I bethought me of the way I had escaped before and rushed thither, only to find it blocked by a huge contrivance of stone. Yards and yards of solid rock were between me and the upper air, and yet through it all came the crash and whistle of the storm. If I were at my wits' end in this inner darkness, there was also high commotion among the powers of the air in that upper world.

As I stood I heard the soft steps of my tormentors. They seemed to think I was meditating escape, for they flung themselves on me and bore me to the ground. I did not struggle, and when they saw me quiet, they squatted round and began to speak. They told me of the holy season and its sacrifices. At first I could not follow them; then when I caught familiar words I found some clue, and they became intelligible. They spoke of a woman, and I asked, "What woman?" With all frankness they told me of the custom which prevailed—how every twentieth summer a woman was sacrificed to some devilish god, and by the hand of one of the stranger race. I said nothing, but my whitening face must have told them a tale, though I strove hard to keep my composure. I asked if they had found the victims. "She is in this place," they said; "and as for the man, thou art he." And with this they left me.

I had still some hours; so much I gathered from their talk, for the sacrifice was at sunset. Escape was cut off for ever. I have always been something of a fatalist, and at the prospect of the irrevocable end my cheerfulness returned. I had my pistol, for they had taken nothing from me. I took out the little weapon and fingered it lovingly. Hope of the lost, refuge of the vanquished, ease to the coward—blessed be he who first conceived it!

The time dragged on, the minutes grew to hours, and still I was left solitary. Only the mad violence of the storm broke the quiet. It had increased in fury, for the stones at the mouth of the exit by which I had formerly escaped seemed to rock with some external pressure, and cutting shafts of wind slipped past and cleft the heat of the passage. What a sight the ravine outside must be, I thought, set in the forehead of a great hill, and swept clean by every breeze! Then came a crashing, and the long hollow echo of a fall. The rocks are splitting, said I; the road down the corrie will be impassable now and for evermore.

I began to grow weak with the nervousness of the waiting, and by-and-by I lay down and fell into a sort of doze. When I next knew consciousness I was being roused by two of the Folk, and bidden get ready. I stumbled to my feet, felt for the pistol in the hollow of my sleeve, and prepared to follow.

When we came out into the wider chamber the noise of the storm was deafening. The roof rang like a shield which has been struck. I noticed, perturbed as I was, that my guards cast anxious eyes around them, alarmed, like myself, at the murderous din. Nor was the world quieter when we entered the last chamber, where the fire burned and the remnant of the Folk waited. Wind had found an entrance from somewhere or other, and the flames blew here and there, and the smoke gyrated in odd circles. At the back, and apart from the rest, I saw the dazed eyes and the white old drawn face of the woman.

They led me up beside her to a place where there was a rude flat stone, hollowed in the centre, and on it a rusty iron knife, which seemed once to have formed part of a scythe-blade. Then I saw the ceremonial which was marked out for me. It was the very rite which I had dimly figured as current among a rude people, and even in that moment of horror I had something of the scholar's satisfaction.

The oldest of the Folk, who seemed to be a sort of priest, came to my side and mumbled a form of words. His fetid breath sickened me; his dull eyes, glassy like a brute's with age, brought my knees together. He put the knife in my hands, dragged the terror-stricken woman forward to the altar, and bade me begin.

I began by sawing her bonds through. When she felt herself free she would have fled back, but stopped when I bade her. At that moment there came a noise of rending and crashing as if the hills were falling, and for one second the eyes of the Folk were averted from the frustrated sacrifice.

Only for a moment. The next they saw what I had done, and with one impulse rushed towards me. Then began the last scene in the play. I sent a bullet through the right eye of the first thing that came on. The second shot went wide but the third shattered the hand of an elderly ruffian with a club. Never for an instant did they stop, and now they were clutching at me. I pushed the woman behind, and fired three rapid shots in blind panic, and then, clutching the scythe, I struck right and left like a madman.

Suddenly I saw the foreground sink before my eyes. The roof sloped down, and with a sickening hiss a mountain of rock and earth seemed to precipitate itself on the foremost of my assailants. One, nipped in the middle by a rock, caught my eye by his hideous writhings. Two only remained in what was now a little suffocating chamber, with embers from the fire still smoking on the floor.

The woman caught me by the hand and drew me with her, while the two seemed mute with fear. "There's a road at the back," she screamed. "I ken it. I fand it out." And she pulled me up a narrow hole in the rock.

How long we climbed I do not know. We were both fighting for air, with the tightness of throat and chest, and the craziness of limb which mean suffocation. I cannot tell when we first came to the surface, but I remember the woman, who seemed to have the strength of extreme terror, pulling me from the edge of a crevasse and laying me on a flat rock. It seemed to be the depth of winter, with sheer-falling rain and a wind that shook the hills.

Then I was once more myself and could look about me. From my feet yawned a sheer abyss, where once had been a hill-shoulder. Some great mass of rock on the brow of the mountain had been loosened by the storm, and in its fall had caught the lips of the ravine and blocked the upper outlet from the nest of dwellings. For a moment I feared that all had been destroyed.

My feeling—Heaven help me!—was not thankfulness for God's mercy and my escape, but a bitter mad regret. I rushed frantically to the edge, and when I saw only the blackness of darkness I wept weak tears. All the time the storm was tearing at my body, and I had to grip hard by hand and foot to keep my place. Suddenly on the brink of the ravine I saw a third figure. We two were not the only fugitives. One of the Folk had escaped.

I ran to it, and to my surprise the thing as soon as it saw me rushed to meet me. At first I thought it was with some instinct of self-preservation, but when I saw its eyes I knew the purpose of fight. Clearly one or other should go no more from the place.

We were some ten yards from the brink when I grappled with it. Dimly I heard the woman scream with fright, and saw her scramble across the hillside. Then we were tugging in a death-throe, the hideous smell of the thing in my face, its red eyes burning into mine, and its hoarse voice muttering. Its strength seemed incredible; but I, too, am no weakling. We tugged and strained, its nails biting into my flesh, while I choked its throat unsparingly. Every second I dreaded lest we should plunge together over the ledge, for it was thither my adversary tried to draw me. I caught my heel in a nick of rock, and pulled madly against it.

And then, while I was beginning to glory with the pride of conquest, my hope was dashed in pieces. The thing seemed to break from my arms, and, as if in despair, cast itself headlong into the impenetrable darkness. I stumbled blindly after it, saved myself on the brink, and fell back, sick and ill, into a merciful swoon.

CHAPTER VIII

NOTE IN CONCLUSION BY THE EDITOR

AT this point the narrative of my unfortunate friend, Mr. Graves of St. Chad's, breaks off abruptly. He wrote it shortly before his death, and was prevented from completing it by the attack of heart failure which carried him off. In accordance with the instructions in his will, I have prepared it for publication, and now in much fear and hesitation give it to the world. First, however, I must supplement it by such facts as fall within my knowledge.

The shepherd seems to have gone to Allermuir and by the help of the letter convinced the inhabitants. A body of men was collected under the landlord, and during the afternoon set out for the hills. But unfortunately the great midsummer storm—the most terrible of recent climatic disturbances—had filled the mosses and streams, and they found themselves unable to proceed by any direct road. Ultimately late in the evening they arrived at the cottage of Farawa, only to find there a raving woman, the shepherd's sister, who seemed crazy with brain-fever. She told some rambling story about her escape, but her narrative said nothing of Mr. Graves. So they treated her with what skill they possessed, and sheltered for the night in and around the cottage. Next morning the storm had abated a little, and the woman had recovered something of her wits. From her they learned that Mr. Graves was lying in a ravine on the side of the Muneraw in imminent danger of his life. A body set out to find him; but so immense was the landslip, and so dangerous the whole mountain, that it was nearly evening when they recovered him from the ledge of rock. He was alive, but unconscious, and on bringing him back to the cottage it was clear that he was, indeed, very ill. There he lay for three months, while the best skill that could be got was procured for him. By dint of an uncommon toughness of constitution he survived; but it was an old and feeble man who returned to Oxford in the early winter.

The shepherd and his sister immediately left the countryside, and were never more heard of, unless they are the pair of unfortunates who are at present in a Scottish pauper asylum, incapable of remembering even their names. The people who last spoke with them declared that their minds seemed weakened by a great shock, and that it was hopeless to try to get any connected or rational statement.

The career of my poor friend from that hour was little short of a tragedy. He awoke from his illness to find the world incredulous; even the country-folk of Allermuir set down the story to the shepherd's craziness and my friend's credulity. In Oxford his argument was received with polite scorn. An account of his experiences which he drew up for *The Times* was refused by the editor; and an article on "Primitive Peoples of the North", embodying what he believed to be the result of his discoveries, was unanimously rejected by every responsible journal in Europe. At first he bore the treatment bravely. Reflection convinced him that the colony had not been destroyed. Proofs were still awaiting his hand, and with courage and caution he might yet triumph over his enemies. But unfortunately, though the ardour of the scholar burned more fiercely than ever and all fear seemed to have been purged from his soul, the last adventure had grievously sapped his bodily strength. In the spring following his accident he made an effort to reach the spot—alone, for no one could be persuaded to follow him in what was regarded as a childish madness. He slept at the now deserted cottage of Farawa, but in the morning found himself unable to continue, and with difficulty struggled back to the shepherd's cottage at Allercleuch, where he was confined to bed for a fortnight. Then it became necessary for him to seek health abroad, and it was not till the following autumn that he attempted the journey again. He fell sick a second time at the inn of Allermuir, and during his convalescence had himself carried to a knoll in the inn garden, whence a glimpse can be obtained of the shoulder of the Muneraw. There he would sit for hours with his eyes fixed on the horizon, and at times he would be found weeping with weakness and vexation. The last attempt was made but two months before his last illness. On this occasion he got no farther than Carlisle, where he was taken ill with what proved to be a premonition of death. After that he shut his lips tightly, as though recognising the futility of his hopes. Whether he had been soured by the treatment he received, or whether his brain had already been weakened, he had become a morose silent man, and for the two years before his death had few friends and no society. From the obituary notice in *The Times* I take the following paragraph, which shows in what light the world had come to look upon him:—

"At the outset of his career he was regarded as a rising scholar in one department of archaeology, and his Taffert lectures were a real contribution to an obscure subject. But in after-life he was led into fantastic speculations; and when he found himself unable to convince his colleagues, he gradually retired into himself, and lived practically a hermit's life till his death. His career, thus broken short, is a sad instance of the fascination which the recondite and the quack can exercise even over men of approved ability."

And now his own narrative is published, and the world can judge as it pleases about the amazing romance. The view which will doubtless find general acceptance is that the whole is a figment of the brain, begotten of some harmless moorland adventure and the company of such religious maniacs as the shepherd and his sister. But some who knew the former sobriety and calmness of my friend's mind may be disposed timorously and with deep hesitation to another verdict. They may accept the narrative, and believe that somewhere in those moorlands he met with a horrible primitive survival, passed through the strangest adventure, and had his fingers on an epoch-making discovery. In this case they will be inclined to sympathise with the loneliness and misunderstanding of his latter days. It is not for me to decide the question. Though a fellow-historian, the Picts are outside my period, and I dare not advance an opinion on a matter with which I am not fully familiar. But I would point out that the means of settling the question are still extant, and I would call upon some young archaeologist, with a reputation to make, to seize upon the chance of the century. Most of the expresses for the North stop at Allerfoot; a ten-miles' drive will bring him to Allermuir; and then with a fifteen-miles' walk he is at Farawa and on the threshold of discovery. Let him follow the burn and cross the ridge and ascend the Scarts of the Muneraw, and, if he return at all, it may be with a more charitable judgment of my unfortunate friend.

FOUNTAINBLUE

I

ONCE upon a time, as the story-books say, a boy came over a ridge of hill, from which a shallow vale ran out into the sunset. It was a high, wind-blown country, where the pines had a crook in their backs and the rocks were scarred and bitten with winter storms. But below was the beginning of pastoral. Soft birch-woods, shady beeches, meadows where cattle had browsed for generations, fringed the little brown river as it twined to the sea. Farther, and the waves broke on white sands, the wonderful billows of the West which cannot bear to be silent. And between, in a garden wilderness, with the evening flaming in its windows, stood Fountainblue, my little four-square castle which guards the valley and the beaches.

The boy had torn his clothes, scratched his face, cut one finger deeply, and soaked himself with bog-water, but he whistled cheerfully and his eyes were happy. He had had an afternoon of adventure, startling emprises achieved in solitude; assuredly a day to remember and mark with a white stone. And the beginning had been most unpromising. After lunch he had been attired in his best raiment, and, in the misery of a broad white collar, despatched with his cousins to take tea with the small lady who domineered in Fountainblue. The prospect had pleased him greatly, the gardens fed his fancy, the hostess was an old confederate, and there were sure to be excellent things to eat. But his curious temper had arisen to torment him. On the way he quarrelled with his party, and in a moment found himself out of sympathy with the future. The enjoyment crept out of the prospect. He knew that he did not shine in society, he foresaw an afternoon when he would be left out in the cold and his

125

hilarious cousins treated as the favoured guests. He reflected that tea was a short meal at the best, and that games on a lawn were a poor form of sport. Above all, he felt the torture of his collar and the straitness of his clothes. He pictured the dreary return in the twilight, when the afternoon, which had proved, after all, such a dismal failure, had come to a weary end. So, being a person of impulses, he mutinied at the gates of Fountainblue and made for the hills. He knew he should get into trouble, but trouble, he had long ago found out, was his destiny, and he scorned to avoid it. And now, having cast off the fear of God and man, he would for some short hours do exactly as he pleased.

Half-crying with regret for the delights he had forsworn, he ran over the moor to the craggy hills which had always been forbidden him. When he had climbed among the rocks awe fell upon the desolate little adventurer, and he bewailed his choice. But soon he found a blue hawk's nest, and the possession of a coveted egg inspired him to advance. By-and-by he had climbed so high that he could not return, but must needs scale Stob Ghabhar itself. With a quaking heart he achieved it, and then, in the pride of his heroism, he must venture down the Grey Correi where the wild goats lived. He saw a bearded ruffian, and pursued him with stones, stalking him cunningly till he was out of breath. Then he found odd little spleenwort ferns, which he pocketed, and high up in the rocks a friendly raven croaked his encouragement. And then, when the shadows lengthened, he set off cheerily homewards, hungry, triumphant, and very weary.

All the way home he flattered his soul. In one afternoon he had been hunter and trapper, and what to him were girls' games and pleasant things to eat? He pictured himself the hardy outlaw, feeding on oatmeal and goat's flesh, the terror and pride of his neighbourhood. Could the little mistress of Fountainblue but see him now, how she would despise his prosaic cousins! And then, as he descended on the highway, he fell in with his forsaken party.

For a wonder they were in good spirits—so good that they forgot to remind him, in their usual way, of the domestic terrors awaiting him. A man had been there who had told them stories and shown them tricks, and there had been coconut cake, and Sylvia had a new pony on which they had ridden races. The children were breathless with excitement, very much in love with each other as common sharers in past joys. And as they talked all the colour went out of his afternoon. The blue hawk's egg was cracked, and it looked a stupid, dingy object as it lay in his cap. His rare ferns were crumpled and withered, and who was to believe his stories of Stob Ghabhar and the Grey Correi? He had been a fool to barter ponies and tea and a man who knew tricks for the barren glories of following his own fancy. But at any rate he would show no sign. If he was to be an outlaw, he would carry his outlawry well; so with a catch in his voice and tears in his eyes he jeered at his inattentive companions, upbraiding himself all the while for his folly.

II

THE sun was dipping behind Stob Ghabhar when Maitland drove over the ridge of hill, whence the moor-road dips to Fountainblue. Twenty long miles from the last outpost of railway to the western sea-loch, and twenty of the barest, steepest miles in the bleak North. And all the way he had been puzzling himself with the half-painful, half-pleasing memories of a childhood which to the lonely man still overtopped the present. Every wayside bush was the home of recollection. In every burn he had paddled and fished; here he had found the jack-snipe's nest, there he had hidden when the shepherds sought him for burning the heather in May. He lost for a little the burden of his years and cares, and lived again in that old fresh world which had no boundaries, where sleep and food were all his thought at night, and adventure the sole outlook of the morning. The western sea lay like a thin line of gold beyond the moorland, and down in the valley in a bower of trees lights began to twinkle from the little castle. The remote mountains, hiding deep corries and woods in their bosom, were blurred by twilight to a single wall of hazy purple, which shut off this fairy glen impenetrably from the world. Fountainblue—the name rang witchingly in his ears.

Fountainblue, the last home of the Good Folk, the last hold of the vanished kings, where the last wolf in Scotland was slain, and, as stories go, the last saint of the Great Ages taught the people— what had Fountainblue to do with his hard world of facts and figures? The thought woke him to a sense of the present, and for a little he relished the paradox. He had left it long ago, an adventurous child; now he was returning with success behind him and a portion of life's good things his own. He was rich, very rich and famous. Few men of forty had his power, and he had won it all in fair struggle with enemies and rivals and a niggardly world. He had been feared and hated, as he had been extravagantly admired; he had been rudely buffeted by fortune, and had met the blows with a fighter's joy. And out of it all something hard and austere had shaped itself, something very much a man, but a man with little heart and a lack of kindly human failings. He was master of himself in a curious degree, but the mastery absorbed his interests. Nor had he ever regretted it, when suddenly in this outlandish place the past swept over him, and he had a vision of a long avenue of vanished hopes. It pleased and disquieted him, and as the road dipped into the valley he remembered the prime cause of this mood of vagaries.

He had come up into the North with one purpose in view, he frankly told himself. The Etheridges were in Fountainblue, and ever since, eight months before, he had met Clara Etheridge, he had forgotten his ambitions. A casual neighbour at a dinner-party, a chance partner at a ball—and then he had to confess that this slim, dark, bright-eyed girl had broken in irrevocably upon his contentment. At first he hated it for a weakness, then he welcomed the weakness with feverish ecstasy. He did nothing by halves, so he sought her company eagerly, and, being a great man in his way, found things made easy for him. But the girl remained shy and distant, flattered doubtless by his atten-tion, but watching him curiously as an intruder from an alien world. It was characteristic of the man that he never thought of a rival. His whole aim was to win her love; for rivalry with other men he had the contempt of a habitual conqueror. And so the uneasy wooing went on till the Etheridges left town, and he found himself a fortnight later with his work done and a visit before him to which he looked forward with all the vehemence of a nature whose strong point had always been its hope. As the road wound among the fir-trees, he tried to forecast the life at Fountainblue, and map out the future in his usual business-like way. But now the future refused to be thus shorn and parcelled: there was an unknown quantity in it which defied his efforts.

The house-party were sitting round the hall-fire when he entered. The high-roofed place, the flagged floor strewn with rugs, and the walls bright with the glow of fire on armour gave him a boyish sense of comfort. Two men in knickerbockers were lounging on a settle, and at his entrance came forward to greet him. One was Sir Hugh Clanroyden, a follower of his own; the other he recognised as a lawyer named Durward. From the circle of women Miss Etheridge rose and welcomed him. Her mother was out, but would be back for dinner; meantime he should be shown his room. He noticed that her face was browner, her hair a little less neat, and there seemed something franker and kindlier in her smile. So in a very good humour he went to rid himself of the dust of the roads.

Durward watched him curiously, and then turned, laughing, to his companion, as the girl came back to her friends with a heightened colour in her cheeks.

"Romeo the second," he said. "We are going to be spectators of a comedy. And yet, Heaven knows! Maitland is not cast for comedy."

The other shook his head. "It will never come off. I've known Clara Etheridge most of my life, and I would as soon think of marrying a dancing-girl to a bishop. She is a delightful person, and my very good friend, but how on earth is she ever to understand Maitland? And how on earth can he see anything in her? Besides, there's another man."

Durward laughed. "Despencer! I suppose he will be a serious rival with a woman; but imagine him Maitland's rival in anything else! He'd break him like a rotten stick in half an hour. I like little Despencer, and I don't care about Maitland; but all the same it is absurd to compare the two, except in love-making."

"Lord, it will be comic," and Clanroyden stretched his long

legs and lay back on a cushion. The girls were still chattering beside the fire, and the twilight was fast darkening into evening.

"You dislike Maitland?" he asked, looking up. "Now, I wonder why?"

Durward smiled comically at the ceiling. "Oh, I know I oughtn't to. I know he's supposed to be a man's man, and that it's bad form for a man to say he dislikes him. But I'm honest enough to own to detesting him. I suppose he's great, but he's not great enough yet to compel one to fall down and worship him, and I hate greatness in the making. He goes through the world with his infernal arrogance and expects everybody to clear out of his way. I am told we live in an age of reason, but that fellow has burked reason. He never gives a reason for a thing he does, and if you try to argue he crushes you. He has killed good talk for ever with his confounded rudeness. All the little sophistries and conventions which make life tolerable are so much rubbish to him, and he shows it. The plague of him is that he can never make-believe. He is as hard as iron, and as fierce as the devil, and about as unpleasant. You may respect the sledgehammer type, but it's confoundedly dull. Why, the man has not the imagination of a rabbit except in his description of people he dislikes. I liked him when he said that Layden reminded him of a dissipated dove, because I disliked Layden; but when Freddy Alton played the fool and people forgave him, because he was a good sort, Maitland sent him about his business, saying he had no further use for weaklings. He is so abominably cold-blooded and implacable that everyone must fear him, and yet most people can afford to despise him. All the kind simple things of life are shut out of his knowledge. He has no nature, only a heart of stone and an iron will and a terribly subtle brain. Of course he is a great man—in a way, but at the best he is only half a man. And to think that he should have fallen in love, and be in danger of losing to Despencer! It's enough to make one forgive him."

Clanroyden laughed. "I can't think of Despencer. It's too absurd. But, seriously, I wish I saw Maitland well rid of this mood, married or cured. That sort of man doesn't take things easily."

"It reminds one of Theocritus and the Cyclops in love. Who would have thought to see him up in this moorland place, running after a girl? He doesn't care for sport."

"Do you know that he spent most of his childhood in this glen, and that he *is* keen about sport? He is too busy for many holidays, but he once went with Burton to the Caucasus and Burton said the experience nearly killed him. He said that the fellow was tireless, and as mad and reckless as a boy with nothing to lose."

"Well, that simply bears out what I say of him. He does not understand the meaning of sport. When he gets keen about anything he pursues it as carefully and relentlessly as if it were something on the Stock Exchange. Now little Despencer is a genuine sportsman in his canary-like way. He loves the art of the thing and the being out-of-doors. Maitland, I don't suppose, ever thinks whether it is a ceiling or the sky above his august head. Despencer—"

But at that moment Clanroyden uncrossed his legs, bringing his right foot down heavily upon his companion's left. Durward looked up and saw a young man coming towards him, smiling.

The newcomer turned aside to say something to the girls round the fire, and then came and sat on an arm of the settle. He was a straight, elegant person, with a well-tanned, regular face, and very pleasant brown eyes.

"I've had such an afternoon," he said. "You never saw a place like Cairnlora. It's quite a little stone tower all alone in a fir-wood, and nothing else between the moor and the sea. It is furnished as barely as a prison, except for the chairs, which are priceless old Dutch things. Oh, and the silver at tea was the sort of thing that only Americans can buy nowadays. Mrs. Etheridge is devoured with envy. But the wonder of the house is old Miss Elphinstone. She must be nearly seventy, and she looks forty-five, except for her hair. She speaks broad Scots, and she has the manners of a *marquise*. I would give a lot to have had Raeburn paint her. She reminded me of nothing so much as a hill-wind with her keen high-coloured old face. Yes, I have enjoyed the afternoon."

"Jack has got a new enthusiasm," said Durward. "I wish I

were like you to have a new one once a week. By the way, Maitland has arrived at last."

"Really!" said Despencer. "Oh, I forgot to tell you something which you would never have guessed. Miss Elphinstone is Maitland's aunt, and he was brought up a good deal at Cairnlora. He doesn't take his manners from her, but I suppose he gets his cleverness from that side of the family. She disapproves of him strongly, so of course I had to defend him. And what do you think she said? 'He has betrayed his tradition. He has sold his birthright for a mess of pottage, and I wish him joy of his bargain!' Nice one for your party, Hugh."

Miss Etheridge had left the group at the fire and was standing at Despencer's side. She listened to him with a curious air of solicitude, like an affectionate sister. At the mention of Maitland's name Clanroyden had watched her narrowly, but her face did not change. And when Despencer asked, "Where is the new arrival?" she talked of him with the utmost nonchalance.

Maitland came down to dinner, ravenously hungry and in high spirits. Nothing was changed in this house since he had stared at the pictures and imagined terrible things about the armour and broken teacups with childish impartiality. His own favourite seat was still there, where, hidden by a tapestry screen, he had quarrelled with Sylvia while their elders gossiped. This sudden flood of memories mellowed him towards the world. He was cordial to Despencer, forbore to think Durward a fool, and answered every one of Mr. Etheridge's many questions. For the first time he felt the success of his life. The old house recalled his childhood, and the sight of Clanroyden, his devoted follower, reminded him of his power. Somehow the weariful crying for the moon, which had always tortured him, was exchanged for a glow of comfort, a shade of complacency in his haggard soul. . . . And then the sight of Clara dispelled his satisfaction.

Here in this cheerful homely party of friends he found himself out of place. On state occasions he could acquit himself with credit, for the man had a mind. He could make the world listen to him when he chose, and the choice was habitual. But now his loneliness claimed its lawful consequences, and he longed for the little friendly graces which he had so often despised. Despencer talked of scenery and weather with a tenderness to which this man, who loved nature as he loved little else, was an utter stranger. This elegant and appropriate sentiment would have worried him past endurance, if Miss Clara had not shared it. It was she who told some folk-tale about the Grey Correi with the prettiest hesitancy which showed her feeling. And then the talk drifted to books and people, flitting airily about their petty world. Maitland felt himself choked by their accomplishments. Most of the subjects were ones no sane man would trouble to think of, and yet here were men talking keenly about trifles and disputing with nimble-witted cleverness on the niceties of the trivial. Feeling miserably that he was the only silent one, he plunged desperately into the stream, found himself pulled up by Despencer and deftly turned. The event gave him the feeling of having been foiled by a kitten.

Angry with the world, angrier with his own angularity, he waited for the end of the meal. Times had not changed in this house since he had been saved by Sylvia from social disgrace. But when the women left the room he found life easier. His host talked of sport, and he could tell him more about Stob Ghabhar than any keeper. Despencer, victorious at dinner, now listened like a docile pupil. Durward asked a political question, and the answer came sharp and definite. Despencer demurred gently, after his fashion. "Well, but surely—" and a grimly smiling "What do you know about it?" closed the discussion. The old Maitland had returned for the moment.

The night was mild and impenetrably dark, and the fall of waters close at hand sounded like a remote echo. An open hall-door showed that some of the party had gone out to the garden, and the men followed at random. A glimmer of white frocks betrayed the women on the lawn, standing by the little river which slipped by cascade and glide from the glen to the low pasture-lands. In the featureless dark there was no clue to locality. The place might have been Berkshire or a suburban garden.

Suddenly the scream of some animal came from the near thicket. The women started and asked what it was.

"It was a hill-fox," said Maitland to Clara. "They used to keep me awake at nights on the hill. They come and bark close to your ear and give you nightmare."

The lady shivered. "Thank Heaven for the indoors," she said. "Now, if I had been the daughter of one of your old Donalds of the Isles, I should have known that cry only too well. Wild nature is an excellent background, but give me civilisation in front."

Maitland was looking into the wood. "You will find it creep far into civilisation if you look for it. There is a very narrow line between the warm room and the savage out-of-doors."

"There are miles of luxuries," the girl cried, laughing. "People who are born in the wrong century have to hunt over half the world before they find their savagery. It is all very tame, but I love the tameness. You may call yourself primitive, Mr. Maitland, but you are the most complex and modern of us all. What would Donald of the Isles have said to politics and the Stock Exchange?"

They had strolled back to the house. "Nevertheless I maintain my belief," said the man. "You call it miles of rampart; I call the division a line, a thread, a sheet of glass. But then, you see, you only know one side, and I only know the other."

"What preposterous affectation!" the girl said, as with a pretty shiver she ran indoors. Maitland stood for a moment looking back at the darkness. Within the firelit hall, with its rugs and little tables and soft chairs, he had caught a glimpse of Despencer smoking a cigarette. As he looked towards the hills he heard the fox's bark a second time, and then somewhere from the black distance came a hawk's scream, hoarse, lonely, and pitiless. The thought struck him that the sad elemental world of wood and mountain was far more truly his own than this cosy and elegant civilisation. And, oddly enough, the thought pained him.

III

THE day following was wet and windy, when a fire was grateful, and the hills, shrouded in grey mist, had no attractions. The party read idly in armchairs during the morning, and in the afternoon Maitland and Clanroyden went down to the stream-mouth after sea-trout. So Despencer remained to talk to Clara, and, having played many games of picquet and grown heartily tired of each other, as tea-time approached they fell to desultory comments on their friends. Maitland was beginning to interest the girl in a new way. Formerly he had been a great person who was sensible enough to admire her, but something remote and unattractive, for whom friendship (much less love) was impossible. But now she had begun to feel his power, his manhood. The way in which other men spoke of him impressed her unconsciously, and she began to ask Despencer questions which were gall and worm-wood to that young man. But he answered honestly, after his fashion.

"Isn't he very rich?" she asked. "And I suppose he lives very plainly?"

"Rich as Croesus, and he sticks in his ugly rooms in the Albany because he never thinks enough about the thing to change. I've been in them once, and you never saw such a place. He's a maniac for fresh air, so they're large enough, but they're littered like a stable with odds and ends of belongings. He must have several thousand books, and yet he hasn't a decent binding among them. He hasn't a photograph of a single soul, and only one picture, which, I believe, was his father. But you never saw such a collection of whips and spurs and bits. It smells like a harness-room and there you find Maitland, when by any chance he is at home, working half the night and up to the eyes in papers. I don't think the man has any expenses except food and rent, for he wears the same clothes for years. And he has given up horses."

"Was he fond of horses?" Miss Clara asked.

"Oh, you had better ask him. I really can't tell you any more about him."

"But how do his friends get on with him?"

"He has hardly any, but his acquaintances, who are all the world, say he is the one great man of the future. If you want to read what people think of him, you had better look at the *Monthly*."

Under cover of this one ungenerous word Despencer made his escape, for he hated the business, but made it the rule of his life "never to crab a fellow". Miss Clara promptly sought out the *Monthly*, and found twenty pages of superfine analysis and bitter, grudging praise. She read it with interest, and then lay back in her chair and tried to fix her thoughts. It is only your unhealthy young woman who worships strength in the abstract, and the girl tried to determine whether she admired the man as a power or disliked him as a brute. She chose a compromise, and the feeling which survived was chiefly curiosity.

The result of the afternoon was that when the fishermen returned, and Maitland, in dry clothes, appeared for tea, she settled herself beside him and prepared to talk. Maitland, being healthily tired, was in an excellent temper, and he found himself enticed into what for him was a rare performance—talk about himself. They were sitting apart from the others, and, ere ever he knew, he was answering the girl's questions with an absent-minded frankness. In a little she had drawn from him the curious history of his life, which most men knew, but never from his own lips. "I was at school for a year," he said, "and then my father died and our affairs went to pieces. I had to come back and go into an office, a sort of bank. I hated it, but it was good for me, for it taught me something, and my discontent made me ambitious. I had about eighty pounds a year, and I saved from that. I worked too at books incessantly, and by-and-by I got an Oxford scholarship, at an obscure college. I went up there, and found myself in a place where everyone seemed well-off, while I was a pauper. However, it didn't trouble me much, for I had no ambition to play the fool. I only cared about two things— horses and metaphysics. I hated all games, which I thought only fit for children. I daresay it was foolish, but then you see I had had a queer upbringing. I managed to save a little money, and one vacation when I was wandering about in Norfolk, sleeping under haystacks and working in harvest-fields when my supplies ran down, I came across a farmer. He was a good fellow and a sort of sportsman, and I took a fancy to him. He had a colt to sell which I fancied more, for I saw it had blood in it. So I bought it for what seemed a huge sum to me in those days, but I kept it at his farm and I superintended its education. I broke it myself and taught it to jump, and by-and-by in my third year I brought it to Oxford and entered for the Grind on it. People laughed at me, but I knew my own business. The little boys who rode in the thing knew nothing about horses, and not one in ten could ride; so I entered and won. It was all I wanted, for I could sell my horse then, and the fellow who rode second bought it. It was decent of him, for I asked a big figure, and I think he had an idea of doing me a kindness. I made him my private secretary the other day."

"You mean Lord Drapier?" she asked.

"Yes—Drapier. That gave me money to finish off and begin in town. Oh, and I had got a first in my Schools. I knew very little about anything except metaphysics, and I never went to tutors. I suppose I knew a good deal more than the examiners in my own subject, and anyhow they felt obliged to give me my first after some grumbling. Then I came up to town with just sixty pounds in my pocket, but I had had the education of a gentleman."

Maitland looked out of the window, and the sight of the mist-clad hills recalled him to himself. He wondered why he was telling the girl this story, and he stopped suddenly.

"And what did you do in town?" she asked, with interest.

"I hung round and kept my eyes open. I nearly starved, for I put half my capital on a horse which I thought was safe, and lost it. By-and-by, quite by accident, I came across a curious fellow, Ransome—you probably have heard his name. I met him in some stables where he was buying a mare, and he took a liking to me. He made me his secretary, and then, because I liked hard work, he let me see his business. It was enormous, for the man was a genius after a fashion; and I slaved away in his office and down at the docks for about three years. He paid me just enough to keep body and soul together and cover them with clothes; but I didn't grumble, for I had a sort of idea that I was on my probation. And then my apprenticeship came to an end."

"Yes," said the girl.

"Yes; for you see Ransome was an odd character. He had a sort of genius for finance, and within his limits he was even a

137

great administrator. But in everything else he was as simple as a child. His soul was idyllic: he loved green fields and Herrick and sheep. So it had always been his fancy to back out some day and retire with his huge fortune to some country place and live as he pleased. It seemed that he had been training me from the first day I went into the business, and now he cut the rope and left the whole enormous concern in my hands. I needed every atom of my wits, and the first years were a hard struggle. I became of course very rich; but I had to do more, I had to keep the thing at its old level. I had no natural turn for the work, and I had to acquire capacity by sheer grind. However, I managed it, and then, when I felt my position sure, I indulged myself with a hobby and went into politics."

"You call it a hobby?"

"Certainly. The ordinary political career is simply a form of trifling. There's no trade on earth where a man has to fear so few able competitors. Of course it's very public and honourable and that sort of thing, and I like it; but sometimes it wearies me to death."

The girl was looking at him with curious interest. "Do you always get what you want?" she asked.

"Never," he said.

"Then is your success all disappointment?"

"Oh, I generally get a bit of my ambitions, which is all one can hope for in this world."

"I suppose your ambitions are not idyllic, like Mr. Ransome's?"

He laughed. "No, I suppose not. I never could stand your Corot meadows and ivied cottages and village church bells. But I am at home in this glen, or used to be."

"You said that last night, and I thought it was affectation," said the girl; "but perhaps you are right. I'm not at home in this scenery, at any rate in this weather. Ugh, look at that mist driving and that spur of Stob Ghabhar! I really must go and sit by the fire."

IV

THE next day dawned clear and chill, with a little frost to whiten the heather; but by midday the sun had turned August to June, and sea and land drowsed in a mellow heat. Maitland was roused from his meditations with a pipe on a garden-seat by the appearance of Miss Clara, her eyes bright with news. He had taken her in to dinner the night before, and for the first time in his life had found himself talking easily to a woman. Her interest of the afternoon had not departed; and Despencer in futile disgust shunned the drawing-room, his particular paradise, and played billiards with Clanroyden in the spirit of an unwilling martyr.

"We are going out in the yacht," Miss Clara cried, as she emerged from the shadow of a fuchsia-hedge, "to the Isles of the Waves, away beyond the Seal's Headland. Do you know the place, Mr. Maitland?"

"Eilean na Cille? Yes. It used to be dangerous for currents, but a steam-yacht does not require to fear them."

"Well, we'll be ready to start at twelve, and I must go in to give orders about lunch."

A little later she came out with a bundle of letters in her hands. "Here are your letters, Mr. Maitland; but you mustn't try to answer them, or you'll be late."

He put the lot in his jacket pocket and looked up at the laughing girl. "My work is six hundred miles behind me," he said, "and today I have only the Eilean na Cille to think of." And, as she passed by, another name took the place of the Eilean and it seemed to him that at last he had found the link which was to bind together the two natures—his boyhood and his prime.

Out on the loch the sun was beating with that steady August blaze which is more torrid than midsummer. But as the yacht slipped between the horns of the land, it came into a broken green sea with rollers to the north where the tireless Atlantic fretted on the reefs. In a world of cool salt winds and the golden weather of afternoon, with the cries of tern and gull about the bows and the foam and ripple of green water in the wake, the party fell into a mood of supreme contentment. The restless Miss

Clara was stricken into a figure of contemplation, which sat in the bows and watched the hazy blue horizon and the craggy mainland hills in silent delight. Maitland was revelling in the loss of his isolation. He had ceased to be alone, a leader, and for the moment felt himself one of the herd, a devotee of humble pleasures. His mind was blank, his eyes filled only with the sea, and the lady of his devotion, in that happy moment of romance, seemed to have come at last within the compass of his hopes.

The Islands of the Waves are low green ridges which rise little above the highest tidemark. The grass is stiff with salt, the sparse heather and rushes are crooked with the winds, but there are innumerable little dells where a light wild scrub flourishes, and in one a spring of sweet water sends a tiny stream to the sea. The yacht's company came ashore in boats, and tea was made with a great bustle beside the well, while the men lay idly in the bent and smoked. All wind seemed to have died down, a soft, cool, airless peace like a June evening was abroad, and the heavy surging of the tides had sunk to a distant whisper. Maitland lifted his head, sniffed the air, and looked uneasily to the west, meeting the eye of one of the sailors engaged in the same scrutiny. He beckoned the man to him.

"What do you make of the weather?" he asked.

The sailor, an East-coast man from Arbroath, shook his head. "It's ower lown a' of a sudden," he said. "It looks like mair wind nor we want, but I think it'll haud till the morn."

Maitland nodded and lay down again. He smiled at the return of his old sea craft and weather-lore, on which he had prided himself in his boyhood; and when Miss Clara came up to him with tea she found him grinning vacantly at the sky.

"What a wonderful lull in the wind," she said. "When I was here last these were real isles of the waves, with spray flying over them and a great business to land. But now they might be the island in Fountainblue lake."

"Did you ever hear of the Ocean Quiet?" he asked. "I believe it to be a translation of a Gaelic word which is a synonym for death, but it is also a kind of natural phenomenon. Old people at Cairnlora used to talk of it. They said that sometimes fishermen far out at sea in blowing weather came into a place of extraordinary peace, where the whole world was utterly still and they could hear their own hearts beating."

"What a pretty fancy!" said the girl.

"Yes; but it had its other side. The fishermen rarely came home alive, and if they did they were queer to the end of their days. Another name for the thing was the Breathing of God. It is an odd idea, the passing from the wholesome turmoil of nature to the uncanny place where God crushes you by His silence."

"All the things to eat are down by the fire," she said, laughing. "Do you know, if you weren't what you are, people might think you a poet, Mr. Maitland. I thought you cared for none of these things."

"What things?" he asked. "I don't care for poetry. I am merely repeating the nonsense I was brought up on. Shall I talk to you about politics?"

"Heaven forbid! And now I will tell you my own story about these isles. There is a hermit's cell on one of them and crosses, like Iona. The hermit lived alone all winter, and was fed by boats from the shore when the weather was calm. When one hermit died another took his place, and no one knew where he came from. Now one day a great lord in Scotland disappeared from his castle. He was the King's Warden of the Marches and the greatest soldier of his day, but he disappeared utterly out of men's sight, and people forgot about him. Long years after, the Northmen in a great fleet came down upon these isles, and the little chiefs fled before them. But suddenly among them there appeared an old man, the hermit of the Wave Islands, who organised resistance and gathered a strong army. No one dared oppose him, and the quarrelsome petty chiefs forgot their quarrels under his banner, for he had the air of one born to command. At last he met the invaders in the valley of Fountainblue, and beat them so utterly that few escaped to their ships. He fell himself in the first charge, but not before his followers had heard his battle-cry of 'Saint Bride', and known that the hermit of the Isles and the great King's Warden were the same."

"That was a common enough thing in wild times. Men grew tired of murder and glory and waving banners, and wanted quiet to make their peace with their own souls. I should have thought the craving scarcely extinct yet."

"Then here is your chance, Mr. Maitland," said the girl, laughing. "A little trouble would make the hut habitable, and you could simply disappear, leaving no address to forward your letters to. Think of the sensation, 'Disappearance of a Secretary of State', and the wild theories and the obituaries. Then some day when the land question became urgent on the mainland, you would turn up suddenly, settle it with extraordinary wisdom, and die after confiding your life-story to some country reporter. But I am afraid it would scarcely do, for you would be discovered by Scotland Yard, which would be ignominious."

"It is a sound idea, but the old device is too crude. However, it could be managed differently. Some day, when civilisation grows oppressive, Miss Clara, I will remember your advice."

The afternoon shadows were beginning to lengthen, and from the west a light sharp wind was crisping the sea. The yacht was getting up steam, and boats were coming ashore for the party. The deep blue waters were flushing rose-pink as the level westering sun smote them from the summit of a cloudbank. The stillness had gone, and the air was now full of sounds and colour. Miss Clara, with an eye on the trim yacht, declared her disapproval. "It is an evening for the cutter," she cried, and in spite of Mrs. Etheridge's protests she gave orders for it to be made ready. Then the self-willed young woman looked round for company. "Will you come, Mr. Maitland?" she said. "You can sail a boat, can't you? And Mr. Despencer, I shall want you to talk to me when Mr. Maitland is busy. We shall race the yacht, for we ought to be able to get through the Scart's Neck with this wind."

"I am not sure if you are wise, Miss Clara," and Maitland pulled down his brows as he looked to the west. "It will be wind—in a very little, and you stand the chance of a wetting."

"I don't mind. I want to get the full good of such an evening. You want to be near the water to understand one of our sunsets. I can be a barbarian too, you know."

It was not for Maitland to grumble at this friendliness; so he followed her into the cutter with Despencer, who had no love for the orders but much for her who gave them. He took the helm and steered, with directions from the lady, from his memory of the intricate coast. Despencer with many rugs looked to Miss Clara's comfort, and, having assured his own, was instantly entranced with the glories of the evening.

The boat tripped along for a little in a dazzle of light into the silvery grey of the open water. Far in front lay the narrow gut called the Scart's Neck, which was the by-way to the loch of Fountainblue. Then Maitland at the helm felt the sheets suddenly begin to strain, and, looking behind, saw that the Isles of the Waves were almost lost in the gloom, and that the roseate heavens were quickly darkening behind. The wind which he had feared was upon them; a few seconds more and it was sending the cutter staggering among billows. He could hardly make himself heard in the din, as he roared directions to Despencer about disposing of his person in another part of the boat. The girl with flushed face was laughing in pure joy of the storm. She caught a glimpse of Maitland's serious eye and looked over the gunwale at the threatening west. Then she too became quiet, and meekly sat down on the thwart to which he motioned her.

The gale made the Scart's Neck impossible, and the murky sky seemed to promise greater fury ere the morning. Twilight was falling, and the other entrance to the quiet loch meant the rounding of a headland and a difficult course through a little archipelago. It was the only way, for return was out of the question, and it seemed vain to risk the narrow chances of the short-cut. Maitland looked down at his two companions, and reflected with pleasure that he was the controller of their fates. He had sailed much as a boy, and he found in this moment of necessity that his old lore returned to him. He felt no mistrust of his powers: whatever the gale he could land them at Fountainblue, though it might take hours and involve much discomfort. He remembered the coast like his own name; he relished the grim rage of the elements, and he kept the cutter's head out to sea with a delight in the primeval conflict.

The last flickering rays of light, coming from the screen of cloud, illumined the girl's pale face, and the sight disquieted him. There was a hint of tragedy in this game. Despencer, nervously self-controlled, was reassuring Clara. Ploughing onward in the blackening night in a frail boat on a wind-threshed sea was no work for a girl. But it was Despencer who was comforting her! Well, it was his proper work. He was made for the business of talking soft things to women. Maitland, his face hard with spray, looked into the darkness with a kind of humour in his heart. And then, as the boat shore and dipped into the storm, its human occupants seemed to pass out of the picture, and it was only a shell tossed on great waters in the unfathomable night. The evening had come, moonless and starless, and Maitland steered as best he could by the deeper blackness which was the configuration of the shore. Something loomed up that he knew for the headland, and they were drifting in a quieter stretch of sea, with the breakers grumbling ahead from the little tangle of islands.

Suddenly he fell into one of the abstractions which had always dogged him through his strenuous life. His mind was clear, he chose his course with a certain precision, but the winds and waves had become to him echoes of echoes. Wet with spray and shifting his body constantly with the movement of the boat, it yet was all a phantasmal existence, while his thoughts were following an airy morrice in a fairyland world. The motto of his house, the canting motto of old reivers, danced in his brain— *"Parmi ceu haut bois conduyrai m'amie"*—"Through the high wood I will conduct my love"—and in a land of green forests, dragon-haunted, he was piloting Clara robed in a quaint medieval gown, himself in speckless plate-armour. His fancy fled through a score of scenes, sometimes on a dark heath, or by a lonely river, or among great mountains, but always the lady and her protector. Clara, looking up from Despencer's side, saw his lips moving, noted that his eyes were glad, and for a moment hoped better things of their chances.

Then suddenly she was dumb with alarm, for the cutter heeled over, and but that Maitland woke to clear consciousness and swung the sheet loose, all would have been past. The adventure nerved him and quickened his senses. The boat seemed to move more violently than the wind drove her, and in the utter blackness he felt for the first time the grip of the waters. The ugly cruel monster had wakened, and was about to wreak its anger on the toy. And then he remembered the currents which raced round Eilean Righ and the scattered isles. Dim shapes loomed up, shapes strange and unfriendly, and he felt miserably that he was as helpless now as Despencer. To the left night had wholly shut out the coast; his one chance was to run for one of the isles and risk a landing. It would be a dreary waiting for the dawn, but safety had come before any comfort. And yet, he remembered, the little islands were rock-bound and unfriendly, and he was hurrying forward in the grip of a black current with a gale behind and unknown reefs before.

And then he seemed to remember something of this current which swept along the isles. In a little—so he recalled a boyish voyage in clear weather—they would come to a place where the sea ran swift and dark beside a kind of natural wharf. Here he had landed once upon a time, but it was a difficult enterprise, needing a quick and a far leap at the proper moment, for the stream ran very fast. But if this leap were missed there was still a chance. The isle was the great Eilean Righ, and the current swung round its southern end, and then, joining with another stream, turned up its far side, and for a moment washed the shore. But if this second chance were missed, then nothing remained but to fall into the great sea-going stream and be carried out to death in the wide Atlantic. He strained his eyes to the right for Eilean Righ. Something seemed to approach, as they bent under an access of the gale. They bore down upon it, and he struggled to keep the boat's head away, for at this pace to grate upon rock would mean upsetting. The sail was down, fluttering amidships like a captive bird, and the gaunt mast bowed with the wind. A horrible fascination, the inertia of nightmare, seized him. The motion was so swift and beautiful; why not go on and onward, listlessly? And then, conquering the weakness, he leaned forward and called to Clara. She caught his arm like a child, and he pulled her up beside him. Then he beckoned Despencer, and, shrieking against the din, told him to follow him when he jumped. Despencer nodded, his teeth chattering with cold and the novel business. Suddenly out of the darkness, a yard on their right, loomed a great flat rock along which the current raced like a mill-lade. The boat made to strike, but Maitland forced her nose out to sea, and then as the stern swung round he seized his chance. Holding Clara with his left arm he stood up, balanced himself for a moment on the gunwale, and jumped. He landed sprawling on his side on some wet seaweed, over which the sea was lipping, but undeniably on land. As he pulled himself up he had a vision of the cutter, dancing like a cork, vanishing down the current into the darkness.

Holding the girl in his arms he picked his way across the rock-pools to the edge of the island heather. For a moment he thought Clara had fainted. She lay still and inert, her eyes shut, her hair falling foolishly over her brow. He sprinkled some water on her face, and she revived sufficiently to ask her whereabouts. He was crossing the island to find Despencer, but he did not tell her. "You are safe," he said, and he carried her over the rough ground as lightly as a child. An intense exhilaration had seized him. He ran over the flats and strode up the low hillocks with one thought possessing his brain. To save Despencer, that of course was the far-off aim on his mind's horizon, but all the foreground was filled with the lady. "*Parmi ceu haut bois*"—the old poetry of the world had penetrated to his heart. The black night and the wild wind and the sea were the ministrants of love. The hollow shams of life with their mincing conventions had departed, and in this savage out-world a man stood for a man. The girl's light tweed jacket was no match for this chill gale, so he stopped for a moment, took off his own shooting-coat and put it round her. And then, as he came over a little ridge, he was aware of a grumbling of waters and the sea.

The beach was hidden in a veil of surf which sprinkled the very edge of the bracken. Beyond, the dark waters were boiling like a caldron, for the tides in this little bay ran with the fury of a river in spate. A moon was beginning to struggle through the windy clouds, and surf, rock, and wave began to shape themselves out of the night. Clara stood on the sand, a slim, desolate figure, and clung to Maitland's arm. She was still dazed with the storm and the baffling suddenness of change. Maitland, straining his eyes out to sea, was in a waking dream. With the lady no toil was too great, no darkness terrible; for her he would scale the blue air and plough the hills and do all the lover's feats of romance. And then suddenly he shook her hand roughly from his arm and ran forward, for he saw something coming down the tide.

Before he left the boat he had lowered the sail, and the cutter swung to the current, an odd amorphous thing, now heeling over with a sudden gust and now pulled back to balance by the strong grip of the water. A figure seemed to sit in the stern, making feeble efforts to steer. Maitland knew the coast and the ways of the sea. He ran through the surf-ring into the oily-black eddies, shouting to Despencer to come overboard. Soon he was not ten yards from the cutter's line, where the current made a turn towards the shore before it washed the iron rocks to the right. He found deep water, and in two strokes was in the grip of the tides and borne wildly towards the reef. He prepared himself for what was coming, raising his feet and turning his right shoulder to the front. And then with a shock he was pinned against the rock-wall, with the tides tugging at his legs, while his hands clung desperately to a shelf. Here he remained, yelling directions to the coming boat. Surf was in his eyes, so that at first he could not see, but at last in a dip of the waves he saw the cutter, a man's form in the stern, plunging not twenty yards away. Now was his chance or never, for while the tide would take a boat far from his present place of vantage, it would carry a lighter thing, such as a man's body, in a circle nearer to the shore. He yelled again, and the world seemed to him quiet for a moment, while his voice echoed eerily in the void. Despencer must have heard it, for the next moment he saw him slip pluckily overboard, making the cutter heel desperately with his weight. And then—it seemed an age—a man, choking and struggling weakly, came down the current, and, pushing his right arm out against the rush of water, he had caught the swimmer by the collar and drawn him in to the side of the rock.

Then came the harder struggle. Maitland's left hand was numbing, and though he had a foothold, it was too slight to lean on with full weight. A second lassitude oppressed him, a supreme desire to slip into those racing tides and rest. He was in no panic about death, but he had the practical man's love of an accomplished task, and it nerved him to the extreme toil. Slowly by inches he drew himself up the edge of the reef, cherishing jealously each grip and foothold, with Despencer, half-choked and all but fainting, hanging heavily on his right arm. Blind with spray, sick with seawater, and aching with his labours, he gripped at last the tangles of seaweed, which meant the flat surface, and with one final effort raised himself and Despencer to the top. There he lay for a few minutes with his head in a rock-pool till the first weariness had passed.

He staggered with his burden in his arms along the ragged reef to the strip of sand where Clara was weeping hysterically. The sight of her restored Maitland to vigour, the appeal of her lonely figure there in the wet brackens. She must think them all dead, he reflected, and herself desolate, for she could not have interpreted rightly his own wild rush into the waves. When she heard his voice she started, as if at a ghost, and then seeing his burden, ran towards him. "Oh, he is dead!" she cried. "Tell me! tell me!" and she clasped the inert figure so that her arm crossed Maitland's. Despencer, stupefied and faint, was roused to consciousness by a woman's kisses on his cheek, and still more by his bearer abruptly laying him on the heather. Clara hung over him like a mother, calling him by soft names, pushing his hair from his brow, forgetful of her own wet and sorry plight. And meanwhile Maitland stood watching, while his palace of glass was being shivered about his ears.

Aforetime his arrogance had kept him from any thought of jealousy; now the time and place were too solemn for trifling, and facts were laid bare before him. Sentiment does not bloom readily in a hard nature, but if it once comes to flower it does not die without tears and agonies. The wearied man, who stood quietly beside the hysterical pair, had a moment of peculiar anguish. Then he conquered sentiment, as he had conquered all other feelings of whose vanity he was assured. He was now, as he was used to be, a man among children, and as a man he had his work. He bent over Clara. "I know a hollow in the middle of the island," he said, "where we can camp the night. I'll carry Despencer, for his ankle is twisted. Do you think you could try to walk?"

The girl followed obediently, her eyes only on her lover. Her trust in the other was infinite, her indifference to him impenetrable; while he, hopelessly conscious of his fate, saw in the slim dishevelled figure at his side the lost lady, the mistress for him of all romance and generous ambitions. The new springs in his life were choked; he had still his work, his power, and, thank God, his courage; but the career which ran out to the horizon of his vision was black and loveless, And he held in his arms the thing which had frustrated him, the thing he had pulled out of the deep in peril of his body; and at the thought life for a moment seemed to be only a comic opera with tragedy to shift the scenes.

He found a cleft between two rocks with a soft floor of heather. There had been no rain, so the bracken was dry, and he gathered great armfuls and driftwood logs from the shore. Soon he had a respectable pile of timber, and then in the nick of the cleft he built a fire. His matches, being in his jacket pocket, had escaped the drenchings of salt water, and soon with a smoke and crackling and sweet scent of burning wood, a fire was going cheerily in the darkness. Then he made a couch of bracken, and laid there the still feeble Despencer. The man was more weak than ill; but for his ankle he was unhurt; and a little brandy would have brought him to himself. But this could not be provided, and Clara saw in his condition only the sign of mortal sickness. With haggard eyes she watched by him, easing his head, speaking soft kind words, forgetful of her own cold and soaking clothes. Maitland drew her gently to the fire, shook down the bracken to make a rest for her head, and left a pile of logs ready for use. "I am going to the end of the island," he said, "to light a fire for a signal. It is the only part which they can see on the mainland, and if they see the blaze they will come off for us as soon as it is light." The pale girl listened obediently. This man was the master, and in his charge was the safety of her lover and herself.

Maitland turned his back upon the warm nook, and stumbled along the ridge to the northern extremity of the isle. It was not a quarter of a mile away, but the land was so rough with gullies and crags that the journey took him nearly an hour. Just off the extreme point was a flat rock, sloping northward to a considerable height, a place from which a beacon could penetrate far over the mainland. He gathered brackens for kindling, and driftwood which former tides had heaped on the beach; and then with an armful he splashed through the shallow surf to the rock. Scrambling to the top, he found a corner where a fire might be lit, a place conspicuous and yet sheltered. Here he laid his kindling, and then in many wet journeys he carried his stores of firewood from the mainland to the rock. The lighting was nervous work, for he had few matches; but at last the dampish wood had caught, and tongues of flame shot up out of the smoke. Meantime the wind had sunk lower, the breakers seemed to have been left behind, and the eternal surge of the tides became the dominant sound to the watcher by the beacon.

And then, it seemed to him, the great convulsions of the night died away, and a curious peace came down upon the waters. The fire leaped in the air, the one living thing in a hushed and expectant world. It was not the quiet of sleep but of a sudden cessation, like the lull after a great flood or a snowslip. The tides still eddied and swayed, but it was noiselessly; the world moved, yet without sound or friction. The bitter wind which chilled his face and stirred up the red embers was like a phantom blast, without the roughness of a common gale. For a moment he seemed to be set upon a high mountain with the world infinitely remote beneath his feet. To all men there come moments of loneliness of body, and to some few the mingled ecstasy and grief of loneliness of soul. The child-tale of the Ocean Quiet came back to him, the hour of the Breathing of God. Surely the great silence was now upon the world. But it was an evil presage, for all who sailed into it were homeless wanderers for ever after. Ah well! he had always been a wanderer, and the last gleam of home had been left behind, where by the firelight in the cold cranny a girl was crooning over her lover.

His past, his monotonous, brilliant past, slipped by with the knotless speed of a vision. He saw a boy, haunted with dreams, chafing at present delights, clutching evermore at the faint things of fancy. He saw a man, playing with the counters which others played with, fighting at first for bare existence and then for power and the pride of life. Success came over his path like a false dawn, but he knew in his heart that he had never sought it. What was that remote ineffable thing he had followed? Here in the quiet of the shadowy waters he had the moment of self-revelation which comes to all, and hopes and dim desires seemed to stand out with the clearness of accomplished facts. There had always been something elect and secret at the back of his fiercest ambitions. The ordinary cares of men had been to him but little things to be played with; he had won by despising them; casting them from him, they had fallen into the hollow of his hand. And he had held them at little, finding his reward in his work, and in a certain alertness and freshness of spirit which he had always cherished. There is a story of island-born men who carry into inland places and the streets of cities the noise of sea-water in their ears, and hear continually the tern crying and the surf falling. So from his romantic boyhood this man had borne an arrogance towards the things of the world which had given him a contemptuous empire over a share of them. As he saw the panorama of his life no place or riches entered into it, but only himself, the haggard, striving soul, growing in power, losing, perhaps, in wisdom. And then, at the end of the way, Death, to shrivel the power to dust, and with the might of his sunbeam to waken to life the forgotten world of the spirit.

In the hush he seemed to feel the wheel and the drift of things, the cosmic order of nature. He forgot his weariness and his plashing clothes as he put more wood on the beacon and dreamed into the night. The pitiless sea, infinite, untamable, washing the Poles and hiding Earth's secrets in her breast, spoke to him with a far-remembered voice. The romance of the remote isles, the homes of his people, floating still in a twilight of old story, rose out of the darkness. His life, with its routine and success, seemed in a moment hollow, a child's game, unworthy of a man. The little social round, the manipulation of half-truths, the easy victories over fools—surely this was not the task for him. He was a dreamer, but a dreamer with an iron hand; he was scarcely in the prime of life; the world was wide and his chances limitless. One castle of cards had already been over-thrown; the Ocean Quiet was undermining another. He was sick of domesticity of every sort—of town, of home, of civilisation. The sad elemental world was his, the fury and the tenderness of nature, the peace of the wilds which old folk had called the Breathing of God. *"Parmi ceu haut bois conduyrai m'amie"*—this was still his motto, to carry untarnished to the end an austere and beautiful dream. His little ambitions had been but shreds and echoes and shadows of this supreme reality. And his love had been but another such simulacrum; for what he had sought was no foolish, laughing girl, but the Immortal Shepherdess, who, singing the old songs of youth, drives her flocks to the hill in the first dewy dawn of the world.

Suddenly he started and turned his head. Day was breaking in a red windy sky, and somewhere a boat's oars were plashing in the sea. And then he realised for the first time that he was cold and starving and soaked to the bone.

V

MR. HENRY DURWARD TO LADY CLAUDIA ETHERIDGE

". . . Things have happened, my dear Clo, since I last wrote; time has passed; tomorrow I leave this place and go to stalk with Drapier; and yet in the stress of departure I take time to answer the host of questions with which you assailed me. I am able to give you the best of news. You have won your bet. Your prophecy about the conduct of the 'other Etheridge girl' has come out right. They are both here, as it happens, having come on from Fountainblue—both the hero and the heroine, I mean, of this most reasonable romance. You know Jack Despencer, one of the best people in the world, though a trifle given to chirping. But I don't think the grasshopper will become a burden to Miss Clara, for she likes that sort of thing. She must, for there is reason to believe that she refused for its sake the greatest match—I speak with all reverence—which this happy country could offer. I know you like Maitland as little as I do, but we agree in admiring the Colossus from a distance. Well, the Colossus has, so to speak, been laid low by a frivolous member of your sex. It is all a most romantic tale. Probably you have heard the gist of it, but here is the full and circumstantial account.

"We found Maitland beside the fire he had been feeding all night, and I shall never forget his figure alone in the dawn on that rock, drenched and dishevelled, but with his haggard white face set like a Crusader's. He took us to a kind of dell in the centre of the island, where we found Clara and Despencer shivering beside a dying fire. He had a twisted ankle and had got a bad scare, while she was perfectly composed, though she broke down when we got home. It must have been an awful business for both, but Maitland never seems to have turned a hair. I want to know two things. First, how in the presence of great danger he managed to get his dismissal from the lady?—for get it he assuredly did, and Despencer at once appeared in the part of the successful lover; second, what part he played in the night's events? Clara remembered little, Despencer only knew that he had been pulled out of the sea, but over all Maitland seems to have brooded like a fate. As usual he told us nothing. It was always his way to give the world results and leave it to find out his methods for itself.

"Despencer overwhelmed him with gratitude. His new happiness made him in love with life, and he included Maitland in the general affection. The night's events seemed to have left their mark on the great man also. He was very quiet, forgot to be rude to anybody, and was kind to both Clara and Despencer. It is his way of acknowledging defeat, the great gentleman's way, for, say what we like about him, he is a tremendous gentleman, one of the last of the breed. . . .

"And then he went away—two days later. Just before he went Hugh Clanroyden and myself were talking in the library, which has a window opening on a flower-garden. Despencer was lying in an invalid's chair under a tree and Clara was reading to him. Maitland was saying goodbye, and he asked for Despencer. We told him that he was with Clara in the garden. He smiled one of those odd scarce smiles of his, and went out to them. When I saw his broad shoulders bending over the chair and the strong face looking down at the radiant Jack with his amiable good looks, confound it, Clo, I had to contrast the pair, and admit with Shakespeare the excellent foppery of the world. Well-a-day! 'Smooth Jacob still robs homely Esau.' And perhaps it is a good thing, for we are most of us Jacobs, and Esau is an uncomfortable fellow in our midst.

"A week later came the surprising, the astounding news that he had taken the African Governorship. A career ruined, everyone said, the finest chance in the world flung away; and then people speculated, and the story came out in bits, and there was only one explanation. It is the right one, as I think you will agree, but it points to some hidden weakness in that iron soul that he could be moved to fling over the ambitions of years because of a girl's choice. He will go and bury himself in the wilds, and our party will have to find another leader. Of course he will do his work well, but it is just as if I were to give up my chances of the Woolsack for a county-court judgeship. He will probably be killed, for he has a million enemies; he is perfectly fearless, and he does not understand the arts of compromise. It was a privilege, I shall always feel, to have known him. He was a great man, and yet—intellect, power, character, were at the mercy of a girl's caprice. As I write, I hear Clara's happy laugh below in the garden, probably at some witticism of the fortunate Jack's. Upon which, with my usual pride in the obvious, I am driven to reflect that the weak things in life may confound the strong, and that, after all, the world is to the young. . . ."

VI

SIR HUGH CLANROYDEN TO MR. HENRY DURWARD— SOME YEARS LATER

". . . I am writing this on board ship, as you will see from the heading, and shall post it when I get to the Cape. You have heard of my appointment, and I need not tell you how deep were my searchings of heart before I found courage to accept. Partly I felt that I had got my chance; partly I thought—an inconsequent feeling—that Maitland, if he had lived, would have been glad to see me in the place. But I am going to wear the Giant's Robe, and Heaven knows I have not the shoulders to fill it. Yet I am happy in thinking that I am in a small sense faithful to his memory.

"No further news, I suppose, has come of the manner of his death? Perhaps we shall never know, for it was on one of those Northern expeditions with a few men by which he held the frontier. I wonder if anyone will ever write fully the history of all that he did? It must have been a titanic work, but his methods were always so quiet that people accepted his results like a gift from Providence. He was given, one gathers, a practically free hand, and he made the country—four years' work of a man of genius. They wished to bring his body home, but he made them bury him where he fell—a characteristic last testament, And so he has gone out of the world into the world's history.

"I am still broken by his death, but, now that he is away, I begin to see him more clearly. Most people, I think, misunderstood him. I was one of his nearest friends, and I only knew bits of the man. For one thing—and I hate to use the vulgar word—he was the only aristocrat I ever heard of. Our classes are three-fourths of them of yesterday's growth, without the tradition, character, manner, or any trait of an aristocracy. And the few, who are nominally of the blood, have gone to seed in mind, or are spoilt by coarse marriages, or, worst of all, have the little trifling superior airs of incompetence. But he, he had the most transcendent breeding in mind and spirit. He had no need for self-assertion, for his most casual acquaintances put him at once in a different class from all other men. He had never a trace of a vulgar ideal; men's opinions, worldly honour, the common pleasures of life, were merely degrees of the infinitely small. And yet he was no bloodless mystic. If race means anything, he had it to perfection. Dreams and fancies to him were the realities, while facts were the shadows which he made dance as it pleased him.

"The truth is, that he was that rarest of mortals, the iron dreamer. He thought in aeons and cosmic cycles, and because of it he could do what he pleased in life. We call a man practical if he is struggling in the crowd with no knowledge of his whereabouts, and yet in our folly we deny the name to the clear-sighted man who can rule the crowd from above. And here I join issue with you and everybody else. You thought it was Miss Clara's refusal which sent him abroad and interrupted his career. I read the thing otherwise. His love for the girl was a mere accident, a survival of the domestic in an austere spirit. Something, I do not know what, showed him his true desires. She may have rejected him; he may never have spoken to her; in any case the renunciation had to come. You must remember that that visit to Fountainblue was the first that he had paid since his boyhood to his boyhood's home. Those revisitings have often a strange trick of self-revelation. I believe that in that night on the island he saw our indoor civilisation and his own destiny in so sharp a contrast that he could not choose but make the severance. He found work where there could be small hope of honour or reward, but many a chance for a hero. And I am sure that he was happy, and that it was the longed-for illumination that dawned on him with the bullet which pierced his heart.

"But, you will say, the fact remains that he was once in love with Miss Clara, and that she would have none of him. I do not deny it. He was never a favourite with women; but, thank Heaven, I have better things to do than study their peculiarities."

THE FAR ISLANDS

"Lady Alice, Lady Louise,
Between the wash of the tumbling seas—"

I

WHEN Bran the Blessed, as the story goes, followed the white bird on the Last Questing, knowing that return was not for him, he gave gifts to his followers. To Heliodorus he gave the gift of winning speech, and straightaway the man went south to the Italian seas, and, becoming a scholar, left many descendants who sat in the high places of the Church. To Raymond he gave his steel battle-axe, and bade him go out to the warrior's path and hew his way to a throne; which the man forthwith accomplished, and became an ancestor in the fourth degree of the first king of Scots. But to Colin, the youngest and the dearest, he gave no gift, whispering only a word in his ear and laying a finger on his eyelids. Yet Colin was satisfied, and he alone of the three, after their master's going, remained on that coast of rock and heather.

In the third generation from Colin, as our elders counted years, came one Colin the Red, who built his keep on the cliffs of Acharra and was a mighty sea-rover in his day. Five times he sailed to the rich parts of France, and a good score of times he carried his flag of three stars against the easterly vikings. A mere name in story, but a sounding piece of nomenclature well garnished with tales. A mastermind by all accounts, but cursed with a habit of fantasy; for, hearing in his old age of a land to the westward, he forthwith sailed into the sunset, and three days later was washed up, a twisted body, on one of the outer isles.

So far it is but legend, but with his grandson, Colin the Red, we fall into the safer hands of the chroniclers. To him God gave

157

the unnumbered sorrows of story-telling, for he was a bard, cursed with a bard's fervours, and none the less a mighty warrior among his own folk. He it was who wrote the lament called "The White Waters of Usna", and the exquisite chain of romances, "Glede-red Gold and Grey Silver." His tales were told by many fires, down to our grandfathers' time, and you will find them still pounded at by the folklorists. But his airs—they are eternal. On harp and pipe they have lived through the centuries; twisted and tortured, they survive in many song-books; and I declare that the other day I heard the most beautiful of them all murdered by a band at a German watering-place. This Colin led the wanderer's life, for he disappeared at middle-age, no one knew whither, and his return was long looked for by his people. Some thought that he became a Christian monk, the holy man living in the sea-girt isle of Cuna, who was found dead in extreme old age, kneeling on the beach, with his arms, contrary to the fashion of the Church, stretched to the westward.

As history narrowed into bonds and forms the descendants of Colin took Raden for their surname, and settled more firmly on their lands in the long peninsula of crag and inlets which runs west to the Atlantic. Under Donald of the Isles they harried the Kings of Scots, or, on their own authority, made war on Macleans and Macranalds, till their flag of the three stars, their badge of the grey-goose feather, and their on-cry of "Cuna" were feared from Lochalsh to Cantire. Later they made a truce with the king, and entered into the royal councils. For years they warded the western coast, and as king's lieutenants smoked out the inferior pirates of Eigg and Toronsay. A Raden was made a Lord of Sleat, another was given lands in the low country and the name Baron of Strathyre, but their honours were transitory and short as their lives. Rarely one of the house saw middle age. A bold, handsome, and stirring race, it was their fate to be cut off in the rude warfare of the times, or, if peace had them in its clutches, to man vessel and set off once more on those mad western voyages which were the weird of the family. Three of the name were found drowned on the far shore of Cuna; more than one sailed straight out of the ken of mortals. One rode with the Good Lord James on the pilgrimage of the Heart of Bruce, and died by his leader's side in the Saracen battle. Long afterwards a Raden led the western men against the Cheshire archers at Flodden and was slain himself in the steel circle around the king.

But the years brought peace and a greater wealth, and soon the cold stone tower was left solitary on the headland and the new house of Kinlochuna rose by the green links of the stream. The family changed its faith, and an Episcopal chaplain took the place of the old mass-priest in the tutoring of the sons. Radens were in the '15 and the '45. They rose with Bute to power, and they long disputed the pride of Dundas in the northern capital. They intermarried with great English houses till the sons of the family were Scots only in name, living much abroad or in London, many of them English landowners by virtue of a mother's blood. Soon the race was of the common over-civilised type, graceful, well-mannered, with abundant good looks, but only once in a generation reverting to the rugged northern strength. Eton and Oxford had in turn displaced the family chaplain, and the house by the windy headland grew emptier and emptier save when grouse and deer brought home its fickle masters.

II

A CHILDLESS illness brought Colin to Kinlochuna when he had reached the mature age of five, and delicate health kept him there for the greater part of the next six years. During the winter he lived in London, but from the late northern spring, through all the long bright summers, he lived in the great tenantless place without company—for he was an only child. A French nurse had the charge of his doings, and when he had passed through the formality of lessons there were the long pine-woods at his disposal, the rough moor, the wonderful black holes with the rich black mud in them, and best of all the bay of Acharra, below the headland, with Cuna lying in the waves a mile to the west. At such times his father was busy elsewhere; his mother was dead; the family had few near relatives; so he passed a solitary childhood in the company of seagulls and the birds of the moor.

His time for the beach was the afternoon. On the left as you go down through the woods from the house there runs out the great headland of Acharra, red and grey with mosses, and with a nimbus always of screaming sea-fowl. To the right runs a low beach of sand, passing into rough limestone boulders and then into the heather of the wood. This in turn is bounded by a reef of low rocks falling by gentle breaks to the water's edge. It is crowned with a tangle of heath and fern, bright at most seasons with flowers, and dwarf pine-trees straggle on its crest till one sees the meaning of its Gaelic name, "The Ragged Cock's-Comb". This place was Colin's playground in fine weather. When it blew rain or snow from the north he dwelt indoors among dogs and books, puzzling his way through great volumes from his father's shelves. But when the mild west-wind weather fell on the sea, then he would lie on the hot sand—Amelie the nurse reading a novel on the nearest rock—and kick his small heels as he followed his fancy. He built great sand castles to the shape of Acharra old tower, and peopled them with preposterous knights and ladies; he drew great moats and rivers for the tide to fill; he fought battles innumerable with crackling seaweed, till Amelie, with her sharp cry of "Colin, Colin," would carry him houseward for tea.

Two fancies remained in his mind through those boyish years. One was about the mysterious shining sea before him. In certain weathers it seemed to him a solid pathway. Cuna, the little ragged isle, ceased to block the horizon, and his own white road ran away down into the west, till suddenly it stopped and he saw no farther. He knew he ought to see more, but always at one place, just when his thoughts were pacing the white road most gallantly, there came a baffling mist to his sight, and he found himself looking at a commonplace sea with Cuna lying very real and palpable in the offing. It was a vexatious limitation; for all his dreams were about this pathway. One day in June, when the waters slept in a deep heat, he came down the sands barefoot, and lo! there was his pathway. For one moment things seemed clear, the mist had not gathered on the road and with a cry he ran down to the tide's edge and waded in. The touch of water dispelled the illusion, and almost in tears he saw the cruel back of Cuna blotting out his own magic way.

The other fancy was about the low ridge of rocks which bounded the bay on the right. His walks had never extended beyond it, either on the sands or inland, for that way lay a steep hillside and a perilous bog. But often on the sands he had come to its foot and wondered what country lay beyond. He made many efforts to explore it, difficult efforts, for the vigilant Amelie had first to be avoided. Once he was almost at the top when some seaweed to which he clung gave way, and he rolled back again to the soft warm sand. By-and-by he found that he knew what was beyond. A clear picture had built itself up in his brain of a mile of reefs, with sand in bars between them, and beyond all a sea-wood of alders slipping from the hill's skirts to the water's edge. This was not what he wanted in his explorations, so he stopped, till one day it struck him that the westward view might reveal something beyond the hog-backed Cuna. One day, pioneering alone, he scaled the steepest heights of the seaweed and pulled his chin over the crest of the ridge. There, sure enough, was his picture—a mile of reefs and the tattered sea-wood. He turned eagerly seawards. Cuna still lay humped on the waters, but beyond it he seemed to see his shining pathway running far to a speck which might be an island. Crazy with pleasure he stared at the vision, till slowly it melted into the waves, and Cuna the inexorable once more blocked the skyline. He climbed down, his heart in a doubt between despondency and hope.

It was the last day of such fancies, for on the morrow he had to face the new world of school.

At Cecil's Colin found a new life and a thousand new interests. His early delicacy had been driven away by the sea-winds of Acharra, and he was rapidly growing up a tall, strong child, straight of limb like all his house, but sinewy and alert beyond his years. He learned new games with astonishing facility, became a fast-bowler with a genius for twists, and a Rugby three-quarters full of pluck and cunning. He soon attained to the modified popularity of a private school, and, being essentially clean, strong, and healthy, found himself a mark for his juniors' worship and a favourite with masters. The homage did not spoil him, for no boy was ever less self-possessed. On the cricket-ground and the football-field he was a leader, but in private he had the nervous, sensitive manners of the would-be recluse. No one ever accused him of "side"—his polite, halting address was the same to junior and senior; and the result was that wild affection which simplicity in the great is wont to inspire.

He spoke with a pure accent, in which lurked no northern trace; in a little he had forgotten all about his birthplace and his origin. His name had at first acquired for him the sobriquet of "Scottie", but the title was soon dropped from its manifest inaptness.

In his second year at Cecil's he caught a prevalent fever, and for days lay very near the brink of death. At his worst he was wildly delirious, crying ceaselessly for Acharra and the beach at Kinlochuna. But as he grew convalescent the absorption remained, and for the moment he seemed to have forgotten his southern life. He found himself playing on the sands, always with the boundary ridge before him, and the hump of Cuna rising in the sea. When dragged back to his environment by the inquiries of Bellew, his special friend, who came to sit with him, he was so abstracted and forgetful that the good Bellew was seriously grieved. "The chap's a bit cracked, you know," he announced in hall. "Didn't know me. Asked me what 'footer' meant when I told him about the Bayswick match, and talked about nothing but a lot of heathen Scotch names."

One dream haunted Colin throughout the days of his recovery. He was tormented with a furious thirst, poorly assuaged at long intervals by watered milk. So when he crossed the borders of dreamland his first search was always for a well. He tried the brushwood inland from the beach, but it was dry as stone. Then he climbed with difficulty the boundary ridge, and found little pools of salt water, while far on the other side gleamed the dark black bog-holes. Here was not what he sought, and he was in deep despair, till suddenly over the sea he caught a glimpse of his old path running beyond Cuna to a bank of mist. He rushed down to the tide's edge, and to his amazement found solid ground. Now was the chance for which he had long looked, and he ran happily westwards, till of a sudden the solid earth seemed to sink with him, and he was in the waters struggling. But two curious things he noted. One was that the far bank of mist seemed to open for a pin-point of time, and he had a gleam of land. He saw nothing distinctly, only a line which was not mist and was not water. The second was that the water was fresh, and as he was drinking from this curious new fresh sea he awoke. The dream was repeated three times before he left the sick-room. Always he wakened at the same place, always he quenched his thirst in the fresh sea, but never again did the mist open for him and show him the strange country.

From Cecil's he went to the famous school which was the tradition in his family. The Head spoke to his house-master of his coming. "We are to have another Raden here," he said, "and I am glad of it, if the young one turns out to be anything like the others. There's a good deal of dry-rot among the boys just now. They are all too old for their years and too wise in the wrong way. They haven't anything like the enthusiasm in games they had twenty years ago when I first came here. I hope this young Raden will stir them up." The house-master agreed, and when he first caught sight of Colin's slim, well-knit figure, looked into the handsome kindly eyes, and heard his curiously diffident speech, his doubts vanished. "We have got the right stuff now," he told himself, and the senior for whom the new boy fagged made the same comment.

From the anomalous insignificance of fagdom Colin climbed up the School, leaving everywhere a record of honest good nature. He was allowed to forget his cricket and football, but in return he was initiated into the mysteries of the river. Water had always been his delight, so he went through the dreary preliminaries of being coached in a tub-pair till he learned to swing steadily and get his arms quickly forward. Then came the stages of scratch fours and scratch eights, till after a long apprenticeship he was promoted to the dignity of a thwart in the Eight itself. In his last year he was Captain of Boats, a position which joins the responsibility of a Cabinet Minister to the rapturous popular applause of a successful warrior. Nor was he the least distinguished of a great band. With Colin at seven the School won the Ladies' after the closest race on record.

The Head's prophecy fell true, for Colin was a born leader. For all his good-humour and diffidence of speech, he had a trick of shutting his teeth which all respected. As Captain he was the idol of the School, and he ruled it well and justly. For the rest, he was a curious boy with none of the ordinary young enthusiasms, reserved for all his kindliness. At house "shouters" his was not the voice which led the stirring strains of "Stroke out all you know", though his position demanded it. He cared little about work, and the School-house scholar, who fancied him from his manner a devotee of things intellectual, found in Colin but an affected interest. He read a certain amount of modern poetry with considerable boredom; fiction he never opened. The truth was that he had a romance in his own brain which, willy nilly, would play itself out, and which left him small relish for the pale secondhand inanities of art. Often, when with others he would lie in the deep meadows by the river on some hot summer's day, his fancies would take a curious colour. He adored the soft English landscape, the lush grasses, the slow streams, the ancient secular trees. But as he looked into the hazy green distance a colder air would blow on his cheek, a pungent smell of salt and pines would be for a moment in his nostrils, and he would be gazing at a line of waves on a beach, a ridge of low rocks, and a shining sea-path running out to—ah, that he could not tell! The envious Cuna would suddenly block all the vistas. He had constantly the vision before his eyes, and he strove to strain into the distance before Cuna should intervene. Once or twice he seemed almost to achieve it. He found that by keeping on the top of the low rock-ridge he could cheat Cuna by a second or two, and get a glimpse of a misty something out in the west. The vision took odd times for recurring—once or twice in lecture, once on the cricket-ground, many times in the fields of a Sunday, and once while he paddled down to the start in a Trials race. It gave him a keen pleasure: it was his private domain, where at any moment he might make some enchanting discovery.

At this time he began to spend his vacations at Kinlochuna. His father, an elderly ex-diplomat, had permanently taken up his abode there, and was rapidly settling into the easy life of the Scots laird. Colin returned to his native place without enthusiasm.

His childhood there had been full of lonely hours, and he had come to like the warm south country. He found the house full of people, for his father entertained hugely, and the talk was of sport and sport alone. As a rule, your very great athlete is bored by Scots shooting. Long hours of tramping and crouching among heather cramp without fully exercising the body; and unless he has the love of the thing ingrained in him, the odds are that he will wish himself home. The father, in his new-found admiration for his lot, was content to face all weathers; the son found it an effort to keep pace with such vigour. He thought upon the sunlit fields and reedy water-courses with regret, and saw little in the hills but a rough waste scarred with rock and sour with mosses.

He read widely throughout these days, for his father had a taste for modern letters, and new books lay littered about the rooms. He read queer Celtic tales which he thought "sickening rot", and mild Celtic poetry which he failed to understand. Among the guests was a noted manufacturer of fiction, whom the elder Raden had met somewhere and bidden to Kinlochuna. He had heard the tale of Colin's ancestors and the sea headland of Acharra, and one day he asked the boy to show him the place, as he wished to make a story of it. Colin assented unwillingly, for he had been slow to visit this place of memories, and he did not care to make his first experiment in such company. But the gentleman would not be gainsaid, so the two scrambled through the sea-wood and climbed the low ridge which looked over the bay. The weather was mist and drizzle; Cuna had wholly hidden herself, and the bluff Acharra loomed hazy and far. Colin was oddly disappointed: this reality was a poor place compared with his fancies. His companion stroked his peaked beard, talked nonsense about Colin the Red and rhetoric about "the spirit of the misty grey weather having entered into the old tale."

"Think," he cried; "to those old warriors beyond that bank of mist was the whole desire of life, the Golden City, the Far Islands, whatever you care to call it." Colin shivered, as if his holy places had been profaned, set down the man in his mind most unjustly as an "awful little cad", and hurried him back to the house.

Oxford received the boy with open arms, for his reputation had long preceded him. To the majority of men he was the one freshman of his year, and gossip was busy with his prospects.

Nor was gossip disappointed. In his first year he rowed seven in the Eight. The next year he was captain of his college boats, and a year later the O.U.B.C. made him its president. For three years he rowed in the winning Eight, and old coaches agreed that in him the perfect seven had been found. It was he who in the famous race of 18— caught up in the last three hundred yards the quickened stroke which gave Oxford victory. As he grew to his full strength he became a splendid figure of a man—tall, supple, deep-chested for all his elegance. His quick dark eyes and his kindly hesitating manners made people think his face extraordinarily handsome, when really it was in no way above the common. But his whole figure, as he stood in his shorts and sweater on the raft at Putney, was so full of youth and strength that people involuntarily smiled when they saw him—a smile of pleasure in so proper a piece of manhood.

Colin enjoyed life hugely at Oxford, for to one so frank and well equipped the place gave of its best. He was the most distinguished personage of his day there, but, save to school friends and the men he met officially on the river, he was little known. His diffidence and his very real exclusiveness kept him from being the centre of a host of friends. His own countrymen in the place were utterly nonplussed by him. They claimed him eagerly as a fellow, but he had none of the ordinary characteristics of the race. There were Scots of every description around him—pale-faced Scots who worked incessantly, metaphysical Scots who talked in the Union, robustious Scots who played football. They were all men of hearty manners and many enthusiasms—who quoted Burns and dined to the immortal bard's honour every 25th of January; who told interminable Scotch stories, and fell into fervours over national sports, dishes, drinks, and religions. To the poor Colin it was all inexplicable. At the remote house of Kinlochuna he had never heard of a Free Kirk or a haggis. He had never read a line of Burns, Scott bored him exceedingly, and in all honesty he thought Scots games inferior to southern sports. He had no great love for the bleak country, he cared nothing for the traditions of his house, so he was promptly set down by his compatriots as "denationalised and degenerate".

He was idle, too, during these years as far as his Schools were concerned, but he was always very intent upon his own private business. Whenever he sat down to read, when he sprawled on the grass at river picnics, in chapel, in lecture—in short, at any moment when his body was at rest and his mind at leisure his fancies were off on the same old path. Things had changed, however, in that country. The boyish device of a hard road running over the waters had gone, and now it was invariably a boat which he saw beached on the shingle. It differed in shape. At first it was an ugly salmon-coble, such as the fishermen used for the nets at Kinlochuna. Then it passed, by rapid transitions, through a canvas skiff which it took good watermanship to sit, a whiff, an ordinary dinghy, till at last it settled itself into a long rough boat, pointed at both ends, with oar-holes in the sides instead of row-locks. It was the devil's own business to launch it, and launch it anew he was compelled to for every journey; for though he left it bound in a little rock hollow below the ridge after landing, yet when he returned, lo! there was the clumsy thing high and dry upon the beach.

The odd point about the new venture was that Cuna had ceased to trouble him. As soon as he had pulled his first stroke the island disappeared, and nothing lay before him but the sea-fog. Yet, try as he might, he could come little nearer. The shores behind him might sink and lessen, but the impenetrable mist was still miles to the westward. Sometimes he rowed so far that the shore was a thin line upon the horizon, but when he turned the boat it seemed to ground in a second on the beach. The long laboured journey out and the instantaneous return puzzled him at first, but soon he became used to them. His one grief was the mist, which seemed to grow denser as he neared it. The sudden glimpse of land which he had got from the ridge of rock in the old boyish days was now denied him, and with the denial came a keener exultation in the quest. Somewhere in the west, he knew, must be land, and in this land a well of sweet water—for so he had interpreted his feverish dream. Sometimes, when the wind blew against him, he caught scents from it—generally the scent of pines, as on the little ridge on the shore behind him.

One day on his college barge, while he was waiting for a picnic party to start, he seemed to get nearer than before. Out on that western sea, as he saw it, it was fresh, blowing weather, with a clear hot sky above. It was hard work rowing, for the wind was against him, and the sun scorched his forehead. The air seemed full of scents—and sounds, too, sounds of far-away surf and wind in trees. He rested for a moment on his oars and turned his head. His heart beat quickly, for there was a rift in the mist, and far through a line of sand ringed with snow-white foam.

Somebody shook him roughly—"Come on, Colin, old man. They're all waiting for you. Do you know you've been half asleep?"

Colin rose and followed silently, with drowsy eyes. His mind was curiously excited. He had looked inside the veil of mist. Now he knew what was the land he sought.

He made the voyage often, now that the spell was broken. It was short work to launch the boat, and, whereas it had been a long pull formerly, now it needed only a few strokes to bring him to the Rim of the Mist. There was no chance of getting farther, and he scarcely tried. He was content to rest there, in a world of curious scents and sounds, till the mist drew down and he was driven back to shore.

The change in his environment troubled him little. For a man who has been an idol at the University to fall suddenly into the comparative insignificance of Town is often a bitter experience; but Colin, whose thoughts were not ambitious, scarcely noticed it. He found that he was less his own master than before, but he humbled himself to his new duties without complaint. Many of his old friends were about him; he had plenty of acquaintances; and, being "sufficient unto himself", he was unaccustomed to ennui. Invitations showered upon him thick and fast. Match-making mothers, knowing his birth and his father's income, and reflecting that he was the only child of his house, desired him as a son-in-law. He was bidden welcome everywhere, and the young girls, for whose sake he was thus courted, found in him an attractive mystery. The tall good-looking athlete, with the kind eyes and the preposterously nervous manner, wakened their maidenly sympathies. As they danced with him or sat next to him at dinner, they talked fervently of Oxford, of the North, of the army, of his friends. "Stupid, but nice, my dear," was Lady Afflint's comment; and Miss Clara Etheridge, the beauty of the year, declared to her friends that he was a "dear boy, but so awkward." He was always forgetful, and ever apologetic; and when he forgot the Shandwicks' theatre-party, the Herapaths' dance, and at least a dozen minor matters, he began to acquire the reputation of a cynic and a recluse.

"You're a queer chap, Col," Lieutenant Bellew said in expostulation.

Colin shrugged his shoulders; he was used to the description.

"Do you know that Clara Etheridge was trying all she knew to please you this afternoon, and you looked as if you weren't listening? Most men would have given their ears to be in your place."

"I'm awfully sorry, but I thought I was very polite to her."

"And why weren't you at the Marshams' show?"

"Oh, I went to polo with Collinson and another man. And, I say, old chap, I'm not coming to the Logans' tomorrow. I've got a fence on with Adair at the school."

Little Bellew who was a tremendous mirror of fashion and chevalier in general, looked up curiously at his tall friend.

"Why don't you like the women, Col, when they're so fond of you?"

"They aren't," said Colin hotly, "and I don't dislike 'em. But, Lord! they bore me. I might be doing twenty things when I talk nonsense to one of 'em for an hour. I come back as stupid as an owl, and besides there's heaps of things better sport."

The truth was that, while among men he was a leader and at his ease, among women his psychic balance was so oddly upset that he grew nervous and returned unhappy. The boat on the beach, ready in general to appear at the slightest call, would delay long after such experiences, and its place would be taken by some woman's face for which he cared not a straw. For the boat, on the other hand, he cared a very great deal. In all his frank wholesome existence there was this enchanting background, this pleasure-garden which he cherished more than anything in life. He had come of late to look at it with somewhat different eyes. The eager desire to search behind the mist was ever with him, but now he had also some curiosity about the details of the picture. As he pulled out to the Rim of the Mist, sounds seemed to shape themselves on his lips, which by-and-by grew into actual words in his memory. He wrote them down in scraps, and after some sorting they seemed to him a kind of Latin. He remembered a college friend of his, one Medway, now reading for the Bar, who had been the foremost scholar of his acquaintance; so with the scrap of paper in his pocket he climbed one evening to Medway's rooms in the Temple.

The man read the words curiously, and puzzled for a bit. "What's made you take to Latin comps so late in life, Colin? It's baddish, you know, even for you. I thought they'd have licked more into you at Eton."

Colin grinned with amusement. "I'll tell you about it later," he said. "Can you make out what it means?"

"It seems to be a kind of dog-Latin or monkish Latin or something of the sort," said Medway. "It reads like this: '*Soles occidere solent*' (that's cribbed from Catullus, and besides it's the regular monkish pun) . . . *qua* . . . then *blandula* something. Then there's a lot of Choctaw, and then *illæ insulæ dilectæ in quas festinant somnia animulæ gaudia*. That's pretty fair rot. Hullo, by George! here's something better—*Insula pomorum insula vitæ*. That's Geoffrey of Monmouth."

He made a dive to a bookcase and pulled out a battered little calf-bound duodecimo. "Here's all about your Isle of Apple-trees. Listen. 'Situate far out in the Western ocean, beyond the Utmost Islands, beyond even the little Isle of Sheep where the cairns of dead men are, lies the Island of Apple-trees where the heroes and princes of the nations live their second life.'" He closed the book and put it back. "It's the old ancient story, the Greek Hesperides, the British Avilion, and this Apple-tree Island is the Northern equivalent."

Colin sat entranced, his memory busy with a problem. Could he distinguish the scents of apple-trees among the perfumes of the Rim of the Mist? For the moment he thought he could. He was roused by Medway's voice asking the story of the writing.

"Oh, it's just some nonsense that was running in my head, so I wrote it down to see what it was."

"But you must have been reading. A new exercise for you, Colin!"

"No, I wasn't reading. Look here. You know the sort of pictures you make for yourself of places you like."

"Rather! Mine is a Yorkshire moor with a little red shooting-box in the heart of it."

"Well, mine is different. Mine is a sort of beach with a sea and a lot of islands somewhere far out. It is a jolly place, fresh, you know, and blowing, and smells good. 'Pon my word, now I think of it, there's always been a scent of apples."

"Sort of cider-press? Well, I must be off. You'd better come round to the club and see the telegrams about the war. *You* should be keen about it."

One evening, a week later, Medway met a friend called Tillotson at the club, and, being lonely, they dined together. Tillotson was a man of some note in science, a dabbler in psychology, an amateur historian, a ripe genealogist. They talked of politics and the war, of a new book, of Mrs. Runnymede, and finally of their hobbies.

"I am writing an article," said Tillotson. "Craikes asked me to do it for the *Monthly*. It's on a nice point in psychics. I call it 'The Transmission of Fallacies', but I do not mean the logical kind. The question is, Can a particular form of hallucination run in a family for generations? The proof must, of course, come from my genealogical studies. I maintain it can. I instance the Douglas-Ernotts, not one of whom can see straight with the left eye. That is one side. In another class of examples I take the Drapiers, who hate salt water and never go on board ship if they can help it. Then you remember the Durwards? Old Lady Balcrynie used to tell me that no one of the lot could ever stand the sight of a green frock. There's a chance for the romancer. The Manorwaters have the same madness, only their colour is red."

A vague remembrance haunted Medway's brain.

"I know a man who might give you points from his own case. Did you ever meet a chap Raden—Colin Raden?"

Tillotson nodded. "Long chap—in the Guards? 'Varsity oar, and used to be a crack bowler? No, I don't know him. I know him well by sight, and I should like to meet him tremendously—as a genealogist, of course."

"Why?" asked Medway.

"Why? Because the man's family is unique. You never hear much about them nowadays, but away up in that north-west corner of Scotland they have ruled since the days of Noah. Why, man, they were aristocrats when our Howards and Nevilles were greengrocers. I wish you would get this Raden to meet me some night."

"I am afraid there's no chance of it just at present," said Medway, taking up an evening paper. "I see that his regiment has gone to the front. But remind me when he comes back, and I'll be delighted."

III

AND now there began for Colin a curious divided life—without, a constant shifting of scene, days of heat and bustle and toil—within, a slow, tantalising, yet exquisite adventure. The Rim of the Mist was now no more the goal of his journeys, but the starting-point. Lying there, amid cool, fragrant sea-winds, his fanciful ear was subtly alert for the sounds of the dim land before him. Sleeping and waking the quest haunted him. As he flung himself on his bed the kerosene-filled air would change to an ocean freshness, the old boat would rock beneath him, and with dear eye and a boyish hope he would be waiting and watching. And then suddenly he would be back on shore, Cuna and the Acharra headland shining grey in the morning light, and with gritty mouth and sand-filled eyes he would awaken to the heat of the desert camp.

He was kept busy, for his good-humour and energy made him a willing slave, and he was ready enough for volunteer work when others were weak with heat and despair. A thirty-mile ride left him untired; more, he followed the campaign with a sharp intelligence and found a new enthusiasm for his profession. Discomforts there might be, but the days were happy; and then—the cool land, the bright land, which was his for the thinking of it.

Soon they gave him reconnoitring work to do, and his wits were put to the trial. He came well out of the thing, and earned golden praise from the silent colonel in command. He enjoyed it as he had enjoyed a hard race on the river or a good cricket match, and when his worried companions marvelled at his zeal he stammered and grew uncomfortable.

"How the deuce do you keep it up, Colin?" the major asked him. "I'm an old hand at the job, and yet I've got a temper like devilled bones. You seem as chirpy as if you were going out to fish a chalk-stream on a June morning."

"Well, the fact is—" and Colin pulled himself up short, knowing that he could never explain. He felt miserably that he had an unfair advantage of the others. Poor Bellew, who groaned and swore in the heat at his side, knew nothing of the Rim of the Mist. It was really rough luck on the poor beggars, and who but himself was the fortunate man?

As the days passed a curious thing happened. He found fragments of the Other world straying into his common life. The barriers of the two domains were falling, and more than once he caught himself looking at a steel-blue sea when his eyes should have found a mustard-coloured desert. One day, on a reconnoitring expedition, they stopped for a little on a hillock above a jungle of scrub, and, being hot and tired, scanned listlessly the endless yellow distances.

"I suppose yon hill is about ten miles off," said Bellew with dry lips. Colin looked vaguely. "I should say five."

"And what's that below it—the black patch? Stones or scrub?"

Colin was in a day-dream. "Why do you call it black? It's blue, quite blue."

"Rot," said the other. "It's grey-black."

"No, it's water with the sun shining on it. It's blue, but just at the edges it's very near sea-green."

173

Bellew rose excitedly. "Hullo, Col, you're seeing the mirage! And you the fittest of the lot of us! You've got the sun in your head, old man!"

"Mirage!" Colin cried in contempt. He was awake now, but the thought of confusing his own bright western sea with a mirage gave him a curious pain. For a moment he felt the gulf of separation between his two worlds, but only for a moment. As the party remounted he gave his fancies the rein, and ere he reached camp he had felt the oars in his hand and sniffed the apple-tree blossom from the distant beaches. The major came to him after supper.

"Bellew told me you were a bit odd today, Colin," he said. "I expect your eyes are getting baddish. Better get your sand-spectacles out."

Colin laughed. "Thanks. It's awfully good of you to bother, but I think Bellew took me up wrong. I never was fitter in my life."

By-and-by the turn came for pride to be humbled. A low desert fever took him, and though he went through the day as usual, it was with dreary lassitude; and at night, with hot hands clasped above his damp hair, he found sleep a hard goddess to conquer.

It was the normal condition of the others, so he had small cause to complain, but it worked havoc with his fancies. He had never been ill since his childish days, and this little fever meant much to one whose nature was poised on a needle-point. He found himself confronted with a hard bare world, with the gilt rubbed from its corners. The Rim of the Mist seemed a place of vague horrors; when he reached it his soul was consumed with terror; he struggled impotently to advance; behind him Cuna and the Acharra coast seemed a place of evil dreams. Again, as in his old fever, he was tormented with a devouring thirst, but the sea beside him was not fresh, but brackish as a rock-pool. He yearned for the apple-tree beaches in front; there, he knew, were cold springs of water; the fresh smell of it was blown towards him in his nightmare.

But as the days passed and the misery for all grew more intense, an odd hope began to rise in his mind. It could not last, coolness and health were waiting near, and his reason for the hope came from the odd events at the Rim of the Mist. The haze was clearing from the foreground, the surf-lined coast seemed nearer, and though all was obscure save the milk-white sand and the foam, yet here was earnest enough for him. Once more he became cheerful; weak and light-headed he rode out again; and the major, who was recovering from sun-stroke, found envy take the place of pity in his soul.

The hope was near fulfilment. One evening when the heat was changing into the cooler twilight, Colin and Bellew were sent with a small picked body to scour the foot-hills above the river in case of a flank attack during the night-march. It was work they had done regularly for weeks, and it is possible that precautions were relaxed. At any rate, as they turned a corner of hill, in a sandy pass where barren rocks looked down on more barren thorn thickets, a couple of rifle-shots rang out from the scarp, and above them appeared a line of dark faces and white steel. A mere handful, taken at a disadvantage, they could not hope to disperse numbers, so Colin gave the word to wheel about and return. Again shots rang out, and little Bellew had only time to catch at his friend's arm to save him from falling from the saddle.

The word of command had scarcely left Colin's mouth when a sharp pain went through his chest, and his breath seemed to catch and stop. He felt as in a condensed moment of time the heat, the desert smell, the dust in his eyes and throat, while he leaned helplessly forward on his horse's mane. Then the world vanished for him. . . . The boat was rocking under him, the oars in his hand. He pulled and it moved, straight, arrow-like towards the forbidden shore. As if under a great wind the mist furled up and fled. Scents of pines, of apple-trees, of great fields of thyme and heather, hung about him; the sound of wind in a forest, of cool waters falling in showers, of old moorland music, came thin and faint with an exquisite clearness. A second and the boat was among the surf, its gunwale ringed with white foam; as it leaped to the still waters beyond. Clear and deep and still the water lay, and then the white beaches shelved downward, and the boat grated on the sand. He turned, every limb alert with a strange new life, crying out words which had shaped themselves on his lips and which an echo seemed to catch and answer. There was the green forest before him, the hills of peace, the cold white waters. With a passionate joy he leaped on the beach, his arms outstretched to this new earth, this light of the world, this old desire of the heart—youth, rapture, immortality.

Bellew brought the body back to camp, himself half-dead with fatigue and whimpering like a child. He almost fell from his horse, and when others took his burden from him and laid it reverently in his tent, he stood beside it, rubbing sand and sweat from his poor purblind eyes, his teeth chattering with fever. He was given something to drink, but he swallowed barely a mouthful.

"It was some d-d-damned sharpshooter," he said. "Right through the breast, and he never spoke to me again. My poor old Col! He was the best chap God ever created, and I do-don't care a dash what becomes of me now. I was at school with him, you know, you men."

"Was he killed outright?" asked the major hoarsely.

"N-no. He lived for about five minutes. But I think the sun had got into his head or he was mad with pain, for he d-d-didn't know where he was. He kept crying out about the smell of pine-trees and heather and a lot of pure nonsense about water."

"*Et dulces reminiscitur Argos*," somebody quoted mournfully, as they went out to the desert evening.

THE OUTGOING OF THE TIDE[1]

"Between the hours of twelve and one,
even at the turning of the tide."

MEN come from distant parts to admire the tides of
Solloway, which race in at flood and retreat at ebb with
a greater speed than a horse can follow. But nowhere are there
queerer waters than in our own parish of Caulds, at the place
called the Sker Bay, where between two horns of land a shallow
estuary receives the stream of the Sker. I never daunder by its
shores, and see the waters hurrying like messengers from the
great deep, without solemn thoughts and a memory of Scripture
words on the terror of the sea. The vast Atlantic may be fearful
in its wrath, but with us it is no clean open rage, but the deceit
of the creature, the unholy ways of quicksands when the waters
are gone, and their stealthy return like a thief in the night-
watches. But in the times of which I write there were more awful
fears than any from the violence of nature. It was before the day
of my ministry in Caulds, for then I was a bit callant in short
clothes in my native parish of Lesmahagow; but the worthy
Doctor Chrystal, who had charge of spiritual things, has told me
often of the power of Satan and his emissaries in that lonely
place. It was the day of warlocks and apparitions, now happily
driven out by the zeal of the General Assembly. Witches pursued
their wanchancy calling, bairns were spirited away, young lassies
selled their souls to the evil one, and the Accuser of the Brethren
in the shape of a dark tyke was seen about cottage-doors in the
gloaming. Many and earnest were the prayers of good Doctor
Chrystal, but the evil thing in spite of his wrestling, grew and

[1] From the unpublished Remains of the Reverend John Dennistoun, sometime
minister of the Gospel in the parish of Caulds, and author of *Satan's Artifices against
the Elect*.

flourished in his midst. The parish stank of idolatry, abominable rites were practised in secret, and in all the bounds there was no one had a more evil name for this black traffic than one Alison Sempill, who bode at the Skerburnfoot.

The cottage stood nigh the burn in a little garden with lilyoaks and grosart-bushes lining the pathway. The Sker ran by in a linn among hollins, and the noise of its waters was ever about the place. The highroad on the other side was frequented by few, for a nearer-hand way to the west had been made through the Lowe Moss. Sometimes a herd from the hills would pass by with sheep, sometimes a tinkler or a wandering merchant, and once in a long while the laird of Heriotside on his grey horse riding to Gledsmuir. And they who passed would see Alison hirpling in her garden, speaking to herself like the ill wife she was, or sitting on a cutty-stool by the doorside with her eyes on other than mortal sights. Where she came from no man could tell. There were some said she was no woman, but a ghost haunting some mortal tenement. Others would threep she was gentrice, come of a persecuting family in the west, that had been ruined in the Revolution wars. She never seemed to want for siller; the house was as bright as a new preen, the yaird better delved than the manse garden; and there was routh of fowls and doos about the small steading, forbye a wheen sheep and milk-kye in the fields. No man ever saw Alison at any market in the countryside, and yet the Skerburnfoot was plenished yearly in all proper order. One man only worked on the place, a doited lad who had long been a charge to the parish, and who had not the sense to fear danger or the wit to understand it. Upon all other the sight of Alison, were it but for a moment, cast a cold grue, not to be remembered without terror. It seems she was not ordinarily ill-faured, as men use the word. She was maybe sixty years in age, small and trig, with her grey hair folded neatly under her mutch. But the sight of her eyes was not a thing to forget. John Dodds said they were the een of a deer with the devil ahint them, and indeed they would so appal an onlooker that a sudden unreasoning terror came into his heart, while his feet would impel him to flight. Once John, being overtaken in drink on the roadside by the cottage, and dreaming that he was burning in hell, woke, and saw the old wife hobbling towards him. Thereupon he fled soberly to the hills, and from that day became a quiet-living humble-minded Christian. She moved about the country like a wraith, gathering herbs in dark loanings, lingering in kirkyairds, and casting a blight on innocent bairns. Once Robert Smillie found her in a ruinous kirk on the Lang Muir where of old the idolatrous rites of Rome were practised. It was a hot day, and in the quiet place the flies buzzed in crowds, and he noted that she sat clothed in them as with a garment, yet suffering no discomfort. Then he, having mind of Beelzebub, the god of flies, fled without a halt homewards; but, falling in the Coo's Loan, broke two ribs and a collarbone, the whilk misfortune was much blessed to his soul. And there were darker tales in the country-side, of weans stolen, of lassies misguided, of innocent beasts cruelly tortured, and in one and all there came in the name of the wife of the Skerburnfoot. It was noted by them that kenned best that her cantrips were at their worst when the tides in the Sker Bay ebbed between the hours of twelve and one. At this season of the night the tides of mortality run lowest, and when the outgoing of these unco waters fell in with the setting of the current of life, then indeed was the hour for unholy revels. While honest men slept in their beds, the auld rudas carlines took their pleasure. That there is a delight in sin no man denies, but to most it is but a broken glint in the pauses of their conscience. But what must be the hellish joy of those lost beings who have forsworn God and trysted with the Prince of Darkness, it is not for a Christian to say. Certain it is that it must be great, though their master waits at the end of the road to claim the wizened things they call their souls. Serious men, notably Gidden Scott in the Back of the Hill and Simon Wauch in the Shieling of Chasehope, have seen Alison wandering on the wet sands, dancing to no earthly music, while the heavens, they said, were full of lights and sounds which betokened the presence of the prince of the powers of the air. It was a season of heart-searching for God's saints in Caulds, and the dispensation was blessed to not a few.

It will seem strange that in all this time the presbytery was idle, and no effort was made to rid the place of so fell an influence.

But there was a reason, and the reason, as in most like cases, was a lassie. Forbye Alison there lived at the Skerburnfoot a young maid, Ailie Sempill, who by all accounts was as good and bonnie as the other was evil. She passed for a daughter of Alison's, whether born in wedlock or not I cannot tell; but there were some said she was no kin to the auld witch-wife, but some bairn spirited away from honest parents. She was young and blithe, with a face like an April morning and a voice in her that put the laverocks to shame. When she sang in the kirk folk have told me that they had a foretaste of the music of the New Jerusalem, and when she came in by the village of Caulds old men stottered to their doors to look at her. Moreover, from her earliest days the bairn had some glimmerings of grace. Though no minister would visit the Skerburnfoot, or if he went, departed quicker than he came, the girl Ailie attended regular at the catechising at the Mains of Sker. It may be that Alison thought she would be a better offering for the devil if she were given the chance of forswearing God, or it may be that she was so occupied in her own dark business that she had no care of the bairn. Meanwhile the lass grew up in the nurture and admonition of the Lord. I have heard Doctor Chrystal say that he never had a communicant more full of the things of the Spirit. From the day when she first declared her wish to come forward to the hour when she broke bread at the table, she walked like one in a dream. The lads of the parish might cast admiring eyes on her bright cheeks and yellow hair as she sat in her white gown in the kirk, but well they knew she was not for them. To be the bride of Christ was the thought that filled her heart; and when at the fencing of the tables Doctor Chrystal preached from Matthew nine and fifteen, "Can the children of the bridechamber mourn, as long as the bridegroom is with them?" it was remarked by sundry that Ailie's face was liker the countenance of an angel than of a mortal lass.

It is with the day of her first communion that this narrative of mine begins. As she walked home after the morning table she communed in secret and her heart sang within her. She had mind of God's mercies in the past, how He had kept her feet from the snares of evil-doers which had been spread around her youth. She had been told unholy charms like the seven south streams and the nine rowan berries, and it was noted when she went first to the catechising that she prayed "Our Father which wert in Heaven," the prayer which the ill wife Alison had taught her, meaning by it Lucifer who had been in Heaven and had been cast out therefrom. But when she had come to years of discretion she had freely chosen the better part, and evil had ever been repelled from her soul like Gled water from the stones of Gled brig. Now she was in a rapture of holy content. The drucken bell—for the ungodly fashion lingered in Caulds—was ringing in her ears as she left the village, but to her it was but a kirk-bell and a goodly sound. As she went through the woods where the primroses and the whitethorn were blossoming, the place seemed as the land of Elam, wherein there were twelve wells and three-score and ten palm-trees. And then, as it might be, another thought came into her head, for it is ordained that frail mortality cannot long continue in holy joy. In the kirk she had been only the bride of Christ; but as she came through the wood, with the birds lilting and the winds of the world blowing, she had mind of another lover. For this lass, though so cold to men, had not escaped the common fate. It seemed that the young Heriotside, riding by one day, stopped to speir something or other, and got a glisk of Ailie's face, which caught his fancy. He passed the road again many times, and then he would meet her in the gloaming or of a morning in the field as she went to fetch the kye. "Blue are the hills that are far away" is an owercome in the countryside, and while at first on his side it may have been but a young man's fancy, to her he was like the god Apollo descending from the skies. He was good to look on, brawly dressed, and with a tongue in his head that would have wiled the bird from the tree. Moreover he was of gentle kin, and she was a poor lass biding in a cot-house with an ill-reputed mother. It seems that in time the young man, who had begun the affair with no good intentions, fell honestly in love, while she went singing about the doors as innocent as a bairn, thinking of him when her thoughts were not on higher things. So it came about that long ere Ailie reached home it was on young Heriotside that her mind dwelt, and it was the love of him that made her eyes glow and her cheeks redden.

Now it chanced that at that very hour her master had been with Alison, and the pair of them were preparing a deadly pit. Let no man say that the devil is not a cruel tyrant. He may give his folk some scrapings of unhallowed pleasure; but he will exact tithes, yea of anise and cummin, in return, and there is aye the reckoning to pay at the hinder end. It seems that now he was driving Alison hard. She had been remiss of late, fewer souls sent to hell, less zeal in quenching the Spirit, and above all the crowning offence that her bairn had communicated in Christ's kirk. She had waited overlong, and now it was like that Ailie would escape her toils. I have no skill of fancy to tell of that dark collogue, but the upshot was that Alison swore by her lost soul and the pride of sin to bring the lass into thrall to her master. The fiend had bare departed when Ailie came over the threshold to find the auld carline glunching by the fire.

It was plain she was in the worst of tempers. She flyted on the lass till the poor thing's cheek paled. "There you gang," she cried, "troking wi' thae wearifu' Pharisees o' Caulds, whae daurna darken your mither's door. A bonnie dutiful child, quotha! Wumman, hae ye nae pride?—no even the mense o' a tinkler-lass?" And then she changed her voice, and would be as soft as honey. "My puir wee Ailie! was I thrawn till ye? Never mind, my bonnie. You and me are a' that's left, and we maunna be ill to ither." And then the two had their dinner, and all the while the auld wife was crooning over the lass. "We maun 'gree weel," she says, "for we're like to be our lee-lane for the rest o' our days. They tell me Heriotside is seeking Joan o' the Croft, and they're sune to be cried in Gledsmuir kirk."

It was the first the lass had heard of it, and you may fancy she was struck dumb. And so with one thing and other the auld witch raised the fiends of jealousy in that innocent heart. She would cry out that Heriotside was an ill-doing wastrel, and had no business to come and flatter honest lassies. And then she would speak of his gentle birth and his leddy mother, and say it was indeed presumption to hope that so great a gentleman could mean all that he said. Before long Ailie was silent and white, while her mother rhymed on about men and their ways. And then she could thole it no longer, but must go out and walk by the burn to cool her hot brow and calm her thoughts, while the witch indoors laughed to herself at her devices.

For days Ailie had an absent eye and a sad face, and it so fell out that in all that time young Heriotside, who had scarce missed a day, was laid up with a broken arm and never came near her. So in a week's time she was beginning to hearken to her mother when she spoke of incantations and charms for restoring love. She kenned it was sin; but though not seven days syne she had sat at the Lord's table, so strong is love in a young heart that she was on the very brink of it. But the grace of God was stronger than her weak will. She would have none of her mother's runes and philters, though her soul cried out for them. Always when she was most disposed to listen some merciful power stayed her consent. Alison grew thrawner as the hours passed. She kenned of Heriotside's broken arm, and she feared that any day he might recover and put her stratagems to shame. And then it seems that she collogued with her master and heard word of a subtler device. For it was approaching that uncanny time of year, the festival of Beltane, when the auld pagans were wont to sacrifice to their god Baal. In this season warlocks and carlines have a special dispensation to do evil, and Alison waited on its coming with graceless joy. As it happened, the tides in the Sker Bay ebbed at this time between the hours of twelve and one, and, as I have said, this was the hour above all others when the powers of darkness were most potent. Would the lass but consent to go abroad in the unhallowed place at this awful season and hour of the night, she was as firmly handfasted to the devil as if she had signed a bond with her own blood. For there, it seemed, the forces of good fled far away, the world for one hour was given over to its ancient prince, and the man or woman who willingly sought the spot was his bond-servant for ever. There are deadly sins from which God's people may recover. A man may even communicate unworthily, and yet, so be it he sin not against the Holy Ghost, he may find forgiveness. But it seems that for this Beltane sin there could be no pardon, and I can testify from my own knowledge that they who once committed it became lost souls from that day. James Deuchar, once a promising professor, fell thus out of sinful bravery and died blaspheming; and of Kate Mallison, who went the same road, no man can tell. Here, indeed, was the witch-wife's chance, and she was the more keen, for her master had warned her that this was her last chance. Either Ailie's soul would be his, or her auld wrinkled body and black heart would be flung from this pleasant world to their apportioned place.

Some days later it happened that young Heriotside was stepping home over the Lang Muir about ten at night—it being his first jaunt from home since his arm had mended. He had been to the supper of the Forest Club at the Cross Keys in Gledsmuir, a clamjamfry of wild young blades who passed the wine and played at cartes once a fortnight. It seems he had drunk well, so that the world ran round about and he was in the best of tempers. The moon came down and bowed to him, and he took off his hat to it. For every step he travelled miles, so that in a little he was beyond Scotland altogether and pacing the Arabian desert. He thought he was the Pope of Rome, so he held out his foot to be kissed, and rolled twenty yards to the bottom of a small brae. Syne he was the King of France, and fought hard with a whin-bush till he had banged it to pieces. After that nothing would content him but he must be a bogle, for he found his head dunting on the stars and his legs were knocking the hills together. He thought of the mischief he was doing to the auld earth, and sat down and cried at his wickedness. Then he went on, and maybe the steep road to the Moss Rig helped him, for he began to get soberer and ken his whereabouts.

On a sudden he was aware of a man linking along at his side. He cried "A fine night," and the man replied. Syne, being merry from his cups, he tried to slap him on the back. The next he kenned he was rolling on the grass; for his hand had gone clean through the body and found nothing but air.

His head was so thick with wine that he found nothing droll in this. "Faith, friend," he says, "that was a nasty fall for a fellow that has supped weel. Where might your road be gaun to?"

"To the World's End," said the man; "but I stop at the Skerburnfoot."

"Bide the night at Heriotside," says he. "It's a thought out of your way, but it's a comfortable bit."

"There's mair comfort at the Skerburnfoot," said the dark man.

Now the mention of the Skerburnfoot brought back to him only the thought of Ailie and not of the witch-wife, her mother. So he jaloused no ill, for at the best he was slow in the uptake.

The two of them went on together for a while, Heriotside's fool head filled with the thought of the lass. Then the dark man broke silence. "Ye're thinkin' o' the maid Ailie Sempill," says he.

"How ken ye that?" asked Heriotside.

"It is my business to read the herts o' men," said the other.

"And who may ye be?" said Heriotside, growing eerie.

"Just an auld packman," said he—"nae name ye wad ken, but kin to mony gentle houses."

"And what about Ailie, you that ken sae muckle?" asked the young man.

"Naething," was the answer—"naething that concerns you, for ye'll never get the lass."

"By God, and I will!" says Heriotside, for he was a profane swearer.

"That's the wrong name to seek her in, anyway," said the man.

At this the young laird struck a great blow at him with his stick, but found nothing to resist him but the hill-wind.

When they had gone on a bit the dark man spoke again. "The lassie is thirled to holy things," says he. "She has nae care for flesh and blood, only for devout contemplation."

"She loves me," says Heriotside.

"Not you," says the other, "but a shadow in your stead." At this the young man's heart began to tremble, for it seemed that there was truth in what his companion said, and he was ower drunk to think gravely.

"I kenna whatna man ye are," he says, "but ye have the skill of lassies' hearts. Tell me truly, is there no way to win her to common love?"

"One way there is," said the man, "and for our friendship's sake I will tell it you. If ye can ever tryst wi' her on Beltane's Eve on the Sker sands, at the green link o' the burn where the sands begin, on the ebb o' the tide when the midnight is bye but afore cockcrow, she'll be yours, body and soul, for this world and for ever."

And then it appeared to the young man that he was walking his lone up the grass walk of Heriotside with the house close by him. He thought no more of the stranger he had met, but the word stuck in his heart.

It seems that about this very time Alison was telling the same tale to poor Ailie. She cast up to her every idle gossip she could think of. "It's Joan o' the Croft," was aye her owercome, and she would threep that they were to be cried in kirk on the first Sabbath of May. And then she would rhyme on about the black cruelty of it, and cry down curses on the lover, so that her daughter's heart grew cauld with fear. It is terrible to think of the power of the world even in a redeemed soul. Here was a maid who had drunk of the well of grace and tasted of God's mercies, and yet there were moments when she was ready to renounce her hope. At those awful seasons God seemed far off and the world very nigh, and to sell her soul for love looked a fair bargain. At other times she would resist the devil and comfort herself with prayer; but aye when she woke there was the sore heart, and when she went to sleep there were the weary eyes. There was no comfort in the goodliness of spring or the bright sunshine weather, and she who had been wont to go about the doors lightfoot and blithe was now as dowie as a widow woman.

And then one afternoon in the hinder end of April came young Heriotside riding to the Skerburnfoot. His arm was healed, he had got him a fine new suit of green, and his horse was a mettle beast that well set off his figure. Ailie was standing by the doorstep as he came down the road, and her heart stood still with joy. But a second thought gave her anguish. This man, so gallant and braw, would never be for her; doubtless the fine suit and the capering horse were for Joan o' the Croft's pleasure. And he in turn, when he remarked her wan cheek and dowie eyes, had mind of what the dark man said on the muir, and saw in her a maid sworn to no mortal love. Yet the passion for her had grown fiercer than ever, and he swore to himself that he would win her back from her phantasies. She, one may believe, was ready enough to listen. As she walked with him by the Sker Water his words were like music to her ears, and Alison within-doors laughed to herself and saw her devices prosper.

He spoke to her of love and his own heart, and the girl hearkened gladly. Syne he rebuked her coldness and cast scorn upon her piety, and so far was she beguiled that she had no answer. Then from one thing and another he spoke of some true token of their love. He said he was jealous, and craved something to ease his care. "It's but a small thing I ask," says he; "but it will make me a happy man, and nothing ever shall come atween us. Tryst wi' me for Beltane's Eve on the Sker sands, at the green link o' the burn where the sands begin; on the ebb o' the tide when midnight is bye but afore cockcrow. For," said he, "that was our forebears' tryst for true lovers, and wherefore no for you and me?"

The lassie had grace given her to refuse, but with a woful heart, and Heriotside rode off in black discontent, leaving poor Ailie to sigh her lone. He came back the next day and the next, but aye he got the same answer. A season of great doubt fell upon her soul. She had no dearness in her hope, nor any sense of God's promises. The Scriptures were an idle tale to her, prayer brought her no refreshment, and she was convicted in her conscience of the unpardonable sin. Had she been less full of pride she would have taken her troubles to good Doctor Chrystal and got comfort; but her grief made her silent and timorous, and she found no help anywhere. Her mother was ever at her side, seeking with coaxings and evil advice to drive her to the irrevocable step. And all the while there was her love for the man riving in her bosom and giving her no ease by night or day. She believed she had driven him away and repented her denial. Only her pride held her back from going to Heriotside and seeking him herself. She watched the road hourly for a sight of his face, and when the darkness came she would sit in a corner brooding over her sorrows.

At last he came, speiring the old question. He sought the same tryst, but now he had a further tale. It seemed he was eager to get her away from the Skerburnside and auld Alison. His aunt, the Lady Balcrynie, would receive her gladly at his request till the day of their marriage. Let her but tryst with him at the hour and place he named, and he would carry her straight to Balcrynie, where she would be safe and happy. He named that hour, he said, to escape men's observation for the sake of her own good name. He named that place, for it was near her dwelling, and on the road between Balcrynie and Heriotside, which fords the Sker Burn. The temptation was more than mortal heart could resist. She gave him the promise he sought, stifling the voice of conscience; and as she clung to his neck it seemed to her that Heaven was a poor thing compared with a man's love.

Three days remained till Beltane's Eve, and throughout the time it was noted that Heriotside behaved like one possessed. It may be that his conscience pricked him, or that he had a glimpse of his sin and its coming punishment. Certain it is that, if he had been daft before, he now ran wild in his pranks, and an evil report of him was in every mouth. He drank deep at the Cross Keys, and fought two battles with young lads that had angered him. One he let off with a touch on the shoulder, the other goes lame to this day from a wound he got in the groin. There was word of the procurator-fiscal taking note of his doings, and troth, if they had continued long he must have fled the country. For a wager he rode his horse down the Dow Craig, wherefore the name of the place is the Horseman's Craig to this day. He laid a hundred guineas with the laird of Slipperfield that he would drive four horses through the Slipperfield loch, and in the prank he had his bit chariot dung to pieces and a good mare killed. And all men observed that his eyes were wild and his face grey and thin, and that his hand would twitch as he held the glass, like one with the palsy.

The eve of Beltane was lown and hot in the low country, with fire hanging in the clouds and thunder grumbling about the heavens. It seems that up in the hills it had been an awesome deluge of rain, but on the coast it was still dry and lowering. It is a long road from Heriotside to the Skerburnfoot. First you go down the Heriot Water, and syne over the Lang Muir to the edge of Mucklewhan. When you pass the steadings of Mirehope and Cockmalane you turn to the right and ford the Mire Burn. That brings you on to the turnpike road, which you will ride till it bends inland, while you keep on straight over the Whinny Knowes to the Sker Bay. There, if you are in luck, you will find the tide out and the place fordable dryshod for a man on a horse. But if the tide runs, you will do well to sit down on the sands and content yourself till it turn, or it will be the solans and scarts of the Solloway that will be seeing the next of you. On this Beltane's Eve the young man, after supping with some wild young blades, bade his horse be saddled about ten o'clock. The company were eager to ken his errand, but he waved them back. "Bide here," he says, "and birl the wine till I return. This is a ploy of my own on which no man follows me." And there was that in his face as he spoke which chilled the wildest, and left them well content to keep to the good claret and the soft seat and let the daft laird go his own ways.

Well and on, he rode down the bridle-path in the wood, along the top of the Heriot glen, and as he rode he was aware of a great noise beneath him. It was not wind, for there was none, and it was not the sound of thunder, and aye as he speired at himself what it was it grew the louder till he came to a break in the trees. And then he saw the cause, for Heriot was coming down in a furious flood, sixty yards wide, tearing at the roots of the aiks, and flinging red waves against the drystone dykes. It was a sight and sound to solemnise a man's mind, deep calling unto deep, the great waters of the hills running to meet with the great waters of the sea. But Heriotside recked nothing of it, for his heart had but one thought and the eye of his fancy one figure. Never had he been so filled with love of the lass, and yet it was not happiness but a deadly secret fear.

As he came to the Lang Muir it was geyan dark, though there was a moon somewhere behind the clouds. It was little he could see of the road, and ere long he had tried many moss-pools and sloughs, as his braw new coat bare witness. Aye in front of him was the great hill of Mucklewhan, where the road turned down by the Mire. The noise of the Heriot had not long fallen behind him ere another began, the same eerie sound of burns crying to ither in the darkness. It seemed that the whole earth was overrun with waters. Every little runnel in the bog was astir, and yet the land around him was as dry as flax, and no drop of rain had fallen. As he rode on the din grew louder, and as he came over the top of Mirehope he kenned by the mighty rushing noise that something uncommon was happening with the Mire Burn. The light from Mirehope shieling twinkled on his left, and had the man not been dozened with his fancies he might have observed that the steading was deserted and men were crying below in the fields. But he rode on, thinking of but one thing, till he came to the cot-house of Cockmalane, which is nigh the fords of the Mire.

John Dodds, the herd who bode in the place, was standing at the door, and he looked to see who was on the road so late.

"Stop," says he, "stop, Laird Heriotside. I kenna what your errand is, but it is to no holy purpose that ye're out on Beltane Eve. D'ye no hear the warning o' the waters?"

And then in the still night came the sound of Mire like the clash of armies.

"I must win over the ford," says the laird quietly, thinking of another thing.

"Ford!" cried John in scorn. "There'll be nae ford for you the nicht unless it be the ford o' the river Jordan. The burns are up, and bigger than man ever saw them. It'll be a Beltane's Eve that a' folk will remember. They tell me that Gled valley is like a loch, and that there's an awesome folk drooned in the hills. Gin ye were ower the Mire, what about crossin' the Caulds and the Sker?" says he, for he jaloused he was going to Gledsmuir.

And then it seemed that that word brought the laird to his senses. He looked the airt the rain was coming from, and he saw it was the airt the Sker flowed. In a second, he has told me, the works of the devil were revealed to him. He saw himself a tool in Satan's hands, he saw his tryst a device for the destruction of the body, as it was assuredly meant for the destruction of the soul, and there came on his mind the picture of an innocent lass borne down by the waters with no place for repentance. His heart grew cold in his breast. He had but one thought, a sinful and reckless one—to get to her side, that the two might go together to their account. He heard the roar of the Mire as in a dream, and when John Dodds laid hands on his bridle he felled him to the earth. And the next seen of it was the laird riding the floods like a man possessed.

The horse was the grey stallion he aye rode, the very beast he had ridden for many a wager with the wild lads of the Cross Keys. No man but himself durst back it, and it had lamed many a hostler lad and broke two necks in its day. But it seemed it had the mettle for any flood, and took the Mire with little spurring. The herds on the hillside looked to see man and steed swept into eternity; but though the red waves were breaking about his shoulders and he was swept far down, he aye held on for the shore. The next thing the watchers saw was the laird struggling up the far bank, and casting his coat from him, so that he rode in his sark. And then he set off like a wildfire across the muir towards the turnpike road. Two men saw him on the road and have recorded their experience. One was a gangrel, by name M'Nab, who was travelling from Gledsmuir to Allerkirk with a heavy pack on his back and a bowed head. He heard a sound like wind afore him, and, looking up, saw coming down the road a grey horse stretched out to a wild gallop and a man on its back with a face like a soul in torment. He kenned not whether it was devil or mortal, but flung himself on the roadside, and lay like a corp for an hour or more till the rain aroused him. The other was one Sim Doolittle, the fish-hawker from Allerfoot, jogging home in his fish-cart from Gledsmuir fair. He had drunk more than was fit for him, and he was singing some light song, when he saw approaching, as he said, the pale horse mentioned in the Revelations, with Death seated as the rider. Thoughts of his sins came on him like a thunder-clap, fear loosened his knees, he leaped from the cart to the road, and from the road to the back of a dyke. Thence he flew to the hills, and was found the next morning far up among the Mire Craigs, while his horse and cart were gotten on the Aller sands, the horse lamed and the cart without the wheels.

At the tollhouse the road turns inland to Gledsmuir, and he who goes to Sker Bay must leave it and cross the wild land called the Whinny Knowes, a place rough with bracken and foxes' holes and old stone cairns. The tollman, John Gilzean, was opening his window to get a breath of air in the lown night when he heard or saw the approaching horse. He kenned the beast for Heriotside's, and, being a friend of the laird's, he ran down in all haste to open the yett, wondering to himself about the laird's errand on this night. A voice came down the road to him bidding him hurry; but John's old fingers were slow with the keys, and so it happened that the horse had to stop, and John had time to look up at the gash and woful face.

"Where away the nicht sae late, laird?" says John.

"I go to save a soul from hell," was the answer.

And then it seems that through the open door there came the chapping of a clock.

"Whatna hour is that?" asks Heriotside.

"Midnicht," says John, trembling, for he did not like the look of things.

There was no answer but a groan, and horse and man went racing down the dark hollows of the Whinny Knowes.

How he escaped a broken neck in that dreadful place no human being will ever tell. The sweat, he has told me, stood in cold drops upon his forehead; he scarcely was aware of the saddle in which he sat; and his eyes were stelled in his head, so that he saw nothing but the sky ayont him. The night was growing colder, and there was a small sharp wind stirring from the east. But, hot or cold, it was all one to him, who was already cold as death. He heard not the sound of the sea nor the peesweeps startled by his horse, for the sound that ran in his ears was the roaring Sker Water and a girl's cry. The thought kept goading him, and he spurred the grey till the creature was madder than himself. It leaped the hole which they call the Devil's Mull as I would step over a thistle, and the next he kenned he was on the edge of the Sker Bay.

It lay before him white and ghastly, with mist blowing in wafts across it and a slow swaying of the tides. It was the better part of a mile wide, but save for some fathoms in the middle where the Sker current ran, it was no deeper even at flood than a horse's fetlocks. It looks eerie at bright midday when the sun is shining and whaups are crying among the seaweeds; but think what it was on that awesome night with the powers of darkness brooding over it like a cloud. The rider's heart quailed for a moment in natural fear. He stepped his beast a few feet in, still staring afore him like a daft man. And then something in the sound or the feel of the waters made him look down, and he perceived that the ebb had begun and the tide was flowing out to sea.

He kenned that all was lost, and the knowledge drove him to stark despair. His sins came in his face like birds of night, and his heart shrank like a pea. He knew himself for a lost soul, and all that he loved in the world was out in the tides. There, at any rate, he could go too, and give back that gift of life he had so blackly misused. He cried small and soft like a bairn, and drove the grey out into the waters. And aye as he spurred it the foam should have been flying as high as his head; but in that uncanny hour there was no foam, only the waves running sleek like oil. It was not long ere he had come to the Sker channel, where the red moss-waters were roaring to the sea, an ill place to ford in midsummer heat, and certain death, as folks reputed it, at the smallest spate. The grey was swimming, but it seemed the Lord had other purposes for him than death, for neither man nor horse could drown. He tried to leave the saddle, but he could not; he flung the bridle from him, but the grey held on, as if some strong hand were guiding. He cried out upon the devil to help his own, he renounced his Maker and his God; but whatever his punishment, he was not to be drowned. And then he was silent, for something was coming down the tide.

It came down as quiet as a sleeping bairn, straight for him as he sat with his horse breasting the waters, and as it came the moon crept out of a cloud and he saw a glint of yellow hair. And then his madness died away and he was himself again, a weary and stricken man. He hung down over the tides and caught the body in his arms, and then let the grey make for the shallows. He cared no more for the devil and all his myrmidons, for he kenned brawly he was damned. It seemed to him that his soul had gone from him and he was as toom as a hazel-shell. His breath rattled in his throat, the tears were dried up in his head, his body had lost its strength, and yet he clung to the drowned maid as to a hope of salvation. And then he noted something at which he marvelled dumbly. Her hair was drookit back from her clay-cold brow, her eyes were shut, but in her face there was the peace of a child. It seemed even that her lips were smiling. Here, certes, was no lost soul, but one who had gone joyfully to meet her Lord. It may be in that dark hour at the burn-foot, before the spate caught her, she had been given grace to resist her adversary and flung herself upon God's mercy.

And it would seem that it had been granted, for when he came to the Skerburnfoot there in the corner sat the weird-wife Alison dead as a stone and shrivelled like a heather-birn.

For days Heriotside wandered the country or sat in his own house with vacant eye and trembling hands. Conviction of sin held him like a vice: he saw the lassie's death laid at his door, her face haunted him by day and night, and the word of the Lord dirled in his ears telling of wrath and punishment. The greatness of his anguish wore him to a shadow, and at last he was stretched on his bed and like to perish. In his extremity worthy Doctor Chrystal went to him unasked and strove to comfort him. Long, long the good man wrestled, but it seemed as if his ministrations were to be of no avail. The fever left his body, and he rose to stotter about the doors; but he was still in his torments, and the mercy-seat was far from him. At last in the back-end of the year came Mungo Muirhead to Caulds to the autumn communion, and nothing would serve him but he must try his hand at this storm-tossed soul. He spoke with power and unction, and a blessing came with his words, the black cloud lifted and showed a glimpse of grace, and in a little the man had some assurance of salvation. He became a pillar of Christ's Kirk, prompt to check abominations, notably the sin of witchcraft, foremost in good works; but with it all a humble man, who walked contritely till his death. When I came first to Caulds I sought to prevail upon him to accept the eldership, but he aye put me by, and when I heard his tale I saw that he had done wisely. I mind him well as he sat in his chair or daundered through Caulds, a kind word for everyone and sage counsel in time of distress, but withal a severe man to himself and a crucifier of the body. It seems that this severity weakened his frame, for three years syne come Martinmas he was taken ill with a fever, and after a week's sickness he went to his account, where I trust he is accepted.

THE WIND IN THE PORTICO

(HENRY NIGHTINGALE'S STORY)

A dry wind of the high places . . . not to fan nor to cleanse,
even a full wind from those places shall come unto me.

JEREMIAH IV: 11-12

NIGHTINGALE was a hard man to draw. His doings with the Bedawin had become a legend, but he would as soon have talked about them as claimed to have won the War. He was a slim dark fellow about thirty-five years of age, very short-sighted, and wearing such high-powered double glasses that it was impossible to tell the colour of his eyes. This weakness made him stoop a little and peer, so that he was the strangest figure to picture in a burnous leading an army of desert tribesmen. I fancy his power came partly from his oddness, for his followers thought that the hand of Allah had been laid on him, and partly from his quick imagination and his flawless courage. After the War he had gone back to his Cambridge fellowship, declaring that, thank God, that chapter in his life was over.

As I say, he never mentioned the deeds which had made him famous. He knew his own business, and probably realised that to keep his mental balance he had to drop the curtain on what must have been the most nerve-racking four years ever spent by man. We respected his decision and kept off Arabia. It was a remark of Hannay's that drew from him the following story. Hannay was talking about his Cotswold house, which was on the Fosse Way, and saying that it always puzzled him how so elaborate a civilisation as Roman Britain could have been destroyed utterly and left no mark on the national history beyond a few roads and ruins and place-names. Peckwether, the historian, demurred, and had a good deal to say about how much the Roman tradition was woven into the Saxon culture. "Rome only sleeps," he said; "she never dies."

Nightingale nodded. "Sometimes she dreams in her sleep and talks. Once she scared me out of my senses."

After a good deal of pressing he produced this story. He was not much of a talker, so he wrote it out and read it to us.

There is a place in Shropshire which I do not propose to visit again. It lies between Ludlow and the hills, in a shallow valley full of woods. Its name is St. Sant, a village with a big house and park adjoining, on a stream called the Vaun, about five miles from the little town of Faxeter. They have queer names in those parts, and other things queerer than the names.

I was motoring from Wales to Cambridge at the close of the long vacation. All this happened before the War, when I had just got my fellowship and was settling down to academic work. It was a fine night in early October, with a full moon, and I intended to push on to Ludlow for supper and bed. The time was about half-past eight, the road was empty and good going, and I was trundling pleasantly along when something went wrong with my headlights. It was a small thing, and I stopped to remedy it beyond a village and just at the lodge-gates of a house.

On the opposite side of the road a carrier's cart had drawn up, and two men, who looked like indoor servants, were lifting some packages from it on to a big barrow. The moon was up, so I didn't need the feeble light of the carrier's lamp to see what they were doing. I suppose I wanted to stretch my legs for a moment, for when I had finished my job I strolled over to them. They did not hear me coming, and the carrier on his perch seemed to be asleep.

The packages were the ordinary consignments from some big shop in town. But I noticed that the two men handled them very gingerly, and that, as each was laid in the barrow, they clipped off the shop label and affixed one of their own. The new labels were odd things, large and square, with some address written on them in very black capital letters. There was nothing in that, but the men's faces puzzled me. For they seemed to do their job in a fever, longing to get it over and yet in a sweat lest they should make some mistake. Their commonplace task seemed to be for them a matter of tremendous importance. I moved so as to get a view of their faces, and I saw that they were white and strained. The two were of the butler or valet class, both elderly, and I could have sworn that they were labouring under something like fear.

I shuffled my feet to let them know of my presence and remarked that it was a fine night. They started as if they had been robbing a corpse. One of them mumbled something in reply, but the other caught a package which was slipping, and in a tone of violent alarm growled to his mate to be careful. I had a notion that they were handling explosives.

I had no time to waste, so I pushed on. That night, in my room at Ludlow, I had the curiosity to look up my map and identify the place where I had seen the men. The village was St. Sant, and it appeared that the gate I had stopped at belonged to a considerable demesne called Vauncastle. That was my first visit.

At that time I was busy on a critical edition of Theocritus, for which I was making a new collation of the manuscripts. There was a variant of the Medicean Codex in England, which nobody had seen since Gaisford, and after a good deal of trouble I found that it was in the library of a man called Dubellay. I wrote to him at his London club, and got a reply to my surprise from Vauncastle Hall, Faxeter. It was an odd letter, for you could see that he longed to tell me to go to the devil, but couldn't quite reconcile it with his conscience. We exchanged several letters, and the upshot was that he gave me permission to examine his manuscript. He did not ask me to stay, but mentioned that there was a comfortable little inn in St. Sant.

My second visit began on the 27th of December, after I had been home for Christmas. We had had a week of severe frost, and then it had thawed a little; but it remained bitterly cold, with leaden skies that threatened snow. I drove from Faxeter, and as we ascended the valley I remember thinking that it was a curiously sad country. The hills were too low to be impressive, and their outlines were mostly blurred with woods; but the tops showed clear, funny little knolls of grey bent that suggested a volcanic origin. It might have been one of those backgrounds you find in Italian primitives, with all the light and colour left out. When I got a glimpse of the Vaun in the bleached meadows it looked like the "wan water" of the Border ballads. The woods, too, had not the friendly bareness of English copses in winter-time. They remained dark and cloudy, as if they were hiding secrets. Before I reached St. Sant, I decided that the landscape was not only sad, but ominous.

I was fortunate in my inn. In the single street of one-storied cottages it rose like a lighthouse, with a cheery glow from behind the red curtains of the bar parlour. The inside proved as good as the outside. I found a bedroom with a bright fire, and I dined in a wainscoted room full of preposterous old pictures of lanky hounds and hollow-backed horses. I had been rather depressed on my journey, but my spirits were raised by this comfort, and when the house produced a most respectable bottle of port I had the landlord in to drink a glass. He was an ancient man who had been a gamekeeper, with a much younger wife, who was respon-sible for the management. I was curious to hear something about the owner of my manuscript, but I got little from the landlord. He had been with the old squire, and had never served the present one. I heard of Dubellays in plenty—the landlord's master, who had hunted his own hounds for forty years, the Major his brother, who had fallen at Abu Klea; Parson Jack, who had had the living till he died, and of all kinds of collaterals. The "Deblays" had been a high-spirited, open-handed stock, and much liked in the place. But of the present master of the Hall he could or would tell me nothing. The Squire was a "great scholard", but I gathered that he followed no sport and was not a convivial soul like his predecessors. He had spent a mint of money on the house, but not many people went there. He, the landlord, had never been inside the grounds in the new master's time, though in the old days there had been hunt breakfasts on the lawn for the whole countryside, and mighty tenantry dinners. I went to bed with a clear picture in my mind of the man I was to interview on the morrow. A scholarly and autocratic recluse, who collected treasures and beautified his dwelling and probably lived in his library. I rather looked forward to meeting him, for the bonhomous sporting squire was not much in my line.

After breakfast next morning I made my way to the Hall. It was the same leaden weather, and when I entered the gates the air seemed to grow bitterer and the skies darker. The place was muffled in great trees which even in their winter bareness made a pall about it. There was a long avenue of ancient sycamores, through which one caught only rare glimpses of the frozen park. I took my bearings, and realised that I was walking nearly due south, and was gradually descending. The house must be in a hollow. Presently the trees thinned, I passed through an iron gate, came out on a big untended lawn, untidily studden with laurels and rhododendrons, and there before me was the house front.

I had expected something beautiful—an old Tudor or Queen Anne façade or a dignified Georgian portico. I was disappointed, for the front was simply mean. It was low and irregular, more like the back parts of a house, and I guessed that at some time or another the building had been turned round, and the old kitchen door made the chief entrance. I was confirmed in my conclusion by observing that the roofs rose in tiers, like one of those recessed New York sky-scrapers, so that the present back parts of the building were of an impressive height.

The oddity of the place interested me, and still more its dilapidation. What on earth could the owner have spent his money on? Everything—lawn, flower-beds, paths—was neglected. There was a new stone doorway, but the walls badly needed pointing, the window woodwork had not been painted for ages, and there were several broken panes. The bell did not ring, so I was reduced to hammering on the knocker, and it must have been ten minutes before the door opened. A pale butler, one of the men I had seen at the carrier's cart the October before, stood blinking in the entrance.

He led me in without question, when I gave my name, so I was evidently expected. The hall was my second surprise. What had become of my picture of the collector? The place was small and poky, and furnished as barely as the lobby of a farm-house. The only thing I approved was its warmth. Unlike most English country-houses there seemed to be excellent heating arrangements.

I was taken into a little dark room with one window that looked out on a shrubbery, while the man went to fetch his master. My chief feeling was of gratitude that I had not been asked to stay, for the inn was paradise compared with this sepulchre. I was examining the prints on the wall, when I heard my name spoken and turned round to greet Mr. Dubellay.

He was my third surprise. I had made a portrait in my mind of a fastidious old scholar, with eye-glasses on a black cord, and a finical *weltkind*-ish manner. Instead I found a man still in early middle age, a heavy fellow dressed in the roughest country tweeds. He was as untidy as his demesne, for he had not shaved that morning, his flannel collar was badly frayed, and his finger-nails would have been the better for a scrubbing brush. His face was hard to describe. It was high-coloured, but the colour was not healthy; it was friendly, but it was also wary; above all, it was *unquiet*. He gave me the impression of a man whose nerves were all wrong, and who was perpetually on his guard.

He said a few civil words, and thrust a badly tied brown paper parcel at me. "That's your manuscript," he said jauntily.

I was staggered. I had expected to be permitted to collate the codex in his library, and in the last few minutes had realised that the prospect was distasteful. But here was this casual owner offering me the priceless thing to take away.

I stammered my thanks, and added that it was very good of him to trust a stranger with such a treasure.

"Only as far as the inn," he said. "I wouldn't like to send it by post. But there's no harm in your working at it at the inn. There should be confidence among scholars." And he gave an odd cackle of a laugh.

"I greatly prefer your plan," I said. "But I thought you would insist on my working at it here."

"No, indeed," he said earnestly. "I shouldn't think of such a thing. . . . Wouldn't do at all. . . . An insult to our free-masonry. . . . That's how I should regard it."

We had a few minutes' further talk. I learned that he had inherited under the entail from a cousin, and had been just over ten years at Vauncastle. Before that he had been a London solicitor. He asked me a question or two about Cambridge—

wished he had been at the University—much hampered in his work by a defective education. I was a Greek scholar?—Latin, too he presumed. Wonderful people the Romans. . . . He spoke quite freely, but all the time his queer restless eyes were darting about, and I had a strong impression that he would have liked to say something to me very different from these commonplaces— that he was longing to broach some subject but was held back by shyness or fear. He had such an odd appraising way of looking at me.

I left without his having asked me to a meal, for which I was not sorry, for I did not like the atmosphere of the place. I took a short cut over the ragged lawn, and turned at the top of the slope to look back. The house was in reality a huge pile, and I saw that I had been right and that the main building was all at the back. Was it, I wondered, like the Alhambra, which behind a front like a factory concealed a treasure-house? I saw, too, that the woodland hollow was more spacious than I had fancied. The house, as at present arranged, faced due north, and behind the south front was an open space in which I guessed that a lake might lie. Far beyond I could see in the December dimness the lift of high dark hills.

That evening the snow came in earnest, and fell continuously for the better part of two days. I banked up the fire in my bedroom and spent a happy time with the codex. I had brought only my working books with me and the inn boasted no library, so when I wanted to relax I went down to the tap-room, or gossiped with the landlady in the bar parlour. The yokels who congregated in the former were pleasant fellows, but, like all the folk on the Marches, they did not talk readily to a stranger and I heard little from them of the Hall. The old squire had reared every year three thousand pheasants, but the present squire would not allow a gun to be fired on his land and there were only a few wild birds left. For the same reason the woods were thick with vermin. This they told me when I professed an interest in shooting. But of Mr. Dubellay they would not speak, declaring that they never saw him. I dare say they gossiped wildly about him, and their public reticence struck me as having in it a touch of fear.

The landlady, who came from a different part of the shire, was more communicative. She had not known the former Dubellays and so had no standard of comparison, but she was inclined to regard the present squire as not quite right in the head. "They do say," she would begin, but she, too, suffered from some inhibition, and what promised to be sensational would tail off into the commonplace. One thing apparently puzzled the neighbourhood above others, and that was his rearrangement of the house. "They do say," she said in an awed voice, "that he have built a great church." She had never visited it—no one in the parish had, for Squire Dubellay did not allow intruders—but from Lyne Hill you could see it through a gap in the woods. "He's no good Christian," she told me, "and him and Vicar has quarrelled this many a day. But they do say as he worships summat there." I learned that there were no women servants in the house, only the men he had brought from London. "Poor benighted souls, they must live in a sad hobble," and the buxom lady shrugged her shoulders and giggled.

On the last day of December I decided that I needed exercise and must go for a long stride. The snow had ceased that morning, and the dull skies had changed to a clear blue. It was still very cold, but the sun was shining, the snow was firm and crisp underfoot, and I proposed to survey the country. So after luncheon I put on thick boots and gaiters, and made for Lyne Hill. This meant a considerable circuit, for the place lay south of the Vauncastle park. From it I hoped to get a view of the other side of the house.

I was not disappointed. There was a rift in the thick woodlands, and below me, two miles off, I suddenly saw a strange building, like a classical temple. Only the entablature and the tops of the pillars showed above the trees, but they stood out vivid and dark against the background of snow. The spectacle in that lonely place was so startling that for a little I could only stare. I remember that I glanced behind me to the snowy line of the Welsh mountains, and felt that I might have been looking at a winter-view of the Apennines two thousand years ago.

My curiosity was now alert, and I determined to get a nearer view of this marvel. I left the track and ploughed through the snowy fields down to the skirts of the woods. After that my troubles began. I found myself in a very good imitation of a primeval forest, where the undergrowth had been unchecked and the rides uncut for years. I sank into deep pits, I was savagely torn by briars and brambles, but I struggled on, keeping a line as best I could. At last the trees stopped. Before me was a flat expanse which I knew must be a lake, and beyond rose the temple.

It ran the whole length of the house, and from where I stood it was hard to believe that there were buildings at its back where men dwelt. It was a fine piece of work—the first glance told me that—admirably proportioned, classical, yet not following exactly any of the classical models. One could imagine a great echoing interior dim with the smoke of sacrifice, and it was only by reflecting that I realised that the peristyle could not be continued down the two sides, that there was no interior, and that what I was looking at was only a portico.

The thing was at once impressive and preposterous. What madness had been in Dubellay when he embellished his house with such a grandiose garden front? The sun was setting and the shadow of the wooded hills darkened the interior, so I could not even make out the back wall of the porch. I wanted a nearer view, so I embarked on the frozen lake.

Then I had an odd experience. I was not tired, the snow lay level and firm, but I was conscious of extreme weariness. The biting air had become warm and oppressive. I had to drag boots that seemed to weigh tons across that lake. The place was utterly silent in the stricture of the frost, and from the pile in front no sign of life came.

I reached the other side at last and found myself in a frozen shallow of bulrushes and skeleton willow-herbs. They were taller than my head, and to see the house I had to look upward through their snowy traceries. It was perhaps eighty feet above me and a hundred yards distant and, since I was below it, the delicate pillars seemed to spring to a great height. But it was still dusky, and the only detail I could see was on the ceiling, which seemed either to be carved or painted with deeply-shaded monochrome figures.

Suddenly the dying sun came slanting through the gap in the hills, and for an instant the whole portico to its farthest recesses was washed in clear gold and scarlet. That was wonderful enough, but there was something more. The air was utterly still with not the faintest breath of wind—so still that when I had lit a cigarette half an hour before the flame of the match had burned steadily upward like a candle in a room. As I stood among the sedges not a single frost crystal stirred. . . . But there was a wind blowing in the portico.

I could see it lifting feathers of snow from the base of the pillars and fluffing the cornices. The floor had already been swept clean, but tiny flakes drifted on to it from the exposed edges. The interior was filled with a furious movement, though a yard from it was frozen peace. I felt nothing of the action of the wind, but I knew that it was hot, hot as the breath of a furnace.

I had only one thought, dread of being overtaken by night near that place. I turned and ran. Ran with labouring steps across the lake, panting and stifling with a deadly hot oppression, ran blindly by a sort of instinct in the direction of the village. I did not stop till I had wrestled through the big wood, and come out on some rough pasture above the highway. Then I dropped on the ground, and felt again the comforting chill of the December air.

The adventure left me in an uncomfortable mood. I was ashamed of myself for playing the fool, and at the same time hopelessly puzzled, for the oftener I went over in my mind the incidents of that afternoon the more I was at a loss for an explanation. One feeling was uppermost, that I did not like this place and wanted to be out of it. I had already broken the back of my task, and by shutting myself up for two days I completed it; that is to say, I made my collation as far as I had advanced myself in my commentary on the text. I did not want to go back to the Hall, so I wrote a civil note to Dubellay, expressing my gratitude and saying that I was sending up the manuscript by the landlord's son, as I scrupled to trouble him with another visit.

I got a reply at once, saying that Mr. Dubellay would like to give himself the pleasure of dining with me at the inn before I went, and would receive the manuscript in person.

It was the last night of my stay in St. Sant, so I ordered the best dinner the place could provide, and a magnum of claret, of which I discovered a bin in the cellar. Dubellay appeared promptly at eight o'clock, arriving to my surprise in a car. He had tidied himself up and put on a dinner jacket, and he looked exactly like the city solicitors you see dining in the Junior Carlton.

He was in excellent spirits, and his eyes had lost their air of being on guard. He seemed to have reached some conclusion about me, or decided that I was harmless. More, he seemed to be burning to talk to me. After my adventure I was prepared to find fear in him, the fear I had seen in the faces of the men-servants. But there was none; instead there was excitement, overpowering excitement.

He neglected the courses in his verbosity. His coming to dinner had considerably startled the inn, and instead of a maid the landlady herself waited on us. She seemed to want to get the meal over, and hustled the biscuits and the port on to the table as soon as she decently could. Then Dubellay became confidential.

He was an enthusiast, it appeared, an enthusiast with a single hobby. All his life he had pottered among antiquities, and when he succeeded to Vauncastle he had the leisure and money to indulge himself. The place, it seemed, had been famous in Roman Britain—Vauni Castra—and Faxeter was a corruption of the same. "Who was Vaunus?" I asked. He grinned, and told me to wait.

There had been an old temple up in the high woods. There had always been a local legend about it, and the place was supposed to be haunted. Well, he had had the site excavated and he had found— Here he became the cautious solicitor, and explained to me the law of treasure trove. As long as the objects found were not intrinsically valuable, not gold or jewels, the finder was entitled to keep them. He had done so—had not published the results of his excavations in the proceedings of any learned society—did not want to be bothered by tourists. I was different, for I was a scholar.

What had he found? It was really rather hard to follow his babbling talk, but I gathered that he had found certain carvings and sacrificial implements. And—he sunk his voice—most important of all, an altar, an altar of Vaunus, the tutelary deity of the vale. When he mentioned this word his face took on a new look—not of fear but of secrecy, a kind of secret excitement. I have seen the same look on the face of a street-preaching Salvationist.

Vaunus had been a British god of the hills, whom the Romans in their liberal way appear to have identified with Apollo. He gave me a long confused account of him, from which it appeared that Mr. Dubellay was not an exact scholar. Some of his derivations of place-names were absurd—like St. Sant from Sancta Sanctorum—and in quoting a line of Ausonius he made two false quantities. He seemed to hope that I could tell him something more about Vaunus, but I said that my subject was Greek, and that I was deeply ignorant about Roman Britain. I mentioned several books, and found that he had never heard of Haverfield.

One word he used, "hypocaust", which suddenly gave me a clue. He must have heated the temple, as he heated his house, by some very efficient system of hot air. I know little about science, but I imagined that the artificial heat of the portico, as contrasted with the cold outside, might create an air current. At any rate that explanation satisfied me, and my afternoon's adventure lost its uncanniness. The reaction made me feel friendly towards him, and I listened to his talk with sympathy, but I decided not to mention that I had visited his temple.

He told me about it himself in the most open way. "I couldn't leave the altar on the hillside," he said. "I had to make a place for it, so I turned the old front of the house into a sort of temple. I got the best advice, but architects are ignorant people, and I often wished I had been a better scholar. Still the place satisfies me."

"I hope it satisfies Vaunus," I said jocularly.

"I think so," he replied quite seriously, and then his thoughts seemed to go wandering, and for a minute or so he looked through me with a queer abstraction in his eyes.

"What do you do with it now you've got it?" I asked.

He didn't reply, but smiled to himself.

"I don't know if you remember a passage in Sidonius Apollinaris," I said, "a formula for consecrating pagan altars to Christian uses. You begin by sacrificing a white cock or something suitable, and tell Apollo with all friendliness that the old dedication is off for the present. Then you have a Christian invocation—"

He nearly jumped out of his chair.

"That wouldn't do—wouldn't do at all! . . . Oh Lord, no! . . . Couldn't think of it for one moment!"

It was as if I had offended his ears by some horrid blasphemy, and the odd thing was that he never recovered his composure. He tried, for he had good manners, but his ease and friendliness had gone. We talked stiffly for another half-hour about trifles, and then he rose to leave. I returned him his manuscript neatly parcelled up, and expanded in thanks, but he scarcely seemed to heed me. He stuck the thing in his pocket, and departed with the same air of shocked absorption.

After he had gone I sat before the fire and reviewed the situation. I was satisfied with my hypocaust theory, and had no more perturbation in my memory about my afternoon's adventure. Yet a slight flavour of unpleasantness hung about it, and I felt that I did not quite like Dubellay. I set him down as a crank who had tangled himself up with a half-witted hobby, like an old maid with her cats, and I was not sorry to be leaving the place.

My third and last visit to St. Sant was in the following June— the midsummer of 1914. I had all but finished my Theocritus, but I needed another day or two with the Vauncastle manuscript, and, as I wanted to clear the whole thing off before I went to Italy in July, I wrote to Dubellay and asked if I might have another sight of it. The thing was a bore, but it had to be faced, and I fancied that the valley would be a pleasant place in that hot summer.

I got a reply at once, inviting, almost begging me to come, and insisting that I should stay at the Hall. I couldn't very well refuse, though I would have preferred the inn. He wired about my train, and wired again saying he would meet me. This time I seemed to be a particularly welcome guest.

I reached Faxeter in the evening, and was met by a car from a Faxeter garage. The driver was a talkative young man, and, as the car was a closed one, I sat beside him for the sake of fresh air. The term had tired me, and I was glad to get out of stuffy Cambridge, but I cannot say that I found it much cooler as we ascended the Vaun valley. The woods were in their summer magnificence but a little dulled and tarnished by the heat, the river was shrunk to a trickle, and the curious hilltops were so scorched by the sun that they seemed almost yellow above the green of the trees. Once again I had the feeling of a landscape fantastically un-English.

"Squire Dubellay's been in a great way about your coming, sir," the driver informed me. "Sent down three times to the boss to make sure it was all right. He's got a car of his own, too, a nice little Daimler, but he don't seem to use it much. Haven't seen him about in it for a month of Sundays."

As we turned in at the Hall gates he looked curiously about him. "Never been here before, though I've been in most gentlemen's parks for fifty miles round. Rum old-fashioned spot, isn't it, sir?"

If it had seemed a shuttered sanctuary in midwinter, in that June twilight it was more than ever a place enclosed and guarded. There was almost an autumn smell of decay, a dry decay like touchwood. We seemed to be descending through layers of ever-thickening woods. When at last we turned through the iron gate I saw that the lawns had reached a further stage of neglect, for they were as shaggy as a hayfield.

The white-faced butler let me in, and there, waiting at his back, was Dubellay. But he was not the man whom I had seen in December. He was dressed in an old baggy suit of flannels, and his unwholesome red face was painfully drawn and sunken. There were dark pouches under his eyes, and these eyes were no longer excited, but dull and pained. Yes, and there was more than pain in them—there was fear. I wondered if his hobby were becoming too much for him.

He greeted me like a long-lost brother. Considering that I scarcely knew him, I was a little embarrassed by his warmth. "Bless you for coming, my dear fellow," he cried. "You want a wash and then we'll have dinner. Don't bother to change, unless you want to. I never do." He led me to my bedroom, which was clean enough but small and shabby like a servant's room. I guessed that he had gutted the house to build his absurd temple.

We dined in a fair-sized room which was a kind of library. It was lined with old books, but they did not look as if they had been there long; rather it seemed like a lumber room in which a fine collection had been stored. Once no doubt they had lived in a dignified Georgian chamber. There was nothing else, none of the antiques which I had expected.

"You have come just in time," he told me. "I fairly jumped when I got your letter, for I had been thinking of running up to Cambridge to insist on your coming down here. I hope you're in no hurry to leave."

"As it happens," I said, "I *am* rather pressed for time, for I hope to go abroad next week. I ought to finish my work here in a couple of days. I can't tell you how much I'm in your debt for your kindness."

"Two days," he said. "That will get us over midsummer. That should be enough." I hadn't a notion what he meant.

I told him that I was looking forward to examining his collection. He opened his eyes. "Your discoveries, I mean," I said, "the altar of Vaunus . . ."

As I spoke the words his face suddenly contorted in a spasm of what looked like terror. He choked and then recovered himself. "Yes, yes," he said rapidly. "You shall see it—you shall see everything—but not now—not tonight. Tomorrow—in broad daylight—that's the time."

After that the evening became a bad dream. Small talk deserted him, and he could only reply with an effort to my commonplaces. I caught him often looking at me furtively, as if he were sizing me up and wondering how far he could go with me. The thing fairly got on my nerves, and to crown all it was abominably stuffy. The windows of the room gave on a little paved court with a background of laurels, and I might have been in Seven Dials for all the air there was.

When coffee was served I could stand it no longer. "What

about smoking in the temple?" I said. "It should be cool there with the air from the lake."

I might have been proposing the assassination of his mother. He simply gibbered at me. "No, no," he stammered. "My God, no!" It was half an hour before he could properly collect himself. A servant lit two oil lamps, and we sat on in the frowsty room.

"You said something when we last met," he ventured at last, after many a sidelong glance at me. "Something about a ritual for re-dedicating an altar."

I remembered my remark about Sidonius Apollinaris.

"Could you show me the passage? There is a good classical library here, collected by my great-grandfather. Unfortunately my scholarship is not equal to using it properly."

I got up and hunted along the shelves, and presently found a copy of Sidonius, the Plantin edition of 1609. I turned up the passage, and roughly translated it for him. He listened hungrily and made me repeat it twice.

"He says a cock," he hesitated. "Is that essential?"

"I don't think so. I fancy any of the recognised ritual stuff would do."

"I am glad," he said simply. "I am afraid of blood."

"Good God, man," I cried out, "are you taking my nonsense seriously? I was only chaffing. Let old Vaunus stick to his altar!"

He looked at me like a puzzled and rather offended dog.

"Sidonius was in earnest . . ."

"Well, I'm not," I said rudely. "We're in the twentieth century and not in the third. Isn't it about time we went to bed?"

He made no objection, and found me a candle in the hall. As I undressed I wondered into what kind of lunatic asylum I had strayed. I felt the strongest distaste for the place, and longed to go straight off to the inn; only I couldn't make use of a man's manuscripts and insult his hospitality. It was fairly clear to me that Dubellay was mad. He had ridden his hobby to the death of his wits and was now in its bondage. Good Lord! he had talked of his precious Vaunus as a votary talks of a god. I believed he had come to worship some figment of his half-educated fancy.

I think I must have slept for a couple of hours. Then I woke dripping with perspiration, for the place was simply an oven. My window was as wide open as it would go, and, though it was a warm night, when I stuck my head out the air was fresh. The heat came from indoors. The room was on the first floor near the entrance and I was looking on to the overgrown lawns. The night was very dark and utterly still, but I could have sworn that I heard wind. The trees were as motionless as marble, but somewhere close at hand I heard a strong gust blowing. Also, though there was no moon, there was somewhere near me a steady glow of light; I could see the reflection of it round the end of the house. That meant that it came from the temple. What kind of saturnalia was Dubellay conducting at such an hour?

When I drew in my head I felt that if I was to get any sleep something must be done. There could be no question about it; some fool had turned on the steam heat, for the room was a furnace. My temper was rising. There was no bell to be found, so I lit my candle and set out to find a servant.

I tried a cast downstairs and discovered the room where we had dined. Then I explored a passage at right angles, which brought me up against a great oak door. The light showed me that it was a new door, and that there was no apparent way of opening it. I guessed that it led into the temple, and, though it fitted close and there seemed to be no key-hole, I could hear through it a sound like a rushing wind. . . . Next I opened a door on my right and found myself in a big store cupboard. It had a funny, exotic, spicy smell, and, arranged very neatly on the floor and shelves, was a number of small sacks and coffers. Each bore a label, a square of stout paper with very black lettering. I read "*Pro servitio Vauni.*"

I had seen them before, for my memory betrayed me if they were not the very labels that Dubellay's servants had been attaching to the packages from the carrier's cart that evening in the past autumn. The discovery made my suspicions an unpleasant certainty. Dubellay evidently meant the labels to read "For the service of Vaunus." He was no scholar, for it was an impossible use of the word "servitium," but he was very patently a madman.

However, it was my immediate business to find some way to sleep, so I continued my quest for a servant. I followed another corridor, and discovered a second staircase. At the top of it I saw an open door and looked in. It must have been Dubellay's, for his flannels were tumbled untidily on a chair, but Dubellay himself was not there and the bed had not been slept in.

I suppose my irritation was greater than my alarm—though I must say I was getting a little scared—for I still pursued the evasive servant. There was another stair which apparently led to attics, and in going up it I slipped and made a great clatter. When I looked up the butler in his nightgown was staring down at me, and if ever a mortal face held fear it was his. When he saw who it was he seemed to recover a little.

"Look here," I said, "for God's sake turn off that infernal hot air. I can't get a wink of sleep. What idiot set it going?"

He looked at me owlishly, but he managed to find his tongue.

"I beg your pardon, sir," he said, "but there is no heating apparatus in this house."

There was nothing more to be said. I returned to my bedroom and it seemed to me that it had grown cooler. As I leaned out of the window, too, the mysterious wind seemed to have died away, and the glow no longer showed from beyond the corner of the house. I got into bed and slept heavily till I was roused by the appearance of my shaving water about half-past nine. There was no bathroom, so I bathed in a tin pannikin.

It was a hazy morning which promised a day of blistering heat. When I went down to breakfast I found Dubellay in the dining-room. In the daylight he looked a very sick man, but he seemed to have taken a pull on himself, for his manner was considerably less nervy than the night before. Indeed, he appeared almost normal, and I might have reconsidered my view but for the look in his eyes.

I told him that I proposed to sit tight all day over the manuscript, and get the thing finished. He nodded. "That's all right. I've a lot to do myself, and I won't disturb you."

"But first," I said, "you promised to show me your discoveries."

He looked at the window where the sun was shining on the laurels and on a segment of the paved court.

"The light is good," he said—an odd remark. "Let us go there now. There are times and seasons for the temple."

He led me down the passage I had explored the previous night. The door opened not by a key but by some lever in the wall. I found myself looking suddenly at a bath of sunshine with the lake below as blue as a turquoise.

It is not easy to describe my impressions of that place. It was unbelievably light and airy, as brilliant as an Italian colonnade in midsummer. The proportions must have been good, for the columns soared and swam, and the roof (which looked like cedar) floated as delicately as a flower on its stalk. The stone was some local limestone, which on the floor took a polish like marble. All around was a vista of sparkling water and summer woods and far blue mountains. It should have been as wholesome as the top of a hill.

And yet I had scarcely entered before I knew that it was a prison. I am not an imaginative man, and I believe my nerves are fairly good, but I could scarcely put one foot before the other, so strong was my distaste. I felt shut off from the world, as if I were in a dungeon or on an ice-floe. And I felt, too, that though far enough from humanity, we were not alone.

On the inner wall there were three carvings. Two were imperfect friezes sculptured in low relief, dealing apparently with the same subject. It was a ritual procession, priests bearing branches, the ordinary *dendrophori* business. The faces were only half-human, and that was from no lack of skill, for the artist had been a master. The striking thing was that the branches and the hair of the hierophants were being tossed by a violent wind, and the expression of each was of a being in the last stage of endurance, shaken to the core by terror and pain.

Between the friezes was a great roundel of a Gorgon's head. It was not a female head, such as you commonly find, but a male head, with the viperous hair sprouting from chin and lip. It had once been coloured, and fragments of a green pigment remained in the locks. It was an awful thing, the ultimate horror of fear, the last dementia of cruelty made manifest in stone. I hurriedly averted my eyes and looked at the altar.

That stood at the west end on a pediment with three steps.

It was a beautiful piece of work, scarcely harmed by the centuries, with two words inscribed on its face—APOLL. VAUN. It was made of some foreign marble, and the hollow top was dark with ancient sacrifices. Not so ancient either, for I could have sworn that I saw there the mark of recent flame.

I do not suppose I was more than five minutes in the place. I wanted to get out, and Dubellay wanted to get me out. We did not speak a word till we were back in the library.

"For God's sake give it up!" I said. "You're playing with fire, Mr. Dubellay. You're driving yourself into Bedlam. Send these damned things to a museum and leave this place. Now, now, I tell you. You have no time to lose. Come down with me to the inn straight off and shut up this house."

He looked at me with his lip quivering like a child about to cry.

"I will. I promise you I will. . . . But not yet. . . . After tonight. . . . Tomorrow I'll do whatever you tell me. . . . You won't leave me?"

"I won't leave you, but what earthly good am I to you if you won't take my advice?"

"Sidonius . . ." he began.

"Oh, damn Sidonius! I wish I had never mentioned him. The whole thing is arrant nonsense, but it's killing you. You've got it on the brain. Don't you know you're a sick man?"

"I'm not feeling very grand. It's so warm today. I think I'll lie down."

It was no good arguing with him, for he had the appalling obstinacy of very weak things. I went off to my work in a shocking bad temper.

The day was what it had promised to be, blisteringly hot. Before midday the sun was hidden by a coppery haze, and there was not the faintest stirring of wind. Dubellay did not appear at luncheon—it was not a meal he ever ate, the butler told me. I slogged away all the afternoon, and had pretty well finished my job by six o'clock. That would enable me to leave next morning, and I hoped to be able to persuade my host to come with me. The conclusion of my task put me into a better humour, and I went for a walk before dinner. It was a very close evening, for the heat haze had not lifted; the woods were as silent as a grave, not a bird spoke, and when I came out of the cover to the burnt pastures the sheep seemed too languid to graze. During my walk I prospected the environs of the house, and saw that it would be very hard to get access to the temple except by a long circuit. On one side was a mass of outbuildings, and then a high wall, and on the other the very closest and highest quickset hedge I have ever seen, which ended in a wood with savage spikes on its containing wall. I returned to my room, had a cold bath in the exiguous tub, and changed.

Dubellay was not at dinner. The butler said that his master was feeling unwell and had gone to bed. The news pleased me, for bed was the best place for him. After that I settled myself down to a lonely evening in the library. I browsed among the shelves and found a number of rare editions which served to pass the time. I noticed that the copy of Sidonius was absent from its place.

I think it was about ten o'clock when I went to bed, for I was unaccountably tired. I remember wondering whether I oughtn't to go and visit Dubellay, but decided that it was better to leave him alone. I still reproach myself for that decision. I know now I ought to have taken him by force and haled him to the inn.

Suddenly I came out of heavy sleep with a start. A human cry seemed to be ringing in the corridors of my brain. I held my breath and listened. It came again, a horrid scream of panic and torture.

I was out of bed in a second, and only stopped to get my feet into slippers. The cry must have come from the temple. I tore downstairs expecting to hear the noise of an alarmed household. But there was no sound, and the awful cry was not repeated.

The door in the corridor was shut, as I expected. Behind it pandemonium seemed to be loose, for there was a howling like a tempest—and something more, a crackling like fire. I made for the front door, slipped off the chain, and found myself in the still, moonless night. Still, except for the rending gale that seemed to be raging in the house I had left.

From what I had seen on my evening's walk I knew that my one chance to get to the temple was by way of the quickset hedge. I thought I might manage to force a way between the end of it and the wall. I did it, at the cost of much of my raiment and my skin. Beyond was another rough lawn set with tangled shrubberies, and then a precipitous slope to the level of the lake. I scrambled along the sedgy margin, not daring to lift my eyes till I was on the temple steps.

The place was brighter than day with a roaring blast of fire. The very air seemed to be incandescent and to have become a flaming ether. And yet there were no flames—only a burning brightness. I could not enter, for the waft from it struck my face like a scorching hand and I felt my hair singe. . . . I am short-sighted, as you know, and I may have been mistaken, but this is what I think I saw. From the altar a great tongue of flame seemed to shoot upwards and lick the roof, and from its pediment ran flaming streams. In front of it lay a body—Dubellay's—a naked body, already charred and black. There was nothing else, except that the Gorgon's head in the wall seemed to glow like a sun in hell.

I suppose I must have tried to enter. All I know is that I found myself staggering back, rather badly burned. I covered my eyes, and as I looked through my fingers I seemed to see the flames flowing under the wall, where there may have been lockers, or possibly another entrance. Then the great oak door suddenly shrivelled like gauze, and with a roar the fiery river poured into the house.

I ducked myself in the lake to ease the pain, and then ran back as hard as I could by the way I had come. Dubellay, poor devil, was beyond my aid. After that I am not very clear what happened. I know that the house burned like a haystack. I found one of the men-servants on the lawn, and I think I helped to get the other down from his room by one of the rain-pipes. By the time the neighbours arrived the house was ashes, and I was pretty well mother-naked. They took me to the inn and put me to bed, and I remained there till after the inquest. The coroner's jury were puzzled, but they found it simply death by misadventure; a lot of country-houses were burned that summer. There was nothing found of Dubellay; nothing remained of the house except a few blackened pillars; the altar and the sculptures were so cracked and scarred that no museum wanted them. The place has not been rebuilt and for all I know they are there today. I am not going back to look for them.

Nightingale finished his story and looked round his audience.

"Don't ask me for an explanation," he said, "for I haven't any. You may believe if you like that the god Vaunus inhabited the temple which Dubellay built for him, and, when his votary grew scared and tried Sidonius's receipt for shifting the dedication, became angry and slew him with his flaming wind. That wind seems to have been a perquisite of Vaunus. We know more about him now, for last year they dug up a temple of his in Wales."

"Lightning," someone suggested.

"It was a quiet night, with no thunderstorm," said Nightingale.

"Isn't the countryside volcanic?" Peckwether asked. "What about pockets of natural gas or something of the kind?"

"Possibly. You may please yourself in your explanation. I'm afraid I can't help you. All I know is that I don't propose to visit that valley again!"

"What became of your Theocritus?"

"Burned, like everything else. However, that didn't worry me much. Six weeks later came the War, and I had other things to think about."

THE GROVE OF ASHTAROTH

*"C'est enfin que dans leurs prunelles
Rit et pleure—fastidieux—
L'amour des choses éternelles,
Des vieux morts et des anciens dieux!"*

PAUL VERLAINE

I

WE were sitting around the camp-fire, some thirty miles north of a place called Taqui, when Lawson announced his intention of finding a home. He had spoken little the last day or two, and I had guessed that he had struck a vein of private reflection. I thought it might be a new mine or irrigation scheme, and I was surprised to find that it was a country-house.

"I don't think I shall go back to England," he said, kicking a sputtering log into place. "I don't see why I should. For business purposes I am far more useful to the firm in South Africa than in Throgmorton Street. I have no relations left except a third cousin, and I have never cared a rush for living in town. That beastly house of mine in Hill Street will fetch what I gave for it—Isaacson cabled about it the other day, offering for furniture and all. I don't want to go into Parliament, and I hate shooting little birds and tame deer. I am one of those fellows who are born Colonial at heart, and I don't see why I shouldn't arrange my life as I please. Besides, for ten years I have been falling in love with this country, and now I am up to the neck."

He flung himself back in the camp-chair till the canvas creaked, and looked at me below his eyelids. I remember glancing at the lines of him, and thinking what a fine make of a man he was. In his untanned field-boots, breeches, and grey shirt he looked the born wilderness-hunter, though less than two months before he had been driving down to the City every morning in the sombre regimentals of his class. Being a fair man, he was gloriously tanned, and there was a clear line at his shirt-collar to mark the limits of his sunburn. I had first known him years ago, when he was a broker's clerk working on half-commission. Then he had gone to South Africa, and soon I heard he was a partner in a mining house which was doing wonders with some gold areas in the North. The next step was his return to London as the new millionaire—young, good-looking, wholesome in mind and body, and much sought after by the mothers of marriageable girls. We played polo together, and hunted a little in the season, but there were signs that he did not propose to become the conventional English gentleman. He refused to buy a place in the country, though half the Homes of England were at his disposal. He was a very busy man, he declared, and had not time to be a squire. Besides, every few months he used to rush out to South Africa. I saw that he was restless, for he was always badgering me to go big-game hunting with him in some remote part of the earth. There was that in his eyes, too, which marked him out from the ordinary blond type of our countrymen. They were large and brown and mysterious, and the light of another race was in their odd depths.

To hint such a thing would have meant a breach of friendship, for Lawson was very proud of his birth. When he first made his fortune he had gone to the Heralds to discover his family, and these obliging gentlemen had provided a pedigree. It appeared that he was a scion of the house of Lowson or Lowieson, an ancient and rather disreputable clan on the Scottish side of the Border. He took a shooting in Teviotdale on the strength of it, and used to commit lengthy Border ballads to memory. But I had known his father, a financial journalist who never quite succeeded, and I had heard of a grandfather who sold antiques in a back street at Brighton. The latter, I think, had not changed his name, and still frequented the synagogue. The father was a progressive Christian, and the mother had been a blonde Saxon from the Midlands. In my mind there was no doubt, as I caught Lawson's heavy-lidded eyes fixed on me. My friend was of a more ancient race than the Lowsons of the Border.

"Where are you thinking of looking for your house?" I asked. "In Natal or in the Cape Peninsula? You might get the Fishers' place if you paid a price."

"The Fishers' place be hanged!" he said crossly. "I don't want any stuccoed, overgrown Dutch farm. I might as well be at Roehampton as in the Cape."

He got up and walked to the far side of the fire, where a lane ran down through thorn-scrub to a gully of the hills. The moon was silvering the bush of the plains, forty miles off and three thousand feet below us. "I am going to live somewhere hereabouts," he answered at last.

I whistled. "Then you've got to put your hand in your pocket, old man. You'll have to make everything, including a map of the countryside."

"I know," he said; "that's where the fun comes in. Hang it all, why shouldn't I indulge my fancy? I'm uncommonly well off, and I haven't chick or child to leave it to. Supposing I'm a hundred miles from railhead, what about it? I'll make a motor-road and fix up a telephone. I'll grow most of my supplies, and start a colony to provide labour. When you come and stay with me, you'll get the best food and drink on earth, and sport that will make your mouth water. I'll put Lochleven trout in these streams—at 6000 feet you can do anything. We'll have a pack of hounds, too, and we can drive pig in the woods, and if we want big game there are the Mangwe flats at our feet. I tell you I'll make such a country-house as nobody ever dreamed of. A man will come plumb out of stark savagery into lawns and rose-gardens." Lawson flung himself into his chair again and smiled dreamily at the fire.

"But why here, of all places?" I persisted. I was not feeling very well and did not care for the country.

"I can't quite explain. I think it's the sort of land I have always been looking for. I always fancied a house on a green plateau in a decent climate looking down on the tropics. I like heat and colour, you know, but I like hills too, and greenery, and the things that bring back Scotland. Give me a cross between Teviotdale and the Orinoco, and, by Gad! I think I've got it here."

I watched my friend curiously, as with bright eyes and eager voice he talked of his new fad. The two races were very clear in him—the one desiring gorgeousness, the other athirst for the soothing spaces of the North. He began to plan out the house. He would get Adamson to design it, and it was to grow out of the landscape like a stone on the hillside. There would be wide verandahs and cool halls, but great fireplaces against winter-time. It would all be very simple and fresh—"clean as morning" was his odd phrase; but then another idea supervened, and he talked of bringing the Tintorets from Hill Street. "I want it to be a civilised house, you know. No silly luxury, but the best pictures and china and books. . . . I'll have all the furniture made after the old plain English models out of native woods. I don't want second-hand sticks in a new country. Yes, by Jove, the Tintorets are a great idea, and all those Ming pots I bought. I had meant to sell them, but I'll have them out here."

He talked for a good hour of what he would do, and his dream grew richer as he talked, till by the time we went to bed he had sketched something liker a palace than a country-house. Lawson was by no means a luxurious man. At present he was well content with a Wolseley valise, and shaved cheerfully out of a tin mug. It struck me as odd that a man so simple in his habits should have so sumptuous a taste in bric-à-brac. I told myself, as I turned in, that the Saxon mother from the Midlands had done little to dilute the strong wine of the East.

It drizzled next morning when we inspanned, and I mounted my horse in a bad temper. I had some fever on me, I think, and I hated this lush yet frigid tableland, where all the winds on earth lay in wait for one's marrow. Lawson was, as usual, in great spirits. We were not hunting, but shifting our hunting ground, so all morning we travelled fast to the north along the rim of the uplands.

At midday it cleared, and the afternoon was a pageant of pure colour. The wind sank to a low breeze; the sun lit the infinite green spaces, and kindled the wet forest to a jewelled coronal. Lawson gaspingly admired it all, as he cantered bareheaded up a bracken-clad slope. "God's country," he said twenty times.

"I've found it." Take a piece of Sussex downland; put a stream in every hollow and a patch of wood; and at the edge, where the cliffs at home would fall to the sea, put a cloak of forest muffling the scarp and dropping thousands of feet to the blue plains. Take the diamond air of the Gornergrat, and the riot of colour which you get by a West Highland loch-side in late September. Put flowers everywhere, the things we grow in hothouses, geraniums like sunshades, and arums like trumpets. That will give you a notion of the countryside we were in. I began to see that after all it was out of the common.

And just before sunset we came over a ridge and found something better. It was a shallow glen, half a mile wide, down which ran a blue-grey stream in linns like the Spean, till at the edge of the plateau it leaped into the dim forest in a snowy cascade. The opposite side ran up in gentle slopes to a rocky knoll, from which the eye had a noble prospect of the plains. All down the glen were little copses, half-moons of green edging some silvery shore of the burn, or delicate clusters of tall trees nodding on the hill brow. The place so satisfied the eye that for the sheer wonder of its perfection we stopped and stared in silence for many minutes.

Then "The House," I said, and Lawson replied softly, "The House!"

We rode slowly into the glen in the mulberry gloaming. Our transport waggons were half an hour behind, so we had time to explore. Lawson dismounted and plucked handfuls of flowers from the water-meadows. He was singing to himself all the time—an old French catch about *Cadet Rousselle* and his *trois maisons*.

"Who owns it?" I asked.

"My firm, as like as not. We have miles of land about here. But whoever the man is, he has got to sell. Here I build my tabernacle, old man. Here, and nowhere else!"

In the very centre of the glen, in a loop of the stream, was one copse which even in that half light struck me as different from the others. It was of tall, slim, fairy-like trees, the kind of wood the monks painted in old missals. No, I rejected the thought. It was no Christian wood. It was not a copse, but a "grove"—one such as Artemis may have flitted through in the moonlight. It was small, forty or fifty yards in diameter, and there was a dark something at the heart of it which for a second I thought was a house.

We turned between the slender trees, and—was it fancy?—an odd tremor went through me. I felt as if I were penetrating the *temenos* of some strange and lovely divinity, the goddess of this pleasant vale. There was a spell in the air, it seemed, and an odd dead silence.

Suddenly my horse started at a flutter of light wings. A flock of doves rose from the branches, and I saw the burnished green of their plumes against the opal sky. Lawson did not seem to notice them. I saw his keen eyes staring at the centre of the grove and what stood there.

It was a little conical tower, ancient and lichened, but, so far as I could judge, quite flawless. You know the famous Conical Temple at Zimbabwe, of which prints are in every guide-book. This was of the same type, but a thousandfold more perfect. It stood about thirty feet high, of solid masonry, without door or window or cranny, as shapely as when it first came from the hands of the old builders. Again I had the sense of breaking in on a sanctuary. What right had I, a common vulgar modern, to be looking at this fair thing, among these delicate trees, which some white goddess had once taken for her shrine?

Lawson broke in on my absorption. "Let's get out of this," he said hoarsely, and he took my horse's bridle (he had left his own beast at the edge) and led him back to the open. But I noticed that his eyes were always turning back, and that his hand trembled.

"That settles it," I said after supper. "What do you want with your medieval Venetians and your Chinese pots now? You will have the finest antique in the world in your garden—a temple as old as time, and in a land which they say has no history. You had the right inspiration this time."

I think I have said that Lawson had hungry eyes. In his enthusiasm they used to glow and brighten; but now, as he sat looking down at the olive shades of the glen, they seemed ravenous in their fire. He had hardly spoken a word since we left the wood.

"Where can I read about these things?" he asked, and I gave him the names of books.

Then, an hour later, he asked me who were the builders. I told him the little I knew about Phœnician and Sabæan wanderings, and the ritual of Sidon and Tyre. He repeated some names to himself and went soon to bed.

As I turned in, I had one last look over the glen, which lay ivory and black in the moon. I seemed to hear a faint echo of wings, and to see over the little grove a cloud of light visitants. "The Doves of Ashtaroth have come back," I said to myself. "It is a good omen. They accept the new tenant." But as I fell asleep I had a sudden thought that I was saying something rather terrible.

II

THREE years later, pretty nearly to a day, I came back to see what Lawson had made of his hobby. He had bidden me often to Welgevonden, as he chose to call it—though I do not know why he should have fixed a Dutch name to a countryside where Boer never trod. At the last there had been some confusion about dates, and I wired the time of my arrival, and set off without an answer. A motor met me at the queer little wayside station of Taqui, and after many miles on a doubtful highway I came to the gates of the park, and a road on which it was a delight to move. Three years had wrought little difference in the landscape. Lawson had done some planting—conifers and flowering shrubs and suchlike—but wisely he had resolved that Nature had for the most part forestalled him. All the same, he must have spent a mint of money. The drive could not have been beaten in England, and fringes of mown turf on either hand had been pared out of the lush meadows. When we came over the edge of the hill and looked down on the secret glen, I could not repress a cry of pleasure. The house stood on the farther ridge, the viewpoint of the whole neighbourhood; and its brown timbers and white rough-cast walls melted into the hillside as if it had been there from the beginning of things. The vale below was ordered in lawns and gardens. A blue lake received the rapids of the stream, and its banks were a maze of green shades and glorious masses of blossom. I noticed, too, that the little grove we had explored on our first visit stood alone in a big stretch of lawn, so that its perfection might be clearly seen. Lawson had excellent taste, or he had had the best advice.

The butler told me that his master was expected home shortly, and took me into the library for tea. Lawson had left his Tintorets and Ming pots at home after all. It was a long, low room, panelled in teak half-way up the walls, and the shelves held a multitude of fine bindings. There were good rugs on the parquet floor, but no ornaments anywhere, save three. On the carved mantelpiece stood two of the old soapstone birds which they used to find at Zimbabwe, and between, on an ebony stand, a half-moon of alabaster, curiously carved with zodiacal figures. My host had altered his scheme of furnishing, but I approved the change.

He came in about half-past six, after I had consumed two cigars and all but fallen asleep. Three years make a difference in most men, but I was not prepared for the change in Lawson. For one thing, he had grown fat. In place of the lean young man I had known, I saw a heavy, flaccid being, who shuffled in his gait, and seemed tired and listless. His sunburn had gone, and his face was as pasty as a city clerk's. He had been walking, and wore shapeless flannel clothes, which hung loose even on his enlarged figure. And the worst of it was, that he did not seem over-pleased to see me. He murmured something about my journey, and then flung himself into an armchair and looked out of the window. I asked him if he had been ill.

"Ill! No!" he said crossly. "Nothing of the kind. I'm perfectly well."

"You don't look as fit as this place should make you. What do you do with yourself? Is the shooting as good as you hoped?"

He did not answer, but I thought I heard him utter something like "shooting be damned."

Then I tried the subject of the house. I praised it extravagantly, but with conviction. "There can be no place like it in the world," I said.

He turned his eyes on me at last, and I saw that they were as deep and restless as ever. With his pallid face they made him look curiously Semitic. I had been right in my theory about his ancestry. "Yes," he said slowly, "there is no place like it—in the world."

Then he pulled himself to his feet. "I'm going to change," he said. "Dinner is at eight. Ring for Travers, and he'll show you your room."

I dressed in a noble bedroom, with an outlook over the garden-vale and the escarpment to the far line of the plains, now blue and saffron in the sunset. I dressed in an ill temper, for I was seriously offended with Lawson, and also seriously alarmed. He was either very unwell or going out of his mind, and it was clear, too, that he would resent any anxiety on his account. I ransacked my memory for rumours, but found none. I had heard nothing of him except that he had been extraordinarily successful in his speculations; and that from his hilltop he directed his firm's operations with uncommon skill. If Lawson was sick or mad, nobody knew of it.

Dinner was a trying ceremony. Lawson, who used to be rather particular in his dress, appeared in a kind of smoking suit with a flannel collar. He spoke scarcely a word to me, but cursed the servants with a brutality which left me aghast. A wretched footman in his nervousness spilt some sauce over his sleeve. Lawson dashed the dish from his hand, and volleyed abuse with a sort of epileptic fury. Also he, who had been the most abstemious of men, swallowed disgusting quantities of champagne and old brandy.

He had given up smoking, and half an hour after we left the dining-room he announced his intention of going to bed. I watched him as he waddled upstairs with a feeling of angry bewilderment. Then I went to the library and lit a pipe. I would leave first thing in the morning—on that I was determined. But as I sat gazing at the moon of alabaster and the soapstone birds my anger evaporated, and concern took its place. I remembered what a fine fellow Lawson had been, what good times we had had together. I remembered especially that evening when we had found this valley and given rein to our fancies. What horrid alchemy in the place had turned a gentleman into a brute? I thought of drink and drugs and madness and insomnia, but I could fit none of them into my conception of my friend. I did not consciously rescind my resolve to depart, but I had a notion that I would not act on it.

The sleepy butler met me as I went to bed. "Mr. Lawson's room is at the end of your corridor, sir," he said. "He don't sleep over well, so you may hear him stirring in the night. At what hour would you like breakfast, sir? Mr. Lawson mostly has his in bed."

My room opened from the great corridor, which ran the full length of the front of the house. So far as I could make out, Lawson was three rooms off, a vacant bedroom and his servant's room being between us. I felt tired and cross, and tumbled into bed as fast as possible. Usually I sleep well, but now I was soon conscious that my drowsiness was wearing off and that I was in for a restless night. I got up and laved my face, turned the pillows, thought of sheep coming over a hill and clouds crossing the sky; but none of the old devices were of any use. After about an hour of make-believe I surrendered myself to facts, and, lying on my back, stared at the white ceiling and the patches of moonshine on the walls.

It certainly was an amazing night. I got up, put on a dressing-gown, and drew a chair to the window. The moon was almost at its full, and the whole plateau swam in a radiance of ivory and silver. The banks of the stream were black, but the lake had a great belt of light athwart it, which made it seem like a horizon, and the rim of land beyond it like a contorted cloud. Far to the right I saw the delicate outlines of the little wood which I had come to think of as the Grove of Ashtaroth. I listened. There was not a sound in the air. The land seemed to sleep peacefully beneath the moon, and yet I had a sense that the peace was an illusion. The place was feverishly restless.

I could have given no reason for my impression, but there it was. Something was stirring in the wide moonlit landscape under its deep mask of silence. I felt as I had felt on the evening three years ago when I had ridden into the grove. I did not think that the influence, whatever it was, was maleficent. I only knew that it was very strange, and kept me wakeful.

By-and-by I bethought me of a book. There was no lamp in the corridor save the moon, but the whole house was bright as I slipped down the great staircase and across the hall to the library. I switched on the lights and then switched them off. They seemed a profanation, and I did not need them.

I found a French novel, but the place held me and I stayed. I sat down in an armchair before the fireplace and the stone birds. Very odd those gawky things, like prehistoric Great Auks, looked in the moonlight. I remember that the alabaster moon shimmered like translucent pearl, and I fell to wondering about its history. Had the old Sabæans used such a jewel in their rites in the Grove of Ashtaroth?

Then I heard footsteps pass the window. A great house like this would have a watchman, but these quick shuffling footsteps were surely not the dull plod of a servant. They passed on to the grass and died away. I began to think of getting back to my room.

In the corridor I noticed that Lawson's door was ajar, and that a light had been left burning. I had the unpardonable curiosity to peep in. The room was empty, and the bed had not been slept in. Now I knew whose were the footsteps outside the library window.

I lit a reading-lamp and tried to interest myself in *La Cruelle Enigme*. But my wits were restless, and I could not keep my eyes on the page. I flung the book aside and sat down again by the window. The feeling came over me that I was sitting in a box at some play. The glen was a huge stage, and at any moment the players might appear on it. My attention was strung as high as if I had been waiting for the advent of some world-famous actress. But nothing came. Only the shadows shifted and lengthened as the moon moved across the sky.

Then quite suddenly the restlessness left me, and at the same moment the silence was broken by the crow of a cock and the rustling of trees in a light wind. I felt very sleepy, and was turning to bed when again I heard footsteps without. From the window I could see a figure moving across the garden towards the house. It was Lawson, got up in the sort of towel dressing-gown that one wears on board ship. He was walking slowly and painfully, as if very weary. I did not see his face, but the man's whole air was that of extreme fatigue and dejection.

I tumbled into bed and slept profoundly till long after daylight.

III

THE man who valeted me was Lawson's own servant. As he was laying out my clothes I asked after the health of his master, and was told that he had slept ill and would not rise till late. Then the man, an anxious-faced Englishman, gave me some information on his own account. Mr. Lawson was having one of his bad turns. It would pass away in a day or two, but till it had gone he was fit for nothing. He advised me to see Mr. Jobson, the factor, who would look to my entertainment in his master's absence.

Jobson arrived before luncheon, and the sight of him was the first satisfactory thing about Welgevonden. He was a big, gruff Scot from Roxburghshire, engaged, no doubt, by Lawson as a duty to his Border ancestry. He had short grizzled whiskers, a weather-worn face, and a shrewd, calm blue eye. I knew now why the place was in such perfect order.

We began with sport, and Jobson explained what I could have in the way of fishing and shooting. His exposition was brief and businesslike, and all the while I could see his eye searching me. It was clear that he had much to say on other matters than sport.

I told him that I had come here with Lawson three years before, when he chose the site. Jobson continued to regard me curiously. "I've heard tell of ye from Mr. Lawson. Ye're an old friend of his, I understand."

"The oldest," I said. "And I am sorry to find that the place does not agree with him. Why it doesn't I cannot imagine, for you look fit enough. Has he been seedy for long?"

"It comes and goes," said Mr. Jobson. "Maybe once a month he has a bad turn. But on the whole it agrees with him badly. He's no' the man he was when I first came here."

Jobson was looking at me very seriously and frankly. I risked a question. "What do you suppose is the matter?"

He did not reply at once, but leaned forward and tapped my knee.

"I think it's something that doctors canna cure. Look at me, sir. I've always been counted a sensible man, but if I told you what was in my head you would think me daft. But I have one word for you. Bide till tonight is past and then speir your question. Maybe you and me will be agreed."

The factor rose to go. As he left the room he flung me back a remark over his shoulder—"Read the eleventh chapter of the First Book of Kings."

After luncheon I went for a walk. First I mounted to the crown of the hill and feasted my eyes on the unequalled loveliness of the view. I saw the far hills in Portuguese territory, a hundred miles away, lifting up thin blue fingers into the sky. The wind blew light and fresh, and the place was fragrant with a thousand delicate scents. Then I descended to the vale, and followed the stream up through the garden. Poinsettias and oleanders were blazing in coverts, and there was a paradise of tinted water-lilies in the slacker reaches. I saw good trout rise at the fly, but I did not think about fishing. I was searching my memory for a recollection which would not come. By-and-by I found myself beyond the garden, where the lawns ran to the fringe of Ashtaroth's Grove.

It was like something I remembered in an old Italian picture. Only, as my memory drew it, it should have been peopled with strange figures—nymphs dancing on the sward, and a prick-eared faun peeping from the covert. In the warm afternoon sunlight it stood, ineffably gracious and beautiful, tantalising with a sense of some deep hidden loveliness. Very reverently I walked between the slim trees, to where the little conical tower stood half in sun and half in shadow. Then I noticed something new. Round the tower ran a narrow path, worn in the grass by human feet. There had been no such path on my first visit, for I remembered the grass growing tall to the edge of the stone. Had the Kaffirs made a shrine of it, or were there other and stranger votaries?

When I returned to the house I found Travers with a message

for me. Mr. Lawson was still in bed, but he would like me to go to him. I found my friend sitting up and drinking strong tea—a bad thing, I should have thought, for a man in his condition. I remember that I looked about the room for some sign of the pernicious habit of which I believed him a victim. But the place was fresh and clean, with the windows wide open, and, though I could not have given my reasons, I was convinced that drugs or drink had nothing to do with the sickness.

He received me more civilly, but I was shocked by his looks. There were great bags below his eyes, and his skin had the wrinkled puffy appearance of a man in dropsy. His voice, too, was reedy and thin. Only his great eyes burned with some feverish life.

"I am a shocking bad host," he said, "but I'm going to be still more inhospitable. I want you to go away. I hate anybody here when I'm off colour."

"Nonsense," I said; "you want looking after. I want to know about this sickness. Have you had a doctor?"

He smiled wearily. "Doctors are no earthly use to me. There's nothing much the matter, I tell you. I'll be all right in a day or two, and then you can come back. I want you to go off with Jobson and hunt in the plains till the end of the week. It will be better fun for you, and I'll feel less guilty."

Of course I pooh-poohed the idea, and Lawson got angry. "Damn it, man," he cried, "why do you force yourself on me when I don't want you? I tell you your presence here makes me worse. In a week I'll be as right as the mail, and then I'll be thankful for you. But get away now; get away, I tell you."

I saw that he was fretting himself into a passion. "All right," I said soothingly; "Jobson and I will go off hunting. But I am horribly anxious about you, old man."

He lay back on his pillows. "You needn't trouble. I only want a little rest. Jobson will make all arrangements, and Travers will get you anything you want. Goodbye."

I saw it was useless to stay longer, so I left the room. Outside I found the anxious-faced servant. "Look here," I said, "Mr. Lawson thinks I ought to go, but I mean to stay. Tell him I'm gone if he asks you. And for Heaven's sake keep him in bed."

The man promised, and I thought I saw some relief in his face.

I went to the library, and on the way remembered Jobson's remark about 1st Kings. With some searching I found a Bible and turned up the passage. It was a long screed about the misdeeds of Solomon, and I read it through without enlightenment. I began to re-read it, and a word suddenly caught my attention—

"For Solomon went after Ashtaroth, the goddess of the Zidonians."

That was all, but it was like a key to a cipher. Instantly there flashed over my mind all that I had heard or read of that strange ritual which seduced Israel to sin. I saw a sunburnt land and a people vowed to the stern service of Jehovah. But I saw, too, eyes turning from the austere sacrifice to lonely hilltop groves and towers and images, where dwelt some subtle and evil mystery. I saw the fierce prophets, scourging the votaries with rods, and a nation penitent before the Lord; but always the backsliding again, and the hankering after forbidden joys. Ashtaroth was the old goddess of the East. Was it not possible that in all Semitic blood there remained, transmitted through the dim generations, some craving for her spell? I thought of the grandfather in the back street at Brighton and of those burning eyes upstairs.

As I sat and mused my glance fell on the inscrutable stone birds. They knew all those old secrets of joy and terror. And that moon of alabaster! Some dark priest had worn it on his forehead when he worshipped, like Ahab, "all the host of Heaven". And then I honestly began to be afraid. I, a prosaic, modern Christian gentleman, a half-believer in casual faiths, was in the presence of some hoary mystery of sin far older than creeds or Christendom. There was fear in my heart—a kind of uneasy disgust, and above all a nervous eerie disquiet. Now I wanted to go away, and yet I was ashamed of the cowardly thought. I pictured Ashtaroth's Grove with sheer horror. What tragedy was in the air? what secret awaited twilight? For the night was coming, the night of the Full Moon, the season of ecstasy and sacrifice.

I do not know how I got through that evening. I was disinclined for dinner, so I had a cutlet in the library and sat smoking till my tongue ached. But as the hours passed a more manly resolution grew up in my mind. I owed it to old friendship to stand by Lawson in this extremity. I could not interfere—God knows, his reason seemed already rocking—but I could be at hand in case my chance came. I determined not to undress but to watch through the night. I had a bath, and changed into light flannels and slippers. Then I took up my position in a corner of the library close to the window, so that I could not fail to hear Lawson's footsteps if he passed.

Fortunately I left the lights unlit, for as I waited I grew drowsy, and fell asleep. When I woke the moon had risen, and I knew from the feel of the air that the hour was late. I sat very still, straining my ears, and as I listened I caught the sound of steps. They were crossing the hall stealthily, and nearing the library door. I huddled into my corner as Lawson entered.

He wore the same towel dressing-gown, and he moved swiftly and silently as if in a trance. I watched him take the alabaster moon from the mantelpiece and drop it in his pocket. A glimpse of white skin showed that the gown was his only clothing. Then he moved past me to the window, opened it, and went out.

Without any conscious purpose I rose and followed, kicking off my slippers that I might go quietly. He was running, running fast, across the lawns in the direction of the Grove—an odd shapeless antic in the moonlight. I stopped, for there was no cover, and I feared for his reason if he saw me. When I looked again he had disappeared among the trees.

I saw nothing for it but to crawl, so on my belly I wormed my way over the dripping sward. There was a ridiculous suggestion of deer-stalking about the game which tickled me and dispelled my uneasiness. Almost I persuaded myself I was tracking an ordinary sleep-walker. The lawns were broader than I imagined, and it seemed an age before I reached the edge of the Grove. The world was so still that I appeared to be making a most ghastly amount of noise. I remember that once I heard a rustling in the air, and looked up to see the green doves circling about the tree tops.

There was no sign of Lawson. On the edge of the Grove I think that all my assurance vanished. I could see between the trunks to the little tower, but it was quiet as the grave, save for the wings above. Once more there came over me the unbearable sense of anticipation I had felt the night before. My nerves tingled with mingled expectation and dread. I did not think that any harm would come to me, for the powers of the air seemed not malignant. But I knew them for powers, and felt awed and abased. I was in the presence of the "host of Heaven", and I was no stern Israelitish prophet to prevail against them.

I must have lain for hours waiting in that spectral place, my eyes riveted on the tower and its golden cap of moonshine. I remember that my head felt void and light, as if my spirit were becoming disembodied and leaving its dew-drenched sheath far below. But the most curious sensation was of something drawing me to the tower, something mild and kindly and rather feeble, for there was some other and stronger force keeping me back. I yearned to move nearer, but I could not drag my limbs an inch. There was a spell somewhere which I could not break. I do not think I was in any way frightened now. The starry influence was playing tricks with me, but my mind was half asleep. Only I never took my eyes from the little tower. I think I could not, if I had wanted to.

Then suddenly from the shadows came Lawson. He was stark-naked, and he wore, bound across his brow, the half-moon of alabaster. He had something, too, in his hand—something which glittered.

He ran round the tower, crooning to himself, and flinging wild arms to the skies. Sometimes the crooning changed to a shrill cry of passion, such as a mænad may have uttered in the train of Bacchus. I could make out no words, but the sound told its own tale. He was absorbed in some infernal ecstasy. And as he ran, he drew his right hand across his breast and arms, and I saw that it held a knife.

I grew sick with disgust—not terror, but honest physical loathing. Lawson, gashing his fat body, affected me with an overpowering repugnance. I wanted to go forward and stop him, and I wanted, too, to be a hundred miles away. And the result was that I stayed still. I believe my own will held me there, but I doubt if in any case I could have moved my legs.

The dance grew swifter and fiercer. I saw the blood dripping from Lawson's body, and his face ghastly white above his scarred breast. And then suddenly the horror left me; my head swam; and for one second—one brief second—I seemed to peer into a new world. A strange passion surged up in my heart. I seemed to see the earth peopled with forms—not human, scarcely divine, but more desirable than man or god. The calm face of Nature broke up for me into wrinkles of wild knowledge. I saw the things which brush against the soul in dreams, and found them lovely. There seemed no cruelty in the knife or the blood. It was a delicate mystery of worship, as wholesome as the morning song of birds. I do not know how the Semites found Ashtaroth's ritual; to them it may well have been more rapt and passionate than it seemed to me. For I saw in it only the sweet simplicity of Nature, and all riddles of lust and terror soothed away as a child's nightmares are calmed by a mother. I found my legs able to move, and I think I took two steps through the dusk towards the tower.

And then it all ended. A cock crew, and the homely noises of earth were renewed. While I stood dazed and shivering, Lawson plunged through the Grove towards me. The impetus carried him to the edge, and he fell fainting just outside the shade.

My wits and common sense came back to me with my bodily strength. I got my friend on my back, and staggered with him towards the house. I was afraid in real earnest now, and what frightened me most was the thought that I had not been afraid sooner. I had come very near the "abomination of the Zidonians".

At the door I found the scared valet waiting. He had apparently done this sort of thing before.

"Your master has been sleep-walking, and has had a fall," I said. "We must get him to bed at once."

We bathed the wounds as he lay in a deep stupor, and I dressed them as well as I could. The only danger lay in his utter exhaustion, for happily the gashes were not serious, and no artery had been touched. Sleep and rest would make him well, for he had the constitution of a strong man. I was leaving the room when he opened his eyes and spoke. He did not recognise me, but I noticed that his face had lost its strangeness, and was once more that of the friend I had known. Then I suddenly bethought me of an old hunting remedy which he and I always carried on our expeditions. It is a pill made up from an ancient Portuguese prescription. One is an excellent specific for fever. Two are invaluable if you are lost in the bush, for they send a man for many hours into a deep sleep, which prevents suffering and madness, till help comes. Three give a painless death. I went to my room and found the little box in my jewel-case. Lawson swallowed two, and turned wearily on his side. I bade his man let him sleep till he woke, and went off in search of food.

IV

I HAD business on hand which would not wait. By seven, Jobson, who had been sent for, was waiting for me in the library. I knew by his grim face that here I had a very good substitute for a prophet of the Lord.

"You were right," I said. "I have read the 11th chapter of 1st Kings, and I have spent such a night as I pray God I shall never spend again."

"I thought you would," he replied. "I've had the same experience myself."

"The Grove?" I said.

"Ay, the wud," was the answer in broad Scots.

I wanted to see how much he understood. "Mr. Lawson's family is from the Scottish Border?"

"Ay. I understand they come off Borthwick Water side," he replied, but I saw by his eyes that he knew what I meant.

"Mr. Lawson is my oldest friend," I went on, "and I am going to take measures to cure him. For what I am going to do I take the sole responsibility. I will make that plain to your master. But if I am to succeed I want your help. Will you give it me? It sounds like madness, and you are a sensible man and may like to keep out of it. I leave it to your discretion."

Jobson looked me straight in the face. "Have no fear for me," he said; "there is an unholy thing in that place, and if I have the strength in me I will destroy it. He has been a good master to me, and, forbye, I am a believing Christian. So say on, sir." There was no mistaking the air. I had found my Tishbite.

"I want men," I said, "as many as we can get."

Jobson mused. "The Kaffirs will no' gang near the place, but there's some thirty white men on the tobacco farm. They'll do your will, if you give them an indemnity in writing."

"Good," said I. "Then we will take our instructions from the only authority which meets the case. We will follow the example of King Josiah." I turned up the 23rd chapter of 2nd Kings, and read—

> "And the high places that were before Jerusalem, which were on the right hand of the Mount of Corruption, which Solomon the king of Israel had builded for Ashtaroth the abomination of the Zidonians . . . did the king defile.
>
> "And he brake in pieces the images, and cut down the groves, and filled their places with the bones of men.
>
> "Moreover the altar that was at Beth-el, and the high place which Jeroboam the son of Nebat, who made Israel to sin, had made, both that altar and the high place he brake down, and burned the high place, and stamped it small to powder, and burned the grove."

Jobson nodded. "It'll need dinnymite. But I've plenty of yon down at the workshops. I'll be off to collect the lads."

*   *   *

Before nine the men had assembled at Jobson's house. They were a hardy lot of young farmers from home, who took their instructions docilely from the masterful factor. On my orders they had brought their shotguns. We armed them with spades and woodman's axes, and one man wheeled some coils of rope in a handcart.

In the clear, windless air of morning the Grove, set amid its lawns, looked too innocent and exquisite for ill. I had a pang of regret that a thing so fair should suffer; nay, if I had come alone, I think I might have repented. But the men were there, and the grim-faced Jobson was waiting for orders. I placed the guns, and sent beaters to the far side. I told them that every dove must be shot.

It was only a small flock, and we killed fifteen at the first drive. The poor birds flew over the glen to another spinney, but we brought them back over the guns and seven fell. Four more were got in the trees, and the last I killed myself with a long shot. In half an hour there was a pile of little green bodies on the sward.

Then we went to work to cut down the trees. The slim stems were an easy task to a good woodman, and one after another they toppled to the ground. And meantime, as I watched, I became conscious of a strange emotion.

It was as if someone were pleading with me. A gentle voice, not threatening, but pleading—something too fine for the sensual ear, but touching inner chords of the spirit. So tenuous it was and distant that I could think of no personality behind it. Rather it was the viewless, bodiless grace of this delectable vale, some old exquisite divinity of the groves. There was the heart of all sorrow in it, and the soul of all loveliness. It seemed a woman's voice, some lost lady who had brought nothing but goodness unrepaid to the world. And what the voice told me was that I was destroying her last shelter.

That was the pathos of it—the voice was homeless. As the axes flashed in the sunlight and the wood grew thin, that gentle spirit was pleading with me for mercy and a brief respite. It seemed to be telling of a world for centuries grown coarse and pitiless, of long sad wanderings, of hardly-won shelter, and a peace which was the little all she sought from men. There was nothing terrible in it. No thought of wrong-doing. The spell which to Semitic blood held the mystery of evil, was to me, of the Northern race, only delicate and rare and beautiful. Jobson and the rest did not feel it, I with my finer senses caught nothing but the hopeless sadness of it. That which had stirred the passion in Lawson was only wringing my heart. It was almost too pitiful to bear. As the trees crashed down and the men wiped the sweat

238

from their brows, I seemed to myself like the murderer of fair women and innocent children. I remember that the tears were running over my cheeks. More than once I opened my mouth to countermand the work, but the face of Jobson, that grim Tishbite, held me back.

I knew now what gave the Prophets of the Lord their mastery, and I knew also why the people sometimes stoned them.

The last tree fell, and the little tower stood like a ravished shrine, stripped of all defence against the world. I heard Jobson's voice speaking. "We'd better blast that stane thing now. We'll trench on four sides and lay the dinnymite. Ye're no' looking weel, sir. Ye'd better go and sit down on the brae-face."

I went up the hillside and lay down. Below me, in the waste of shorn trunks, men were running about, and I saw the mining begin. It all seemed like an aimless dream in which I had no part. The voice of that homeless goddess was still pleading. It was the innocence of it that tortured me. Even so must a merciful Inquisitor have suffered from the plea of some fair girl with the aureole of death on her hair. I knew I was killing rare and unrecoverable beauty. As I sat dazed and heart-sick, the whole loveliness of Nature seemed to plead for its divinity. The sun in the heavens, the mellow lines of upland, the blue mystery of the far plains, were all part of that soft voice. I felt bitter scorn for myself. I was guilty of blood; nay, I was guilty of the sin against light which knows no forgiveness. I was murdering innocent gentleness, and there would be no peace on earth for me. Yet I sat helpless. The power of a sterner will constrained me. And all the while the voice was growing fainter and dying away into unutterable sorrow.

Suddenly a great flame sprang to Heaven, and a pall of smoke. I heard men crying out, and fragments of stone fell around the ruins of the grove. When the air cleared, the little tower had gone out of sight.

The voice had ceased and there seemed to me to be a bereaved silence in the world. The shock moved me to my feet, and I ran down the slope to where Jobson stood rubbing his eyes.

"That's done the job. Now we maun get up the tree-roots. We've no time to howk. We'll just blast the feck o' them."

The work of destruction went on, but I was coming back to my senses. I forced myself to be practical and reasonable. I thought of the night's experience and Lawson's haggard eyes, and I screwed myself into a determination to see the thing through. I had done the deed; it was my business to make it complete. A text in Jeremiah came into my head: "*Their children remember their altars and their groves by the green trees upon the high hills.*" I would see to it that this grove should be utterly forgotten.

We blasted the tree-roots, and, yoking oxen, dragged the debris into a great heap. Then the men set to work with their spades, and roughly levelled the ground. I was getting back to my old self, and Jobson's spirit was becoming mine.

"There is one thing more," I told him. "Get ready a couple of ploughs. We will improve upon King Josiah." My brain was a medley of Scripture precedents, and I was determined that no safeguard should be wanting.

We yoked the oxen again and drove the ploughs over the site of the grove. It was rough ploughing, for the place was thick with bits of stone from the tower, but the slow Afrikander oxen plodded on, and sometime in the afternoon the work was finished. Then I sent down to the farm for bags of rock-salt, such as they use for cattle. Jobson and I took a sack apiece, and walked up and down the furrows, sowing them with salt.

The last act was to set fire to the pile of tree-trunks. They burned well, and on the top we flung the bodies of the green doves. The birds of Ashtaroth had an honourable pyre.

Then I dismissed the much-perplexed men, and gravely shook hands with Jobson. Black with dust and smoke I went back to the house, where I bade Travers pack my bags and order the motor. I found Lawson's servant, and heard from him that his master was sleeping peacefully. I gave him some directions, and then went to wash and change.

Before I left I wrote a line to Lawson. I began by transcribing the verses from the 23rd chapter of 2nd Kings. I told him what I had done, and my reason. "I take the whole responsibility upon myself," I wrote. "No man in the place had anything to do with it but me. I acted as I did for the sake of our old friendship, and you will believe it was no easy task for me. I hope you will understand. Whenever you are able to see me send me word, and I will come back and settle with you. But I think you will realise that I have saved your soul."

The afternoon was merging into twilight as I left the house on the road to Taqui. The great fire, where the Grove had been, was still blazing fiercely, and the smoke made a cloud over the upper glen, and filled all the air with a soft violet haze. I knew that I had done well for my friend, and that he would come to his senses and be grateful. My mind was at ease on that score, and in something like comfort I faced the future. But as the car reached the ridge I looked back to the vale I had outraged. The moon was rising and silvering the smoke, and through the gaps I could see the tongues of fire. Somehow, I know not why, the lake, the stream, the garden-coverts, even the green slopes of hill, wore an air of loneliness and desecration.

And then my heartache returned, and I knew that I had driven something lovely and adorable from its last refuge on earth.

THE LEMNIAN

H E pushed the matted locks from his brow as he peered into
the mist. His hair was thick with salt, and his eyes smarted
from the green-wood fire on the poop. The four slaves who
crouched beside the thwarts—Carians with thin birdlike faces—
were in a pitiable case, their hands blue with oar-weals and the
lash marks on their shoulders beginning to gape from sun and
sea. The Lemnian himself bore marks of ill-usage. His cloak was
still sopping, his eyes heavy with watching, and his lips black and
cracked with thirst. Two days before the storm had caught him
and swept his little craft into mid-Ægean. He was a sailor, come
of sailor stock, and he had fought the gale manfully and well.
But the sea had burst his water-jars, and the torments of drought
had been added to his toil. He had been driven south almost to
Scyros, but had found no harbour. Then a weary day with the
oars had brought him close to the Eubœan shore, when a freshet
of storm drove him seaward again. Now at last in this northerly
creek of Sciathos he had found shelter and a spring. But it was
a perilous place, for there were robbers in the bushy hills—
mainland men who loved above all things to rob an islander: and
out at sea, as he looked towards Pelion, there seemed something
adoing which boded little good. There was deep water beneath
a ledge of cliff, half covered by a tangle of wildwood. So Atta
lay in the bows, looking through the trails of vine at the racing
tides now reddening in the dawn.

The storm had hit others besides him, it seemed. The channel
was full of ships, aimless ships that tossed between tide and
wind. Looking closer, he saw that they were all wreckage. There
had been tremendous doings in the north, and a navy of some
sort had come to grief. Atta was a prudent man, and knew that
a broken fleet might be dangerous. There might be men lurking

in the maimed galleys who would make short work of the owner of a battered but navigable craft. At first he thought that the ships were those of the Hellenes. The troublesome fellows were everywhere in the islands, stirring up strife and robbing the old lords. But the tides running strongly from the east were bringing some of the wreckage in an eddy into the bay. He lay closer and watched the spars and splintered poops as they neared him. These were no galleys of the Hellenes. Then came a drowned man, swollen and horrible: then another—swarthy, hook-nosed fellows, all yellow with the sea. Atta was puzzled. They must be the men from the East about whom he had been hearing. Long ere he left Lemnos there had been news about the Persians. They were coming like locusts out of the dawn, swarming over Ionia and Thrace, men and ships numerous beyond telling. They meant no ill to honest islanders: a little earth and water were enough to win their friendship. But they meant death to the ὕβρις of the Hellenes. Atta was on the side of the invaders; he wished them well in their war with his ancient foes. They would eat them up, Athenians, Lacedæmonians, Corinthians, Æginetans, men of Argos and Elis, and none would be left to trouble him. But in the meantime something had gone wrong. Clearly there had been no battle. As the bodies butted against the side of the galley he hooked up one or two and found no trace of a wound. Poseidon had grown cranky, and had claimed victims. The god would be appeased by this time, and all would go well.

Danger being past, he bade the men get ashore and fill the water-skins. "God's curse on all Hellenes," he said, as he soaked up the cold water from the spring in the thicket.

About noon he set sail again. The wind sat in the north-east, but the wall of Pelion turned it into a light stern breeze which carried him swiftly westward. The four slaves, still leg-weary and arm-weary, lay like logs beside the thwarts. Two slept; one munched some salty figs; the fourth, the headman, stared wearily forward, with over and again a glance back at his master. But the Lemnian never looked his way. His head was on his breast as he steered, and he brooded on the sins of the Hellenes. He was of the old Pelasgian stock, the first lords of the land, who had come out of the soil at the call of God. The pillaging northmen had crushed his folk out of the mainlands and most of the islands, but in Lemnos they had met their match. It was a family story how every grown male had been slain, and how the women long after had slaughtered their conquerors in the night. "Lemnian deeds," said the Hellenes, when they wished to speak of some shameful thing: but to Atta the shame was a glory to be cherished for ever. He and his kind were the ancient people, and the gods loved old things, as those new folk would find. Very especially he hated the men of Athens. Had not one of their captains, Miltiades, beaten the Lemnians and brought the island under Athenian sway? True, it was a rule only in name, for any Athenian who came alone to Lemnos would soon be cleaving the air from the highest cliff-top. But the thought irked his pride, and he gloated over the Persians' coming. The Great King from beyond the deserts would smite those outrageous upstarts. Atta would willingly give earth and water. It was the whim of a fantastic barbarian, and would be well repaid if the bastard Hellenes were destroyed. They spoke his own tongue, and worshipped his own gods, and yet did evil. Let the nemesis of Zeus devour them!

The wreckage pursued him everywhere. Dead men shouldered the sides of the galley, and the straits were stuck full of things like monstrous buoys, where tall ships had foundered. At Artemision he thought he saw signs of an anchored fleet with the low poops of the Hellenes, and sheered off to the northern shores. There, looking towards Œta and the Malian Gulf, he found an anchorage at sunset. The waters were ugly and the times ill, and he had come on an enterprise bigger than he had dreamed. The Lemnian was a stout fellow, but he had no love for needless danger. He laughed mirthlessly as he thought of his errand, for he was going to Hellas, to the shrine of the Hellenes.

It was a woman's doing, like most crazy enterprises. Three years ago his wife had laboured hard in childbirth, and had had the whims of labouring women. Up in the keep of Larisa, on the windy hillside, there had been heart-searching and talk about the gods. The little olive-wood Hermes, the very private and particular god of Atta's folk, was good enough in simple things

244

like a lambing or a harvest but he was scarcely fit for heavy tasks. Atta's wife declared that her lord lacked piety. There were mainland gods who repaid worship, but his scorn of all Hellenes made him blind to the merits of those potent divinities. At first Atta resisted. There was Attic blood in his wife, and he strove to argue with her unorthodox craving. But the woman persisted, and a Lemnian wife, as she is beyond other wives in virtue and comeliness, excels them in stubbornness of temper. A second time she was with child, and nothing would content her but that Atta should make his prayers to the stronger gods. Dodona was far away, and long ere he reached it his throat would be cut in the hills. But Delphi was but two days' journey from the Malian coast, and the god of Delphi, the Far-Darter, had surprising gifts, if one were to credit travellers' tales. Atta yielded with an ill grace, and out of his wealth devised an offering to Apollo. So on this July day he found himself looking across the gulf to Kallidromos, bound for a Hellenic shrine, but hating all Hellenes in his soul. A verse of Homer consoled him—the words which Phocion spoke to Achilles. "Verily even the gods may be turned, they whose excellence and honour and strength are greater than thine; yet even these do men, when they pray, turn from their purpose with offerings of incense and pleasant vows." The Far-Darter must hate the ὕβρις of those Hellenes, and be the more ready to avenge it since they dared to claim his countenance. "No race has ownership in the gods," a Lemnian song-maker had said when Atta had been questioning the ways of Poseidon.

The following dawn found him coasting past the north end of Euboea in the thin fog of a windless summer morn. He steered by the peak of Othrys and a spur of Œta, as he had learnt from a slave who had travelled the road. Presently he was in the muddy Malian waters, and the sun was scattering the mist on the landward side. And then he became aware of a greater commotion than Poseidon's play with the ships off Pelion. A murmur like a winter's storm came seawards. He lowered the sail, which he had set to catch a chance breeze, and bade the men rest on their oars. An earthquake seemed to be tearing at the roots of the hills.

The mist rolled up, and his hawk eyes saw a strange sight. The water was green and still around him, but shoreward it changed its colour. It was a dirty red, and things bobbed about in it like the Persians in the creek of Sciathos. On the strip of shore, below the sheer wall of Kallidromos, men were fighting—myriads of men, for away toward Locris they stretched in ranks and banners and tents till the eye lost them in the haze. There was no sail on the queer, muddy, red-edged sea; there was no man on the hills: but on that one flat ribbon of sand all the nations of the earth were warring. He remembered about the place: Thermopylæ they called it, the Gate of the Hot Springs. The Hellenes were fighting the Persians in the pass for their Fatherland.

Atta was prudent and loved not other men's quarrels. He gave the word to the rowers to row seaward. In twenty strokes they were in the mist again. . . .

Atta was prudent, but he was also stubborn. He spent the day in a creek on the northern shore of the gulf, listening to the weird hum which came over the waters out of the haze. He cursed the delay. Up on Kallidromos would be clear dry air and the path to Delphi among the oak woods. The Hellenes could not be fighting everywhere at once. He might find some spot on the shore, far in their rear, where he could land and gain the hills. There was danger indeed, but once on the ridge he would be safe; and by the time he came back the Great King would have swept the defenders into the sea, and be well on the road for Athens. He asked himself if it were fitting that a Lemnian should be stayed in his holy task by the struggles of Hellene and Barbarian. His thoughts flew to his steading at Larisa, and the dark-eyed wife who was awaiting his homecoming. He could not return without Apollo's favour: his manhood and the memory of his lady's eyes forbade it. So late in the afternoon he pushed off again and steered his galley for the south.

About sunset the mist cleared from the sea; but the dark falls swiftly in the shadow of the high hills, and Atta had no fear. With the night the hum sank to a whisper; it seemed that the invaders were drawing off to camp, for the sound receded to the west. At the last light the Lemnian touched a rock-point well to the rear of the defence. He noticed that the spume at the tide's edge was reddish and stuck to his hands like gum. Of a surety much blood was flowing on that coast.

He bade his slaves return to the north shore and lie hidden to await him. When he came back he would light a signal fire on the topmost bluff of Kallidromos. Let them watch for it and come to take him off. Then he seized his bow and quiver, and his short hunting-spear, buckled his cloak about him, saw that the gift to Apollo was safe in the folds of it, and marched sturdily up the hillside.

The moon was in her first quarter, a slim horn which at her rise showed only the faint outline of the hill. Atta plodded steadfastly on, but he found the way hard. This was not like the crisp sea-turf of Lemnos, where among the barrows of the ancient dead sheep and kine could find sweet fodder. Kallidromos ran up as steep as the roof of a barn. Cytisus and thyme and juniper grew rank, but above all the place was strewn with rocks, leg-twisting boulders, and great cliffs where eagles dwelt. Being a seaman, Atta had his bearings. The path to Delphi left the shore road near the Hot Springs, and went south by a rift of the mountain. If he went up the slope in a bee-line he must strike it in time and find better going. Still it was an eerie place to be tramping after dark. The Hellenes had strange gods of the thicket and hillside, and he had no wish to intrude upon their sanctuaries. He told himself that next to the Hellenes he hated this country of theirs, where a man sweltered in hot jungles or tripped among hidden crags. He sighed for the cool beaches below Larisa, where the surf was white as the snows of Samothrace, and the fisher-boys sang round their smoking broth-pots.

Presently he found a path. It was not the mule road, worn by many feet, that he had looked for, but a little track which twined among the boulders. Still it eased his feet, so he cleared the thorns from his sandals, strapped his belt tighter, and stepped out more confidently. Up and up he went, making odd detours among the crags. Once he came to a promontory, and, looking down, saw lights twinkling from the Hot Springs. He had thought the course lay more southerly, but consoled himself by remembering that a mountain path must have many windings.

247

The great matter was that he was ascending, for he knew that he must cross the ridge of Œta before he struck the Locrian glens that led to the Far-Darter's shrine.

At what seemed the summit of the first ridge he halted for breath, and, prone on the thyme, looked back to sea. The Hot Springs were hidden, but across the gulf a single light shone from the far shore. He guessed that by this time his galley had been beached and his slaves were cooking supper. The thought made him homesick. He had beaten and cursed these slaves of his times without number, but now in this strange land he felt them kinsfolk, men of his own household. Then he told himself he was no better than a woman. Had he not gone sailing to Chalcedon and distant Pontus, many months' journey from home, while this was but a trip of days? In a week he would be welcomed by a smiling wife, with a friendly god behind him.

The track still bore west, though Delphi lay in the south. Moreover, he had come to a broader road running through a little tableland. The highest peaks of Œta were dark against the sky, and around him was a flat glade where oaks whispered in the night breezes. By this time he judged from the stars that midnight had passed, and he began to consider whether, now that he was beyond the fighting, he should not sleep and wait for dawn. He made up his mind to find a shelter, and, in the aimless way of the night traveller, pushed on and on in the quest of it. The truth is his mind was on Lemnos, and a dark-eyed, white-armed dame spinning in the evening by the threshold. His eyes roamed among the oak-trees, but vacantly and idly, and many a mossy corner was passed unheeded. He forgot his ill-temper, and hummed cheerfully the song his reapers sang in the barley-fields below his orchard. It was a song of seamen turned husbandmen, for the gods it called on were the gods of the sea.

Suddenly he found himself crouching among the young oaks, peering and listening. There was something coming from the west. It was like the first mutterings of a storm in a narrow harbour, a steady rustling and whispering. It was not wind; he knew winds too well to be deceived. It was the tramp of light-shod feet among the twigs—many feet, for the sound remained steady, while the noise of a few men will rise and fall. They were coming fast and coming silently. The war had reached far up Kallidromos.

Atta had played this game often in the little island wars. Very swiftly he ran back and away from the path up the slope which he knew to be the first ridge of Kallidromos. The army, whatever it might be, was on the Delphian road. Were the Hellenes about to turn the flank of the Great King?

A moment later he laughed at his folly. For the men began to appear, and they were coming to meet him, coming from the west. Lying close in the brushwood he could see them clearly. It was well he had left the road, for they stuck to it, following every winding—crouching, too, like hunters after deer. The first man he saw was a Hellene, but the ranks behind were no Hellenes. There was no glint of bronze or gleam of fair skin. They were dark, long-haired fellows, with spears like his own, and round Eastern caps, and egg-shaped bucklers. Then Atta rejoiced. It was the Great King who was turning the flank of the Hellenes. They guarded the gate, the fools, while the enemy slipped through the roof.

He did not rejoice long. The van of the army was narrow and kept to the path, but the men behind were straggling all over the hillside. Another minute and he would be discovered. The thought was cheerless. It was true that he was an islander and friendly to the Persian, but up on the heights who would listen to his tale? He would be taken for a spy, and one of those thirsty spears would drink his blood. It must be farewell to Delphi for the moment, he thought, or farewell to Lemnos for ever. Crouching low, he ran back and away from the path to the crest of the sea-ridge of Kallidromos.

The men came no nearer him. They were keeping roughly to the line of the path, and drifted through the oak wood before him, an army without end. He had scarcely thought there were so many fighting men in the world. He resolved to lie there on the crest, in the hope that ere the first light they would be gone. Then he would push on to Delphi, leaving them to settle their quarrels behind him. These were the hard times for a pious pilgrim. But another noise caught his ear from the right. The

249

army had flanking squadrons, and men were coming along the ridge. Very bitter anger rose in Atta's heart. He had cursed the Hellenes, and now he cursed the Barbarians no less. Nay, he cursed all war, that spoiled the errands of peaceful folk. And then, seeking safety, he dropped over the crest on to the steep shoreward face of the mountain.

In an instant his breath had gone from him. He slid down a long slope of screes, and then with a gasp found himself falling sheer into space. Another second and he was caught in a tangle of bush, and then dropped once more upon screes, where he clutched desperately for hand-hold. Breathless and bleeding he came to anchor on a shelf of greensward, and found himself blinking up at the crest which seemed to tower a thousand feet above. There were men on the crest now. He heard them speak, and felt that they were looking down.

The shock kept him still till the men had passed. Then the terror of the place gripped him, and he tried feverishly to retrace his steps. A dweller all his days among gentle downs, he grew dizzy with the sense of being hung in space. But the only fruit of his efforts was to set him slipping again. This time he pulled up at a root of gnarled oak, which overhung the sheerest cliff on Kallidromos. The danger brought his wits back. He sullenly reviewed his case, and found it desperate.

He could not go back, and, even if he did, he would meet the Persians. If he went on he would break his neck, or at the best fall into the Hellenes' hands. Oddly enough he feared his old enemies less than his friends. He did not think that the Hellenes would butcher him. Again, he might sit perched in his eyrie till they settled their quarrel, or he fell off. He rejected this last way. Fall off he should for certain, unless he kept moving. Already he was retching with the vertigo of the heights. It was growing lighter. Suddenly he was looking not into a black world, but to a pearl-grey floor far beneath him. It was the sea, the thing he knew and loved. The sight screwed up his courage. He remembered that he was a Lemnian and a seafarer. He would be conquered neither by rock, nor by Hellene, nor by the Great King. Least of all by the last, who was a barbarian. Slowly, with clenched teeth and narrowed eyes, he began to clamber down a ridge which flanked the great cliff of Kallidromos. His plan was to reach the shore and take the road to the east before the Persians completed their circuit. Some instinct told him that a great army would not take the track he had mounted by. There must be some longer and easier way debouching farther down the coast. He might yet have the good luck to slip between them and the sea.

The two hours which followed tried his courage hard. Thrice he fell, and only a juniper-root stood between him and death. His hands grew ragged, and his nails were worn to the quick. He had long ago lost his weapons; his cloak was in shreds, all save the breast-fold which held the gift to Apollo. The heavens brightened, but he dared not look around. He knew he was traversing awesome places, where a goat could scarcely tread. Many times he gave up hope of life. His head was swimming, and he was so deadly sick that often he had to lie gasping on some shoulder of rock less steep than the rest. But his anger kept him to his purpose. He was filled with fury at the Hellenes. It was they and their folly that had brought him these mischances. Some day . . .

He found himself sitting blinking on the shore of the sea. A furlong off the water was lapping on the reefs. A man, larger than human in the morning mist, was standing above him.

"Greeting, stranger," said the voice. "By Hermes, you choose the difficult roads to travel."

Atta felt for broken bones, and, reassured, struggled to his feet. "God's curse upon all mountains," he said. He staggered to the edge of the tide and laved his brow. The savour of salt revived him. He turned to find the tall man at his elbow, and noted how worn and ragged he was, and yet how upright.

"When a pigeon is flushed from the rocks there is a hawk near," said the voice.

Atta was angry. "A hawk!" he cried. "Nay, an army of eagles. There will be some rare flushing of Hellenes before evening."

"What frightened you, Islander?" the stranger asked. "Did a wolf bark up on the hillside?"

"Ay, a wolf. The wolf from the East with a multitude of wolflings. There will be fine eating soon in the pass."

The man's face grew dark. He put his hand to his mouth and called. Half a dozen sentries ran to join him. He spoke to them in the harsh Lacedæmonian speech which made Atta sick to hear. They talked with the back of the throat, and there was not an "s" in their words.

"There is mischief in the hills," the first man said. "This islander has been frightened down over the rocks. The Persian is stealing a march on us."

The sentries laughed. One quoted a proverb about island courage. Atta's wrath flared and he forgot himself. He had no wish to warn the Hellenes, but it irked his pride to be thought a liar. He began to tell his story hastily, angrily, confusedly: and the men still laughed.

Then he turned eastward and saw the proof before him. The light had grown and the sun was coming up over Pelion. The first beam fell on the eastern ridge of Kallidromos, and there, clear on the sky-line, was the proof. The Persian was making a wide circuit, but moving shoreward. In a little he would be at the coast, and by noon at the Hellenes' rear.

His hearers doubted no more. Atta was hurried forward through the lines of the Greeks to the narrow throat of the pass, where behind a rough rampart of stones lay the Lacedæmonian headquarters. He was still giddy from the heights and it was in a giddy dream that he traversed the misty shingles of the beach amid ranks of sleeping warriors. It was a grim place, for there were dead and dying in it, and blood on every stone. But in the lee of the wall little fires were burning and slaves were cooking breakfast. The smell of roasting flesh came pleasantly to his nostrils, and he remembered that he had had no meal since he crossed the gulf.

Then he found himself the centre of a group who had the air of kings. They looked as if they had been years in war. Never had he seen faces so worn and so terribly scarred. The hollows in their cheeks gave them the air of smiling; and yet they were grave. Their scarlet vests were torn and muddied, and the armour which lay near was dinted like the scrap-iron before a smithy door. But what caught his attention were the eyes of the men. They glittered as no eyes he had ever seen before glittered. The sight cleared his bewilderment and took the pride out of his heart. He could not pretend to despise a folk who looked like Ares fresh from the wars of the Immortals.

They spoke among themselves in quiet voices. Scouts came and went, and once or twice one of the men, taller than the rest, asked Atta a question. The Lemnian sat in the heart of the group, sniffing the smell of cooking, and looking at the rents in his cloak and the long scratches on his legs. Something was pressing on his breast, and he found that it was Apollo's gift. He had forgotten all about it. Delphi seemed beyond the moon, and his errand a child's dream. Then the King, for so he thought of the tall man, spoke—

"You have done us a service, Islander. The Persian is at our back and front, and there will be no escape for those who stay. Our allies are going home, for they do not share our vows. We of Lacedæmon wait in the pass. If you go with the men of Corinth you will find a place of safety before noon. No doubt in the Euripus there is some boat to take you to your own land."

He spoke courteously, not in the rude Athenian way; and somehow the quietness of his voice and his glittering eyes roused wild longings in Atta's heart. His island pride was face to face with a greater—greater than he had ever dreamed of.

"Bid yon cooks give me some broth," he said gruffly. "I am faint. After I have eaten I will speak with you."

He was given food, and as he ate he thought. He was on trial before these men of Lacedæmon. More, the old faith of the islands, the pride of the first masters, was at stake in his hands. He had boasted that he and his kind were the last of the men; now these Hellenes of Lacedæmon were preparing a great deed, and they deemed him unworthy to share in it. They offered him safety. Could he brook the insult? He had forgotten that the cause of the Persian was his; that the Hellenes were the foes of his race. He saw only that the last test of manhood was preparing, and the manhood in him rose to greet the trial. An odd wild ecstasy surged in his veins. It was not the lust of battle, for he had no love of slaying, or hate for the Persian, for he was his friend. It was the sheer joy of proving that the Lemnian stock had a starker pride than these men of Lacedæmon. They would die for their fatherland and their vows; but he, for a whim, a scruple, a delicacy of honour. His mind was so clear that no other course occurred to him. There was only one way for a man. He, too, would be dying for his fatherland, for through him the island race would be ennobled in the eyes of gods and men. Troops were filing fast to the east—Thebans, Corinthians.

"Time flies, Islander," said the King's voice. "The hours of safety are slipping past."

Atta looked up carelessly. "I will stay," he said. "God's curse on all Hellenes! Little I care for your quarrels. It is nothing to me if your Hellas is under the heel of the East. But I care much for brave men. It shall never be said that a man of Lemnos, a son of the old race, fell back when Death threatened. I stay with you, men of Lacedæmon."

The King's eyes glittered; they seemed to peer into his heart.

"It appears they breed men in the islands," he said. "But you err. Death does not threaten. Death awaits us."

"It is all one," said Atta. "But I crave a boon. Let me fight my last fight by your side. I am of older stock than you, and a king in my own country. I would strike my last blow among kings."

There was an hour of respite before battle was joined, and Atta spent it by the edge of the sea. He had been given arms, and in girding himself for the fight he had found Apollo's offering in his breastfold. He was done with the gods of the Hellenes. His offering should go to the gods of his own people. So, calling upon Poseidon, he flung the little gold cup far out to sea. It flashed in the sunlight, and then sank in the soft green tides so noiselessly that it seemed as if the hand of the sea-god had been stretched to take it. "Hail, Poseidon!" the Lemnian cried. "I am bound this day for the Ferryman. To you only I make prayer, and to the little Hermes of Larisa. Be kind to my kin when they travel the sea, and keep them islanders and seafarers for ever. Hail and farewell, God of my own folk!"

Then, while the little waves lapped on the white sand, Atta made a song. He was thinking of the homestead far up in the green downs, looking over to the snows of Samothrace. At this hour in the morning there would be a tinkle of sheep-bells as the flocks went down to the low pastures. Cool winds would be blowing, and the noise of the surf below the cliffs would come faint to the ear. In the hall the maids would be spinning, while their dark-haired mistress would be casting swift glances to the doorway, lest it might be filled any moment by the form of her returning lord. Outside in the chequered sunlight of the orchard the child would be playing with his nurse, crooning in childish syllables the chanty his father had taught him. And at the thought of his home a great passion welled up in Atta's heart. It was not regret, but joy and pride and aching love. In his antique island creed the death he was awaiting was not other than a bridal. He was dying for the things he loved, and by his death they would be blessed eternally. He would not have long to wait before bright eyes came to greet him in the House of Shadows.

So Atta made the Song of Atta, and sang it then, and later in the press of battle. It was a simple song, like the lays of seafarers. It put into rough verse the thought which cheers the heart of all adventurers—nay, which makes adventure possible for those who have much to leave. It spoke of the shining pathway of the sea which is the Great Uniter. A man may lie dead in Pontus or beyond the Pillars of Herakles, but if he dies on the shore there is nothing between him and his fatherland. It spoke of a battle all the long dark night in a strange place— a place of marshes and black cliffs and shadowy terrors.

"In the dawn the sweet light comes," said the song, *"and the salt winds and the tides will bear me home. . . ."*

When in the evening the Persians took toll of the dead, they found one man who puzzled them. He lay among the tall Lacedæmonians, on the very lip of the sea, and around him were swathes of their countrymen. It looked as if he had been fighting his way to the water, and had been overtaken by death as his feet reached the edge. Nowhere in the pass did the dead lie so thick, and yet he was no Hellene. He was torn like a deer that the dogs have worried, but the little left of his garments and his features spoke of Eastern race. The survivors could tell nothing

255

except that he had fought like a god and had been singing all the while. The matter came to the ear of the Great King, who was sore enough at the issue of the day. That one of his men had performed feats of valour beyond the Hellenes was a pleasant tale to tell. And so his captains reported it. Accordingly when the fleet from Artemision arrived next morning, and all but a few score Persians were shovelled into holes, that the Hellenes might seem to have been conquered by a lesser force, Atta's body was laid out with pomp in the midst of the Lacedæmonians. And the seamen rubbed their eyes and thanked their strange gods that one man of the East had been found to match those terrible warriors whose name was a nightmare. Further, the Great King gave orders that the body of Atta should be embalmed and carried with the army, and that his name and kin should be sought out and duly honoured. This latter was a task too hard for the staff, and no more was heard of it till months later, when the King, in full flight after Salamis, bethought him of the one man who had not played him false. Finding that his lieutenants had nothing to tell him, he eased five of them of their heads.

As it happened, the deed was not quite forgotten. An islander, a Lesbian and a cautious man, had fought at Thermopylæ in the Persian ranks, and had heard Atta's singing and seen how he fell. Long afterwards some errand took this man to Lemnos, and in the evening, speaking with the Elders, he told his tale and repeated something of the song. There was that in the words which gave the Lemnians a clue, the mention, I think, of the olive-wood Hermes and the snows of Samothrace. So Atta came to great honour among his own people, and his memory and his words were handed down to the generations. The song became a favourite island lay, and for centuries throughout the Ægean seafaring men sang it when they turned their prows to wild seas. Nay, it travelled farther, for you will find part of it stolen by Euripides and put in a chorus of the *Andromache*. There are echoes of it in some of the epigrams of the *Anthology*; and, though the old days have gone, the simple fisher-folk still sing snatches in their barbarous dialect. The Klephts used to make a catch of it at night round their fires in the hills, and only the other day I met a man in Scyros who had collected a dozen variants, and was publishing them in a dull book on island folklore.

In the centuries which followed the great fight, the sea fell away from the roots of the cliffs and left a mile of marshland. About fifty years ago a peasant, digging in a rice-field, found the cup which Atta had given to Poseidon. There was much talk about the discovery, and scholars debated hotly about its origin. Today it is in the Berlin Museum, and according to the new fashion in archaeology it is labelled "Minoan", and kept in the Cretan Section. But anyone who looks carefully will see behind the rim a neat little carving of a dolphin; and I happen to know that that was the private badge of Atta's house.

ATTA'S SONG

(Roughly translated)

I will sing of thee,
Great Sea-Mother,
Whose white arms gather
Thy sons in the ending:
And draw them homeward
From far sad marches—
Wild lands in the sunset,
Bitter shores of the morning
Soothe them and guide them
By shining pathways
Homeward to thee.

All day I have striven in dark glens
With parched throat and dim eyes,
Where the red crags choke the stream
And dank thickets hide the spear.
I have spilled the blood of my foes
And their wolves have torn my flanks.
I am faint, O Mother,
Faint and aweary.
I have longed for thy cool winds
And thy kind grey eyes
And thy lover's arms.

At the even I came
To a land of terrors,
Of hot swamps where the feet mired
And waters that flowed red with blood.
There I strove with thousands,
Wild-eyed and lost,
As a lion among serpents.

—But sudden before me
I saw the flash
Of the sweet wide waters
That wash my homeland
And mirror the stars of home.
Then sang I for joy,
For I knew the Preserver,
Thee, the Uniter,
The great Sea-Mother.
Soon will the sweet light come,
And the salt winds and the tides
Will bear me home.

Far in the sunrise,
Nestled in thy bosom,
Lies my own green isle.
Thither wilt thou bear me
To where, above the sea-cliffs,
Stretch mild meadows, flower-decked,
    thyme-scented,
Crisp with sea breezes.
There my flocks feed
On sunny uplands,
Looking over thy waters
To where the mount Saos
Raises pure snows to God.

Hermes, guide of souls,
I made thee a shrine in my orchard,
And round thy olive-wood limbs
The maidens twined Spring blossoms—
Violet and helichryse
And the pale wind flowers.
Keep thou watch for me,
For I am coming.

Tell to my lady
And to all my kinsfolk
That I who have gone from them
Tarry not long, but come swift o'er the sea-path,
My feet light with joy,
My eyes bright with longing.
For little it matters
Where a man may fall,
If he fall by the sea-shore;
The kind waters await him,
The white arms are around him,
And the wise Mother of Men
Will carry him home.

I who sing
Wait joyfully on the morning.
Ten thousand beset me
And their spears ache for my heart.
They will crush me and grind me to mire,
So that none will know the man that once was
me.
But at the first light I shall be gone,
Singing, flitting, o'er the grey waters,
Outward, homeward,
To thee, the Preserver,
Thee, the Uniter,
Mother the Sea.

THE GREEN GLEN

I

I FIRST saw the Glen when I was eleven years old, a small boy consumed with a passion for trout. Adventuring on a rusty bicycle I had penetrated to remote dales, and made baskets in streams which no Anglers' Guide ever heard of. One day I had fished the sources of the Cauldshaw, and, the sun being yet high, bethought me of the Fawn, which flowed on the other side of the narrow watershed. I shouldered my rod and tramped up the mossy spaces of the burn-head, till I waded deep in the bracken of the ridge. There on the summit the heather ended as if ruled by a gardener's line. I was looking into a narrow glen which ran from a round hope till a broad green hill baulked the view. From beginning to end there was no house, not even a sheep-fold or a dyke. I remember my amazement at its indescribable greenness. There was the yellow-green of moss, the old velvet of mountain turf, the grey-green of bent on the hill-brow; but all was green, without tree or crag or heather bush to distract the eye. Through the middle of it ran the Fawn, a very fishable stream to my notion, and I ran down the brae with hope high in my heart.

But I never cast a fly in those waters. Long before I was down the hill the eeriness and the solitariness of the place weighed on my mind. There was no man here, and no sign of man. There were no whaups crying, or grouse to upbraid my presence. It was still as the grave, but for the lilt of the stream; and it was terribly green. I remembered a line of a song that ploughmen used to whistle—"The wild glen sae green"—and I thought how much deeper this green wildness was than any rock and heather. The still slopes and folds of hill seemed to my unquiet eye to stretch to eternity.

At the edge of the burn was a rude mound, embanked like some Roman fort. With a fluttering heart I began to put my rod together. The Fawn dashed and swirled in noble pools, but I could not keep my eyes on it. The green hills shut me in, and the awe of them brooded over me. I was mortally afraid, and not ashamed of my fear. I could not give a name to it, but something uncanny was in the air: not terrible exactly, or threatening, but inhumanly strange. I clutched my rod—the butt and middle piece were put together—and fled the way I had come. I do not think I stopped running till I fell panting by the side of the Cauldshaw among the friendly heather.

II

TWENTY years later, when the doings of eleven are a faint memory, chance set me fishing the lower streams of the Fawn. It was a clear June day, but the waters were too low and my basket was light. I fished like an epicure, a cast in each pool sufficing for me; and presently I had rounded the shoulder of the green hill which cuts the valley in two. They call it the Green Dod, and there is no greener hill in that green country. I found myself in an upland glen, where the Fawn had sunk to a mountain burn. The place was very soothing and quiet, and idly I wandered on, drinking in the peace of the hills. Then something in the contours awakened a memory, and I recalled my boyish escapade. The years have their consolations, for what had once terrified now charmed. I laughed at the scared little sinner, whose trembling legs had once twinkled up those braes. I put by my rod and abandoned myself to the delights of the greenness. Far up on the hill shoulders white sheep were dotted, but the waterside was empty. Not even a water-crow was visible, and in the patches of bog there was no sign of snipe. The place was full of a delicious desolation. There were the strait green sides, the Green Dod at the foot, a green hope at the head, and only the clear singing water stirred in the sunny afternoon.

I found a seat on a mound, and basked in deep content. It was the height of pastoral, yet without sheep or shepherd. The

Fawn was a true Border stream, jewelled in sunlight, but wan as death under grey skies. I wondered how I had hitherto missed this happy valley. Nature had wrought it in a kindly mood, and hidden it very far from men. It must, I thought, have had a gracious history. There was no terror in its solitude. I could not imagine the cry of death from the burn, or harsh deeds done on those green lawns. Who had owned it in old days? Perhaps some Roman, pushing north with his bronze soldiers against the Picts, had been caught by its grace, and christened it by the name of his woodland god. True Thomas may have walked by its streams. But its story must have been chiefly of elves and fairy folk, for it wore the fairy livery.

I looked at the mound on which I sat, and saw that it had once been the site of a dwelling. It was all crisp moorland turf, gemmed with eyebright and milkwort, but the rampart had been made by man. Scraping with the butt-end of my rod, I laid bare a chiselled block. This had been no sheepfold or shepherd's cot, but a tower.

The discovery stirred a fresh strain of fancy. Some old raider had his keep here, and filled the glen with ill-gotten cattle. I pictured the forays returning over the green hills in some autumn twilight. I saw beacons fired on the tops, and the winter snows reddened with blood. Just then a cloud came over the sun, and the grace of the valley vanished. Now the stream ran wan, and I saw that the glen was wild and very lonely. Terror had dwelt here as well as peace. I remembered the boy of eleven, who on this very mound had picked up his rod and run.

That evening at Hardriding I hunted the library for local histories. They could not tell me much, being mostly the casual compilations of local ministers. But I found one thing of interest. I had been right about True Thomas. It seemed that the Rhymer had honoured the Fawn with a couplet of doubtful Latin:

> *Ubi Faunus fluit*
> *Spes mortalis ruit.*

I had no notion what he meant, and suspected the hand of the Reverend Mr. Gilfillan *circa* 1780.

FORTUNE and a broken leg gave me some leisure that winter, and I spent it in searching for the history of what I had come to call the Green Glen. For two hundred years back it was plain going. Along with a dozen other valleys it had been swept into the net of the noble house which had built its fortunes on the fall of the turbulent little Border septs. Earlier it had been by turns in the hands of two families, both long perished—Home of Hardriding and Douglas of Cauldshaw. That took me back to the fourteenth century or thereabouts, where the history stopped short. But I found a charter of Melrose a century before, from which it appeared that the lands of Fawn, "the nether and hither glens thereof", had been in the hands of the monks, who had profited by the good grazing. A chapel of Our Lady had stood by the burnside, endowed with a hundred merks a year by a certain Simon de Fries in penance for the slaying of an erring wife. There my tale ended, but I hazarded a guess. Fifty years ago a slab was found near Hadrian's Wall with a list of stations on the great road which ran north to the land of the Picts. You will find it copied in the Berlin *Corpus* and there is much dispute about the identification of the names. One of them is a certain *Fauni Castellum*, which scholars have fastened on a dozen places between Ardoch and Melrose. I was myself convinced that the castellum was the mound in the Green Glen, the more so as Mr. Gilfillan reported a find there of gold coins of the Antonines in 1758. It is true that the place was some miles from the main line of transit, but it would command the hill-roads from the West. Besides, might it not have been a sacred place, half fort, half shrine, an outpost of the dying faith? Why, otherwise, the strange name of the woodland god?

These were all my facts—too few on which to spin the delicate web of history. But my imagination was kindled, and I set to work. If I were right, this glen had a virtue which had drawn to it many races. Little as the recorded history was, it was far more than the due of an inconsiderable howe of the hills. Rome had made it a halting-place and consecrated it to her gods; the Church had built a shrine in it; two famous clans had fought furiously for its sake. My first impression was justified, for it had been no common place. Some ancient *aura* had brooded over its greenness and compelled men's souls.

Bit by bit from monkish Latin, from fragments of ballads, from cumbrous family histories, and from musty chronicles, I built up the shadow of a tale. Rome gave me nothing—the fog of years lay too thick over that greatest of mortal pages; but I hazarded a guess that the broken Satyr's head, found in some unknown Border earthwork and now in the Grange collection, had come from my glen. Perhaps the Melrose monks had found it and copied it in their gargoyles. But of the Christian shrine I had something to tell. The chapel seems to have had an ill reputation for a holy place. The chapter of Melrose in or about 1250 held an inquisition into the doings of a certain John of Fawn, who tended the shrine with unhallowed service. There were complaints of his successor, a monk who bore the name of Lapidarius; and the grand climax was reached in the fate of one Andrew de Faun, a priest, says the record, who had the unpleasing gift "*diabolos convocandi*". He was hand in glove with Lord Soulis, whose castle of Hermitage lay some twenty miles over the hills. Of his iniquities it is recorded that the country folk grew weary, and one October night surprised him at the business. He confessed his sins under the pressure of boiling lead, was duly burned, and his ashes cast into Tweed to be borne to the cleansing sea.

To the monks succeeded the Barons, the first being the tragically fated house of Home. But side by side with the record of their moorland wars I found a ballad history. Fawn had caught the fancy of the wandering minstrel. The heroine of the ghastly "Riding of Etterick" had eyes "grey as Fawn". (The other reading "grey as a fawn" is obvious nonsense.) The tryst for true love on Beltane's E'en was the Fawn side, and it was in the Green Glen that young Brokyn found himself asleep on his return from Fairyland.

"And when ye come to Fawn water,"

says the wise wife in "May Margaret",

"I bid ye lout fu' low,
And say three prayers to Christes grace
Afore ye ride the flow."

In the lovely fragment, "The Thorn of Life", there is a variant,
not given by Child, which tells how on Midsummer morning the
lady washed herself with dew "clear as dawn"—an absurd literary
phrase which spoils the poem. My emendation "Fawn" is, I take
it, certain. In the later riding ballads the name is still more
frequent. The doomed raider in "Carlisle Town" swears that
Fawn will run red as blood ere his wrongs are forgotten. In
"Castle Gay" the dying Home craves, like King David, for a
draught of Fawn water; and in "Lord Archibald's Good-night"
there is a strange line about "the holy wells of Fawn". No doubt
the line is corrupt, but the form of the corruption testifies to the
spell of the Green Glen.

The Homes of Hardriding marched through disorder and
violence to catastrophe. Never more than a hill clan, and kin to
no powerful house, they persisted for three centuries by sheer
audacity and pride. They held the Fawn glen and built a tower
in it, but their real seat was Hardriding in the lower valley. The
wave of Douglas aggression flowed round them, but they stoutly
resisted, and it was only the power of the great Warden of the
Marches that seized Fawnside for the Cauldshaw branch of his
house. The battle in which Piers Home died by the hand of
young Cauldshaw was fought in the Green Glen. Presently the
Douglases were in trouble with the King, and a younger Piers,
under a King's commission, won back his lands and chased
Cauldshaw into Northumberland. The Douglas clan was as often
as not in treaty with the English Warden, while the Hardriding
folk were vehemently Scottish, and, alone of their name, gave a
good account of themselves at Flodden. The fortunes of the two
houses see-sawed so long as lands were won and kept by the
strong arm alone. By-and-by came the day of smooth things,
when a parchment was more potent than the sword, and both
Home and Douglas withered, like hill plants brought into a
lowland garden.

266

It was all an unedifying tale of blood and treason, but in reading it I was struck by one curious fact. Every critical event in the fortunes of the two clans befell in the Green Glen. There the leaders died in battle or in duel, and there a shameless victor celebrated his mastery. It was, so to speak, the citadel, of which the possession was the proof of triumph. It can have had but little value in itself, for the tower by the burn was scarcely a fortalice, and was never seriously dwelled in. Indeed it is referred to not as a castle but as a "bower". When a Douglas defied a Home he summoned him to meet him by the "Bower o' Fawn". This same Bower was the centre of a pretty tale, when for once the bloodstained record emerges into the clear air of pastoral. The Fawn glen did not always pass by war; once it fell to the Douglases by marriage. Marjory of Hardriding, walking one evening by the stream, fell in with the young Douglas, sore wounded in a forest hunt. In the Bower she tended his wounds, and hid him from her fierce clan. Love ripened, and one July morn came the heir of Cauldshaw to Hardriding gates on an errand of peace. But the Home was surly, and the Douglas retired with a bitter denial and an arrow in his corselet. Thereupon Maid Marjory took the matter into her own hands, and rode over the hills to her lover. A gallant lass this, for, after a hurried wedding at the Kirk o' Shaws, she returned with her man to the Fawn Bower to confront an angry father and six angrier brothers. She offered peace or war, but declared that, if war it should be, she herself would fight in the first rank of the Douglases. Whereupon, it is said, old Piers, struck with wonder and delight at the courage he had begotten, declared for peace, and the Green Glen was her dowry.

IV

THE thing became an obsession with me, and I could not let this nook of history alone. Weary hours were spent in the search for Homes and Douglases. Why I wasted my time thus I cannot tell. I told myself it was part of the spell of the Green Glen. "The place was silent and *aware*", as Browning says. I could not think that the virtue had departed and that the romance of Fawn was a past tale. Now it had no visitants save a shepherd taking a short-cut or a fisherman with a taste for moorland trout. But some day a horseman on a fateful errand would stir its waters, or the Bower witness a new pastoral. I told myself that the wise years might ordain a long interval, but sooner or later they would ring up the curtain on the play.

A needle in a haystack was a simple quest compared to mine. History, which loves to leave fringes and loose threads, had cut the record of Home and Douglas with her sharpest shears. The two families disappeared within the same decade. Cauldshaw had chosen the King's side in the Covenant wars, and the head of the house, Sir Adam, had been a noted persecutor of the godly. He came to his end by a bullet of the Black Macmichael's somewhere in the hills of Galloway. His son had fought in the Scots Brigade for the French King, and returned about 1710 to find an estate broken by fines and penalties. We see him last riding south with Mackintosh in the 'Fifteen, but history does not tell us of his fate. He may have died with Derwentwater, or, more likely, he may have escaped and lain low till the hunt passed. Cauldshaw was forfeited and sold, and there was an end of it. Thirty years later I find a Douglas, a locksmith in the High Street of Edinburgh, who may have been his son, since he was gently born and yet clearly of no other known Douglas sept. After that the shears are at work. My note at the end of my researches was, "merged in the burgesses of Edinburgh."

Hardriding showed a similar tale, save that the Homes stood for the Covenant. One of them, Piers or Patrick, swung in the Grassmarket, and was the subject of the eulogies of Wodrow and Patrick Walker. An odd type of saint, his godliness was proved chiefly by his ferocity against the King's officers, for whom he would lie in wait behind a dyke with a musket. He died gallantly, declaiming the 23rd Psalm. The Jacobite rising brought Hardriding round to the side of Cauldshaw. Home and Douglas rode south together, and the fate of the first at any rate is clear. He fell in the rout of Preston, charging with a mouthful of oaths and texts. He left landless sons who disappear into the mist, and the ancient name of Home of Hardriding died in the land. David

Hume, the philosopher, in his cups used to claim kin with the house, but it is recorded that David's friends did not take him seriously.

<h1 style="text-align:center">V</h1>

ABOUT that time I used to try to analyse the impression the Green Glen made upon me. I went to it often and in all weathers, but especially in the soft June days and the flaming twilights of October. At first I thought that the attraction was the peace of it, Wordsworth's "sleep that is among the lonely hills". Certainly it was very quiet and hallowed, with that brooding stillness which is a positive thing and not a mere absence of unrest. I have gone there, worried and distraught, and returned at ease with the world. Once, I remember, I came to it after fighting a forlorn by-election in an English slum, with my brain fagged and dull and my nerves a torment. The Glen healed me, plunging me into the deeps of cool old-world shadows. But I soon discovered that the charm was not an opiate, but a stimulant. Its spell was the spell of life. It stirred the blood, comforting failure and nursing hope, but it did not lull to sleep. Once after a bad illness I went to Hardriding to rest, but I could not face the Glen. It only fevered a sick man. Its call was to action, and its ancient genius had no love for weaklings.

Often I tried to test it, to see if others could feel as I did. I was ridiculously unsuccessful. The sportsmen who frequented Hardriding, finding no grouse in the Glen, fought shy of it, and, if chance took them there, lamented the absence of heather. "Pretty place," one young man observed to me, "but no more Scotch than my hat. It might be Sussex. Where's the brown heath and shaggy wood? What! There isn't cover for a tomtit. It's a nasty big slice out of Harry's shooting to have that long bare place taking up room." It was too remote for ladies to picnic in, but one who penetrated as far called it "sweet", and said it reminded her of Dartmoor. The people of the neighbourhood were no better. Keepers took the same view as the Hardriding sportsmen, and the farmer whose lease covered it spoke of it darkly as "Poaverty Neuk". "Food for neither man nor beast," he said. "Something might be done with phosphates, but I've no money to spend. It would make a grand dam if any town wanted a water-supply." Good business-like views, but no hint anywhere of the strangeness which to me had made it a kind of sanctuary.

There was one exception, the shepherd of the Nine Stane Rig. He was a young man, with a fiery red head and a taste for poetry. He would declaim Burns and Hogg with gusto, and was noted at "kirns" and weddings for his robust rendering of songs like "When the Kye come Hame" and "Robin Tamson's Smiddy". I used to accompany him sometimes on his rounds, and he spoke to me of the Green Glen.

"It's a bonny bit," he once said, waving his arm towards the Green Dod. "And there's ae queer thing about it. Sheep'll no bide in it. Ye may pit a hirsel in at nicht, and every beast'll be on the tap o' the rig by the mornin'. How d'ye account for that? Mr. Yellowlees says the feedin's no guid, and that it wants phosphates. I dinna agree wi' him. I've herdit a' my days, and I never saw better feedin' than by yon burn-side. I've no just fawthomed it yet, but I've an idea o' my ain. I think the glen is an auld kirkyaird. I mind when I herdit in Eskdalemuir there was a bit on the hill whaur Covenanters had been buried, and the sheep were aye sweer to gang near it. Some day I'm thinkin' o' gettin' a spade and howkin'. I micht find something queer. . . ."

VI

I CAME to regard the Green Glen as my own exclusive property, which shared with me a secret. It was a pleasant intimacy, and I had resigned myself to its limits, conscious that the curtain of the past was drawn too close to allow more than one little chink to be seen. Then one day Fate brought Linford across my path. I had known him slightly for several years. I can see him now as I first knew him, a big solemn young man, too heavy for elegance, and an awkward weight for a horse. We met first one spring at Valescure, and a lonely fortnight established a kind of friendship between us. He was a modest being, full of halting sympathies and interests, for which he rarely found words. His family had been settled for two generations in Australia, sheep farming in the good days when the big profits were made. His father had made a second fortune in a gold mine, and, disliking the land legislation of the country, had sold his farms and brought his boy to England. An undistinguished progress through a public school and Oxford had left him without a profession, and, his father having died, with no near relations and a ridiculous amount of money. He should have been a soldier, but somehow had missed his chance. The man was in no way slack, but he gave me the impression of having no niche to fit into. He was very English in speech and manners, but he seemed to stand outside all the ordinary English occupations and look on. Not that he didn't do most things well. He was a magnificent shot, a first-rate horseman, and the best man to sail a boat I have ever met. He read much, had travelled considerably, and had a keen interest in scientific geography. I thought he had found a job when he took a notion of exploring the Brahmaputra gorges, but the expedition fell through and his interest flagged. He belonged to many clubs, and had a few hundred acquaintances; but beyond myself I don't think he had a friend.

He used to come to see me, and I tried to understand what puzzled him. For puzzled he was—not unhappy or disillusioned, but simply puzzled with life. Somehow he did not fit in with the world around him. I used to think it would have been better if he had never left Australia. There he had a ready-made environment; here in England he had to make his own, and he did not seem to have the knack of it. People liked him, and thought him, for all his stiffness, a good fellow. But he never accepted anybody or anything as his own; he was always the observant and sympathetic stranger. I began to realise that my friend, with all his advantages, was desperately homeless.

To myself, as I thought about him, I prescribed marriage. *Vix ea nostra voco* might have been his motto about most things, but in a wife he would find something his very own. The thing was obvious, but I saw also that he would be a hard fellow to marry. He was hopelessly shy and curiously unimpressionable. I do not remember that he ever spoke to me of any woman, and he avoided every chance of meeting them. I only once saw his tall figure at a dance, when he looked like nothing so much as Marius among the ruins of Carthage.

Hunting was his main hobby, and one January I found myself staying under the same roof with him in the Cottesmore country. He was, as I have said, a bold and fine rider, but he had to know his horse, and on this occasion our host mounted both of us. There was an ugly banked fence where he misjudged his animal's powers, and came down in a heap on a hardish bit of ground. I thought his neck was broken, and prepared for the worst, as I helped three other white-faced men to get him clear. But it was only a slight concussion, a broken finger, and a dislocated shoulder. He had a bad night, but next day was little the worse for his fall, and, frost having set in, I spent most of the afternoon in his bedroom.

He wore a ring which I had often noticed, a little engraved carnelian in a heavy setting of Australian gold. In doctoring his hand it had been removed, and now lay on the dressing-table. We were talking idly of runs and spills, and, as we talked, I picked it up and examined it.

The stone was old and curious. There was no motto, and the carving seemed to be a heart transfixed by an arrow. I thought it the ordinary trumpery love-token—Cupid and his darts—when I noticed something more. The heart was crowned, and the barb transfixing it was not an arrow but a spear.

The sight roused me to the liveliest interest. For the cognisance belonged to one house and one house alone. It was Douglas of Cauldshaw who had carried the family badge with this strange difference. Mary of Scots, it was said, had given them the spear, for to the last they had stood by that melancholy lady.

"Where did you get this?" I asked.

"What? The ring? It was my father's. An ugly thing."

I looked at it again. "It has an odd crest. Did you ever inquire about it?"

He said No. He knew little heraldry, and didn't want to pretend to what didn't belong to him. Then he corrected himself. He thought that the thing was a family relic, right enough. His father had got the stone in turn from his mother, and had had it reset. He thought, but he wasn't sure, that it had been a long time in his grandmother's family. "What was her name?" I asked eagerly.

The answer was disappointing. "Brown," he said. "They had the Wooramanga place."

I asked if they came from Scotland. "No," he said. "They were Yorkshire, I think. But wait a bit. I think—yes—I have heard my father say something about the Browns being Scotch—Brouns, you know."

This was a false scent and I tried again. But Linford had nothing to tell me. He had no family papers or jewels or pictures, nothing but the one ring. I could see that he was puzzled at my interest, and to my horror offered to pay the Heralds' College to investigate matters. I made him promise to let the Heralds alone, and tried to get more about his grandmother. She had been a tall thin old lady, as he remembered her, with a north-country accent. She had disliked Melbourne intensely. That was all he could tell; not a saying or a rhyme or a memory to link her with those who had borne the ring's cognisance.

I heard, however, another startling thing that afternoon. Linford, blushing delightfully, confessed that he was in love. He had no chance, of course, wasn't good enough, and all the rest of it. When I heard that the lady was Virginia Dasent I was inclined to agree with him. Miss Dasent was very high game for Linford to fly at—or for anybody.

VII

LANGUAGE is too coarse a medium in which to give a true portrait of Miss Virginia. Airy diaphanous colours and the sharp fineness of marble are needed; and something more, something to recapture that grace, wild and bird-like and only half mortal, which for three seasons turned all our heads. She was an astounding success. Coming from nowhere, and as innocent as a child of ambition, she made every man her most hopeless and humble servant. I think her charm was her pure girlishness—

neither childish nor womanly, you understand. She had the air of one who faces the world frankly but does not accept it. She was a changeling, a wanderer, a dainty solitary figure on the weary old roads of life. I remember thinking, when I first saw her, that she might have stood for a statue of incarnate Wonder.

I knew her a little, well enough to see the hopelessness of my friend's case. She was an American—from one of the Carolinas, I believe; and Lady Amysfort took her about in London. I do not think that they were related. I hope my friends beyond the Atlantic will forgive me for saying that Miss Virginia was like no American I have ever met. Not that she had any of the sad homeless vulgarity of the denationalised. She was a fervent patriot, and had a delicious variety of the national humour. But I could not fit her in with her great continent. Indeed, I could not place her anywhere in any society. She belonged to some fanciful world of her own; but all the time she seemed to me to be looking for something—perhaps for her lost material heritage.

I was more interested, however, in Linford than in Miss Dasent. I could find out no more from him about his forebears, but I wondered if the Glen could tell me anything. Supposing I took him there, unprepared, of course, by any warning of mine, might not he feel the spell of it? If he did, I would be convinced of the Douglas blood; for I was certain that not otherwise would so prosaic a being feel so subtle a charm.

I persuaded him to take the Hardriding shootings; with an option to purchase, too, for Harry's finances were now past praying for. The chance came two days before the Twelfth, when he and I were alone in the house. It was a mild, blue August day, with clear distances and a cool breeze, and as we rounded the Green Dod I thought that my Glen was nobly dressed for us. I had hoped for some cry of delight, but none came. Linford stalked through the bent, muttering something about black-game.

We came to the mound by the waterside, Maid Marjory's Bower, and stretched ourselves on the scented turf. Then a curious thing happened to me. A light wind came up the stream, rippling the pools and sending a grey shiver over the grasses. Suddenly I became oppressed with a mortal fear. I must have lain limp and white, looking dumbly at the opposite hill. I had no notion what I feared, but it was worse than my old boyish adventure, for, though I longed madly to flee, I knew I could not. The Green Glen was trying me, and if I failed I had lost its secret for ever. I shut my teeth, and for a second or two hung at the limit of my endurance. Then it all passed. I found myself lying back on the mound, desperately sleepy and dripping with sweat, as if I had run twenty miles.

I mopped my brow and looked at Linford. He was quite unperturbed, and had got out his pouch and was filling his pipe. He glanced at me curiously.

"You're in pretty bad condition, old chap," he observed. "You'll founder on the Twelfth if you drip like this in an afternoon saunter." He got up and stretched himself. "Let's go back," he said. "There isn't a beast or bird in the place. I am glad I came here, for it will keep us from wasting time over it."

I followed him, still shaky and acutely disappointed. The Glen had nothing to say to him. The ring was an accident, and the Cauldshaw stock was still to find. And yet as we walked home, I began to doubt. The Glen had been not for Douglas or Home alone, but for both. What if a Home were needed to complete the circuit?

It was a possible explanation. Besides, the extraordinary seizure which had befallen me that afternoon seemed to argue that the visit had not been meaningless. I was perfectly well and normal, and I had sat on the mound a hundred times before. Might it not be that the Glen had been stirred, and was striving to tell us its secret? Then I began to laugh, and told myself that I was a fool to treat my fancies as solid facts.

VIII

THAT winter was made memorable to me, and a good many others, by Virginia Dasent. The Amysforts went to Egypt, leaving her very much to her own devices. She hunted a little and spent some time in country-houses; but mostly she was to be found in London, a city for which she had an inordinate love. This was bad for Linford, who stayed devotedly in town, and being deprived of healthful exercise put on flesh and lost spirits. I found him in the club one afternoon in a very bad temper. I alone knew of his hopeless plight, and with me he did not trouble to keep up appearances.

"I get no forrarder," he groaned. "She tolerates me as she tolerates everybody else. Lord, how I hate that kind smile of hers! She isn't a woman, Jack. She's an adorable sort of bird that flits about and never settles. You know the way she holds her head forward and peers away beyond you. She's always preening for another flight."

Love was making him a psychologist, for Miss Virginia's maddening charm lay in just that bird-like detachment. We had become very good friends, she and I; and often of a late afternoon we talked in the Amysforts' big ugly drawing-room. She liked me because I was interested in old things and odd bypaths, for I found that the child bubbled over with romance. A lonely girlhood in some Carolinian manor had given her fancy rich feeding. Half in a world of books, half in a world of pure dreaming, she took her airy way. She had about as much worldliness as St. Theresa, and much less worldly knowledge. Frankly, I was a little afraid for her; some day disillusion would come, and come cruelly. There was a loneliness about her, as about Linford, but it was the loneliness of a happy preoccupation. Some day those wondering eyes would find the world less marvellous, and then her heart would break. Or would she carry her fresh childlike interest undimmed to the end? I could not tell, but I argued badly for Linford's chances. He was far too eligible—young, good-looking, preposterously rich. The man who was to win Miss Virginia's heart, I thought, must come riding in the fearless old fashion. Linford was as romantic in the ordinary sense of the word as a Republican senator of Virginia's native land.

That was my first impression, but I found cause to alter it slightly. As I came to know her better, new avenues opened up in her soul. She had an excellent brain, very clever, shrewd and subtle, and behind all her fancies I was aware of a solid rock of common sense. She was not a ready talker, and never rhapsodised. Little odd phrases, a shrug and a laugh, gave the key to her whimsical world. But on a matter of prosaic fact I found her amazingly practical. More than once she offered me advice; with a little wise air which spoke of youth, but with a penetration, too, which took my breath away. I put my surprise into words. "Of course I'm practical," she said. "I'm more than half Scotch, you know."

I thought nothing of it at the time, for American girls have a habit of being either Scotch or early Norman. I remember asking her if she had ever been to Scotland, and she said—No: not yet. She had not had time. But some day . . .

I was inclined to be a little angry with both her and Linford. He went about like a sheep, a ridiculous figure of purposeless melancholy, and the deeper he sank in this mood the worse it was for his chances. As for the lady, I began to think her almost inhuman. I wondered if she were not perfectly heartless, hollow within like an Ell-woman. She seemed unconscious of the havoc she was causing everywhere. I think I would have preferred a common flirt to this unearthly aloofness. But her eyes used always to make me revise my judgments: they were so innocent and young. Some day she would awaken, I told myself. Some day the sleeping princess would be kissed into life. But I was pretty certain that, unless a miracle happened, it would be none of Linford's doing.

It was one morning in the Park in early May that she exploded the mine under my feet. She had been riding with Linford, and turned, as I came up, to accompany me. I don't know what they had been talking about, but her eyes were shining, her colour high, and her lips very tight.

"We have been discussing Scotch places," she volunteered. "It is very tiresome. I wanted a place, and Mr. Linford seems to have got a long lease of it. He offered to make it over to me, but of course that was impossible. It's a great nuisance, for I had set my heart on it."

I asked the name, and even as I asked I think I guessed the answer.

"Hardriding," she said. "A little old place in the Borders. My family lived there long ago, and I have always meant to make a pilgrimage to it. Caroline Amysfort is going to Bayreuth, so I shall set up as hostess on my own account. If I can't get Hardriding I must have Cauldshaw. Will you come and stay with me?"

I listened to her, I hope, with an impassive face, but inwardly I was a volcano of excitement. Hardriding and Cauldshaw! Home and Douglas! Was the circuit by some amazing chance to be completed? I wondered how soon I could decently make an appointment with Miss Virginia and get the whole story. She was going away for the weekend, but would be free on Tuesday, rather late. I hugged my impatience for three beastly days.

I had expected a fragment, and found instead a complete and well-authenticated tale. I blessed that lovable American serious-ness about genealogies. There was the pedigree neatly inscribed, with excerpts from registers and letters, as businesslike, as irrefutable, as a share certificate. After old Sir Piers fell at Preston his eldest son, Gideon, fled to France, and thence to the Canadas. He fought under the French flag, and rose to a colonelcy before he fell at Quebec. He had married a French-woman, and their son—Lewis, I think—took to the sea and did good trade in the smuggling and privateering line along the New England coast. He settled in North Carolina, and, being rich from his ventures, bought a handsome property, and built a manor-house in the colonial style. With his grand-daughter the male line of Home—Miss Virginia pronounced it to rhyme with "loam"—ended. She married a Dasent, son of a neighbouring squire, and was Miss Virginia's grandmother. There it was, all set down in black and white, and very prettily she expounded it to me. I had found the Hardriding stock at last. It had come back to me out of the mist with ample credentials.

Miss Virginia at Cauldshaw, Linford at Hardriding, and be-tween them the Green Glen! Surely the stage was being set at last for the play. My first impulse was to tell her the whole romance. I pictured her delight; I saw the prosaic Linford take on the colour of poetry. But a scruple deterred me. It would be breaking faith with the Green Glen. If the spell were there it needed no preparation of mine for its working. Those starry influences called for respectful treatment. I would go to Hardriding, and some day—some mellow autumn day—Miss Virginia would cross the hills, and Linford would be there by the Bower to meet her!

Meanwhile all that summer the course of true love ran badly. The two were friends after a fashion, but Linford was such a clumsy and uneasy being, and Miss Virginia so swift and evasive, that it seemed impossible that that friendship could ripen. I got very sick of the whole business, angry with Linford, and puzzled about the lady. At one moment I called her inhuman, at another angelic: but, whatever view one took (and after all they came to the same conclusion), she was the most heartbreaking beauty. Her wild childlike eyes looked through one as if to a pleasant country beyond. There is a Greek fable, isn't there? about some hero who needed the touch of his mother the Earth to give him strength. I wondered if she would ever find that earth-kinship, which means common humanity.

IX

IN early August the Lammas floods were high, so that sultriness was purged from the air and the world left clean and rain-washed and sweet-scented. I was staying at Cauldshaw, in a small party which tried in vain to induce its dancing hostess to be still. She was in wild spirits, out at all hours, a crony of shepherds, already learned in the ways of the moors. She had come back, she said, to her own country, and lived every hour in a whirl of delight and wonder. The long round-shouldered hills, the clear burns, the very homely simplicity of the old land ravished her heart. I counted the days till I could take her to the Green Glen.

Then the party melted away, and it was arranged that she should pay a visit of state to Hardriding. I also was bidden, and Linford spent his days in a fever of expectation. Miss Virginia was scrupulous about the details. She would walk across the hills by the old raiding road from Cauldshaw. I showed her the way, which traversed the Green Glen, and on the map I pointed out the Bower. She clapped her hands with delight at my tale—the barest sketch—of the Home doings. "What an adventure!" she cried. "I shall tell you all about it at dinner. I feel like a princess coming home to her kingdom."

I sincerely hoped that she was. If the Fates were kind this airy spirit should feel the antique spell of earth, and I dared to think that two wanderers might find a home.

To this hour I remember every incident of that autumn day. It was the 3rd of September. The morning broke cold and misty, but by ten o'clock the sun had burned up the rime, and the hills slept in a bright windless calm. I was shooting with Linford, and set out from Cauldshaw at eleven o'clock. Miss Virginia was to leave after luncheon, and, if she followed my directions, would be at Hardriding by six. She would reach the Green Glen about four o'clock, and I laid my plans accordingly.

I shot vilely, for I was full of a curious sense of anticipation. So was Linford, but nothing could impair his skill. We talked very little, I remember; but it took some manœuvring on my part to have the afternoon beat where I wanted it. Linford would have had us try the moors near the house, for his mind was always turning to Hardriding; but after some persuasion I got him to keep to the hills by the Nine Stane Rig, where we looked down on the Green Glen. Had I told him that Miss Virginia was walking, he would have set off then and there to meet her, and spoiled everything. He kept asking me when she would start. "She'll have to go round by the Red Ford," he repeated, "and that means Hardriding at tea-time. We needn't stay too long up here. Hardriding is her family place, so to speak, and I want to be there to welcome her."

Shortly after three we stood on the summit of the Dun Rig, and as I watched the green shoulders of the Fawn Hope I saw a figure cross the sky-line. Then I told Linford the truth. I bade him go up the Glen to meet her and wait for her at the Bower. He looked at me shyly. "You arranged all this?" he asked. "Thanks very much, old man. You've been a pretty good friend to me."

I set off for Hardriding without a glance behind. The Glen was now no place for me. Looking back at my frame of mind, I can see nothing but exhilaration. Some great thing was about to befall two people whom I loved. I had no doubt of the virtue of the place. By devious paths I had brought back to it its old masters. It had whispered its secret to me, and I had repaid it. For the moment I felt that time was not, that death was little, and change a mockery. The wise years let nothing die, and always the circle came full again, bringing back lost hopes and dreams. The still and golden afternoon spoke the same message to my heart. I felt the serene continuance of all things, the sense of something eternal behind the trivial ways of man.

I reached Hardriding a little after four, and according to my plan sat down to read and smoke. But I soon found that idleness was impossible. I was strung too high with expectation. I wandered into the library, and then into the garden, but my eyes were always turning to the shoulder of hill which marked the opening of the Fawn glen. Then I resolved to go to meet Linford. Whatever had happened, it would be right for me to welcome Miss Virginia to Hardriding.

Before I had crossed the lawns my mood changed utterly. I suddenly became a prey to black forebodings. The doggerel Latin of True Thomas rang in my head like the croak of a raven:—

> *Ubi Faunus fluit*
> *Spes mortalis ruit.*

I tried to laugh at it. I told myself that the verses were no doubt the work of a foolish eighteenth-century parson. What harm could follow the meeting of two friends in a hill glen where their forebears had fought and loved? But I reasoned in vain. A deadly depression overmastered me. The light had gone out of the sky, and the bent, all yellow in the westering sun, seemed wan as death.

> Where Fawn flows
> Man's hope goes.

The dolorous refrain would not leave me.

I emerged from the park into the water meadows where Fawn runs deep among flags and meadow-sweet. Beyond them I came to the lower glen, where the fir-clad slopes leave a thin strip of pasture by the stream. Here I should have met the two, but there was no sign of them. I looked at my watch and found it after five.

Then I began to quicken my pace. My depression had turned to acute anxiety. Before me was half a mile of open strath, and then the Green Dod, where the Glen turned sharply to the right. I ran that half-mile with dread in my heart of what I might see beyond it. But when I came to the Green Dod there was still no sign of a human being. The Fawn flows round the shoulder of hill in a narrow defile, at the upper end of which begins the Green Glen. I resolved to wait there, for I realised that I could not enter the Glen. I can give no reason for this, but I knew the truth of it. My feet could not have carried me round the shoulder of hill.

I did not wait long. Suddenly down the defile came a single figure. It was Linford, but even to my distraught sight a different Linford from him I had known. As I have said, he was a big fellow, a little ungainly, a little afraid of his size. But now he was a noble figure of a man, and as he strode along there was a strange mastery and dignity in him. But why was he alone? I blinked my eyes, for I saw that he was not alone. He carried in his arms something slim and white and very quiet. I crouched behind a boulder as he came near, but he had no eyes for anything but his burden. His head was bent over it, and his face was wild and drawn with grief. Then I saw that a fair head lay limply in the crook of his arm and that the face was very pale.

The doctors called it heart failure. Miss Virginia, said one of them in a moment of poetry, had for years had a frail chariot for her body and the horses of her spirit had driven too fiercely. She must have had heart trouble, though no one had diagnosed it. The hill walk from Cauldshaw had been too much for her. The same man spoke wisely about the evils of our modern life. "Most people today," he said, "have temperaments that prey on their bodies. They must live at white heat and the shell cracks."

Years afterwards, when time had taken the edge off his grief, Linford told me something of what happened. "She met me, looking very well and jolly, and we walked to the place you call the Bower. You may laugh at me, but I tell you I had a presentiment that something was going to happen, but I couldn't be sure whether it was good or bad. . . . She looked all round the Glen and sighed happily, as if she had found something she liked very much. Then suddenly she gave a little cry and went very white. I caught her, and saw that she was all in a shiver. She was staring at the burn, and her eyes were round and frightened like a deer's. Then she smiled again, and turned to me with a look—Oh, my God, I can never forget it! It was so kind and happy and . . . She must have cared for me all the time, and like a blind fool I didn't know it. She put her arms round my neck and said, 'My ain true love'—I suppose she was quoting from a Scotch song. And just as I was bursting with joy I felt that her cheek was cold. . . ."

Now it is a curious thing, but in the *Scotichronicon* of Hume of Calzeat—it is in manuscript, and I do not think anyone living has read it besides myself—there is a version of the story of Maid Marjory. And according to that version, when the lady confronted her father in the Green Glen, she put her arm around the Douglas's neck and said, "My ain true love."

THE WISE YEARS

(The monk, LAPIDARIUS, in meditation.)

I, Lapidarius, priest of the Most High
(Called, ere Christ sought me, John of Dinlay-burn),
Now in this shadowy twilight of my days
Give laud and make confession. Yester-eve
I cast lots in the Scriptures, for 'tis right,
As Austin teaches, thus to question God.
Twofold the answer: first I found the text,
"The hour is nigh", a token clear that soon
I must put off these tattered mortal weeds
And don the immortal raiment of the blest.
The second was the Psalm, that "to the just
Peace shall be granted while the moon endures."
A fitting benediction, quoth my soul;
For I have ever loved the moon and sought
The gentle lore that dwelleth in her beams.

Here, in this moorland cell, long years I strove
To pierce the veil that hideth Heaven from man.
By fasts and vigils I wore thin the robe,
The fleshly robe that clogs the soul; in prayer
I from the body soared among the stars
And held high converse with the cherubim.
I moved in ecstasy, and all the land
Spake of my sainthood; people thronged from far
To gaze upon the man who walked with God.
Ah, little knew they! In my heart I wept,
For God was ever distant. Not with Him
I communed, but with fancies self-begot,
Half of sick brain and half of fevered flesh.

And then one eve—'twas at the Lammastide
When every twilight is a taste of Heaven,
While half-distraught I laboured, sudden came
The light that shone on Paul; I caught my breath,
Felt on my forehead the cool hand of God,
And heard His holy accents in my ear:—
"Why troublest thou thyself to mount to Me
When I am with thee always. Love My world,
The good green earth I gave thee for thy joy."
Then through the rushes flowered the rose of eve,
And I went forth into the dewy air,
And made my first communion with God's world.

The robe of flesh wears thin, and with the years
God shines through all things. Time and Death are not,
Nor Change, but all endures even as a tree
Bears in its secular trunk the rings of youth.
I walk by stream and hill, at even and dawn,
In noontide's height, in the first joy of spring,
Through the warm hours of summer, in the ripe
Soft fall of autumn, when the winter's spell
Has stilled the earth to sleep; and as I go
The dear unseen companions walk with me;
The birds and beasts attend me, and their speech,
Wise as the hills, hath opened mysteries.
I hold high fellowship with souls long dead
And souls unborn, for I am one with life,
One with the earth, and almost one with God.
They name me saint no more. The abbot scowls,
The brethren flee me, and the country folk
Call me the devil's minion. Soon, belike,—
For God may will I reach Him through the fire—
They seek to burn me as a brand of hell.

All men have shunned me, but the children come
Stealthily on a holy day with flowers
Or autumn berries; from the hazel shade
They whisper, "Brother John, come play with us,
And tell us stories of your fairy friends."
They know, whose hearts are pure, that mine is kind,
And erreth not in loving all God gave.
They shall have comfort while the moon endures.

The hour is nigh. Behind the wattled strip
Which screens my pallet, lo! the first grey light
Creeps timorous like a fawn. My limbs are moved
To a strange exaltation. . . . Soon the sun
Will steep the moorlands in a holier dawn,
And my thin veil of sense will fade and fall.
I shall be one with Him, and hear His speech
As friend to friend, and see Him face to face.
He findeth God who finds the earth He made . . .
The Green Glen waits the morning, and I go.

THE HERD OF STANDLAN

When the wind is nigh and the moon is high
    And the mist on the riverside,
Let such as fare have a very good care
    Of the Folk who come to ride.
For they may meet with the riders fleet
    Who fare from the place of dread;
And hard it is for a mortal man
    To sort at ease with the Dead.

                    THE BALLAD OF GREY WEATHER

WHEN Standlan Burn leaves the mosses and hags which gave it birth, it tumbles over a succession of falls into a deep, precipitous glen, whence in time it issues into a land of level green meadows, and finally finds its rest in the Gled. Just at the opening of the ravine there is a pool shut in by high, dark cliffs, and black even on the most sunshiny day. The rocks are never dry but always black with damp and shadow. There is scarce any vegetation save stunted birks, juniper bushes, and draggled fern; and the hoot of owls and the croak of hooded crows is seldom absent from the spot. It is the famous Black Linn where in winter sheep stray and are never more heard of, and where more than once an unwary shepherd has gone to his account. It is an Inferno on the brink of a Paradise, for not a stone's throw off is the green, lawn-like turf, the hazel thicket, and the broad, clear pools, by the edge of which on that July day the Herd of Standlan and I sat drowsily smoking and talking of fishing and the hills. There he told me this story, which I here set down as I remember it, and as it bears repetition.

"D'ye mind Airthur Morrant?" said the shepherd, suddenly.

I did remember Arthur Mordaunt. Ten years past he and I had been inseparables, despite some half-dozen summers difference in age. We had fished and shot together, and together we had

287

tramped every hill within thirty miles. He had come up from the South to try sheep-farming, and as he came of a great family and had no need to earn his bread, he found the profession pleasing. Then irresistible fate had swept me southward to college, and when after two years I came back to the place, his father was dead and he had come into his own. The next I heard of him was that in politics he was regarded as the most promising of the younger men, one of the staunchest and ablest upstays of the Constitution. His name was rapidly rising into prominence, for he seemed to exhibit that rare phenomenon of a man of birth and culture in direct sympathy with the wants of the people.

"You mean Lord Brodakers?" said I.

"Dinna call him by that name," said the shepherd, darkly. "I hae nae thocht o' him now. He's a disgrace to his country, servin' the Deil wi' baith hands. But nine year syne he was a bit innocent callant wi' nae Tory deevilry in his heid. Well, as I was sayin', Airthur Morrant has cause to mind that place till his dying day;" and he pointed his finger to the Black Linn.

I looked up the chasm. The treacherous water, so bright and joyful at our feet, was like ink in the great gorge. The swish and plunge of the cataract came like the regular beating of a clock, and though the weather was dry, streams of moisture seamed the perpendicular walls. It was a place eerie even on that bright summer's day.

"I don't think I ever heard the story," I said casually.

"Maybe no," said the shepherd. "It's no yin I like to tell;" and he puffed sternly at his pipe, while I awaited the continuation.

"Ye see it was like this," he said, after a while. "It was just the beginning o' the back-end, and that year we had an awfu' spate o' rain. For near a week it poured hale water, and a' doon by Drummeler and the Mossfennan haughs was yae muckle loch. Then it stopped, and an awfu' heat came on. It dried the grund in nae time, but it hardly touched the burns; and it was rale queer to be pourin' wi' sweat and the grund aneath ye as dry as a potato-sack, and a' the time the water neither to haud nor bind. A' the waterside fields were clean stripped o' stooks, and a guid wheen hay-ricks gaed doon tae Berwick, no to speak o' sheep and nowt beast. But that's anither thing.

"Weel, ye'll mind that Airthur was terrible keen on fishing. He wad gang oot in a' weather, and he wasna feared for ony mortal or naitural thing. Dod, I've seen him in Gled wi' the water rinnin' ower his shouthers yae cauld March day playin' a saumon. He kenned weel aboot the fishings for he had traivelled in Norroway and siccan outlandish places, where there's a heap o' big fish. So that day—and it was a Setterday tae and far ower near the Sabbath—he maun gang awa' up Standlan Burn wi' his rod and creel to try his luck.

"I was bidin' at that time, as ye mind, in the wee cot-house at the back o' the faulds. I was alane, for it was three year afore I mairried Jess, and I wasna begun yet to the coortin'. I had been at Gledsmuir that day for some o' the new stuff for killing sheep-mawks, and I wasna very fresh on my legs when I gaed oot after my tea that night to hae a look at the hill-sheep. I had had a bad year on the hill. First the lambin'-time was snaw, snaw ilka day, and I lost mair than I wad like to tell. Syne the grass a' summer was so short wi' the drought that the puir beasts could scarcely get a bite and were as thin as pipe-stapples. And then, to crown a', auld Will Broun, the man that helpit me, turned ill wi' his back, and had to bide at hame. So I had twae man's work on yae man's shouthers, and was nane so weel pleased.

"As I was saying, I gaed oot that nicht, and after lookin' a' the Dun Rig and the Yellow Mire and the back o' Cramalt Craig, I cam down the burn by the road frae the auld faulds. It was geyan dark, being about seven o'clock o' a September nicht, and I keepit weel back frae that wanchancy hole o' a burn. Weel, I was comin' kind o' quick, thinkin' o' supper and a story-book that I was readin' at the time, when just abune that place there, at the foot o' the Linn, I saw a man fishing. I wondered what ony body in his senses could be daein' at that time o' nicht in sic a dangerous place, so I gave him a roar and bade him come back. He turned his face round and I saw in a jiffey that it was Mr. Airthur.

" 'O, sir,' I cried, 'What for are ye fishing there? The water's awfu' dangerous, and the rocks are far ower slid.'

" 'Never mind, Scott,' he roars back cheery-like. 'I'll take care o' mysel'.'

"I lookit at him for twa-three meenutes, and then I saw by his rod he had yin on, and a big yin tae. He ran it up and doon the pool, and he had uncommon wark wi' 't, for it was strong and there was little licht. But bye and bye he got it almost tae his feet, and was just about to lift it out when a maist awfu' thing happened. The tackets o' his boots maun hae slithered on the stane, for the next thing I saw was Mr. Airthur in the muckle hungry water.

"I dinna exactly ken what happened after that, till I found myself on the very stone he had slipped off. I maun hae come doon the face of the rocks, a thing I can scarcely believe when I look at them, and a thing no man ever did afore. At ony rate I ken I fell the last fifteen feet or sae, and lichted on my left airm, for I felt it crack like a rotten branch, and an awfu' sairness ran up it.

"Now, the pool is a whirlpool as ye ken, and if anything fa's in, the water first smashes it against the muckle rock at the foot, then it brings it round below the fall again, and syne at the second time it carries it doon the burn. Weel, that was what happened to Mr. Airthur. I heard his heid gang dunt on the stane wi' a sound that made me sick. This must hae dung him clean senseless, and indeed it was a wonder it didna knock his brains oot. At ony rate there was nae mair word o' swimming, and he was swirled round below the fa' just like a corp.

"I kenned fine that nae time was to be lost, for if he once gaed doun the burn he wad be in Gled or ever I could say a word, and nae wad ever see him mair in life. So doon I got on my hunkers on the stane, and waited for the turnin'. Round he came, whirling in the foam, wi' a lang line o' blood across his brow where the stane had cut him. It was a terrible meenute. My heart fair stood still. I put out my airm, and as he passed I grippit him and wi' an awfu' pu' got him out o' the current into the side.

"But now I found that a waur thing still was on me. My left airm was broken, and my richt sae numbed and weak wi' my fall that, try as I micht, I couldna raise him ony further. I thocht I wad burst a blood-vessel i' my face and my muscles fair cracked wi' the strain, but I would make nothing o' 't. There he stuck wi' his heid and shouthers abune the water, pu'd close until the edge of a rock.

"What was I to dae? If I once let him slip he wad be into the stream and lost forever. But I couldna hang on here a' nicht, and as far as I could see there wad be naebody near till the mornin', when Ebie Blackstock passed frae the Head o' the Hope. I roared wi' a' my power; but I got nae answer, naething but the rummle o' the water and the whistling o' some whaups on the hill.

"Then I turned very sick wi' terror and pain and weakness and I kenna what. My broken airm seemed a great lump o' burnin' coal. I maun hae given it some extra wrench when I hauled him out, for it was sae sair now that I thocht I could scarcely thole it. Forbye, pain and a', I could hae gone off to sleep wi' fair weariness. I had heard tell o' men sleepin' on their feet, but I never felt it till then. Man, if I hadna warstled wi' mysel, I wad hae dropped off as deid's a peery.

"Then there was the awfu' strain o' keepin' Mr. Airthur up. He was a great big man, twelve stone I'll warrant, and weighing a terrible lot mair wi' his fishing togs and things. If I had had the use o' my ither airm I micht hae taen aff his jacket and creel and lichtened the burden, but I could do naething. I scarcely like to tell ye how I was tempted in that hour. Again and again I says to mysel, 'Gidden Scott,' say I, 'what do ye care for this man? He's no a drap's bluid to you, and forbye ye'll never be able to save him. Ye micht as weel let him gang. Ye've dune a' ye could. Ye're a brave man, Gidden Scott, and ye've nae cause to be ashamed o' givin' up the fecht.' But I says to mysel again: 'Gidden Scott, ye're a coward. Wad ye let a man die, when there's a breath in your body? Think shame o' yoursel, man.' So I aye kept haudin' on, although I was very near bye wi' 't. Whenever I lookit at Mr. Airthur's face, as white's death and a' blood, and his een sae stelled-like, I got a kind o' groo and felt awfu' pitiful for the bit laddie. Then I thocht on his faither, the auld Lord, wha was sae built up in him, and I couldna bear to think o' his son droonin' in that awfu' hole. So I set mysel to the wark o' keepin' him up a' nicht, though I had nae hope in the matter. It wasna what ye ca' bravery that made me dae't, for I had nae ither choice. It was just a kind o' dourness that runs in my folk, and a kind o' vexedness for sae young a callant in sic an ill place.

"The nicht was hot and there was scarcely a sound o' wind. I felt the sweat standin' on my face like frost on tatties, and abune me the sky was a' misty and nae mune visible. I thocht very likely that it micht come a thunder-shower and I kind o' lookit forrit tae 't. For I was aye feared at lichtning, and if it came that nicht I was bound to get clean dazed and likely tummle in. I was a lonely man wi' nae kin to speak o', so it wouldna maitter muckle.

"But now I come to tell ye about the queer side o' that nicht's wark, whilk I never telled to nane but yoursel, though a' the folk about here ken the rest. I maun hae been geyan weak, for I got into a kind o' doze, no sleepin', ye understand, but awfu' like it. And then a' sort o' daft things began to dance afore my een. Witches and bogles and brownies and things oot o' the Bible, and leviathans and brazen bulls—a' cam fleerin' and flauntin' on the tap o' the water straucht afore me. I didna pay muckle heed to them, for I half kenned it was a' nonsense, and syne they gaed awa'. Then an auld wife wi' a mutch and a hale procession o' auld wives passed, and just about the last I saw yin I thocht I kenned.

" 'Is that you, grannie?' says I.

" 'Ay, it's me, Gidden,' says she; and as shure as I'm a leevin' man, it was my auld grannie, whae had been deid thae sax year. She had on the same mutch as she aye wore, and the same auld black stickie in her hand, and, Dod, she had the same snuff-box I made for her out o' a sheep's horn when I first took to the herdin'. I thocht she was lookin' rale weel.

" 'Losh, Grannie,' says I, 'Where in the warld hae ye come frae? It's no canny to see ye danderin' about there.'

" 'Ye've been badly brocht up,' she says, 'and ye ken nocht about it. Is't no a decent and comely thing that I should get a breath o' air yince in the while?'

" 'Deed,' said I, 'I had forgotten. Ye were sae like yoursel I never had a mind ye were deid. And how d'ye like the Guid Place?'

" 'Wheesht, Gidden,' says she, very solemn-like, 'I'm no there.'

"Now at this I was fair flabbergasted. Grannie had aye been a guid contentit auld wumman, and to think that they hadna let her intil Heeven made me think ill o' my ain chances.

" 'Help us, ye dinna mean to tell me ye're in Hell?' I cries.

" 'No exactly,' says she, 'But I'll trouble ye, Gidden, to speak mair respectful about holy things. That's a name ye uttered the noo whilk we dinna daur to mention.'

" 'I'm sorry, Grannie,' says I, 'but ye maun allow it's an astonishin' thing for me to hear. We aye counted ye shure, and ye died wi' the Buik in your hands.'

" 'Weel,' she says, 'it was like this. When I gaed up till the gate o' Heeven a man wi' a lang white robe comes and says, "Wha may ye be?" Says I, "I'm Elspeth Scott." He gangs awa' and consults a wee and then he says, "I think, Elspeth my wumman, ye'll hae to gang doon the brae a bit. Ye're no quite guid eneuch for this place, but ye'll get a very comfortable doonsittin' whaur I tell ye." So off I gaed and cam' to a place whaur the air was like the inside of the glass-houses at the Lodge. They took me in wi'oot a word and I've been rale comfortable. Ye see they keep the bad part o' the Ill Place for the reg'lar bad folk, but they've a very nice half-way house where the likes o' me stop.'

" 'And what kind o' company hae ye?'

" 'No very select,' says she. 'There's maist o' the ministers o' the countryside and a pickle fairmers, tho' the maist o' them are further ben. But there's my son Jock, your ain faither, Gidden, and a heap o' folk from the village, and oh, I'm nane sae bad.'

" 'Is there naething mair ye wad like then, Grannie?'

" 'Oh aye,' says she, 'we've each yae thing which we canna get. It's a' the punishment we hae. Mine's butter. I canna get fresh butter for my bread, for ye see it winna keep, it just melts. So I've to tak jeely to ilka slice, whilk is rale sair on the teeth. Ye'll no hae ony wi' ye?'

" 'No,' I says, 'I've naething but some tobaccy. D'ye want it? Ye were aye fond o' 't.'

" 'Na, na,' says she. 'I get plenty o' tobaccy doon bye. The pipe's never out o' the folks' mouth there. But I'm no speakin' about yoursel, Gidden. Ye're in a geyan ticht place.'

" 'I'm a' that,' I said. 'Can ye no help me?'

" 'I micht try.' And she raxes out her hand to grip mine. I put out mine to tak it, never thinkin' that that wasna the richt side, and that if Grannie grippit it she wad pu' the broken airm and haul me into the water. Something touched my fingers like a hot poker; I gave a great yell; and ere ever I kenned I was awake, a' but off the rock, wi' my left airm aching like hell-fire. Mr. Airthur I had let slunge ower the heid and my ain legs were in the water.

"I gae an awfu' whammle and edged my way back though it was near bye my strength. And now anither thing happened. For the cauld water roused Mr. Airthur frae his dwam. His een opened and he gave a wild look around him. 'Where am I?' he cries, 'Oh God!' and he gaed off intil anither faint.

"I can tell ye, sir, I never felt anything in this warld and I hope never to feel anything in anither sae bad as the next meenutes on that rock. I was fair sick wi' pain and weariness and a kind o' fever. The lip-lap o' the water, curling round Mr. Airthur, and the great *crush* o' the Black Linn itsel dang me fair silly. Then there was my airm, which was bad eneuch, and abune a' I was gotten into sic a state that I was fleyed at ilka shadow just like a bairn. I felt fine I was gaun daft, and if the thing had lasted anither score o' meenutes I wad be in a madhouse this day. But soon I felt the sleepiness comin' back, and I was off again dozin' and dreamin'.

"This time it was nae auld wumman but a muckle black-avised man that was standin' in the water glowrin' at me. I kenned him fine by the bandy-legs o' him and the broken nose (whilk I did mysel), for Dan Kyle the poacher deid thae twae year. He was a man, as I remembered him weel, wi' a great black beard and een that were stuck sae far in his heid that they looked like twae wull-cats keekin' oot o' a hole. He stands and just stares at me, and never speaks a word.

" 'What d'ye want?' I yells, for by this time I had lost a' grip o' mysel. 'Speak, man, and dinna stand there like a dummy.'

" 'I want naething,' he says in a mournfu' sing-song voice; 'I'm just thinkin'.'

" 'Whaur d'ye come frae?' I asked, 'and are ye keepin' weel?'

" 'Weel,' he says bitterly. 'In this warld I was ill to my wife, and twa-three times I near killed a man, and I stole like a pyet, and I was never sober. How d'ye think I should be weel in the next?'

"I was sorry for the man. 'D'ye ken I'm vexed for ye, Dan,' says I; 'I never likit ye when ye were here, but I'm wae to think ye're sae ill off yonder.'

" 'I'm no alane,' he says. 'There's Mistress Courhope o' the Big House, she's waur. Ye mind she was awfu' fond o' gumflowers. Weel, she canna keep them Yonder, for they a' melt wi' the heat. She's in an ill way about it, puir body.' Then he broke off. 'Whae's that ye've got there? Is't Airthur Morrant?'

" 'Ay, it's Airthur Morrant,' I said.

" 'His family's weel kent doon bye,' says he. 'We've maist o' his forebears, and we're expectin' the auld Lord every day. May be we'll sune get the lad himsel.'

" 'That's a damned lee,' says I, for I was angry at the man's presumption.

"Dan lookit at me sorrowfu'-like. 'We'll be gettin' you tae, if ye swear that gate,' says he, 'and then ye'll ken what it's like.'

"Of a sudden I fell into a great fear. 'Dinna say that, Dan,' I cried; 'I'm better than ye think. I'm a deacon, and'll maybe sune be an elder, and I never swear except at my dowg.'

" 'Tak care, Gidden,' said the face afore me. 'Where I am, a' things are taken into account.'

" 'Then they'll hae a gey big account for you,' says I. 'What-like do they treat you, may be?'

The man groaned.

" 'I'll tell ye what they dae to ye doon there,' he said. 'They put ye intil a place a' paved wi' stanes and wi' four square walls around. And there's naething in't, nae grass, nae shadow. And abune you there's a sky like brass. And sune ye get terrible hot and thirsty, and your tongue sticks to your mouth, and your eyes get blind wi' lookin' on the white stane. Then ye gang clean fey, and dad your heid on the ground and the walls to try and kill yoursel. But though ye dae't till a' eternity ye couldna feel pain. A' that ye feel is just the awfu' devourin' thirst, and the heat and the weariness. And if ye lie doon the ground burns ye and ye're fain to get up. And ye canna lean on the walls for the heat, and bye and bye when ye're fair perished wi' the thing, they tak ye out to try some ither ploy.'

" 'Nae mair,' I cried, 'nae mair, Dan!'

"But he went on malicious-like—

" 'Na, na, Gidden, I'm no dune yet. Syne they tak you to a fine room but awfu' warm. And there's a big fire in the grate and thick woollen rugs on the floor. And in the corner there's a braw feather bed. And they lay ye down on't, and then they pile on the tap o' ye mattresses and blankets and sacks and great rolls o' woollen stuff miles wide. And then ye see what they're after, tryin' to suffocate ye as they dae to folk that a mad dowg has bitten. And ye try to kick them off, but they're ower heavy, and ye canna move your feet nor your airms nor gee your heid. Then ye gang clean gyte and skirl to yoursel, but your voice is choked and naebody is near. And the warst o' 't is that ye canna die and get it ower. It's like death a hundred times and yet ye're aye leevin'. Bye and bye when they think ye've got eneuch they tak you out and put ye somewhere else.'

" 'Oh,' I cries, 'stop, man, or you'll ding me silly.'

"But he says never a word, just glowrin' at me.

" 'Aye, Gidden, and waur than that. For they put ye in a great loch wi' big waves just like the sea at the Pier o' Leith. And there's nae chance o' soomin', for as sune as ye put out your airms a billow gulfs ye down. Then ye swallow water and your heid dozes round and ye're chokin'. But ye canna die, ye must just thole. And down ye gang, down, down, in the cruel deep, till your heid's like to burst and your een are fu' o' bluid. And there's a' kind o' fearfu' monsters about, muckle slimy things wi' blind een and white scales, that claw at ye wi' claws just like the paws o' a drooned dog. And ye canna get away though ye fecht and fleech, and bye and bye ye're fair mad wi' horror and choking and the feel o' thae awfu' things. Then—'

"But now I think something snapped in my heid, and I went daft in doonricht earnest. The man before me danced about like a lantern's shine on a windy nicht and then disappeared. And I woke yelling like a pig at a killing, fair wud wi' terror, and my skellochs made the rocks ring. I found mysel in the pool a' but yae airm—the broken yin—which had hankit in a crack o' rock. Nae wonder I had been dreaming o' deep waters among the torments o' the Ill Place, when I was in them mysel. The pain in my airm was sae fearsome and my heid was gaun round sae wi' horror that I just skirled on and on, shrieking and groaning wi'oot a thocht what I was daein'. I was as near death as ever I will be, and as for Mr. Airthur he was on the very nick o' 't, for by this time he was a' in the water, though I still kept a grip o' him.

"When I think ower it often I wonder how it was possible that I could be here the day. But the Lord's very gracious, and he works in a queer way. For it so happened that Ebie Blackstock, whae had left Gledsmuir an hour afore me and whom I thocht by this time to be snorin' in his bed at the Head o' the Hope, had gone intil the herd's house at the Waterfit, and had got sae muckle drink there that he was sweered to start for hame till aboot half-past twal i' the night. Weel, he was comin' up the burnside, gae happy and contentit, for he had nae wife at hame to speir about his ongaeings, when, as he's telled me himsel, he heard sic an uproar doon by the Black Linn that made him turn pale and think that the Deil, whom he had long served, had gotten him at last. But he was a brave man, was Ebie, and he thinks to himsel that some fellow-creature micht be perishin'. So he gangs forrit wi' a' his pith, trying to think on the Lord's Prayer and last Sabbath's sermon. And, lookin' ower the edge, he saw naething for a while, naething but the black water wi' the awfu' yells coming out o' 't. Then he made out something like a heid near the side. So he rins doon by the road, no ower the rocks as I had come, but round by the burnside road, and soon he gets to the pool, where the crying was getting aye fainter and fainter. And then he saw me. And he grips me by the collar, for he was a sensible man, was Ebie, and hauls me oot. If he hadna been geyan strong he couldna hae dune it, for I was a deid wecht, forbye having a heavy man hanging on to me. When he got me up, what was his astonishment to find anither man at the end o' my airm, a man like a corp a' bloody about the heid. So he got us baith out, and we wae baith senseless; and he laid us in a safe bit back frae the water, and syne gaed off for help. So

297

bye and bye we were baith got home, me to my house and Mr. Airthur up to the Lodge."

"And was that the end of it?" I asked.

"Na," said the shepherd. "I lay for twae month there raving wi' brain fever, and when I cam to my senses I was as weak as a bairn. It was many months ere I was mysel again, and my left airm to this day is stiff and no muckle to lippen to. But Mr. Airthur was far waur, for the dad he had gotten on the rock was thocht to have broken his skull, and he lay long atween life and death. And the warst thing was that his faither was sae vexed about him that he never got ower the shock, but dee'd afore Airthur was out o' bed. And so when he cam out again he was My Lord, and a monstrously rich man."

The shepherd puffed meditatively at his pipe for a few minutes.

"But that's no a' yet. For Mr. Airthur wad tak nae refusal but that I maun gang awa' doon wi' him to his braw house in England and be a land o' factor or steward or something like that. And I had a rale fine cottage a' to mysel, wi' a very bonny gairden and guid wages, so I stayed there maybe sax month and then I gaed up till him. 'I canna bide nae longer,' says I. 'I canna stand this place. It's far ower laigh, and I'm fair sick to get hills to rest my een on. I'm awfu' gratefu' to ye for your kindness, but I maun gie up my job.' He was very sorry to lose me, and was for giein' me a present o' money or stockin' a fairm for me, because he said that it was to me he owed his life. But I wad hae nane o' his gifts. 'It wad be a terrible thing,' I says, 'to tak siller for daein' what ony body wad hae dune out o' pity.' So I cam awa' back to Standlan, and I maun say I'm rale contentit here. Mr. Airthur used whiles to write to me and ca' in and see me when he cam North for the shooting; but since he's gane sae far wrang wi' the Tories, I've had naething mair to dae wi' him."

I made no answer, being busy pondering in my mind on the depth of the shepherd's political principles, before which the ties of friendship were as nothing.

"Ay," said he, standing up, "I did what I thocht my duty at the time and I was rale glad I saved the callant's life. But now, when I think on a' the ill he's daein' to the country and the Guid Cause, I whiles think I wad hae been daein' better if I had just drappit him in.

"But whae kens? It's a queer warld." And the shepherd knocked the ashes out of his pipe.

SPACE

"Est impossible? Certum est."

TERTULLIAN[1]

L EITHEN told me this story one evening in early September
as we sat beside the pony track which gropes its way from
Glenavelin up the Correi na Sidhe. I had arrived that afternoon
from the South, while he had been taking an off-day from a
week's stalking, so we had walked up the glen together after tea
to get the news of the forest. A rifle was out on the Correi na
Sidhe beat, and a thin spire of smoke had risen from the top
of Sgurr Dearg to show that a stag had been killed at the burn-
head. The lumpish hill pony with its deer-saddle had gone up the
Correi in a gillie's charge, while we followed at leisure, picking
our way among the loose granite rocks and the patches of wet
bogland. The track climbed high on one of the ridges of Sgurr
Dearg, till it hung over a caldron of green glen with the Alt-na-
Sidhe churning in its linn a thousand feet below. It was a
breathless evening, I remember, with a pale-blue sky just clearing
from the haze of the day. West-wind weather may make the
North, even in September, no bad imitation of the Tropics, and
I sincerely pitied the man who all these stifling hours had been
toiling on the screes of Sgurr Dearg. By-and-by we sat down on
a bank of heather, and idly watched the trough swimming at our
feet. The clatter of the pony's hoofs grew fainter, the drone of
bees had gone, even the midges seemed to have forgotten their
calling. No place on earth can be so deathly still as a deer-forest
early in the season before the stags have begun roaring, for there
are no sheep with their homely noises, and only the rare croak
of a raven breaks the silence. The hillside was far from sheer—
one could have walked down with a little care—but something
in the shape of the hollow and the remote gleam of white water

gave it an air of extraordinary depth and space. There was a shimmer left from the day's heat, which invested bracken and rock and scree with a curious airy unreality. One could almost have believed that the eye had tricked the mind, that all was mirage, that five yards from the path the solid earth fell away into nothingness. I have a bad head, and instinctively I drew farther back into the heather. Leithen's eyes were looking vacantly before him.

"Did you ever know Hollond?" he asked.

Then he laughed shortly. "I don't know why I asked that, but somehow this place reminded me of Hollond. That glimmering hollow looks as if it were the beginning of eternity. It must be eerie to live with the feeling always on one."

Leithen seemed disinclined for further exercise. He lit a pipe and smoked quietly for a little. "Odd that you didn't know Hollond. You must have heard his name. I thought you amused yourself with metaphysics."

Then I remembered. There had been an erratic genius who had written some articles in *Mind* on that dreary subject, the mathematical conception of infinity. Men had praised them to me, but I confess I never quite understood their argument. "Wasn't he some sort of mathematical professor?" I asked.

"He was, and, in his own way, a tremendous swell. He wrote a book on Number which has translations in every European language. He is dead now, and the Royal Society founded a medal in his honour. But I wasn't thinking of that side of him."

It was the time and place for a story, for the pony would not be back for an hour. So I asked Leithen about the other side of Hollond which was recalled to him by Correi na Sidhe. He seemed a little unwilling to speak. . . .

"I wonder if you will understand it. You ought to, of course, better than me, for you know something of philosophy. But it took me a long time to get the hang of it, and I can't give you any kind of explanation. He was my fag at Eton, and when I began to get on at the Bar I was able to advise him on one or two private matters, so that he rather fancied my legal ability. He came to me with his story because he had to tell someone, and he wouldn't trust a colleague. He said he didn't want a scientist to know, for scientists were either pledged to their own theories and wouldn't understand, or, if they understood, would get ahead of him in his researches. He wanted a lawyer, he said, who was accustomed to weighing evidence. That was good sense, for evidence must always be judged by the same laws, and I suppose in the long run the most abstruse business comes down to a fairly simple deduction from certain data. Anyhow, that was the way he used to talk, and I listened to him, for I liked the man, and had an enormous respect for his brains. At Eton he sluiced down all the mathematics they could give him, and he was an astonishing swell at Cambridge. He was a simple fellow, too, and talked no more jargon than he could help. I used to climb with him in the Alps now and then, and you would never have guessed that he had any thoughts beyond getting up steep rocks.

"It was at Chamonix, I remember, that I first got a hint of the matter that was filling his mind. We had been taking an off-day, and were sitting in the hotel garden, watching the Aiguilles getting purple in the twilight. Chamonix always makes me choke a little—it is so crushed in by those great snow masses. I said something about it—said I liked open spaces like the Gornergrat or the Bel Alp better. He asked me why: if it was the difference of the air, or merely the wider horizon? I said it was the sense of not being crowded, of living in an empty world. He repeated the word "empty" and laughed.

" 'By "empty" you mean,' he said, 'where things don't knock up against you?'

"I told him No. I meant just empty, void, nothing but blank æther.

" 'You don't knock up against things here, and the air is as good as you want. It can't be the lack of ordinary emptiness you feel.'

"I agreed that the word needed explaining. 'I suppose it is mental restlessness,' I said. 'I like to feel that for a tremendous distance there is nothing round me. Why, I don't know. Some men are built the other way and have a terror of space.'

"He said that that was better. 'It is a personal fancy, and depends on your *knowing* that there is nothing between you and the top of the Dent Blanche. And you know because your eyes tell you there is nothing. Even if you were blind, you might have a sort of sense about adjacent matter. Blind men often have it. But in any case, whether got from instinct or sight, the *knowledge* is what matters.'

"Hollond was embarking on a Socratic dialogue in which I could see little point. I told him so, and he laughed.

" 'I am not sure that I am very clear myself. But yes—there *is* a point. Supposing you knew—not by sight or by instinct, but by sheer intellectual knowledge, as I know the truth of a mathematical proposition—that what we call empty space was full, crammed. Not with lumps of what we call matter like hills and houses, but with things as real—as real to the mind. Would you still feel crowded?'

" 'No,' I said, 'I don't think so. It is only what we call matter that signifies. It would be just as well not to feel crowded by the other thing, for there would be no escape from it. But what are you getting at? Do you mean atoms or electric currents or what?'

"He said he wasn't thinking about that sort of thing, and began to talk of another subject.

"Next night, when we were pigging it at the Géant *cabane*, he started again on the same tack. He asked me how I accounted for the fact that animals could find their way back over great tracts of unknown country. I said I supposed it was the homing instinct.

" 'Rubbish, man,' he said. 'That's only another name for the puzzle, not an explanation. There must be some reason for it. They must *know* something that we cannot understand. Tie a cat in a bag and take it fifty miles by train and it will make its way home. That cat has some clue that we haven't.'

"I was tired and sleepy, and told him that I did not care a rush about the psychology of cats. But he was not to be snubbed, and went on talking.

" 'How if Space is really full of things we cannot see and as yet do not know? How if all animals and some savages have a cell in their brain or a nerve which responds to the invisible world? How if all Space be full of these landmarks, not material in our sense, but quite real? A dog barks at nothing, a wild beast makes an aimless circuit. Why? Perhaps because Space is made

303

up of corridors and alleys, ways to travel and things to shun? For all we know, to a greater intelligence than ours the top of Mont Blanc may be as crowded as Piccadilly Circus.'

"But at that point I fell asleep and left Hollond to repeat his questions to a guide who knew no English and a snoring porter.

"Six months later, one foggy January afternoon, Hollond rang me up at the Temple and proposed to come to see me that night after dinner. I thought he wanted to talk Alpine shop, but he turned up in Duke Street about nine with a kitbag full of papers. He was an odd fellow to look at—a yellowish face with the skin stretched tight on the cheekbones, clean-shaven, a sharp chin which he kept poking forward, and deep-set, greyish eyes. He was a hard fellow, too, always in pretty good condition, which was remarkable considering how he slaved for nine months out of the twelve. He had a quiet, slow-spoken manner, but that night I saw that he was considerably excited.

"He said that he had come to me because we were old friends. He proposed to tell me a tremendous secret. 'I must get another mind to work on it or I'll go crazy. I don't want a scientist. I want a plain man.'

"Then he fixed me with a look like a tragic actor's. 'Do you remember that talk we had in August at Chamonix—about Space? I daresay you thought I was playing the fool. So I was in a sense, but I was feeling my way towards something which has been in my mind for ten years. Now I have got it, and you must hear about it. You may take my word that it's a pretty startling discovery.'

"I lit a pipe and told him to go ahead, warning him that I knew about as much science as the dustman.

"I am bound to say that it took me a long time to understand what he meant. He began by saying that everybody thought of Space as an 'empty homogeneous medium'. 'Never mind at present what the ultimate constituents of that medium are. We take it as a finished product, and we think of it as mere extension, something without any quality at all. That is the view of civilised man. You will find all the philosophers taking it for granted. Yes, but every living thing does not take that view. An animal, for instance. It feels a kind of quality in Space. It can find its way over new country, because it perceives certain landmarks, not necessarily material, but perceptible, or if you like intelligible. Take an Australian savage. He has the same power, and, I believe, for the same reason. He is conscious of intelligible landmarks.'

" 'You mean what people call a sense of direction,' I put in.

" 'Yes, but what in Heaven's name is a sense of direction? The phrase explains nothing. However incoherent the mind of the animal or the savage may be, it is there somewhere, working on some data I've been all through the psychological and anthropological side of the business, and after you eliminate clues from sight and hearing and smell and half-conscious memory there remains a solid lump of the inexplicable.'

"Hollond's eye had kindled, and he sat doubled up in his chair, dominating me with a finger.

" 'Here, then, is a power which man is civilising himself out of. Call it anything you like, but you must admit that it is a power. Don't you see that it is a perception of another kind of reality that we are leaving behind us? . . . Well, you know the way nature works. The wheel comes full circle, and what we think we have lost we regain in a higher form. So for a long time I have been wondering whether the civilised mind could not re-create for itself this lost gift, the gift of seeing the quality of Space. I mean that I wondered whether the scientific modern brain could not get to the stage of realising that Space is not an empty homogeneous medium, but full of intricate differences, intelligible and real, though not with our common reality.'

"I found all this very puzzling, and he had to repeat it several times before I got a glimpse of what he was talking about.

" 'I've wondered for a long time,' he went on, 'but now, quite suddenly, I have begun to know.' He stopped and asked me abruptly if I knew much about mathematics.

" 'It's a pity,' he said, 'but the main point is not technical, though I wish you could appreciate the beauty of some of my proofs.' Then he began to tell me about his last six months' work. I should have mentioned that he was a brilliant physicist besides other things. All Hollond's tastes were on the border-lands of sciences, where mathematics fades into metaphysics and physics merges in the abstrusest kind of mathematics. Well, it seems he had been working for years at the ultimate problem of matter, and especially of that rarefied matter we call æther or space. I forget what his view was—atoms or molecules or electric waves. If he ever told me I have forgotten, but I'm not certain that I ever knew. However, the point was that these ultimate constituents were dynamic and mobile, not a mere passive medium but a medium in constant movement and change. He claimed to have discovered—by ordinary inductive experiment— that the constituents of æther possessed certain functions, and moved in certain figures obedient to certain mathematical laws. Space, I gathered, was perpetually 'forming fours' in some fancy way.

"Here he left his physics and became the mathematician. Among his mathematical discoveries had been certain curves or figures or something whose behaviour involved a new dimension. I gathered that this wasn't the ordinary Fourth Dimension that people talk of, but that fourth-dimensional inwardness or involution was part of it. The explanation lay in the pile of manuscripts he left with me, but though I tried honestly I couldn't get the hang of it. My mathematics stopped with desperate finality just as he got into his subject.

"His point was that the constituents of Space moved according to these new mathematical figures of his. They were always changing, but the principles of their change were as fixed as the law of gravitation. Therefore, if you once grasped these principles you knew the contents of the void. What do you make of that?"

I said that it seemed to me a reasonable enough argument, but that it got one very little way forward. "A man," I said, "might know the contents of Space and the laws of their arrangement and yet be unable to see anything more than his fellows. It is a purely academic knowledge. His mind knows it as the result of many deductions, but his senses perceive nothing."

Leithen laughed. "Just what I said to Hollond. He asked the opinion of my legal mind. I said I could not pronounce on his argument, but that I could point out that he had established no *trait d'union* between the intellect which understood and the senses which perceived. It was like a blind man with immense knowledge but no eyes, and therefore no peg to hang his knowledge on and make it useful. He had not explained his savage or his cat. 'Hang it, man,' I said, 'before you can appreciate the existence of your Spacial forms you have to go through elaborate experiments and deductions. You can't be doing that every minute. Therefore you don't get any nearer to the use of the sense you say that man once possessed, though you can explain it a bit.'

"What did he say?" I asked.

"The funny thing was that he never seemed to see my difficulty. When I kept bringing him back to it he shied off with a new wild theory of perception. He argued that the mind can live in a world of realities without any sensuous stimulus to connect them with the world of our ordinary life. Of course that wasn't my point. I supposed that this world of Space was real enough to him, but I wanted to know how he got there. He never answered me. He was the typical Cambridge man, you know—dogmatic about uncertainties, but curiously diffident about the obvious. He laboured to get me to understand the notion of his mathematical forms, which I was quite willing to take on trust from him. Some queer things he said, too. He took our feeling about Left and Right as an example of our instinct for the quality of Space. But when I objected that Left and Right varied with each object, and only existed in connection with some definite material thing, he said that that was exactly what he meant. It was an example of the mobility of the Spacial forms. Do you see any sense in that?"

I shook my head. It seemed to me pure craziness.

"And then he tried to show me what he called the 'involution of Space', by taking two points on a piece of paper. The points were a foot away when the paper was flat, but they coincided when it was doubled up. He said that there were no gaps between the figures, for the medium was continuous, and he took as an illustration the loops on a cord. You are to think of a cord always looping and unlooping itself according to certain mathematical laws. Oh, I tell you, I gave up trying to follow him. And he was so desperately in earnest all the time. By his account Space was a sort of mathematical pandemonium."

*   *   *

Leithen stopped to refill his pipe, and I mused upon the ironic fate which had compelled a mathematical genius to make his sole confidant of a philistine lawyer, and induced that lawyer to repeat it confusedly to an ignoramus at twilight on a Scotch hill. As told by Leithen it was a very halting tale.

"But there was one thing I could see very clearly," Leithen went on, "and that was Hollond's own case. This crowded world of Space was perfectly real to him. How he had got to it I do not know. Perhaps his mind, dwelling constantly on the problem had unsealed some atrophied cell and restored the old instinct. Anyhow, he was living his daily life with a foot in each world.

"He often came to see me, and after the first hectic discussions he didn't talk much. There was no noticeable change in him—a little more abstracted perhaps. He would walk in the street or come into a room with a quick look round him, and sometimes for no earthly reason he would swerve. Did you ever watch a cat crossing a room? It sidles along by the furniture and walks over an open space of carpet as if it were picking its way among obstacles. Well, Hollond behaved like that, but he had always been counted a little odd, and nobody noticed it but me.

"I knew better than to chaff him, and we had stopped argument, so there wasn't much to be said. But sometimes he would give me news about his experiences. The whole thing was perfectly clear and scientific and above-board, and nothing creepy about it. You know how I hate the washy supernatural stuff they give us nowadays. Hollond was well and fit, with an appetite like a hunter. But as he talked, sometimes—well, you know I haven't much in the way of nerves or imagination—but I used to get a little eerie. Used to feel the solid earth dissolving round me. It was the opposite of vertigo, if you understand me—a sense of airy realities crowding in on you—crowding the mind, that is, not the body.

"I gathered from Hollond that he was always conscious of corridors and halls and alleys in Space, shifting, but shifting according to inexorable laws. I never could get quite clear as to what this consciousness was like. When I asked he used to look puzzled and worried and helpless. I made out from him that one landmark involved a sequence, and once given a bearing from an object you could keep the direction without a mistake. He told me he could easily, if he wanted, go in a dirigible from the top of Mont Blanc to the top of Snowdon in the thickest fog and without a compass, if he were given the proper angle to start from. I confess I didn't follow that myself. Material objects had nothing to do with the Spacial forms, for a table or a bed in our world might be placed across a corridor of Space. The forms played their game independent of our kind of reality. But the worst of it was, that if you kept your mind too much in one world you were apt to forget about the other, and Hollond was always barking his shins on stones and chairs and things.

"He told me all this quite simply and frankly. Remember his mind and no other part of him lived in his new world. He said it gave him an odd sense of detachment to sit in a room among people, and to know that nothing there but himself had any relation at all to the infinite strange world of Space that flowed around them. He would listen, he said, to a great man talking, with one eye on the cat on the rug, thinking to himself how much more the cat knew than the man."

"How long was it before he went mad?" I asked. It was a foolish question, and made Leithen cross. "He never went mad in your sense. My dear fellow, you're very much wrong if you think there was anything pathological about him—then. The man was brilliantly sane. His mind was as keen as a keen sword. I couldn't understand him, but I could judge of his sanity right enough."

I asked if it made him happy or miserable.

"At first I think it made him uncomfortable. He was restless because he knew too much and too little. The unknown pressed in on his mind, as bad air weighs on the lungs. Then it lightened, and he accepted the new world in the same sober practical way that he took other things. I think that the free exercise of his mind in a pure medium gave him a feeling of extraordinary power and ease. His eyes used to sparkle when he talked. And another odd thing he told me. He was a keen rock-climber, but, curiously enough, he had never a very good head. Dizzy heights always worried him, though he managed to keep hold on himself. But now all that had gone. The sense of the fullness of Space made him as happy—happier I believe—with his legs dangling into eternity, as sitting before his own study fire.

"I remember saying that it was all rather like the medieval wizards who made their spells by means of numbers and figures.

"He caught me up at once, 'Not numbers,' he said. 'Number has no place in Nature. It is an invention of the human mind to atone for a bad memory. But figures are a different matter. All the mysteries of the world are in them, and the old magicians knew that at least, if they knew no more.'

"He had only one grievance. He complained that it was terribly lonely. 'It is the Desolation,' he would quote, 'spoken of by Daniel the prophet.' He would spend hours travelling those eerie shifting corridors of Space with no hint of another human soul. How could there be? It was a world of pure reason, where human personality had no place. What puzzled me was why he should feel the absence of this. One wouldn't, you know, in an intricate problem of geometry or a game of chess. I asked him, but he didn't understand the question. I puzzled over it a good deal, for it seemed to me that if Hollond felt lonely, there must be more in this world of his than we imagined. I began to wonder if there was any truth in fads like psychical research. Also, I was not so sure that he was as normal as I had thought: it looked as if his nerves might be going bad.

"Oddly enough, Hollond was getting on the same track himself. He had discovered, so he said, that in sleep everybody now and then lived in this new world of his. You know how one dreams of triangular railway platforms with trains running simultaneously down all three sides and not colliding. Well, this sort of cantrip was 'common form', as we say at the Bar, in Hollond's Space, and he was very curious about the why and wherefore of Sleep. He began to haunt psychological laboratories, where they experiment with the charwoman and the odd-man, and he used to go up to Cambridge for *séances*. It was a foreign atmosphere to him, and I don't think he was very happy in it. He found so many charlatans that he used to get angry, and declare he would be better employed at Mothers' Meetings!"

From far up the Glen came the sound of the pony's hoofs. The stag had been loaded up, and the gillies were returning. Leithen looked at his watch. "We'd better wait and see the beast," he said.

. . . "Well, nothing happened for more than a year. Then one evening in May he burst into my rooms in high excitement. You understand quite clearly that there was no suspicion of horror or fright or anything unpleasant about this world he had discovered. It was simply a series of interesting and difficult problems. All this time Hollond had been rather extra well and cheery. But when he came in I thought I noticed a different look in his eyes, something puzzled and diffident and apprehensive.

" 'There's a queer performance going on in the other world,' he said. 'It's unbelievable. I never dreamed of such a thing. I— I don't quite know how to put it, and I don't know how to explain it, but—but I am becoming aware that there are other beings—other minds—moving in Space besides mine.'

"I suppose I ought to have realised then that things were beginning to go wrong. But it was very difficult, he was so rational and anxious to make it all clear. I asked him how he knew. There could, of course, on his own showing be no *change* in that world, for the forms of Space moved and existed under inexorable laws. He said he found his own mind failing him at points. There would come over him a sense of fear—intellectual fear—and weakness, a sense of something else, quite alien to Space, thwarting him. Of course he could only describe his impressions very lamely, for they were purely of the mind, and he had no material peg to hang them on, so that I could realise them. But the gist of it was that he had been gradually becoming conscious of what he called 'Presences' in his world. They had no effect on Space—did not leave footprints in its corridors, for instance—but they affected his mind. There was some mysterious contact established between him and them. I asked him if the affection was unpleasant, and he said 'No, not exactly.' But I could see a hint of fear in his eyes.

"Think of it. Try to realise what intellectual fear is. I can't, but it is conceivable. To you and me fear implies pain to ourselves or some other, and such pain is always in the last resort pain of the flesh. Consider it carefully and you will see that it is so. But imagine fear so sublimated and transmuted as to be the tension of pure spirit. I can't realise it, but I think it possible. I don't pretend to understand how Hollond got to know about these Presences. But there was no doubt about the fact. He was positive, and he wasn't in the least mad—not in our sense. In that very month he published his book on Number, and gave a German professor who attacked it a most tremendous public trouncing.

"I know what you are going to say—that the fancy was a weakening of the mind from within. I admit I should have thought of that, but he looked so confoundedly sane and able that it seemed ridiculous. He kept asking me my opinion, as a lawyer, on the facts he offered. It was the oddest case ever put before me, but I did my best for him. I dropped all my own views of sense and nonsense. I told him that, taking all that he had told me as fact, the Presences might be either ordinary minds traversing Space in sleep; or minds such as his which had independently captured the sense of Space's quality; or, finally, the spirits of just men made perfect, behaving as psychical researchers think they do. It was a ridiculous task to set a prosaic man, and I wasn't quite serious. But Hollond was serious enough.

"He admitted that all three explanations were conceivable, but he was very doubtful about the first. The projection of the spirit into Space during sleep, he thought, was a faint and feeble thing, and these were powerful Presences. With the second and the third he was rather impressed. I suppose I should have seen what was happening and tried to stop it; at least, looking back that seems to have been my duty. But it was difficult to think that anything was wrong with Hollond; indeed the odd thing is that all this time the idea of madness never entered my head. I rather backed him up. Somehow the thing took my fancy, though I thought it moonshine at the bottom of my heart. I enlarged on the pioneering before him. 'Think,' I told him, 'what may be waiting for you. You may discover the meaning of Spirit. You may open up a new world, as rich as the old one, but imperishable. You may prove to mankind their immortality and deliver them for ever from the fear of death. Why, man, you are picking at the lock of all the world's mysteries.'

"But Hollond did not cheer up. He seemed strangely languid and dispirited. 'That is all true enough,' he said, 'if you are right, if your alternatives are exhaustive. But suppose they are something else, something . . .' What that 'something' might be he had apparently no idea, and very soon he went away.

"He said another thing before he left. He asked me if I ever read poetry, and I said, Not often. Nor did he: but he had picked up a little book somewhere and found a man who knew about the Presences. I think his name was Traherne, one of the seventeenth-century fellows. He quoted a verse which stuck to my fly-paper memory. It ran something like this:—

> " 'Within the region of the air,
> Compassed about with heavens fair,
> Great tracts of lands there may be found,
>   Where many numerous hosts,
>   In those far distant coasts,
> For other great and glorious ends
> Inhabit, my yet unknown friends.'

Hollond was positive he did not mean angels or anything of the sort. I told him that Traherne evidently took a cheerful view of them. He admitted that, but added: 'He had religion, you see. He believed that everything was for the best. I am not a man of faith, and can only take comfort from what I understand. I'm in the dark, I tell you. . . .'

"Next week I was busy with the Chilian Arbitration case, and saw nobody for a couple of months. Then one evening I ran against Hollond on the Embankment, and thought him looking horribly ill. He walked back with me to my rooms, and hardly uttered one word all the way. I gave him a stiff whisky-and-soda, which he gulped down absent-mindedly. There was that strained, hunted look in his eyes that you see in a frightened animal's. He was always lean, but now he had fallen away to skin and bone.

" 'I can't stay long,' he told me, 'for I'm off to the Alps tomorrow and I have a lot to do.' Before then he used to plunge

313

readily into his story, but now he seemed shy about beginning. Indeed I had to ask him a question.

"'Things are difficult,' he said hesitatingly, 'and rather distressing. Do you know, Leithen, I think you were wrong about—about what I spoke to you of. You said there must be one of three explanations. I am beginning to think that there is a fourth. . . .'

"He stopped for a second or two, then suddenly leaned forward and gripped my knee so fiercely that I cried out. 'That world is the Desolation,' he said in a choking voice, 'and perhaps I am getting near the Abomination of the Desolation that the old prophet spoke of. I tell you, man, I am on the edge of a terror, a terror,' he almost screamed, 'that no mortal can think of and live.'

"You can imagine that I was considerably startled. It was lightning out of a clear sky. How the devil could one associate horror with mathematics? I don't see it yet. . . . At any rate, I— You may be sure I cursed my folly for ever pretending to take him seriously. The only way would have been to have laughed him out of it at the start. And yet I couldn't, you know—it was too real and reasonable. Anyhow, I tried a firm tone now, and told him the whole thing was arrant raving bosh. I bade him be a man and pull himself together. I made him dine with me, and took him home, and got him into a better state of mind before he went to bed. Next morning I saw him off at Charing Cross, very haggard still, but better. He promised to write to me pretty often. . . ."

The pony, with a great eleven-pointer lurching athwart its back, was abreast of us, and from the autumn mist came the sound of soft Highland voices. Leithen and I got up to go, when we heard that the rifle had made direct for the Lodge by a short-cut past the Sanctuary. In the wake of the gillies we descended the Correi road into a glen all swimming with dim purple shadows. The pony minced and boggled; the stag's antlers stood out sharp on the rise against a patch of sky, looking like a skeleton tree. Then we dropped into a covert of birches and emerged on the white glen highway.

Leithen's story had bored and puzzled me at the start, but

314

now it had somehow gripped my fancy. Space a domain of endless corridors and Presences moving in them! The world was not quite the same as an hour ago. It was the hour, as the French say, "between dog and wolf", when the mind is disposed to marvels. I thought of my stalking on the morrow, and was miserably conscious that I would miss my stag. Those airy forms would get in the way. Confound Leithen and his yarns!

"I want to hear the end of your story," I told him, as the lights of the Lodge showed half a mile distant.

"The end was a tragedy," he said slowly. "I don't much care to talk about it. But how was I to know? I couldn't see the nerve going. You see I couldn't believe it was all nonsense. If I could I might have seen. But I still think there was something in it—up to a point. Oh, I agree he went mad in the end. It is the only explanation. Something must have snapped in that fine brain, and he saw the little bit more which we call madness. Thank God, you and I are prosaic fellows. . . .

"I was going out to Chamonix myself a week later. But before I started I got a postcard from Hollond, the only word from him. He had printed my name and address, and on the other side had scribbled six words—'*I know at last—God's mercy.—H. G. H.*' The handwriting was like a sick man of ninety. I knew that things must be pretty bad with my friend.

"I got to Chamonix in time for his funeral. An ordinary climbing accident—you probably read about it in the papers. The Press talked about the toll which the Alps took from intellectuals—the usual rot. There was an inquiry, but the facts were quite simple. The body was only recognised by the clothes. He had fallen several thousand feet.

"It seems that he had climbed for a few days with one of the Kronigs and Dupont, and they had done some hair-raising things on the Aiguilles. Dupont told me that they had found a new route up the Montanvert side of the Charmoz. He said that Hollond climbed like a '*diable fou*', and if you know Dupont's standard of madness you will see that the pace must have been pretty hot. 'But monsieur was sick,' he added; 'his eyes were not good. And I and Franz, we were grieved for him and a little afraid. We were glad when he left us.'

"He dismissed the guides two days before his death. The next day he spent in the hotel, getting his affairs straight. He left everything in perfect order, but not a line to a soul, not even to his sister. The following day he set out alone about three in the morning for the Grèpon. He took the road up the Nantillons glacier to the Col, and then he must have climbed the Mummery crack by himself. After that he left the ordinary route and tried a new traverse across the Mer de Glace face. Somewhere near the top he fell, and next day a party going to the Dent du Requin found him on the rocks thousands of feet below.

"He had slipped in attempting the most foolhardy course on earth, and there was a lot of talk about the dangers of guideless climbing. But I guessed the truth, and I am sure Dupont knew, though he held his tongue. . . ."

We were now on the gravel of the drive, and I was feeling better. The thought of dinner warmed my heart, and drove out the eeriness of the twilight glen. The hour between dog and wolf was passing. After all, there was a gross and jolly earth at hand for wise men who had a mind to comfort.

Leithen, I saw, did not share my mood. He looked glum and puzzled, as if his tale had aroused grim memories. He finished it at the Lodge door.

". . . For, of course, he had gone out that day to die. He had seen the something more, the little bit too much, which plucks a man from his moorings. He had gone so far into the land of pure spirit that he must needs go further and shed the fleshly envelope that cumbered him. God send that he found rest! I believe that he chose the steepest cliff in the Alps for a purpose. He wanted to be unrecognisable. He was a brave man and a good citizen. I think he hoped that those who found him might not see the look in his eyes."

STOCKS AND STONES

(*The Chief* TOPIAWARI *replieth to* Sir WALTER RALEIGH,
who upbraided him for idol worship.)

My gods, you say, are idols dumb,
    Which men have wrought from wood or clay,
Carven with chisel, shaped with thumb,
    A morning's task, an evening's play.
You bid me turn my face on high
    Where the blue Heaven the sun enthrones,
And serve a viewless deity,
    Nor make my bow to stocks and stones.

My lord, I am not skilled in wit
    Nor wise in priestcraft, but I know
That fear to man is spur and bit
    To jog and curb his fancies' flow.
He fears and loves, for love and awe
    In mortal souls may well unite
To fashion forth the perfect law
    Where Duty takes to wife Delight.

But on each man one Fear awaits
    And chills his marrow like the dead—
He cannot worship what he hates
    Or make a god of naked Dread.
The homeless winds that twist and race,
    The heights of cloud that veer and roll,
The unplumb'd Abyss, the drifts of Space—
    These are the fears that drain the soul.

Ye dauntless ones from out the sea
    Fear nought. Perchance your gods are strong
To rule the air where grim things be,
    And quell the deeps with all their throng.
For me, I dread not fire nor steel,
    Nor aught that walks in open light,
But fend me from the endless Wheel,
    The voids of Space, the gulfs of Night.

Wherefore my brittle gods I make
　Of friendly clay and kindly stone,—
Wrought with my hands, to serve or break,
　From crown to toe my work, my own.
My eyes can see, my nose can smell,
　My fingers touch their painted face,
They weave their little homely spell
　To warm me from the cold of Space.

My gods are wrought of common stuff
　For human joys and mortal tears;
Weakly, perchance, yet staunch enough
　To build a barrier 'gainst my fears,
Where, lowly but secure, I wait
　And hear without the strange winds blow.—
I cannot worship what I hate,
　Or serve a god I dare not know.

[1] [Andrew Lownie's *John Buchan: The Complete Short Stories*, vol. 2, p182 uses two different epigraphs. These were not employed in the version of the story published in *Blackwood's Magazine*, May 1911, which instead gave the Tertullian used here. They are, however, equally apt. The brief one from Pascal would be known to Buchan from Walter Pater, *The Renaissance*, first published in 1873, in the chapter on Pico della Mirandola (p43 in Macmillan's 1928 edition). Buchan uses it also in the posthumous *Sick Heart River* (1941). The passage from Poincaré shares with Traherne's poem the generative power of the story.

> *J'ai dit que nous pourrions concevoir, vivant dans notre monde, des êtres pensants dont le tableau de distribution serait à quatre dimensions et qui par conséquent penseraient dans l'hyperespace. Il n'est pas certain toutefois que de pareils êtres, en admettant qu'ils y naissent, pourraient y vivre et s'y défendre contre les mille dangers dont ils y seraient assailis.*
> H. POINCARÉ: *Science et Méthode*

> *Le silence éternel de ces espaces infinis m'effraie.*
> PASCAL]

THE RIME OF TRUE THOMAS

*(Being the Tale of the Respectable Whaup
and the Great Godly Man.)*

THIS is a story that I heard from the King of the Numidians,
who with his tattered retinue encamps behind the peat-ricks.
If you ask me where and when it happened I fear that I am
scarce ready with an answer. But I will vouch my honour for its
truth; and if anyone seek further proof, let him go east the town
and west the town and over the fields of Nomansland to the
Long Muir, and if he find not the King there among the peat-
ricks, and get not a courteous answer to his question, then times
have changed in that part of the country, and he must continue
the quest to his Majesty's castle in Spain.

Once upon a time, says the tale, there was a Great Godly
Man, a shepherd to trade, who lived in a cottage among heather.
If you looked east in the morning, you saw miles of moor
running wide to the flames of sunrise, and if you turned your
eyes west in the evening, you saw a great confusion of dim peaks
with the dying eye of the sun set in a crevice. If you looked
north, too, in the afternoon, when the life of the day is near its
end and the world grows wise, you might have seen a country
of low hills and haughlands with many waters running sweet
among meadows. But if you looked south in the dusty forenoon
or at hot midday, you saw the far-off glimmer of a white road,
the roofs of the ugly little clachan of Kilmaclavers, and the
rigging of the fine new kirk of Threepdaidle.

It was a Sabbath afternoon in the hot weather, and the man
had been to kirk all the morning. He had heard a grand sermon
from the minister (or it may have been the priest, for I am not
sure of the date and the King told the story quickly)—a fine
discourse with fifteen heads and three parentheses. He held all

the parentheses and fourteen of the heads in his memory, but he had forgotten the fifteenth; so for the purpose of recollecting it, and also for the sake of a walk, he went forth in the afternoon into the open heather.

The whaups were crying everywhere, making the air hum like the twanging of a bow. *Poo-eelie*, *Poo-eelie*, they cried, *Kirlew*, *Kirlew*, *Whaup*, *Wha- -up*. Sometimes they came low, all but brushing him, till they drove settled thoughts from his head. Often had he been on the moors, but never had he seen such a stramash among the feathered clan. The wailing iteration vexed him, and he *shoo'd* the birds away with his arms. But they seemed to mock him and whistle in his very face, and at the flaff of their wings his heart grew sore. He waved his great stick; he picked up bits of loose moor-rock and flung them wildly; but the godless crew paid never a grain of heed. The morning's sermon was still in his head, and the grave words of the minister still rattled in his ear, but he could get no comfort for this intolerable piping. At last his patience failed him and he swore unchristian words. "Deil rax the birds' thrapples!" he cried.

At this all the noise was hushed and in a twinkling the moor was empty. Only one bird was left, standing on tall legs before him with its head bowed upon its breast, and its beak touching the heather.

Then the man repented his words and stared at the thing in the moss. "What bird are ye?" he asked thrawnly.

"I am a Respectable Whaup," said the bird, "and I kenna why ye have broken in on our family gathering. Once in a hundred years we foregather for decent conversation, and here we are interrupted by a muckle, sweerin' man."

Now the shepherd was a fellow of great sagacity, yet he never thought it a queer thing that he should be having talk in the mid-moss with a bird.

"What for were ye making siccan a din, then?" he asked. "D'ye no ken ye were disturbing the afternoon of the holy Sabbath?"

The bird lifted its eyes and regarded him solemnly. "The Sabbath is a day of rest and gladness," it said, "and is it no' reasonable that we should enjoy the like?"

The shepherd shook his head, for the presumption staggered him. "Ye little ken what ye speak of," he said. "The Sabbath is for them that have the chance of salvation, and it has been decreed that salvation is for Adam's race and no for the beasts that perish."

The whaup gave a whistle of scorn. "I have heard all that long ago. In my great-grandmother's time, which 'ill be a thousand years and mair syne, there came a people from the south with bright brass things on their heads and breasts, and terrible swords at their thighs. And with them were some lang-gowned men who kenned the stars and would come out o' nights to talk to the deer and the corbies in their ain tongue. And one, I mind, foregathered with my great-grandmother and told her that the souls o' men flitted in the end to braw meadows where the gods bide or gaed down to the black pit which they ca' Hell. But the souls o' birds, he said, die wi' their bodies, and that's the end o' them. Likewise in my mother's time, when there was a great abbey down yonder by the Threepdaidle Burn which they called the House of Kilmaclavers, the auld monks would walk out in the evening to pick herbs for their distillings, and some were wise and kenned the ways of bird and beast. They would crack often o' nights with my ain family, and tell them that Christ had saved the souls o' men, but that birds and beasts were perishable as the dew o' Heaven. And now ye have a black-gowned man in Threepdaidle who threeps on the same owercome. Ye may a' ken something o' your ain kitchen-midden, but certes! ye ken little o' the warld beyond it."

Now this angered the man, and he rebuked the bird. "These are great mysteries," he said, "which are no' to be mentioned in the ears of an unsanctified creature. What can a thing like you wi' a lang neb and twae legs like stilts ken about the next warld?"

"Weel, weel," said the whaup, "we'll let the matter be. Everything to its ain trade, and I will not dispute with ye on metapheesics. But if ye ken something about the next warld, ye ken terrible little about this."

Now this angered the man still more, for he was a shepherd reputed to have great skill in sheep and esteemed the nicest judge of hogg and wether in all the countryside. "What ken ye about that?" he asked. "Ye may gang east to Yetholm and west to Kells, and no find a better herd."

"If sheep were a'," said the bird, "ye micht be right; but what o' the wide warld and the folk in it? Ye are Simon Etterick o' the Lowe Moss. Do ye ken aucht o' your forebears?"

"My father was a God-fearing man at the Kennel-head, and my grandfather and great-grandfather afore him. One o' our name, folk say, was shot at a dyke-back by the Black Westeraw."

"If that's a'," said the bird, "ye ken little. Have ye never heard o' the little man, the fourth back from yoursel', who killed the Miller o' Bewcastle at the Lammas Fair? That was in my ain time, and from my mother I have heard o' the Covenanter who got a bullet in his wame hunkering behind the divot-dyke and praying to his Maker. There were others o' your name rode in the Hermitage forays and burned Naworth and Warkworth and Castle Gay. I have heard o' an Etterick, Sim o' the Redcleuch, who cut the throat o' Jock Johnstone in his ain house by the Annan side. And my grandmother had tales o' auld Ettericks who rade wi' Douglas and the Bruce and the ancient Kings o' Scots; and she used to tell o' others in her mother's time, terrible shock-headed men, hunting the deer and rinnin' on the high moors, and bidin' in the broken stane biggings on the hill-taps."

The shepherd stared, and he, too, saw the picture. He smelled the air of battle and lust and foray, and forgot the Sabbath.

"And you yoursel'," said the bird, "are sair fallen off from the auld stock. Now ye sit and spell in books, and talk about what ye little understand, when your fathers were roaming the warld. But little cause have I to speak, for I too am a downcome. My bill is two inches shorter than my mother's, and my grandmother was taller on her feet. The warld is getting weaklier things to dwell in it, even since I mind mysel'."

"Ye have the gift o' speech, bird," said the man, "and I would hear mair." You will perceive that he had no mind of the Sabbath day or the fifteenth head of the forenoon's discourse.

"What things have I to tell ye when ye dinna ken the very horn-book o' knowledge? Besides, I am no clatter-vengeance to tell stories in the middle o' the muir, where there are ears open high and low. There's others than me wi' mair experience and a better skill at the telling. Our clan was well acquaint wi' the reivers and lifters o' the muirs, and could crack fine o' wars and the taking of cattle. But the blue hawk that lives in the corrie o' the Dreichil can speak o' kelpies and the dwarfs that bide in the hill. The heron, the lang solemn fellow, kens o' the greenwood fairies and the wood elfins, and the wild geese that squatter on the tap o' the Muneraw will croak to ye of the merrymaidens and the girls o' the pool. The wren—him that hops in the grass below the birks—has the story of the *Lost Ladies of the Land*, which is ower auld and sad for any but the wisest to hear; and there is a wee bird bides in the heather—hill-lintie men call him—who sings the *Lay of the West Wind* and the *Glee of the Rowan Berries*. But what am I talking of? What are these things to you, if ye have not first heard True Thomas's Rime, which is the beginning and end o' all things?"

"I have heard no rime," said the man, "save the sacred psalms o' God's Kirk."

"Bonny rimes," said the bird. "Once I flew by the hinder end o' the kirk and I keekit in. A wheen auld wives wi' mutches and a wheen solemn men wi' hoasts! Be sure the Rime is no like yon."

"Can ye sing it, bird?" said the man, "for I am keen to hear it."

"Me sing," cried the bird, "me that has a voice like a craw! Na, na, I canna sing it, but maybe I can tak ye where ye may hear it. When I was young an auld bog-blitter did the same to me, and sae began my education. But are ye willing and brawly willing?—for if ye get but a sough of it ye will never mair have an ear for other music."

"I am willing and brawly willing," said the man.

"Then meet me at the Gled's Cleuch Head at the sun's setting," said the bird, and it flew away.

Now it seemed to the man that in a twinkling it was sunset, and he found himself at the Gled's Cleuch Head with the bird flapping in the heather before him. The place was a long rift in the hill, made green with juniper and hazel, where it was said True Thomas came to drink the water.

323

"Turn ye to the west," said the whaup, "and let the sun fall on your face; then turn ye five times round about and say after me the Rune of the Heather and the Dew." And before he knew, the man did as he was told, and found himself speaking strange words, while his head hummed and danced as if in a fever.

"Now lay ye down and put your ear to the earth," said the bird; and the man did so. Instantly a cloud came over his brain, and he did not feel the ground on which he lay or the keen hill-air which blew about him. He felt himself falling deep into an abysm of space, then suddenly caught up and set among the stars of Heaven. Then slowly from the stillness there welled forth music, drop by drop like the clear falling of rain, and the man shuddered, for he knew that he heard the beginning of the Rime.

High rose the air, and trembled among the tallest pines and the summits of great hills. And in it were the sting of rain and the blatter of hail, the soft crush of snow and the rattle of thunder among crags. Then it quieted to the low sultry croon which told of blazing midday when the streams are parched and the bent crackles like dry tinder. Anon it was evening, and the melody dwelled among the high soft notes which mean the coming of dark and the green light of sunset. Then the whole changed to a great pæan which rang like an organ through the earth. There were trumpet notes in it and flute notes and the plaint of pipes. "Come forth," it cried; "the sky is wide and it is a far cry to the world's end. The fire crackles fine o' nights below the firs, and the smell of roasting meat and wood-smoke is dear to the heart of man. Fine, too, is the sting of salt and the rise of the north wind in the sheets. Come forth, one and all, to the great lands oversea, and the strange tongues and the fremit peoples. Learn before you die to follow the Piper's Son, and though your old bones bleach among grey rocks, what matter, if you have had your bellyful of life and come to your heart's desire?" And the tune fell low and witching, bringing tears to the eyes and joy to the heart; and the man knew (though no one told him) that this was the first part of the Rime, the *Song of the Open Road*, the *Lilt of the Adventurer*, which shall be now and ever and to the end of days.

Then the melody changed to a fiercer and sadder note. He saw his forefathers, gaunt men and terrible, run stark among woody hills. He heard the talk of the bronze-clad invader, and the jar and clangour as stone met steel. Then rose the last coronach of his own people, hiding in wild glens, starving in corries, or going hopelessly to the death. He heard the cry of Border foray, the shouts of the famished Scots as they harried Cumberland, and he himself rode in the midst of them. Then the tune fell more mournful and slow, and Flodden lay before him. He saw the flower of the Scots gentry around their King, gashed to the breast-bone, still fronting the lines of the south, though the paleness of death sat on each forehead. "The flowers of the Forest are gone," cried the lilt, and through the long years he heard the cry of the lost, the desperate, fighting for kings over the water and princes in the heather. "Who cares?" cried the air. "Man must die, and how can he die better than in the stress of fight with his heart high and alien blood on his sword? Heigh-ho! One against twenty, a child against a host, this is the romance of life." And the man's heart swelled, for he knew (though no one told him) that this was the *Song of Lost Battles* which only the great can sing before they die.

But the tune was changing, and at the change the man shivered, for the air ran up to the high notes and then down to the deeps with an eldrich cry, like a hawk's scream at night, or a witch's song in the gloaming. It told of those who seek and never find, the quest that knows no fulfilment. "There is a road," it cried, "which leads to the Moon and the Great Waters. No change-house cheers it, and it has no end; but it is a fine road, a braw road—who will follow it?" And the man knew (though no one told him) that this was the *Ballad of Grey Weather*, which makes him who hears it sick all the days of his life for something which he cannot name. It is the song which the birds sing on the moor in the autumn nights, and the old crow on the tree-top hears and flaps his wing. It is the lilt which men and women hear in the darkening of their days, and sigh for the unforgettable; and love-sick girls get catches of it and play pranks with their lovers. It is a song so old that Adam heard it in the Garden before Eve came to comfort him, so young that from it still flows the whole joy and sorrow of earth.

Then it ceased, and all of a sudden the man was rubbing his eyes on the hillside, and watching the falling dusk. "I have heard the Rime," he said to himself, and he walked home in a daze. The whaups were crying, but none came near him, though he looked hard for the bird that had spoken with him. It may be that it was there and he did not know it, or it may be that the whole thing was only a dream; but of this I cannot say.

The next morning the man rose and went to the manse.

"I am glad to see you, Simon," said the minister, "for it will soon be the Communion Season, and it is your duty to go round with the tokens."

"True," said the man, "but it was another thing I came to talk about," and he told him the whole tale.

"There are but two ways of it, Simon," said the minister. "Either ye are the victim of witchcraft, or ye are a self-deluded man. If the former (whilk I am loth to believe), then it behoves ye to watch and pray lest ye enter into temptation. If the latter, then ye maun put a strict watch over a vagrom fancy, and ye'll be quit o' siccan whigmaleeries."

Now Simon was not listening, but staring out of the window. "There was another thing I had it in my mind to say," said he. "I have come to lift my lines, for I am thinking of leaving the place."

"And where would ye go?" asked the minister, aghast.

"I was thinking of going to Carlisle and trying my luck as a dealer, or maybe pushing on with droves to the South."

"But that's a cauld country where there are no faithfu' ministrations," said the minister.

"Maybe so, but I am not caring very muckle about ministrations," said the man, and the other looked after him in horror.

When he left the manse he went to a Wise Woman, who lived on the left side of the kirkyard above Threepdaidle burn-foot. She was very old, and sat by the ingle day and night, waiting upon death. To her he told the same tale.

She listened gravely, nodding with her head. "Ach," she said, "I have heard a like story before. And where will you be going?"

"I am going south to Carlisle to try the dealing and droving," said the man, "for I have some skill of sheep."

"And will ye bide there?" she asked.

"Maybe ay, and maybe no," he said. "I had half a mind to push on to the big toun or even to the abroad. A man must try his fortune."

"That's the way of men," said the old wife. "I, too, have heard the Rime, and many women who now sit decently spinning in Kilmaclavers have heard it. But a woman may hear it and lay it up in her soul and bide at hame, while a man, if he get but a glisk of it in his fool's heart, must needs up and awa' to the warld's end on some daft-like ploy. But gang your ways and fare-ye-weel. My cousin Francie heard it, and he went north wi' a white cockade in his bonnet and a sword at his side, singing 'Charlie's come hame'. And Tam Crichtoun o' the Bourhopehead got a sough o' it one simmer's morning, and the last we heard o' Tam he was fechting like a deil among the Frenchmen. Once I heard a tinkler play a sprig of it on the pipes, and a' the lads were wud to follow him. Gang your ways, for I am near the end o' mine." And the old wife shook with her coughing.

So the man put up his belongings in a pack on his back and went whistling down the Great South Road.

Whether or not this tale have a moral it is not for me to say. The King (who told it me) said that it had, and quoted a scrap of Latin, for he had been at Oxford in his youth before he fell heir to his kingdom. One may hear tunes from the Rime, said he, in the thick of a storm on the scarp of a rough hill, in the soft June weather, or in the sunset silence of a winter's night. But let none, he added, pray to have the full music; for it will make him who hears it a footsore traveller in the ways o' the world and a masterless man till death.

A LUCID INTERVAL

I

TO adopt the opening words of a more famous tale, "The truth of this strange matter is what the world has long been looking for." The events which I propose to chronicle were known to perhaps a hundred people in London whose fate brings them into contact with politics. The consequences were apparent to all the world, and for one hectic fortnight tinged the soberest newspapers with saffron, drove more than one worthy election agent to an asylum, and sent whole batches of legislators to Continental "cures". But no reasonable explanation of the mystery has been forthcoming until now, when a series of chances gave the key into my hands.

Lady Caerlaverock is my aunt, and I was present at the two remarkable dinner-parties which form the main events in this tale. I was also taken into her confidence during the terrible fortnight which intervened between them. Like everybody else, I was hopelessly in the dark, and could only accept what happened as a divine interposition. My first clue came when James, the Caerlaverocks' second footman, entered my service as valet, and being a cheerful youth chose to gossip while he shaved me. I checked him, but he babbled on, and I could not choose but learn something about the disposition of the Caerlaverock household below-stairs. I learned—what I knew before—that his lordship had an inordinate love for curries, a taste acquired during some troubled years as Indian Viceroy. I had often eaten that admirable dish at his table, and had heard him boast of the skill of the Indian cook who prepared it. James, it appeared, did not hold with the Orient in the kitchen. He described the said Indian gentleman as a "nigger", and expressed profound distrust of his ways. He referred darkly to the events of the year before, which in some distorted way had reached the servants' ears. "We always thought as 'ow it was them niggers as done it," he declared; and when I questioned him on his use of the plural, admitted that at the time in question "there 'ad been more nor one nigger 'anging about the kitchen."

Pondering on these sayings, I asked myself if it were not possible that the behaviour of certain eminent statesmen was due to some strange devilry of the East, and I made a vow to abstain in future from the Caerlaverock curries. But last month my brother returned from India, and I got the whole truth. He was staying with me in Scotland, and in the smoking-room the talk turned on occultism in the East. I declared myself a sceptic, and George was stirred. He asked me rudely what I knew about it, and proceeded to make a startling confession of faith. He was cross-examined by the others, and retorted with some of his experiences. Finding an incredulous audience, his tales became more defiant, until he capped them all with one monstrous yarn. He maintained that in a Hindu family of his acquaintance there had been transmitted the secret of a drug, capable of altering a man's whole temperament until the antidote was administered. It would turn a coward into a bravo, a miser into a spendthrift, a rake into a fakir. Then, having delivered his manifesto, he got up abruptly and went to bed.

I followed him to his room, for something in the story had revived a memory. By dint of much persuasion I dragged from the somnolent George various details. The family in question were Beharis, large landholders dwelling near the Nepal border. He had known old Ram Singh for years, and had seen him twice since his return from England. He got the story from him, under no promise of secrecy, for the family drug was as well known in the neighbourhood as the nine incarnations of Krishna. He had no doubt about the truth of it, for he had positive proof. "And others besides me," said George. "Do you remember when Vennard had a lucid interval a couple of years ago and talked sense for once? That was old Ram Singh's doing, for he told me about it."

Three years ago it seems the Government of India saw fit to

329

appoint a commission to inquire into land tenure on the Nepal border. Some of the feudal Rajahs had been "birsing yont", like the Breadalbanes, and the smaller zemindars were gravely disquieted. The result of the commission was that Ram Singh had his boundaries rectified, and lost a mile or two of country which his hard-fisted fathers had won. I know nothing of the rights of the matter, but there can be no doubt about Ram Singh's dissatisfaction. He appealed to the law courts, but failed to upset the commission's finding, and the Privy Council upheld the Indian judgment. Thereupon in a flowery and eloquent document he laid his case before the Viceroy, and was told that the matter was closed. Now Ram Singh came of a fighting stock, so he straightway took ship to England to petition the Crown. He petitioned Parliament, but his petition went into the bag behind the Speaker's chair, from which there is no return. He petitioned the King, but was courteously informed that he must approach the Department concerned. He tried the Secretary of State for India, and had an interview with Abinger Vennard, who was very rude to him, and succeeded in mortally insulting the feudal aristocrat. He appealed to the Prime Minister, and was warned off by a harassed private secretary. The handful of members of Parliament who make Indian grievances their stock-in-trade fought shy of him, for indeed Ram Singh's case had no sort of platform appeal in it, and his arguments were flagrantly undemocratic. But they sent him to Lord Caerlaverock; for the ex-Viceroy loved to be treated as a kind of consul-general for India. But this Protector of the Poor proved a broken reed. He told Ram Singh flatly that he was a belated feudalist, which was true; and implied that he was a land-grabber, which was not true, Ram Singh having only enjoyed the fruits of his forebears' enterprise. Deeply incensed, the appellant shook the dust of Caerlaverock House from his feet, and sat down to plan a revenge upon the Government which had wronged him. And in his wrath he thought of the heirloom of his house, the drug which could change men's souls.

It happened that Lord Caerlaverock's cook came from the same neighbourhood as Ram Singh. This cook, Lal Muhammad by name, was one of a large poor family, hangers-on of Ram

Singh's house. The aggrieved landowner summoned him, and demanded as of right his humble services. Lal Muhammad, who found his berth to his liking, hesitated, quibbled, but was finally overborne. He suggested a fee for his services, but hastily withdrew when Ram Singh sketched a few of the steps he proposed to take on his return by way of punishing Lal Muhammad's insolence on Lal Muhammad's household. Then he got to business. There was a great dinner next week—so he had learned from Jephson, the butler—and more than one member of the Government would honour Caerlaverock House by his presence. With deference he suggested this as a fitting occasion for the experiment, and Ram Singh was pleased to assent.

I can picture these two holding their meetings in the South Kensington lodgings where Ram Singh dwelt. We know from James, the second footman, that they met also at Caerlaverock House, no doubt that Ram Singh might make certain that his orders were duly obeyed. I can see the little packet of clear grains—I picture them like small granulated sugar—added to the condiments, and soon dissolved out of sight. The deed was done: the cook returned to Bloomsbury and Ram Singh to Gloucester Road, to await with the patient certainty of the East the consummation of a great vengeance.

II

MY wife was at Kissingen, and I was dining with the Caerlaverocks *en garçon*. When I have not to wait upon the adornment of the female person I am a man of punctual habits, and I reached the house as the hall clock chimed the quarter-past. My poor friend, Tommy Deloraine, arrived along with me, and we ascended the staircase together. I call him "my poor friend", for at the moment Tommy was under the weather. He had the misfortune to be a marquis, and a very rich one, and at the same time to be in love with Claudia Barriton. Neither circumstance was in itself an evil, but the combination made for tragedy. For Tommy's twenty-five years of healthy manhood, his cleanly-made upstanding figure, his fresh countenance and cheerful laugh, were of no avail in the lady's eyes when set against the fact that he was an idle peer. Miss Claudia was a charming girl, with a notable bee in her bonnet. She was burdened with the cares of the State, and had no patience with anyone who took them lightly. To her mind the social fabric was rotten beyond repair, and her purpose was frankly destructive. I remember some of her phrases: "A bold and generous policy of social amelioration"; "The development of a civic conscience"; "A strong hand to lop off decaying branches from the trunk of the State". I have no fault to find with her creed, but I objected to its practical working when it took the shape of an inhuman hostility to that devout lover, Tommy Deloraine. She had refused him, I believe, three times, with every circumstance of scorn. The first time she had analysed his character, and described him as a bundle of attractive weaknesses. "The only forces I recognise are those of intellect and conscience," she had said, "and you have neither." The second time—it was after he had been to Canada on the staff—she spoke of the irreconcilability of their political ideals. "You are an Imperialist," she said, "and believe in an empire of conquest for the benefit of the few. I want a little island with a rich life for all." Tommy declared that he would become a Doukhobor to please her, but she said something about the inability of Ethiopians to change their skin. The third time she hinted vaguely that there was "another". The star of Abinger Vennard was now blazing in the firmament, and she had conceived a platonic admiration for him. The truth is that Miss Claudia, with all her cleverness, was very young and—dare I say it?—rather silly.

Caerlaverock was stroking his beard, his legs astraddle on the hearthrug, with something appallingly viceregal in his air, when Mr. and Mrs. Alexander Cargill were announced. The Home Secretary was a joy to behold. He had the face of an elderly and pious bookmaker, and a voice in which lurked the indescribable Scotch quality of "unction". When he was talking you had only to shut your eyes to imagine yourself in some lowland kirk on a hot Sabbath morning. He had been a distinguished advocate before he left the law for politics, and had swayed juries of his countrymen at his will. The man was extraordinarily efficient on a platform. There were unplumbed depths of emotion in his eye, a juicy sentiment in his voice, an overpowering tenderness in his manner, which gave to politics the glamour of a revival meeting. He wallowed in obvious pathos, and his hearers, often unwillingly, wallowed with him. I have never listened to any orator at once so offensive and so horribly effective. There was no appeal too base for him, and none too august: by some subtle alchemy he blended the arts of the prophet and the fishwife. He had discovered a new kind of language. Instead of "the hungry millions", or "the toilers", or any of the numerous synonyms for our masters, he invented the phrase "Goad's people". "I shall never rest," so ran his great declaration, "till Goad's green fields and Goad's clear waters are free to Goad's people." I remember how on this occasion he pressed my hand with his famous cordiality, looked gravely and earnestly into my face, and then gazed sternly into vacancy. It was a fine picture of genius descending for a moment from its hilltop to show how close it was to poor humanity.

Then came Lord Mulross, a respectable troglodytic peer, who represented the one sluggish element in a swiftly progressing Government. He was an oldish man with bushy whiskers and a reputed mastery of the French tongue. A Whig, who had never changed his creed one iota, he was highly valued by the country as a sober element in the nation's councils, and endured by the Cabinet as necessary ballast. He did not conceal his dislike for certain of his colleagues, notably Mr. Vennard and Mr. Cargill.

When Miss Barriton arrived with her step-mother the party was almost complete. She entered with an air of apologising for her prettiness. Her manner with old men was delightful, and I watched with interest the unbending of Caerlaverock and the simplifying of Mr. Cargill in her presence. Deloraine, who was talking feverishly to Mrs. Cargill, started as if to go and greet her, thought better of it, and continued his conversation. The lady swept the room with her eye, but did not acknowledge his presence. She floated off with Mr. Cargill to a window-corner, and metaphorically sat at his feet. I saw Deloraine saying things behind his moustache, while he listened to Mrs. Cargill's new cure for dyspepsia.

333

Last of all, twenty minutes late, came Abinger Vennard. He made a fine stage entrance, walking swiftly with a lowering brow to his hostess, and then glaring fiercely round the room as if to challenge criticism. I have heard Deloraine, in a moment of irritation, describe him as a "Pre-Raphaelite attorney", but there could be no denying his good looks. He had a bad, loose figure, and a quantity of studiously neglected hair, but his face was the face of a young Greek. A certain kind of political success gives a man the manners of an actor, and both Vennard and Cargill bristled with self consciousness. You could see it in the way they patted their hair, squared their shoulders, and shifted their feet to positions loved by sculptors.

"Well, Vennard, what's the news from the House?" Caerlaverock asked.

"Simpson is talking," said Vennard wearily. "He attacks me, of course. He says he has lived forty years in India—as if that mattered! When will people recognise that the truths of democratic policy are independent of time and space? Liberalism is a category, an eternal mode of thought, which cannot be overthrown by any trivial happenings. I am sick of the word 'facts'. I long for truths."

Miss Barriton's eyes brightened, and Cargill said, "Excellent." Lord Mulross, who was a little deaf, and in any case did not understand the language, said loudly to my aunt that he wished there was a close time for legislation. "The open season for grouse should be the close season for politicians." And then we went down to dinner.

Miss Barriton sat on my left hand, between Deloraine and me, and it was clear she was discontented with her position. Her eyes wandered down the table to Vennard, who had taken in an American duchess, and seemed to be amused at her prattle. She looked with complete disfavour at Deloraine, and turned to me as the lesser of two evils.

I was tactless enough to say that I thought there was a good deal in Lord Mulross's view.

"Oh, how can you?" she cried. "Is there a close season for the wants of the people? It sounds to me perfectly horrible the way you talk of government, as if it were a game for idle men of the upper classes. I want professional politicians, men who give their whole heart and soul to the service of the State. I know the kind of member you and Lord Deloraine like—a rich young man who eats and drinks too much, and thinks the real business of life is killing little birds. He travels abroad and shoots some big game, and then comes home and vapours about the Empire. He knows nothing about realities, and will go down before the men who take the world seriously."

I am afraid I laughed, but Deloraine, who had been listening, was in no mood to be amused.

"I don't think you are quite fair to us, Miss Claudia," he said slowly. "We take things seriously enough, the things we know about. We can't be expected to know about everything, and the misfortune is that the things I care about don't interest you. But they are important enough for all that."

"Hush," said the lady rudely. "I want to hear what Mr. Vennard is saying."

Mr. Vennard was addressing the dinner-table as if it were a large public meeting. It was a habit he had, for he had no mind to confine the pearls of his wisdom to his immediate neighbours. His words were directed to Caerlaverock at the far end.

"In my opinion this craze for the scientific standpoint is not merely overdone—it is radically vicious. Human destinies cannot be treated as if they were inert objects under the microscope. The cold-blooded logical way of treating a problem is in almost every case the wrong way. Heart and imagination to me are more vital than intellect. I have the courage to be illogical, to defy facts for the sake of an ideal, in the certainty that in time facts will fall into conformity. My creed may be put in the words of Newman's favourite quotation: *Non in dialectica complacuit Deo salvum facere populum suum*—Not in cold logic is it God's will that His people should find salvation."

"It is profoundly true," sighed Mr. Cargill, and Miss Claudia's beaming eyes proved her assent.

The moment of destiny, though I did not know it, had arrived. The *entrée* course had begun, and of the two *entrées* one was the famous Caerlaverock curry. Now on a hot July evening in London there are more attractive foods than curry seven times

335

heated, *more Indico*. I doubt if any guest would have touched it, had not our host in his viceregal voice called the attention of the three Ministers to its merits, while explaining that under doctor's orders he was compelled to refrain for a season. The result was that Mulross, Cargill, and Vennard alone of the men partook of it. Miss Claudia, alone of the women, followed suit in the fervour of her hero-worship. She ate a mouthful, and then drank rapidly two glasses of water.

My narrative of the events which followed is based rather on what I should have seen than on what I saw. I had not the key, and missed much which otherwise would have been plain to me. For example, if I had known the secret, I must have seen Miss Claudia's gaze cease to rest upon Vennard and the adoration die out of her eyes. I must have noticed her face soften to the unhappy Deloraine. As it was, I did not remark her behaviour till I heard her say to her neighbour—

"Can't you get hold of Mr. Vennard and forcibly cut his hair?"

Deloraine looked round with a start. Miss Barriton's tone was intimate and her face friendly.

"Some people think it picturesque," he said in serious bewilderment.

"Oh, yes, picturesque—like a hairdresser's young man!" she shrugged her shoulders. "He looks as if he had never been out-of-doors in his life."

Now, whatever the faults of Tommy's appearance, he had a wholesome sunburnt face, and he knew it. This speech of Miss Barriton's cheered him enormously, for he argued that if she had fallen out of love with Vennard's looks she might fall in love with his own. Being a philosopher in his way, he was content to take what the gods gave, and ask for no explanations.

I do not know how their conversation prospered, for my attention was distracted by the extraordinary behaviour of the Home Secretary. Mr. Cargill had made himself notorious by his treatment of "political" prisoners. It was sufficient in his eyes for a criminal to confess to political convictions to secure the most lenient treatment and a speedy release. The Irish patriot who cracked skulls in the Scotland Division of Liverpool, the Suffragist who broke windows and the noses of the police, the Social

Democrat whose antipathy to the Tzar revealed itself in assaults upon the Russian Embassy, the "hunger-marchers" who had designs on the British Museum—all were sure of respectful and tender handling. He had announced more than once, amid tumultuous cheering, that he would never be the means of branding earnestness, however mistaken, with the badge of the felon.

He was talking, I recall, to Lady Lavinia Dobson, renowned in two hemispheres for her advocacy of women's rights. And this was what I heard him say. His face had grown suddenly flushed and his eye bright, so that he looked liker than ever to a bookmaker who had had a good meeting. "No, no, my dear lady, I have been a lawyer, and it is my duty in office to see that the law, the palladium of British liberties, is kept sacrosanct. The law is no respecter of persons, and I intend that it shall be no respecter of creeds. If men or women break the laws, to jail they shall go, though their intentions were those of the Apostle Paul. We don't punish them for being Socialists or Suffragists, but for breaking the peace. Why, goodness me, if we didn't, we should have every malefactor in Britain claiming preferential treatment because he was a Christian Scientist or a Pentecostal Dancer."

"Mr. Cargill, do you realise what you are saying?" said Lady Lavinia with a scared face.

"Of course I do. I am a lawyer, and may be presumed to know the law. If any other doctrine were admitted, the Empire would burst up in a fortnight."

"That I should live to hear you name that accursed name!" cried the outraged lady. "You are denying your gods, Mr. Cargill. You are forgetting the principles of a lifetime."

Mr. Cargill was becoming excited, and exchanging his ordinary Edinburgh-English for a broader and more effective dialect.

"Tut, tut, my good wumman, I may be allowed to know my own principles best. I tell ye I've always maintained these views from the day when I first walked the floor of the Parliament House. Besides, even if I hadn't, I'm surely at liberty to change if I get more light. Whoever makes a fetish of consistency is a trumpery body and little use to God or man. What ails ye at the

Empire, too? Is it not better to have a big country than a kailyard, or a house in Grosvenor Square than a but-and-ben in Balham?"

Lady Lavinia folded her hands. "We slaughter our black fellow-citizens, we fill South Africa with yellow slaves, we crowd the Indian prisons with the noblest and most enlightened of the Indian race, and we call it Empire-building!"

"No, we don't," said Mr. Cargill stoutly, "we call it common sense. That is the penal and repressive side of any great activity. D'ye mean to tell me that you never give your maid a good hearing? But would you like it to be said that you spent the whole of your days swearing at the wumman?"

"I never swore in my life," said Lady Lavinia.

"I spoke metaphorically," said Mr. Cargill. "If ye cannot understand a simple metaphor, ye cannot understand the rudiments of politics."

Picture to yourself a prophet who suddenly discovers that his God is laughing at him, a devotee whose saint winks and tells him that the devotion of years has been a farce, and you will get some idea of Lady Lavinia's frame of mind. Her sallow face flushed, her lip trembled, and she slewed round as far as her chair would permit her. Meanwhile Mr. Cargill, redder than before, went on contentedly with his dinner.

I was glad when my aunt gave the signal to rise. The atmosphere was electric, and all were conscious of it save the three Ministers, Deloraine, and Miss Claudia. Vennard seemed to be behaving very badly. He was arguing with Caerlaverock down the table, and the ex-Viceroy's face was slowly getting purple. When the ladies had gone, we remained oblivious to wine and cigarettes, listening to this heated controversy which threatened any minute to end in a quarrel.

The subject was India, and Vennard was discoursing on the follies of all Viceroys.

"Take this idiot we've got now," he declared. "He expects me to be a sort of wet-nurse to the Government of India and do all their dirty work for them. They know local conditions, and they have ample powers if they would only use them, but they won't take an atom of responsibility. How the deuce am I to decide for them, when in the nature of things I can't be half as well informed about the facts!"

"Do you maintain," said Caerlaverock, stuttering in his wrath, "that the British Government should divest itself of responsibility for the government of our great Indian Dependency?"

"Not a bit," said Vennard impatiently; "of course we are responsible, but that is all the more reason why the fellows who know the business at first hand should do their duty. If I am the head of a bank I am responsible for its policy, but that doesn't mean that every local bank-manager should consult me about the solvency of clients I never heard of. Faversham keeps bleating to me that the state of India is dangerous. Well, for God's sake let him suppress every native paper, shut up the schools, and send every agitator to the Andamans. I'll back him up all right. But don't let him ask me what to do, for I don't know."

"You think such a course would be popular?" asked a large, grave man, a newspaper editor.

"Of course it would," said Vennard cheerily. "The British public hates the idea of letting India get out of hand. But they want a lead. They can't be expected to start the show any more than I can."

Lord Caerlaverock rose to join the ladies with an air of outraged dignity. Vennard pulled out his watch and announced that he must get back to the House.

"Do you know what I am going to do?" he asked. "I am going down to tell Simpson what I think of him. He gets up and prates of having been forty years in India. Well, I am going to tell him that it is to him and his forty year lot that all this muddle is due. Oh, I assure you, there's going to be a row," said Vennard, as he struggled into his coat.

Mulross had been sitting next me, and I asked him if he was leaving town. "I wish I could," he said, "but I fear I must stick on over the Twelfth. I don't like the way that fellow Von Kladow has been talking. He's up to no good, and he's going to get a flea in his ear before he is very much older."

Cheerfully, almost hilariously, the three Ministers departed, Vennard and Cargill in a hansom, and Mulross on foot. I can only describe the condition of those left behind as nervous prostration. We looked furtively at each other, each afraid to hint his suspicions, but all convinced that a surprising judgment had befallen at least two members of his Majesty's Government. For myself I put the number at three, for I did not like to hear a respected Whig Foreign Secretary talk about giving the Chancellor of a friendly but jealous Power a flea in his ear.

The only unperplexed face was Deloraine's. He whispered to me that Miss Barriton was going on to the Alvanleys' ball, and had warned him to be there. "She hasn't been to a dance for months, you know," he said. "I really think things are beginning to go a little better, old man."

III

WHEN I opened my paper next morning I read two startling pieces of news. Lord Mulross had been knocked down by a taxi-cab on his way home the night before, and was now in bed suffering from a bad shock and a bruised ankle. There was no cause for anxiety, said the report, but his lordship must keep his room for a week or two.

The second item, which filled leading articles and overflowed into "Political Notes", was Mr. Vennard's speech. The Secretary for India had gone down about eleven o'clock to the House, where an Indian debate was dragging out its slow length. He sat himself on the Treasury Bench and took notes, and the House soon filled in anticipation of his reply. His "tail"—progressive young men like himself—were there in full strength, ready to cheer every syllable which fell from their idol. Somewhere about half-past twelve he rose to wind up the debate, and the House was treated to an unparalleled sensation. He began with his critics, notably the unfortunate Simpson, and, pretty much in Westbury's language to the herald, called them silly old men who did not understand their silly old business. But it was the reasons he gave for this abuse which left his followers aghast. He attacked his critics not for being satraps and reactionaries, but because they had dared to talk second-rate Western politics in

340

connection with India. "Have you lived for forty years with your eyes shut," he cried, "that you cannot see the difference between a Bengali, married at fifteen and worshipping a pantheon of savage gods, and the university-extension young Radical at home? There is a thousand years between them, and you dream of annihilating the centuries with a little dubious popular science!" Then he turned to the other critics of Indian administration— his quondam supporters. He analysed the character of these "members for India" with a vigour and acumen which deprived them of speech. The East, he said, had had its revenge upon the West by making certain Englishmen babus. His honourable friends had the same slipshod minds, and they talked the same pigeon-English, as the patriots of Bengal. Then his mood changed, and he delivered a solemn warning against what he called "the treason begotten of restless vanity and proved incompetence". He sat down, leaving a House deeply impressed and horribly mystified.

The Times did not know what to make of it at all. In a weighty leader it welcomed Mr. Vennard's conversion, but hinted that with a convert's zeal he had slightly overstated his case. *The Daily Chronicle* talked of "nervous breakdown", and suggested "kindly forgetfulness" as the best treatment. *The Daily News*, in a spirited article called "The Great Betrayal", washed its hands of Mr. Vennard unless he donned the white sheet of the penitent. Later in the day I got *The Westminster Gazette*, and found an ingenious leader which proved that the speech in no way conflicted with Liberal principles, and was capable of a quite ordinary explanation. Then I went to see Lady Caerlaverock. I found my aunt almost in tears.

"What has happened?" she cried. "What have we done that we should be punished in this awful way? And to think that the blow fell in this house! Caerlaverock—we all—thought Mr. Vennard so strange last night, and Lady Lavinia told me that Mr. Cargill was perfectly horrible. I suppose it must be the heat and the strain of the session. And that poor Lord Mulross, who was always so wise, should be stricken down at this crisis!"

I did not say that I thought Mulross's accident a merciful dispensation. I was far more afraid of him than of all the others, for if with his reputation for sanity he chose to run amok, he would be taken seriously. He was better in bed than affixing a flea to Von Kladow's ear. "Caerlaverock was with the Prime Minister this morning," my aunt went on. "He is going to make a statement in the Lords tomorrow to try to cover Mr. Vennard's folly. They are very anxious about what Mr. Cargill will do today. He is addressing the National Convention of Young Liberals at Oldham this afternoon, and though they have sent him a dozen telegrams they can get no answer. Caerlaverock went to Downing Street an hour ago to get news."

There was the sound of an electric brougham stopping in the square below, and we both listened with a premonition of disaster. A minute later Caerlaverock entered the room, and with him the Prime Minister. The cheerful, eupeptic countenance of the latter was clouded with care. He shook hands dismally with my aunt, nodded to me, and flung himself down on a sofa.

"The worst has happened," Caerlaverock boomed solemnly. "Cargill has been incredibly and infamously silly." He tossed me an evening paper.

One glance convinced me that the Convention of Young Liberals had had a waking-up. Cargill had addressed them on what he called the true view of citizenship. He had dismissed manhood suffrage as an obsolete folly. The franchise, he maintained, should be narrowed and given only to citizens, and his definition of citizenship was military training combined with a fairly high standard of rates and taxes. I do not know how the Young Liberals received this creed, but it had no sort of success with the Prime Minister. "We must disavow him," said Caerlaverock.

"He is too valuable a man to lose," said the Prime Minister. "We must hope that it is only a temporary aberration. I simply cannot spare him in the House."

"But this is flat treason."

"I know, I know. It is all too horrible, and utterly unexpected. But the situation wants delicate handling, my dear Caerlaverock. I see nothing for it but to give out that he was ill."

"Or drunk?" I suggested.

The Prime Minister shook his head sadly. "I fear it will be the

342

same thing. What we call illness the ordinary man will interpret as intoxication. It is a most regrettable necessity, but we must face it."

The harassed leader rose, seized the evening paper, and departed as swiftly as he had come. "Remember, illness," were his parting words. "An old heart trouble, which is apt to affect the brain. His friends have always known about it."

I walked home, and looked in at the club on my way. There I found Deloraine devouring a hearty tea and looking the picture of virtuous happiness.

"Well, this is tremendous news," I said, as I sat down beside him.

"What news?" he asked with a start.

"This row about Vennard and Cargill."

"Oh, that! I haven't seen the papers today. What's it all about?" His tone was devoid of interest.

Then I knew that something of great private moment had happened to Tommy.

"I hope I may congratulate you," I said.

Deloraine beamed on me affectionately. "Thanks very much, old man. Things came all right quite suddenly, you know. We spent most of the time at the Alvanleys' together, and this morning in the Park she accepted me. It will be in the papers next week, but we mean to keep it quiet for a day or two. However, it was your right to be told—and, besides, you guessed."

I remember wondering, as I finished my walk home, whether there could not be some connection between the stroke of Providence which had driven three Cabinet Ministers demented and that gentler touch which had restored Miss Claudia Barriton to good sense and a reasonable marriage.

IV

THE next week was an epoch in my life. I seemed to live in the centre of a Mad Tea-party, where everyone was convinced of the madness, and yet resolutely protested that nothing had happened. The public events of those days were simple enough. While Lord Mulross's ankle approached convalescence, the hives of politics were humming with rumours. Vennard's speech had dissolved his party into its parent elements, and the Opposition, as nonplussed as the Government, did not dare as yet to claim the recruit. Consequently he was left alone till he should see fit to take a further step. He refused to be interviewed, using blasphemous language about our free Press; and mercifully he showed no desire to make speeches. He went down to golf at Littlestone, and rarely showed himself in the House. The earnest young reformer seemed to have adopted not only the creed but the habits of his enemies.

Mr. Cargill's was a hard case. He returned from Oldham, delighted with himself and full of fight, to find awaiting him an urgent message from the Prime Minister. His chief was sympathetic and kindly. He had long noticed that the Home Secretary looked fagged and ill. There was no Home Office Bill very pressing, and his assistance in general debate could be dispensed with for a little. Let him take a fortnight's holiday—fish, golf, yacht—the Prime Minister was airily suggestive. In vain Mr. Cargill declared he was perfectly well. His chief gently but firmly overbore him, and insisted on sending him his own doctor. That eminent specialist, having been well coached, was vaguely alarming, and insisted on a change. Then Mr. Cargill began to suspect, and asked the Prime Minister point-blank if he objected to his Oldham speech. He was told that there was no objection—a little strong meat, perhaps, for Young Liberals, a little daring, but full of Mr. Cargill's old intellectual power. Mollified and reassured, the Home Secretary agreed to a week's absence, and departed for a little salmon-fishing in Scotland. His wife had meantime been taken into the affair, and privately assured by the Prime Minister that she would greatly ease the mind of the Cabinet if she could induce her husband to take a longer holiday—say three weeks. She promised to do her best and to keep her instructions secret, and the Cargills duly departed for the North. "In a fortnight," said the Prime Minister to my aunt, "he will have forgotten all this nonsense;

but of course we shall have to watch him very carefully in the future."

The Press was given its cue, and announced that Mr. Cargill had spoken at Oldham while suffering from severe nervous breakdown, and that the remarkable doctrines of that speech need not be taken seriously. As I had expected, the public put its own interpretation upon this tale. Men took each other aside in clubs, women gossiped in drawing-rooms, and in a week the Cargill scandal had assumed amazing proportions. The popular version was that the Home Secretary had got very drunk at Caerlaverock House, and still under the influence of liquor had addressed the Young Liberals at Oldham. He was now in an Inebriates' Home, and would not return to the House that session. I confess I trembled when I heard this story, for it was altogether too libellous to pass unnoticed. I believed that soon it would reach the ear of Cargill, fishing quietly at Tomandhoul, and that then there would be the deuce to pay.

Nor was I wrong. A few days later I went to see my aunt to find out how the land lay. She was very bitter, I remember, about Claudia Barriton. "I expected sympathy and help from her, and she never comes near me. I can understand her being absorbed in her engagement, but I cannot understand the frivolous way she spoke when I saw her yesterday. She had the audacity to say that both Mr. Vennard and Mr. Cargill had gone up in her estimation. Young people can be so heartless."

I would have defended Miss Barriton, but at this moment an astonishing figure was announced. It was Mrs. Cargill in travelling-dress, with a purple bonnet and a green motor-veil. Her face was scarlet, whether from excitement or the winds of Tomandhoul, and she charged down on us like a young bull.

"We have come back," she said, "to meet our accusers."

"Accusers!" cried my aunt.

"Yes, accusers!" said the lady. "The abominable rumour about Alexander has reached our ears. At this moment he is with the Prime Minister demanding an official denial. I have come to you, because it was here, at your table, that Alexander is said to have fallen."

"I really don't know what you mean, Mrs. Cargill."

"I mean that Alexander is said to have become drunk while dining here, to have been drunk when he spoke at Oldham, and to be now in a Drunkards' Home." The poor lady broke down. "Alexander," she cried, "who has been a teetotaller from his youth, and for thirty years an elder in the U.P. Church! No form of intoxicant has ever been permitted at our table. Even in illness the thing has never passed our lips."

My aunt by this time had pulled herself together. "If this outrageous story is current, Mrs. Cargill, there was nothing for it but to come back. Your friends know that it is a gross libel. The only denial necessary is for Mr. Cargill to resume his work. I trust his health is better."

"He is well, but heartbroken. His is a sensitive nature, Lady Caerlaverock, and he feels a stain like a wound."

"There is no stain," said my aunt briskly. "Every public man is a target for scandals, but no one but a fool believes them. They will die a natural death when he returns to work. An official denial would make everybody look ridiculous, and encourage the ordinary person to think that there may have been something in them. Believe me, dear Mrs. Cargill, there is nothing to be anxious about now that you are back in London again."

On the contrary, I thought, there was more cause for anxiety than ever. Cargill was back in the House and the illness game could not be played a second time. I went home that night acutely sympathetic towards the worries of the Prime Minister. Mulross would be abroad in a day or two, and Vennard and Cargill were volcanoes in eruption. The Government was in a parlous state, with three demented Ministers on the loose.

The same night I first heard the story of *The* Bill. Vennard had done more than play golf at Littlestone. His active mind—for his bitterest enemies never denied his intellectual energy—had been busy on a great scheme. At that time, it will be remembered, a serious shrinkage of unskilled labour existed not only in the Transvaal, but in the new copper fields of East Africa. Simultaneously a famine was scourging Behar, and Vennard, to do him justice, had made manful efforts to cope with it. He had gone fully into the question, and had been slowly coming to the conclusion that Behar was hopelessly overcrowded. In his new frame of mind—unswervingly logical, utterly unemotional, and wholly unbound by tradition—he had come to connect the African and Indian troubles, and to see in one the relief of the other. The first fruit of his meditations was a letter to *The Times*. In it he laid down a new theory of emigration. The peoples of the Empire, he said, must be mobile, shifting about to suit economic conditions. But if this was true for the white man, it was equally true for the dark races under our tutelage. He referred to the famine, and argued that the recurrence of such disasters was inevitable, unless we assisted the poverty-stricken ryot to emigrate and sell his labour to advantage. He proposed indentures and terminable contracts, for he declared he had no wish to transplant for good. All that was needed was a short season of wage-earning abroad, that the labourer might return home with savings which would set him for the future on a higher economic plane. The letter was temperate and academic in phrasing, the speculation of a publicist rather than the declaration of a Minister. But in Liberals, who remembered the pandemonium raised over the Chinese in South Africa, it stirred up the gloomiest forebodings.

Then, whispered from mouth to mouth, came the news of the Great Bill. Vennard, it was said, intended to bring in a measure at the earliest possible date to authorise a scheme of enforced and State-aided emigration to the African mines. It would apply at first only to the famine districts, but power would be given to extend its working by proclamation to other areas. Such was the rumour, and I need not say it was soon magnified. Questions were asked in the House which the Speaker ruled out of order. Furious articles, inviting denial, appeared in the Liberal Press; but Vennard took not the slightest notice. He spent his time between his office in Whitehall and the links at Littlestone, dropping into the House once or twice for half an hour's slumber while a colleague was speaking. His Under Secretary in the Lords—a young gentleman who had joined the party for a bet, and to his immense disgust had been immediately rewarded with office— lost his temper under cross-examination and swore audibly at the Opposition. In a day or two the story universally believed was that the Secretary for India was about to transfer the bulk of the

Indian people to work as indentured labourers for South African Jews.

It was this popular version, I fancy, which reached the ears of Ram Singh, and the news came on him like a thunderclap. He thought that what Vennard proposed Vennard could do. He saw his native province stripped of its people, his fields left unploughed, and his cattle untended; nay, it was possible, his own worthy and honourable self sent to a far country to dig in a hole. It was a grievous and intolerable prospect. He walked home to Gloucester Road in heavy preoccupation, and the first thing he did was to get out the mysterious brass box in which he kept his valuables. From a pocket-book he took a small silk packet, opened it, and spilled a few clear grains on his hand. It was the antidote.

He waited two days, while on all sides the rumour of the Bill grew stronger and its provisions more stringent. Then he hesitated no longer, but sent for Lord Caerlaverock's cook.

V

I CONCEIVE that the drug did not create new opinions, but elicited those which had hitherto lain dormant. Every man has a creed, but in his soul he knows that that creed has another side, possibly not less logical, which it does not suit him to produce. Our most honest convictions are not the children of pure reason, but of temperament, environment, necessity, and interest. Most of us take sides in life and forget the one we reject. But our conscience tells us it is there, and we can on occasion state it with a fairness and fulness which proves that it is not wholly repellent to our reason. During the crisis I write of, the attitude of Cargill and Vennard was not that of roysterers out for irresponsible mischief. They were eminently reasonable and wonderfully logical, and in private conversation they gave their opponents a very bad time. Cargill, who had hitherto been the hope of the extreme Free-traders, wrote an article for the *Quarterly* on Tariff Reform. It was set up, but long before it could be used it was cancelled and the type scattered. I have seen a proof of it, however, and I confess I have never read a more brilliant defence of a doctrine which the author had hitherto described as a childish heresy. Which proves my contention—that Cargill all along knew that there was a case against Free Trade, but naturally did not choose to admit it, his allegiance being vowed elsewhere. The drug altered temperament, and with it the creed which is based mainly on temperament. It scattered current convictions, roused dormant speculations, and without damaging the reason switched it on to a new track.

I can see all this now, but at the time I saw only stark madness and the horrible ingenuity of the lunatic. While Vennard was ruminating on his Bill, Cargill was going about London arguing like a Scotch undergraduate. The Prime Minister had seen from the start that the Home Secretary was the worse danger. Vennard might talk of his preposterous Bill, but the Cabinet would have something to say to it before its introduction, and he was mercifully disinclined to go near St. Stephen's. But Cargill was assiduous in his attendance at the House, and at any moment might blow the Government sky-high. His colleagues were detailed in relays to watch him. One would hale him to luncheon, and keep him till question-time was over. Another would insist on taking him for a motor-ride, which would end in a break-down about Brentford. Invitations to dinner were showered upon him, and Cargill, who had been unknown in society, found the whole social machinery of his party set at work to make him a lion. The result was that he was prevented from speaking in public, but given far too much encouragement to talk in private. He talked incessantly, before, at, and after dinner, and he did enormous harm. He was horribly clever, too, and usually got the best of an argument, so that various eminent private Liberals had their tempers ruined by his dialectic. In his rich and unabashed accent—he had long discarded his Edinburgh-English—he dissected their arguments and ridiculed their character. He had once been famous for his soapy manners: now he was as rough as a Highland stot.

Things could not go on in this fashion: the risk was too great. It was just a fortnight, I think, after the Caerlaverock dinner-party, when the Prime Minister resolved to bring matters to a head. He could not afford to wait for ever on a return of sanity. He consulted Caerlaverock, and it was agreed that Vennard and Cargill should be asked, or rather commanded, to dine on the following evening at Caerlaverock House. Mulross, whose sanity was not suspected, and whose ankle was now well again, was also invited, as were three other members of the Cabinet and myself as *amicus curiæ*. It was understood that after dinner there would be a settling-up with the two rebels. Either they should recant and come to heel, or they should depart from the fold to swell the wolf-pack of the Opposition. The Prime Minister did not conceal the loss which his party would suffer, but he argued very sensibly that anything was better than a brace of vipers in its bosom.

I have never attended a more lugubrious function. When I arrived I found Caerlaverock, the Prime Minister, and the three other members of the Cabinet standing round a small fire in attitudes of nervous dejection. I remember it was a raw, wet evening, but the gloom out-of-doors was sunshine compared to the gloom within. Caerlaverock's viceregal air had sadly altered. The Prime Minister, once famous for his genial manners, was pallid and preoccupied. We exchanged remarks about the weather and the duration of the session. Then we fell silent till Mulross arrived.

He did not look as if he had come from a sickbed. He came in as jaunty as a boy, limping just a little from his accident. He was greeted by his colleagues with tender solicitude—solicitude, I fear, completely wasted on him.

"Devilish silly thing to do to get run over," he said. "I was in a brown study when a cab came round a corner. But I don't regret it, you know. During the past fortnight I have had leisure to go into this Bosnian Succession business, and I see now that Von Kladow has been playing one big game of bluff. Very well; it has got to stop. I am going to prick the bubble before I am many days older."

The Prime Minister looked anxious. "Our policy towards Bosnia has been one of non-interference. It is not for us, I should have thought, to read Germany a lesson."

"Oh, come now," Mulross said, slapping—yes, actually

slapping—his leader on the back; "we may drop that nonsense when we are alone. You know very well that there are limits to our game of non-interference. If we don't read Germany a lesson, she will read us one—and a damned long unpleasant one too. The sooner we give up all this milk-blooded, blue-spectacled, pacificist talk the better. However, you will see what I have got to say tomorrow in the House."

The Prime Minister's face lengthened. Mulross was not the pillar he had thought him, but a splintering reed. I saw that he agreed with me that this was the most dangerous of the lot.

Then Cargill and Vennard came in together. Both looked uncommonly fit, younger, trimmer, cleaner. Vennard, instead of his sloppy clothes and shaggy hair, was groomed like a Guardsman; had a large pearl-and-diamond solitaire in his shirt, and a white waistcoat with jewelled buttons. He had lost all his self-consciousness, grinned cheerfully at the others, warmed his hands at the fire, and cursed the weather. Cargill, too, had lost his sanctimonious look. There was a bloom of rustic health on his cheek, and a sparkle in his eye, so that he had the appearance of some rosy Scotch laird of Raeburn's painting. Both men wore an air of purpose and contentment.

Vennard turned at once on the Prime Minister. "Did you get my letter?" he asked. "No? Well, you'll find it waiting when you get home. We're all friends here, so I can tell you its contents. We *must* get rid of this ridiculous Radical 'tail'. They think they have the whip-hand of us; well, we have got to prove that we can do very well without them. They are a collection of confounded, treacherous, complacent prigs, but they have no grit in them, and will come to heel if we tackle them firmly. I respect an honest fanatic, but I do not respect those sentiment-mongers. They have the impudence to say that the country is with them. I tell you it is rank nonsense. If you take a strong hand with them, you'll double your popularity, and we'll come back next year with an increased majority. Cargill agrees with me."

The Prime Minister looked grave. "I am not prepared to discuss any policy of ostracism. What you call our 'tail' is a vital section of our party. Their creed may be one-sided, but it is none the less part of our mandate from the people."

"I want a leader who governs as well as reigns," said Vennard. "I believe in discipline, and you know as well as I do that the Rump is infernally out of hand."

"They are not the only members who fail in discipline."

Vennard grinned. "I suppose you mean Cargill and myself. But we are following the central lines of British policy. We are on your side, and we want to make your task easier."

Cargill suddenly began to laugh. "I don't want any ostracism. Leave them alone, and Vennard and I will undertake to give them such a time in the House that they will wish they had never been born. We'll make them resign in batches."

Dinner was announced, and, laughing uproariously, the two rebels went arm-in-arm into the dining-room.

Cargill was in tremendous form. He began to tell Scotch stories, memories of his old Parliament House days. He told them admirably, with a raciness of idiom which I had thought beyond him. They were long tales, and some were as broad as they were long, but Mr. Cargill disarmed criticism. His audience, rather scandalised at the start, were soon captured, and political troubles were forgotten in old-fashioned laughter. Even the Prime Minister's anxious face relaxed. This lasted till the *entrée*, the famous Caerlaverock curry.

As I have said, I was not in the secret, and did not detect the transition. As I partook of the dish I remember feeling a sudden giddiness and a slight nausea. The antidote, to those who had not taken the drug, must have been, I suppose, in the nature of a mild emetic. A mist seemed to obscure the faces of my fellow-guests, and slowly the tide of conversation ebbed away. First Vennard, then Cargill, became silent. I was feeling rather sick, and I noticed with some satisfaction that all our faces were a little green. I wondered casually if I had been poisoned.

The sensation passed, but the party had changed. More especially I was soon conscious that something had happened to the three Ministers. I noticed Mulross particularly, for he was my neighbour. The look of keenness and vitality had died out of him, and suddenly he seemed a rather old, rather tired man, very weary about the eyes. I asked him if he felt seedy.

"No, not specially," he replied, "but that accident gave me a nasty shock."

"You should go off for a change," I said.

"I almost think I will," was the answer. "I had not meant to leave town till just before the Twelfth, but I think I had better get away to Marienbad for a fortnight. There is nothing doing in the House, and work at the Office is at a standstill. Yes, I fancy I'll go abroad before the end of the week."

I caught the Prime Minister's eye and saw that he had forgotten the purpose of the dinner, being dimly conscious that that purpose was now idle. Cargill and Vennard had ceased to talk like rebels. The Home Secretary had subsided into his old, suave, phrasing self. The humour had gone out of his eye, and the looseness had returned to his lips. He was an older and more commonplace man, but harmless, quite harmless. Vennard, too, wore a new air, or rather had recaptured his old one. He was saying little, but his voice had lost its crispness and recovered its half-plaintive unction; his shoulders had a droop in them; once more he bristled with self-consciousness.

We others were still shaky from that detestable curry, and were so puzzled as to be acutely uncomfortable. Relief would come later, no doubt; for the present we were uneasy at this weird transformation. I saw the Prime Minister examining the two faces intently, and the result seemed to satisfy him. He sighed and looked at Caerlaverock, who smiled and nodded.

"What about that Bill of yours, Vennard?" he asked. "There have been a lot of stupid rumours."

"Bill?" Vennard said. "I know of no Bill. Now that my departmental work is over, I can give my whole soul to Cargill's Small Holdings. Do you mean that?"

"Yes, of course. There was some confusion in the popular mind, but the old arrangement holds. You and Cargill will put it through between you."

They began to talk about those weariful small holdings, and I ceased to listen. We left the dining-room and drifted to the library, where a fire tried to dispel the gloom of the weather. There was a feeling of deadly depression abroad, so that, for all its awkwardness, I would really have preferred the former

Caerlaverock dinner. The Prime Minister was whispering to his host. I heard him say something about there being "the devil of a lot of explaining" before him. Vennard and Cargill came last to the library, arm-in-arm as before.

"I should count it a greater honour," Vennard was saying, "to sweeten the lot of one toiler in England than to add a million miles to our territory. While one English household falls below the minimum scale of civic well-being, all talk of Empire is sin and folly."

"Excellent!" said Mr. Cargill.

Then I knew for certain that at last peace had descended upon the vexed tents of Israel.

THE SHORTER CATECHISM

(REVISED VERSION)

When I was young and herdit sheep
    I read auld tales o' Wallace wight;
My heid was fou o' sangs and threip
    O' folk that feared nae mortal might.
But noo I'm auld, and weel I ken
    We're made alike o' gowd and mire;
There's saft bits in the stievest men,
    The bairnliest's got a spunk o' fire.

      Sae hearken to me, lads,
        It's truth that I tell:
      There's nae man a' courage—
        I ken by mysel'.

I've been an elder forty year:
    I've tried to keep the narrow way;
I've walked afore the Lord in fear:
    I've never missed the kirk a day.
I've read the Bible in and oot
    (I ken the feck o't clean by hert),
But, still and on, I sair misdoot
    I'm better noo than at the stert.

      Sae hearken to me, lads,
        It's truth I maintain:
      Man's works are but rags, for
        I ken by my ain.

I hae a name for decent trade:
　　I'll wager a' the countryside
Wad sweer nae trustier man was made,
　　The ford to soom, the bent to bide.
But when it comes to coupin' horse,
　　I'm just like a' that e'er were born;
I fling my heels and tak' my course;
　　I'd sell the minister the morn.

　　　Sae hearken to me, lads,
　　　　It's truth that I tell:
　　　There's nae man deid honest—
　　　　I ken by mysel'.

Other John Buchan titles from B&W:

HUNTINGTOWER

Introduced by Andrew Lownie

Huntingtower is a gloomy, decaying mansion, abandoned by the family who had built it less than twenty years before. But mysterious events in the grounds one evening form the starting-point of one of Buchan's most popular thrillers, involving a Russian Princess, priceless jewellery, a desperate band of foreign agents, and John Buchan's most unlikely hero —the resourceful Dickson McGunn, a middle-aged retired Glasgow grocer.

THE BLANKET OF THE DARK

Introduced by Professor David Daniell

It is 1536, and the Reformation has yet to disrupt the life of the great medieval Abbey of Oseney near Oxford, where Peter Pentecost is completing his education.

But Peter's life is to be changed forever when he uncovers the astonishing secret of his true identity. From that moment, Peter descends into a dangerous world of conspiracy and treason, as powerful men seek to persuade him to risk everything in a rebellion that could overthrow Henry VIII.

'A tour de force'
RUDYARD KIPLING

THE GAP IN THE CURTAIN

Introduced by Dr James Robertson

When Sir Edward Leithen visits Lady Flambard's stately home in the heart of the Cotswolds, he has no idea of the extraordinary sequence of events that is about to unfold.

One of the other guests, the brilliant Professor Moe, enlists the help of Leithen and his companions in a bizarre experiment: he claims he will be able to show each of them a fleeting glimpse of the future. For those who take part, the consequences are dramatic—not least for the ambitious young politition who discovers the exact date of his own death. . . .

THE FREE FISHERS

Introduced by Professor David Daniell

A classic story of espionage and adventure during the Napoleonic Wars, as a ruthless fanatic plots to assassinate the Prime Minister and deliver the country into the hands of its most deadly enemies.

With the action stretching from the shores of Fife to the moors of Northumberland and the Fens of East Anglia, this is one of Buchan's most atmospheric novels, its themes echoing his other great story of conspiracy and adventure, *The Thirty-Nine Steps*.

SICK HEART RIVER

In his final adventure, Sir Edward Leithen travels deep into the arctic wastes of Canada, to investigate the mysterious disappearance of Francis Galliard—a man who seemed to have everything, but had inexplicably abandoned it all to head north in search of the mythical Sick Heart River.

Leithen soon realises that he is unlikely to return alive, and is forced to confront not only the 'terror of the North', but also his own deepest fears.

'A fine story, told with skill and power'
THE SCOTSMAN

JOHN BURNET OF BARNS

Introduced by Dr James Robertson

Set in the Scottish Borders in 1678, *John Burnet of Barns* tells the story of two young noblemen—John Burnet, heir to the ancient house of Barns and the last in a long line of Border reivers; and his cousin, Captain Gilbert Burnet, a dashing but ruthless soldier and adventurer.

A story of honour and loyalty, betrayal and retribution, this is also a marvellous evocation of the Border country during the 'Killing Time' of the Covenanting period.

'A delightful novel of adventure
and old-world heroism'
THE SCOTSMAN

THE POWER-HOUSE

Introduced by Anthony Quinton

When a friend vanishes in mysterious circumstances, Sir Edward Leithen becomes convinced that he has stumbled on the work of a secret society, code-named the Power-House. He soon finds himself in terrible danger, as he stands alone against the might of this unseen enemy.

Written in 1913, just before *The Thirty-Nine Steps*, *The Power-House* is one of John Buchan's finest thrillers, in which Edwardian London is portrayed as a nightmarish landscape, haunted by the brethren of the Power-House—sinister, and seemingly unstoppable. . . .

A LOST LADY OF OLD YEARS

Introduced by Dr James Robertson

A dark, compelling and authentic portrayal of the Jacobite Rebellion, *A Lost Lady of Old Years* is the enthralling tale of one of the most infamous traitors of the 18th century—Murray of Broughton, secretary to Prince Charles Edward Stewart—and of one young man's fight to thwart him, as the battle of Culloden approaches and the Jacobite Cause seems doomed to meet with disaster.

THE COURTS OF THE MORNING

Introduced by Andrew Lownie

The Courts of the Morning begins in the pleasant atmosphere of a Scottish country house, where Richard Hannay is the guest of his old friend, Sandy Arbuthnot. But the scene quickly shifts to a small South American republic in the grip of a dictator, a powerful and charismatic leader whose greed and ruthlessness know no bounds.

First published in 1929, *The Courts of the Morning* was more than just an adventure story—it was also an examination of the nature of dictatorship and a prophetic warning of the corrupting effect of absolute power.

'A thrilling story, original,
finely written and absorbing'
DAILY EXPRESS

MIDWINTER

Introduced by Allan Massie

Midwinter is regarded by many critics as one of the best historical novels ever written, in the tradition of Scott and Stevenson.

The year is 1745, and the Jacobite Rising is in full swing. Alastair Maclean, close confidant of Prince Charles Edward Stewart, sets out on a secret mission to raise support for the Jacobite Cause. He is befriended by two extraordinary men— Dr Samuel Johnson, an aspiring man of letters, and the shadowy figure known only as 'Midwinter', guardian of a twilight world.

> *'It is a book which once read is never forgotten'*
> ALLAN MASSIE

A PRINCE OF THE CAPTIVITY

Introduced by Professor David Daniell

A Prince of the Captivity is the epic story of Adam Melfort, an officer and a gentleman with a brilliant career ahead of him —until he is imprisoned for a crime he did not commit. Determined to salvage something from the wreckage of his life, Adam embarks on a series of spectacular and daring missions in the service of his country.

The gripping story of one man's courage and self-sacrifice, *A Prince of the Captivity* is also a powerful evocation of Europe in turmoil—emerging from the anarchy of the First World War only to face further disaster under the looming shadow of Fascism.

*Available from all good bookshops,
or direct from the publishers:*

*B&W Publishing,
233 Cowgate, Edinburgh,
EH1 1NQ.*

Tel: 0131 220 5551

SUPERNATURA

John Buchan (1875-1940) was b[...]
August 1875, the eldest son of a minister in the Free
Church of Scotland. He spent part of his childhood
in Fife, before the family moved to Glasgow in the
1880s. In 1894 he went to Oxford University and began
to write, publishing several books and many articles
while still a student. After Oxford he had a successful
career as a barrister and Member of Parliament, while
continuing to write highly-acclaimed novels such as
The Thirty-Nine Steps, *Greenmantle* and *The Three
Hostages*. He also wrote widely on other subjects,
including biographies of Cromwell and Montrose, and
an autobiography *Memory Hold-the-Door*. John Buchan
was created Baron Tweedsmuir in 1935 and became
Governor-General of Canada the same year. He died in
Canada in 1940, soon after completing his last great
novel, *Sick Heart River*.

Jim Greig (Rev. James C. G. Greig) first became
interested in John Buchan at the age of twelve.
Educated at the universities of Cambridge and Glasgow, he became a minister of the Church of Scotland,
and has lectured in the New Testament at Westminster
College and in religious education at Jordanhill
College of Education, Glasgow. He has been a member
of the John Buchan Society since its inception in 1979,
is a past chairman of its Council, and provided the
introduction and notes for Buchan's *Witch Wood* in
the Oxford University Press's World Classics series
(1993). Prior to retirement in 1992 he spent almost six
years in Geneva with the World Council of Churches
as a translator, and he still freelances in that field.
He married Elsa Carlile in 1958 and they have three
children and four grandchildren.

Other B&W titles by John Buchan